The Gift of Osiris

by

Francois Napoleon Jones

 New Generation **Publishing**

Dedicated to the love of my life,

Sheryll

Also by Francois Napoleon Jones

The Drug of Hope 2010

Table of Contents

Book One

Chapter One

Three thousand five hundred years before the birth of Jesus, was a land called tWay, which had a ruler, Geb, who ruled wisely with his wife, Nut, who was also his sister. When he knew he was dying, he divided the land between his two sons. Osiris, as the elder, was given the richer lands of Ta-Mehu of Lower tWay, which stretched from the Mediterranean to the region south of Fayoum Oasis. Set was given Ta-Shemau, Upper tWay, the remaining land that stretched along the Nile to Elephantine. His daughter, Isis, was to marry her brother Osiris, as was the custom in the royal household, and the other sister, Nephths, was to be married to Set to rule alongside him.

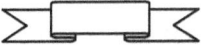

The Pharaoh Set of the Ta-Shemau sat on the imperial throne dressed in the traditional loincloth, his muscular frame a testimony to countless hours of rigorous exercise with his manservant Benipe. Set was large for a tWay man, perhaps five feet nine inches tall. He had very white skin and a mane of golden hair that he wore long. He always wore a scorpion crown to keep his hair in place, and many feared him because of his striking appearance. The throne room of the pharaoh was ornate, with columns of marble supporting the high ceiling painted with several cosmic patterns depicting the God Ra. Set was in his early thirties and a man of vast appetites with a passion for life and power; his impatience was legendry. His two main advisors lay on the polished marble floor in front of him quivering in fear as he spoke to them both in a harsh, hard voice, the venom in his speech evident to all the guards that surrounded the room. Set never went anywhere without his elect body guards and manservant in attendance; even the royal bedchamber and bathing were attended by his inner core of trusted guards. Each man was handpicked for his bravery and loyalty and known to Set during his childhood.

"Ammon, why is Osiris still alive?" Set stated the obvious.

"My Pharaoh, the slave was discovered trying to poison Osiris. He was tortured and killed." Ammon spoke calmly, even though he knew he faced death.

"How?" Set spat the word.

"Osiris usually eats alone after his morning exercise, and the food taster smeared the fresh dates with poison, eating some of the dates that were not poisoned, and leaving the pips for Osiris to clearly see."

"So, why did he not eat the dates?" Set asked, now clearly perplexed.

"His Nubian manservant, Panhsj, wrestles with him each day, and Osiris offered him the dates whilst he dried his body with a cloth. He died choking in front of Osiris; the poison acts immediately," said Ammon, still calm.

"And the slave?" asked Set.

"Osiris had him tortured, peeling the skin from his body until he told him everything he knew," said Ammon.

"What did he know?" asked Set.

"That if Osiris died, his family in your kingdom would be released from prison and each one made rich," said Ammon. "He knew whatever happened, he would die."

"So, why did he not kill himself with the poison when the plot failed?" asked Set.

"The slave offered the plate of dates to Osiris, expecting him just to pick a date to eat, but he took the plate and gave it to Panhsj on the other side of the room, so he could not get to the dates before they arrested him," said Ammon.

"So what did Osiris do when he learned I had tried to kill him?" asked Set.

"Nothing," said Ammon, "he spoke to Isis your sister about the plot, but they decided the best course of action was to remain silent and be more vigilant. He will see the food taster eat before he now tastes food, and drink from his cup before he drinks."

"How do we know this?" asked Set.

"From the slave girl, Tadinanefar, who shares Osiris' bed sometimes in the afternoon when Isis is resting," said Ammon.

"He speaks to her of these matters?" Set was shocked; he never spoke to slaves.

"Yes, he tells her everything," said Ammon.

"How did you persuade her to seek information on our behalf?" asked Set.

"My brother Hakim is a merchant here in El-Kab, and her sister is a slave in his keeping, he has promised they will both be freed if Tadinanefar provides information to help kill Osiris."

"Could the girl kill him?" asked Set.

"Probably not," said Ammon, "and we would lose a valuable informant."

"So, Zosimos, what is to be done?" asked Set.

Zosimos was a small man in his late fifties and had been an advisor at the court of the pharaoh before Set was born. He had always been careful not to be the main advisor, always his assistant. He knew now that whatever he said sealed their fates. "Ammon's plan was sound and he was just unlucky in its execution, my Pharaoh. We now need to lure Osiris away from his private rooms and gardens to some location where we can kill him. Perhaps the sister could be bait to tempt him," said Zosimos, the cold marble floor seeping into his bones as the fear crept up his spine.

"Is the woman beautiful?" asked Set.

"Very beautiful, my Pharaoh," said Ammon. "She is called Nefertiti, and she is the most wondrous woman my brother has ever met."

"Really?" said Set.

"Hakim tried to buy both women, but purchased Nefertiti first, but when her sister was auctioned, Tadinanefar was to be sold, and an aid arrived for Osiris and bought the girl for the pharaoh so the girls were separated," said Ammon.

"I always thought Osiris was above ploughing the slaves," said Set.

"He always plants his seed in your sister every day, I am told, but occasionally takes a slave to his bed," said Ammon. "The girl Tadinanefar is different; she has become a regular visitor to his bedchamber."

"And boys?" asked Set.

"Never," replied Ammon. "He only puts his seed in girls."

Set looked at the two men lying on the floor spread-eagle and remained silent. He was angry and wanted to punish both men, watch them being tortured, crying out in agony and dying before his eyes for this failure, but he hesitated. His advisors were very few, and capable men even less. Ammon and Zosimos were both very clever and proposed several social projects that had been successful. As he got older he learned not to surround himself with merely subservient men, but those worthy of their position.

"Stand," said Set. "Your plan is a good one. You may proceed with it without delay. Now, what news of the Eblan, has their envoy arrived?"

"No, my Pharaoh," said Ammon, relieved he had lived another day.

"When he arrives, bring him to me in all haste," said Set "Now go and do my bidding."

The two men shuffled backwards, their heads bent low towards the ground, and as they approached the door, the guards opened it and the two disappeared from view.

"Will the girl lure Osiris?" Zosimos asked Ammon.

"Probably," said Ammon, "but Osiris is no fool and rarely travels alone. We need a much better plan to kill him which strikes his vanity. Bedding another girl will not make him careless; he can bed any woman with the flick of an eyelash."

"We need to be clever and think quickly," said Zosimos.

"I think best when I am rested following bedding my wife," said Ammon.

"I am told you only bed your wife," said Zosimos, the shock of survival making him incautious with his information.

"It is true," said Ammon. "Fouada has been the love of my life since she was a child. We married when she was only fifteen and I was thirty, and I have ploughed her every day since and never looked at another woman or wanted to."

"You are lucky. I have taken three wives, but none make me happy, and each day I try a new slave girl, but always I am disappointed," said Zosimos.

"Some men prefer boys," said Ammon.

"I tried," said Zosimos, "but it was not for me. I prefer women, but I have not found that special person who makes my heart leap like my beautiful daughter Fatin each time I see her."

"Well, you have one blessing; I do not have children," said Ammon.

"But you have the love of Fouada and are content," said Zosimos.

"That is true," said Ammon. "You go and find the Eblan envoy, and I will ponder on a better plan to kill Osiris."

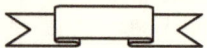

Fouada wore a simple sheath dress falling from the breast to just above the ankle in a pure white linen cloth. She wore papyrus sandals with a leather thong that passed between the first and second toe and was attached to a bar that went across the instep. Her jewellery was of the finest manufactured in gold, using amethyst, garnet, onyx, and turquoise to weave intricate patterns. She wore one broad anklet on the left ankle and a matching bracelet on the right wrist; these both contained amulets to protect her and her family. Her necklace was very ornate and heavy, and it covered her whole chest. It matched the simpler and lighter earrings and headpiece she wore in the ornate wig. Like most women and men, she shaved her head, as was the fashion, and put on a wig as part of her daily dress.

Fouada had been very lucky in her family life. She had a very happy childhood with her mother and father, who were doting parents and very loving. She met Ammon as a family friend when he visited her father Heru, and she immediately liked him. As she grew older, she came to consider him like a family member. When she was fifteen and ready to marry, Ammon surprised her father by asking for her hand in marriage and offering a large dowry of gold and jewels. Her father was overjoyed, but only would consent if Fouada agreed, and so he asked her one evening. She still remembered how the soft rain beat on the roof of a veranda at their house in El-Kab during that meeting with her father.

"My daughter, you are now fifteen and a marriageable age; have you considered who you shall marry?" asked Heru.

"Not really, Father," said Fouada, "but I would like a man, not a boy, somebody a bit older than myself."

"Really, Fouada, why do you say that?" asked Heru, surprised.

"The young boys who came to the house are fun to play with, but are not serious about life, or for that matter the love of a woman, and are very shallow in their opinions," said Fouada. "When I speak to you or Ammon, you speak carefully and with meaning about every subject, and I find that interesting."

"But you must consider with an older man he may die and leave you a widow and you may then be lonely in your old age," said Heru.

"That I have considered, but you start your life at an advantage: Your life partner is already a man and developed, and you know with what type of man you will spend your marriage. With a young boy, he may develop into a wonderful man, or somebody cruel and without honour, so marrying an older man also has many advantages," said Fouada, as the rain seemed to softly chorus her words.

"Ammon, our family friend, has approached me already, Fouada, asking permission to marry you, and is such a man," said Heru. "Would you consider his proposal?"

"There is no need to consider the proposal, Father. I have known Ammon since I was twelve, and already love him as I do you or mother," said Fouada. "I think I could love him as a husband, and know he is a kind and very interesting man."

"You know Ammon is an advisor to the pharaoh. One day he may become the chief advisor, and with that position comes risks," said Heru. "If the pharaoh gets bad advice, he may kill Ammon and even his family as revenge, and who knows who will be pharaoh when Set dies."

"I know this, Father, but we can be stung like a bee like Panhj in the garden and die, or fall under a donkey like Sabeen and be killed by its hoof. Our time here and our time in the afterlife are set by the gods," said Fouda philosophically.

"So you want me to accept Ammon's proposed marriage to you?" asked Heru.

"Yes, Father," said Fouada, as she looked into the dark cloudy sky outside and watched the soft rain wash her childhood innocence away as she accepted the marriage proposal.

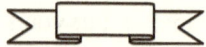

Ammon always ate his afternoon or evening meal with Fouada before they both retired to their bedchamber. As he always started work early in the day, he retired very early to bed each day. Ammon did not exercise, so he had to be careful of how much he ate, and Fouada always had food prepared for his arrival.

He saw her, now sitting like a beautiful princess on her three-legged stool with a woven rush seat, simple in her white sheath dress with her dark black wig high on her head, making her neck seem so long and slender. Her gold and jewels glinted in the afternoon sunlight. In his eyes, Fouada was a goddess, and he had loved her the first time he saw her as a child, and now as a middle-aged man and husband, only death would separate them, he knew.

Fouada knew Ammon hated waste, so unlike many of their friends, she did not prepare a banquet that was wasted. Neither Fouada or Ammon were gluttons, and they ate very little each evening. As was normal, she had the servants prepare only a few dishes, one of vegetables and fruit, both of which had been grown in the irrigated gardens of the house. Today she had selected lettuce, radishes, sweet onions, and beans for the vegetables, and grapes, plums, and dates for the fruit. The fish dish was mullet, caught in the Nile that very morning. The meat was beef from their herd of cows on the family farm. The food was accompanied by bread made from barley and emmer wheat, as was traditional, and baked into a conical shape. All the food was on clay pottery without any ornate patterns, as both Ammon and Fouada loved simplicity in most of their lives.

Fouada saw Ammon arriving and removed her sandals, which was a sign of respect. Ammon had told her several times not to do this, as he was her husband, but she insisted each time that they must obey the custom.

"Welcome, my husband," said Fouada. "You honour me with your presence," and she bowed.

"Fouada, my love," said Ammon, and he kissed her on the cheek.

"How was your day, my husband?" asked Fouada, the formalities now over.

"We survive another day. The pharaoh was very angry at the failure of killing Osiris," said Ammon plainly.

"And he blames you, of course," said Fouada.

"Of course," said Ammon. "As chief advisor, everything is my fault, from famine, disease, to death; all is laid at my door."

"You will succeed in time to kill Osiris and help the pharaoh unite the kingdom again," said Fouada.

"Tonight we forget about the pharaoh and play a game of sonnet and read. I have brought two stories written by Mesopotamians we can read before we retire," said Ammon.

"That will be fun, husband, but let us eat first," and she poured fresh water from the well into a clay goblet for Ammon.

Chapter Two

Ammon rose early before the sun rose in the sky and looked at the beautiful body of Fouada, marvelling at her beauty and perfection in his eyes. He got up to prepare for the day, but always returned to eat his breakfast with Fouada before he left to start work at the palace of the pharaoh. He washed his body sparingly, using a cloth and the cold water his servant had brought for him, and put some ointment on his body that smelled like lavender, but did not colour his face, as was the fashion, with ochre or black eye paint. Dressed in his simple white loincloth, he returned to the bedchamber to see his wife awake and organizing the food with their servants. In the mornings, Ammon and Fouada ate mainly fish and fruit and drank some watered wine. Many TWayians overindulged, but they both were very careful not to become obese by eating small portions and only modestly drinking a little watered wine each day.

"Have you decided what to propose to the pharaoh?" asked Fouada.

"Yes my love," said Ammon, careful to ensure no servants were close by. "The pharaoh must offer Osiris a gift, and that gift must be something that will only be specific to him."

"What gift?" asked Fouada.

"Maybe something that fits him," said Ammon.

"If it is a gift, why does the pharaoh not just send it to him?" asked Fouada.

"Good point," said Ammon. "Why does he need to come here?"

"Have something valuable and make it a prize," said Fouada.

"Yes," said Ammon. "But how?"

"Maybe a coffin of gold and jewels that fits Osiris," said Fouada.

"Very good," said Ammon.

"Ask each of the regions to send a person to fit the box and let the prize be the box itself," said Fouada.

"But why should he come?" asked Ammon. "Osiris is rich; he can have his own box made."

"Have the girl come also to the location of the box, and make the rendezvous the real reason for the visit," said Fouada.

"But how to kill him?" said Ammon.

"Get him to lie in the box, close the lid, and stab him through holes in the box," said Fouada.

"Excellent!" said Ammon. "A very complex plan and yet simple to execute."

"Talk it over with Zosimos first and let him make suggestions first before telling him your decision," said Fouada. "Make it a joint plan if possible."

"I will do that," said Ammon.

"Make sure the pharaoh is there at his death this time, so if something goes wrong, he won't blame you and Zosimos," said Fouada.

"I will, don't worry," said Ammon.

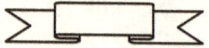

Set sat staring at his two advisors again, their plan to lure Osiris to Ta-Shemau, now revealed, appealed to him, especially as he would be there to see Osiris being killed.

"Why the seventy-two men present?" asked Set.

"This is a symbolic number, my Pharaoh, before a god passes to the afterlife, so does a coffin; seventy-two men must be selected to fit the box," said Ammon. "It was Zosimos' idea, and I think a nice touch."

"And the girl?" asked Set.

"She will be the main bait," said Ammon, "but we need Hakin first to show the girl Nefertiti to Osiris, maybe by a visit to Tadinanefar, and then dangle the coffin."

"How do you propose doing that?" asked Set.

"We will have the girl sent there before the invitation is sent to Osiris," said Ammon.

"When shall this happen?" asked Set.

"Soon, my Pharaoh," said Ammon, "but first we need to make the coffin and gather the seventy-two men to spring the trap."

"Make all haste," said Set. "Now, where is the Eblan envoy?"

"Outside, my Pharaoh," said Zosimos, who had found him whoring in one of the city's brothels.

"Get him," said Set, and waved his hand for the men to stand.

Both men rose and backed to the main door, which opened, and they saw the Eblan envoy with a servant girl, her sheath dress raised to her waist, and the envoy's hand in her crotch area.

"Thoth," said Zosimos, "the pharaoh awaits your words of obedience."

Thoth turned and looked at the two waiting advisors and then the girl's open legs and sighed. Well, he would not plough this girl, he thought, before his death, once Set heard his words.

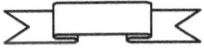

Thoth was a large man, nearly five feet eight inches tall, with a broad, powerful chest and huge biceps and triceps from daily exercise and training in the Eblan army. He had risen slowly from entering the army at the age of fourteen. He became an officer when he was twenty, and at the age of thirty he had risen to the level of captain with a reputation for being fearless, if a little headstrong. The King Inpu decided that Thoth would be ideal for the insult he was to send Set, as he knew no other man would stand and deliver the message knowing certain death followed. He put on his leather helmet over his long hair, worn to the shoulder, and strapped on his leather belt. His sword had been taken from him when Zosimos found him in the whorehouse. He stood his full height now, calm, and ready to face death.

"Take me to your pharaoh," said Thoth. "My message from King Inpu is ready to be delivered."

Ammon and Zosimos led the way into the pharaoh's ceremonial hall, and Thoth marvelled at its size and beauty, as the buildings in Hattisa, the capital of Eblan, were small by comparison. Set was as he imagined him: tall and powerful, with a fierce face and a cruel smile through which he spoke.

"What words do you have from your king, Eblan?" asked Set, impressed with the stature and bearing of the envoy, as most visitors usually were cowed by Set's presence.

"King Inpu of Eblan sends no greetings to Set, the pretender to the throne of tWay whose rightful heir is Osiris. He gives you no tribute and no allegiance, and will stand in the field against you should you cross the desert to Eblan, and then kill you and scatter your bones across the desert sand," said Thoth in a loud, clear voice, the room deathly silent.

Set sat very still, as if struck. His first reaction was to strike off the envoy's head and send it back to King Inpu on a plate. Instead, he hesitated. "What do you think of this insult, Ammon?" asked Set.

"Disgraceful, my Pharaoh," said Ammon, who visibly was shocked that Thoth had the courage to deliver such a message. "Send back this envoy in pieces!"

Thoth looked at Ammon peacefully, as though he was not concerned at what was about to happen to him.

"You, envoy, what is your name?" asked Set

"Thoth, my Lord," said Thoth, surprised he was still alive.

"What did you think was going to happen to you once you delivered your message?" asked Set.

"You would kill me, my Lord," said Thoth.

"Perhaps," said Set, surprised by his bravery. "Guards, take this man to the dungeons, but do not harm him, and see he is treated well."

Two burly guards came and pushed Thoth, who walked unconcerned, his fate sealed in his own mind.

"Why, Ammon is Eblan's king so disrespectful?" asked Set.

"We need to march across the land of Osiris to reach Eblan, and they pay tribute to Osiris, so they do not fear you, my Pharaoh," said Ammon, stating the obvious.

"But why the direct insult? Why not just ignore the request for a tribute?" asked Set, now puzzled.

"Eblan wants to show Osiris he is his friend and your enemy. The insult proves his loyalty to Osiris," said Ammon.

"The messenger? Why send this man to be killed?" asked Set.

"That I do not know, my Pharaoh, but will make enquiries," said Ammon.

"Then go and do my bidding," said Set.

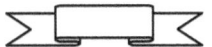

The measurements of Osiris had been obtained from Tadinanefar, and the coffin took nearly a month to prepare. The workmen had fashioned a beautiful coffin, fit for a pharaoh. The coffin was made of wood, but then covered with thin layers of gold in a lattice pattern both inside and outside the coffin. The whole of the outside was covered with elaborate mystical patterns in jewels depicting imagined scenes from the afterlife. Whilst there was a lid and clasp to close the coffin, Ammon could see no holes through which Osiris could be stabbed.

"Where are the holes I requested?" asked Ammon, pointing at the coffin.

"They are hidden my Lord," said the coffin maker, and he turned two of the raised jewels on the front of the coffin to reveal a hole wide enough for a sword blade.

Ammon inspected the work carefully and closed the two holes. He looked inside and could not see any way you would suspect a blade could enter the coffin once shut.

"Good," said Ammon, "so the work is completed."

"Yes, my Lord," said the coffin maker.

"Show Zosimos all the secrets of the coffin," said Ammon, and he handed the coffin maker a purse of gold. Ammon then stepped from the workshop into the street, where a captain of the guard and a number of soldiers stood waiting. Ammon drew his hand across his throat, and the guard captain nodded.

It was a pity that the coffin maker had to die after such wonderful work, but he could not risk the coffin maker getting drunk and speaking the truth about the coffin. His fate and that of his family were sealed the moment he was given the task to make the coffin. Zosimos would make sure that no family member was spared.

Ta-Shemau, which had twenty-two nomes (regions), each had an envoy sent from Set asking for a man of substance and good standing to come to El-Kab, the walled city and capital of Ta-Shemau, and seek the Coffin of Destiny. Ta-Mehu, with its twenty nomes, each had a similar envoy sent, but asked for two men from each of the twenty nomes, except the capital Memphis, from which Osiris himself was invited, and he was to name one man. The sixty-two men each would compete in a tournament to lie in the Coffin of Destiny, and if it fit that man, he would he given the coffin for his afterlife. Ammon knew most men believed in the afterlife as an extension of the real world, and the method of burial was very important. To be buried in a gold and jewelled coffin would be sought after by all men, even Osiris, particularly if it was thought that the coffin had a spell cast on it for their destiny.

Osiris received the invitation with some amusement from the envoy, and would have dismissed him without another thought, but for the compelling reason of the girl. He enjoyed sex with many women, but had been childless like his brother Set, and therefore he had started to plant his seed in Tadinanefar, but she also remained barren. When Tadinanefar came to ask permission for travel with her sister to El-Kab to witness the coffin being given to a righteous man, he was stunned by the beauty of her sister, who accompanied her, and pondered how he could find an excuse to be alone with Nefertiti.

A shy woman servant arrived after her departure with a message for Osiris. "My mistress Nefertiti greets you, great Pharaoh, and wants it to be known that should you come to claim your prize in E-Kab, a willing furrow can be ploughed by your shaft." The maiden spoke in a low voice so that only Osiris could hear in the great hall.

"Thank your mistress," said Osiris, "and tell her I may come and plough both her and her sister at El-Kab."

"I will pass your message to my mistress, my Pharaoh," said the servant, and she bowed and walked backwards out of the hall.

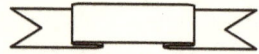

And so, against the will of Isis and his advisors, Osiris travelled to El-Kab to claim his prize of the Coffin of Destiny from his brother Set.

Nearly all of the seventy-two contestants for the coveted prize of the Coffin of Destiny arrived by boat at the El-Kab port, greeted by cheering crowds, as the event had been declared a public holiday by Set. Set also had organized public events at which ten members of the public could be selected to become contestants at the event, which was to be held in the open in the large square within the walled city.

El-Kab was really two cities, one called Nekheb, dedicated to the falcon goddess in the east of the Nile, and Nekhen, dedicated to the falcon god in the west of the Nile. The capital was in Nekhen, as Set preferred its position and had developed the city with help of Ammon and Zosimos during the years of his reign.

Many of the projects were typical of other cities: temples for the gods, water for the city, irrigation for the farms that spread along the plain in either side of the Nile, paving of the streets, and the building of clay dwellings for the workers and stone houses for the rich. The city had many craft workers making furniture, weaving cloth, making jewellery, and making cosmetics, and because of these, both foreign and national traders settled their caravans of donkeys in the city, visiting places all over the known land. The bustling streets encouraged such trade, and as no money existed, sales of the exchange of goods and the exchange of labour were made. Although writing had been invented, most people could not read, so everything was based on a man's word and each man's memory. The trade routes went to Cyprus, Crete, Greece, Syro – Palestine, Pant, and Nabea, and often, slaves were given in exchange for goods; therefore, the city contained many nationalities within its walls, and they brought with them new ideas and concepts.

Medicine was one area much admired by Set and his advisors, and many practitioners came to El Kab to practice the art. Bones could be set, surgery could be performed, and medicines to cure ailments were prescribed. Of course, the oldest profession of prostitution was practiced, and an area in El Kab was dedicated to its practice, with both women and men being offered for sex. The trade was strictly regulated by the pharaoh's advisors, and the owners of the prostitutes were taxed. Tax was a burden for all of the population of the kingdom and it was managed by the monarch of each district. The monarch would appoint a tax collector to collect the taxes and to remember the punishment for unpaid taxes, which usually were instant to avoid the problem of forgetting debts that were owed.

Religion was another important part of life in El-Kab, as the temples were sacred, and the priests, as the pharaoh's representatives, offered food and wine to the gods on a daily basis. As the public were not allowed in the temples, they did not know that the gods did not eat the food, and in fact, the priests consumed everything. The symbolism was what was important in any event in El Kab. Set was well aware of how to create an event to meet the expectations of the public, so when he planned the event with Ammon and Zosimos, he ensured all aspects of the culture and religion were satisfied in the games and rituals that would unfold on the day of the Coffin of Destiny.

Chapter Three

Games in El Kab were organized in different locations around the city. Fowling using a throw stick was conducted in the marshes. Hunting was in the Lower Desert, where the animals were plentiful. Wrestling, running, fencing, archery, and feats of strength all were completed in the city in controlled games, as were the entertainment games of musical instruments, dancing, and singing. Priests and monarchs from the two kingdoms of Ta-Mehu and Ta-Shemau had been selected for their reputations of fairness and honesty to preside over each game, of which there were ten. The winner of each game would receive a prize of gold and jewels and be entered as a contestant in the Coffin of Destiny competition. If the winner was already a contestant, then the runner-up or the next person who was not a contestant in the event would be selected by the judges. The events would be over four days, and a feast would be held each evening to which the public would be invited. On the final night, the winners would be invited to try and see if they fit the Coffin of Destiny.

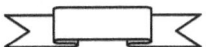

Osiris rose early in the morning of the first event, as he intended to participate in as many events as he could in spite of the fact that he was already qualified as one of the seventy-two people preselected. He and his manservant's would hunt together in the marshes using the throwing sticks he hunted with at his home in Memphis.

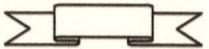

Set had his plans for Osiris, and they involved a new assassin: Thoth, the envoy from Eblan. Thoth had languished in his dungeons for a number of weeks before Set received any information about the man from Eblan. He came from a noble family distantly related to the king, whose father had been disgraced, so the boy had entered the army to make his way. Thoth had excelled in all of the arts of war.

Diplomacy had not been his favourite subject, and therefore had not been popular at any stage in his career. He had never married, and all of his family was dead. One of his weaknesses was women, and he had been found several times coupling with fellow officer's wives or mistresses, which was taboo for the life of a warrior within the Eblan Army. The reason for his assignment to be the envoy to Ta-Shemau stemmed from this proclivity in his nature.

His General Heru had a beautiful wife, Hatshepsut, who was only seventeen, whilst the general was in his late forties and just being selected for his position not because of ability, but because of his family contacts. Thoth, having served under his command, despised Heru as being incompetent and unworthy of command, and sought to punish him by mating with Hatshepsut. Unfortunately for Thoth, he fell under the spell of the girl, and instead of a casual affair, they both fell in love and met frequently for Thoth to plough the furrow of Hatshepsut. Heru discovered them by chance, coupling in his gardens, his wife's legs and arms wrapped around Thoth's powerful body as he thrust into her soft and willing body. Heru was transfixed in horror as he saw his beautiful wife cry in ecstasy as Thoth thrust himself inside her every orifice while she moaned in pleasure, encouraging Thoth to press deeper inside her. When they had finished and Thoth withdrew from Hatshepsut, he saw that Thoth's manhood was long and thick, and this shamed Heru as being inadequate. He wanted to confront Thoth and strike him dead, but he knew he would be killed by the strong and fearless warrior, so he decided he needed to go away and devise a plan to kill and hurt him in a more devious way.

It was, of course, quite easy for Heru to arrange to select the envoy to Ta-Shemau and meet almost certain death and torture with the arrogant message to the Pharaoh Set. Heru had been asked to find a suitable fearless envoy, and he simply asked his whole army for volunteers. Thoth was one of the men who immediately volunteered, and Heru, in front of the whole army, sealed his fate.

"Captain Thoth, you volunteer for the mission as envoy to Ta-Shemau, knowing it is dangerous?" asked Heru.

"Yes, my General," said Thoth.

"Know that you could be killed in this mission, and even be tortured," said Heru, "so a coward is not required."

Thoth visibly winced at the suggestion he might be a coward, but had not considered death or torture. Now, shamed, he answered, "I accept the mission knowing both these things, my General."

"Then it is done," said Heru. "I will tell our king a brave man has volunteered his life in the service of our nation."

Heru could not help smiling at how easily Thoth had been trapped.

Thoth suddenly realized he had been trapped by his vanity into certain death. "I ask one favour, my General."

"Speak, and it will be granted," said Heru, smug in the belief he had now mastered this insolent junior officer.

"I would like a few days of love with a woman of my choice to prepare me for death. Of course, the woman must agree publicly that she is willing to the proposition," said Thoth.

"You have your wish," said Heru, too hurriedly to consider who he might choose.

"I choose your wife, Hatshepsut," said Thoth, "if she agrees."

A murmur of laughter came from the ranks, and Heru's colour went red with embarrassment, as his wife had been brought to witness Thoth's downfall.

"What say you, my lady Hatshepsut?" shouted Thoth above the now open laughter.

"I agree," said Hatshepsut. "We cannot deny a brave man, or refuse my husband's gift given in front of his whole army."

So, for seven full days and nights, Heru had to endure his wife Hatshepsut being ploughed by Thoth, and the whole army knowing the general had been cuckolded by a junior officer.

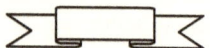

When Set met Thoth again, he had bathed and rested in the palace, and even had some women slaves sent to his bed before the meeting. Thoth came into the chamber as before, but this time bowed low to Set to acknowledge his superiority and removed his sandals before he came into the room.

"So, Thoth, which do you prefer: a dungeon and death, or a young girl or boy to plough and life in the palace?" asked Set.

"The latter, my Pharaoh," said Thoth.

"So have you changed your allegiance?" asked Set.

"I was a dead man after I delivered my message," said Thoth. "If my life is spared, then it is yours."

"Very well, I have a mission for you," said Set. "Come closer, I will whisper it in your ear."

Thoth approached the throne and bent to hear the mission, and then smiled and nodded knowingly.

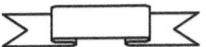

The marshes at El Kab were along the floodplain close to the Nile, and formed part of the regular hunting land used by many of the local residents both as an occupation and for sport. The throw stick was like a boomerang and returned to stun or kill the prey, usually a bird in flight. For sport, wild ducks or geese would be hunted, and the birds would be stalked by a servant who would creep quietly upon a flock and then charge them, banging loud drums or symbols and shouting. When the flock rose into the air, the hunters would use the throw sticks to knock the birds out of the air, and dogs would be used to collect the birds for each hunter.

Osiris had been hunting using a throw stick all of his life and loved the sport, which he practiced often with Bes as his hunting servant who carried a bag of throw sticks strapped to his back. As well as Osiris, the competition was to be with two other men, one each from Ta-Mehu and Ta-Shemau. Each of the kingdoms had held preliminary rounds of the competition to select one contestant for each event. The competition would be simple: each person would select where to stand, and when the birds rose in the air, the man who felled the most birds from a single flock would be the winner.

The three men took their position. All three had a servant who would hand throw sticks to the hunter.

However, Bes would stand to the right of Osiris with the throw sticks in his bag strapped to his back, and Osiris would pick the throw sticks himself. The early morning cold was ebbing, and the water was becoming warmer, and the three men were nearly up to their knees with water as they watched the stalkers in the distance silently surround a flock of ducks. Suddenly, the stalkers charged the birds, and they rose in fright, spreading upwards to the sky. The three men loosed their three throw sticks, and the birds fell from the sky. The hunting dogs from the three hunters immediately leapt forward to find the birds.

Hardly had the first throw stick left his hand when Osiris grabbed the next stick and threw it skyward; the rhythm was quite remarkable, as his aim always was accurate and deadly for every bird. The other hunters were quick in being handed a stick from their companion but the Osiris method was perhaps a second quicker between each throw and Bes' bag had more throw sticks available in the short space of time before the birds rose out of reach. Osiris threw a remarkable twelve sticks, all of which hit a bird and were retrieved. The hunter from Ta-Mehu was the second fastest with nine, having launched ten throw sticks but missing one bird. The hunter from Ta-Shemau had eight kills to his name and had missed no birds. As the men retrieved their sticks from the marshes, a cry came up from the hunter from Ta-Shemau that curdled the air.

Osiris immediately pulled the sword from the side of Bes and the spear he had placed in the soft silt of the march. He spun to see a large crocodile speeding towards him, his jaw wide open, ready for the kill. Using his left hand, he instinctively swung the spear forward and thrust the spear into the throat of the crocodile, the spear going deep into its body. The crocodile wriggled and splashed furiously in its death throes, but its momentum was stopped. He now grabbed the second spear he had and splashed towards the cry, but it was too late; he saw the man from Te-Shemau being ripped apart by three large crocodiles. He turned to see the man from Ta-Mehu fleeing the marshes for the safer, dry land, and he and Bes followed, leaving the crocodiles to their early morning breakfast.

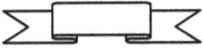

Set watched from the high ground in silence, willing the crocodiles to kill the hunters, but he saw clearly that Osiris was too alert and quick to be trapped and had escaped victorious. He sighed; his plan of trapping crocodiles the previous day and releasing them behind the hunters had failed, even killing his city's finest hunter.

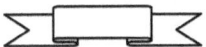

The second hunting game used a similar technique, but was played in the higher ground in the Upper Desert close to a watering hole used by the animals. The stalkers would herd gazelles, stags, ostrich, even lions, and leopards to a watering hole and the hunters would slay the beasts using bows and arrows. The hunters used the self bow. This was a single arched bow made of wood and string with sinews from animals. The bow was between one and two meters in length and narrowed at each end. The bows were strengthened with binding cord by the bowmen. Bows had a single curve or a double curve. Single arched bows were harder to draw than double arched bows, and the draw length was shorter, thus the distance achieved was shorter.

Osiris had imported a bow from Cyrene. This was a composite bow shorter and higher than the self bow. It had a double curve and was made from wood and horn that was glued to the belly of the bow (the part that faces the archer). The strength and lightness of the bow allowed Osiris to fully extend the draw length of the bow to the full distance of his arm. This was not possible with the self bow, which broke when fully extended. This gave Osiris a huge advantage of additional distance with full extension, or higher speed if he did not fully extend the bow string (and still he could achieve a similar distance to a self bow). However the bow was very fragile and required careful maintenance and had to be unstrung when not being used. It usually took two men to string the bow. However because of Osiris' immense strength, he could string the bow by himself, and he made it look easy.

Each archer had different coloured feathers for their arrows, and once the beasts were at the watering hole, they would keep firing arrows until all the animals were dead. The winner would be the archer with the most kills. Osiris wore a pouch strapped to his back—unusual for an archer—and would reach behind his head for arrows. He also had spare pouches carried by Bes, as well as two spears and his sword. It was not unusual for animals to break from the herd and attack hunters, so Osiris and Bes were vigilant at all times.

The archer from Ta-Mehu was well known to Osiris. Thutmose was a fine nobleman who entered many competitions and was a fierce competitor. Like Osiris, he had a composite bow, but unlike Osiris, he needed his slave to help him string the bow. The archer from Ta-Shemau used the long wooden self bow used by most archers in both kingdoms. The three men stood quite close together some hundred meters from the watering hole and watched as a multitude of stalkers surrounded animals and beat the ground to herd them to the watering hole. The beasts were plentiful, and Osiris was pleased that he had brought several quivers of arrows with Bes as well has the ones he wore on his back. They both had the long spears for hunting with the broad steel heads, in addition to their swords and daggers. The crocodile incident was common whilst fowling or hunting, and it was part of the excitement and thrill of the sport.

The two judges for the event raised a flag to signal when the animals were nearing the watering hole; the flag was white. Osiris could see gazelles in their tens nearing the oasis, with ostrich and hyenas. He also saw a confused pride of lions and leopards and nodded towards Bes as the beasts neared the watering hole. "Bes, be ready with the arrows," said Osiris, and Bes nodded, moving to the side of his master. He would fill the pouch on his back with arrows as his master emptied the pouch as he fired arrows into the beasts. The black flag was waved, and the archers all propelled their first arrows, and three beasts fell immediately. It was difficult to miss, as a huge herd was now at the watering hole.

Osiris fired his arrows in a rhythm, clearing his mind of everything except the target he was aiming at and the smooth execution of selecting an arrow from the pouch on his back and drawing back the bow correctly. As the seconds became minutes, the animals fell rhythmically, quivering amongst each other as the slaughter continued relentlessly and the three archers kept firing their arrows. Osiris, with the red feathers in his arrows, never missed a target. With every arrow was a death, and he kept pace with the two other archers. Slowly, as the minutes passed, both the other archers tired, and their pace slowed, and as the animals thinned, only Osiris continued at the same pace and accuracy.

Surprisingly, the archer from Ta-Shemau was his nearest rival, but even he tired to the point of exhaustion, and his arms fell to his side in defeat as he watched Osiris continue relentlessly. *Surely, this was a god in the form of a man*, thought the archer, as he watched the beasts continue to fall as Osiris now fired his final arrows. Then, from the corner of his eye, he saw in horror a pride of lions emerge from the spare coarse vegetation in which they stood and rush towards Osiris and Bes.

"Behind you, lions!" Shouted the Ta- Shemau archer.

Osiris immediately dropped his bow and in one swift, fluid move he picked one of his two spears and threw the spear, pinning a lioness to the ground. His second spear was just as accurate, but did not stop the lioness, who staggered a few feet forward. Bes did not throw either of his spears as the four remaining animals approached. Throwing his first spear to Osiris, who killed a third animal in a final fluid movement, the final spear arrived from Bes as a huge lion leapt . Using the final spear, he thrust it forward, piercing the lion right through its body but not killing it outright, and it roared in defiance. The two lionesses jumped on the massive frame of Bes, who had drawn his sword and struck one of the beasts but only wounded it, and their combined weight brought him to the ground.

Osiris had been wounded by a lion, his giant paw gouging his shoulder, but Osiris ignored the pain, and as he fell to the ground, he threw a knife at one of the lionesses, which severed its throat. It was a magnificent and almost impossible throw, and extremely brave, as the lion he was fighting was still alive and attacking again. Osiris pulled his final hunting knife, and in an amazing jump, he somersaulted in the air and landed on the back of the lion with his dagger in hand. Stabbing at the lion's windpipe, killed the beast with swift strokes.

He leapt from the beast, grabbed his sword, and rushed to Bes, who now lay motionless as the lioness mauled his body. With one mighty blow, he nearly chopped the beast in half, slicing through its spine and releasing its jaw from Bes. He threw the beast from Bes, but saw immediately that he was dead and motionless. A pang of regret struck his heart, as Bes was more than a manservant; he was his closest friend and confidant and even lover. He loved this man more than his own life, and now he was dead and had given his life for Osiris. Unselfishly, he had given both his spears to him, when he could have used them to kill the two lionesses that were attacking him.

Meanwhile, Thutmose watched the events unfold before his eye, and could not believe what he had witnessed. Osiris had killed a pride of six lions single handed. He was surely a god and not a man.

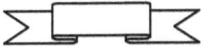

From a safe vantage point, Thoth watched Osiris, and wondered what sort of man could perform such miracles, and wondered if Osiris would be killed even by the deceit they had planned for him. Certainly, the two last attempts had both been defeated, and Osiris' reputation enhanced. Perhaps the only consolation was that Osiris' loyal servant Bes now was dead and could no longer protect him.

Chapter Four

Osiris slept alone for the first time in years, exhausted from the day's events and distraught over the loss of Bes. His shoulder wound had not been serious, and the SWNW (*svono*) stitched his wound neatly and applied a cleansing ointment to clean the wound, which stung. Osiris drank a draft that he carried with him from Ta-Mehu that drugged him and sent him into a deep sleep. His small group of bodyguards surrounded his chambers and none were allowed to pass. In the morning, he woke surprisingly refreshed and he felt recovered from the loss of Bes. His manhood was hard, and he took a girl who delivered his water to bathe to satisfy his lust. He felt alive and ready for the next day's competitions. Through a servant, he sent a message to Nefertiti to join him the next evening in his bed.

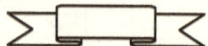

The next event was along the Nile, and Osiris loved the water; swimming and sailing were two of his favourite pastimes and he practiced them often. The three men all were in perfect shape, their bodies rippling with muscles as they stood on the river's edge ready for the swimming race. They swam completely naked, as was the custom, and unlike the other events, there were spectators to witness the three contestants. The ladies in the audience swooned at the size of Osiris' manhood, and his long, athletic, and powerful physique, and they discussed his powers in bed and fantasized him ploughing their furrow the coming night. The men wagered bets on who would win the race, and told of the rumour circulating regarding Osiris exploits the day before. Children ran along the Nile mimicking the crawl stroke, pretending they were in the race, and celebrating when they reached the imaginary finish line.

The three men were to swim to the boat that would be the start of the race, swim to another boat about a mile upstream, turn, and return to the first boat. It was about one mile between the two boats, so the course was two miles in length. Osiris loved competition and now was exhilarated by the race; his manhood stiffened and lengthened and some of the crowd noticed and laughed, but Osiris did not notice, as he now concentrated on the race. He entered the water with the two other men and swam with slow, even strokes to the boat, and then they trod water whilst they awaited the start flag.

The white flag to make ready was raised, and Osiris could see the other two swimmers stroke poses in the water to make ready, pointing their hands forward as though they were going to sprint in the water. Osiris relaxed his muscles, cleared his mind, and thought only of how to keep each stroke smooth and to pull powerfully with each arm, striking the water cleanly with each leg and swimming straight like an arrow. When the black flag fell to start the race, he completed his first stroke unconcerned about the other two swimmers. His concentration was the perfection and power he could get from each individual stroke, dismissing it upon completion and concentrating on the next stroke. Keep his body straight, his breath from the left in the draught was made from his stroke. Then, there were two powerful strokes to rotate and breathe from the right. He needed to keep the body supple, keep the rhythm, and slowly increase the stroke rate as the body acclimates to the water; however, he had to listen and be alert for predators in the water, as large crocodiles frequented the waters. These fearsome creatures reached ten feet in length and could weigh up to fifteen hundred pounds. With only their eyes and nostrils above the water, they were difficult to see while swimming, and Osiris had been taught a sixth sense; with it, he would scan the waters to either side of him to spot crocodiles.

Osiris swam the farthest from the shore. His two competitors swam nearer to the shore line, as the current was slower near the shore and the first leg was against the current. Osiris always preferred the more difficult start, as the swimmer had to keep the same positions on the return leg, and the strong current would help Osiris to the finish line. Both of the other two swimmers were very good and the three men were very close to each other until they reached the half-mile stage. Osiris then very gradually increased his pace, and by the time they reached the boat around which they had to swim, he had clear water between them.

The return leg was easy for Osiris. With the extra speed of the current to aid him, he stretched his lead in the race and reached the finishing boat perhaps a good quarter of a mile in front of the other two swimmers. Instead of swimming to the shore, he surprised the judges by getting into the boat and waiting for the other two swimmers. He pulled each of them aboard when they had finished. When they were both aboard the boat, he pointed to the reeds near the shore. "Crocodiles," said Osiris. "You can take us ashore by boat."

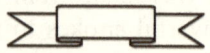

From the shore line, Thoth watched the waiting crocodiles, a pack of twelve huge beasts submerged in the water, and saw Osiris board the boat with the other swimmers. *Today was not going to be the day Osiris died*, he thought to himself. The finish had been selected carefully to be at this position where this fearsome crocodile pack hunted.

The next event was the javelin, and it was to follow directly after the swimming event. Each contestant would throw three spears. The thrower who threw the longest aggregate distance would win.

Osiris knew the man from Ta-Mehu, as he was high born and a famous athlete called Gabir; he often competed in events. Osiris, as he was the ruler, was not permitted to compete in his homeland, and he often had wondered if he would be able to beat Gabir athletically. Gabir was good at all of the events, but famous for the javelin, which he always won against all athletes who competed against him, including the opponent from Ta-Shemau who would compete today. He often challenged his nearest opponent to a death throw. This often was banned from many events. On the final throw, the two opponents nearest each other stand at their rival's furthest spear, and the opponent can throw his spear directly at him, hoping to win the event by killing his opponent.

Gabir was renowned for being able to throw the javelin for sixty paces, which was a prodigious distance to throw the metal-tipped spear of wood. Both Gabir and Osiris had specially designed spears with the traditional wide spear point narrowed and the spear about two and half strides long with the end tapered. There were no rules on the size of the spear or how it

43

was thrown, but the thrower had to be behind a marker made in the ground, and the spear had to spear the ground or the target. The throw was measured in strides by a judge.

Gabir and Osiris both threw the spear with a run-up and an overhead arching of the back. They threw upwards, whilst the man from Te-Shemau spun around to get more force. Osiris had tried spinning, but found you lost accuracy, and often the javelin did not pierce the ground. The first man threw his spear using the spinning technique and it travelled about sixty yards, but did not pierce the ground. Gabir was next, and he removed his loincloth, wearing a short kilt to cover his genitals. Gabir was tall perhaps five feet ten or eleven and very broad with large biceps and triceps. He was a very fast runner, with muscular thighs and calves, and he used a long run-up before launching the javelin. Osiris watched as Gabir covered the ground like an arrow, his back arching back before the throw, his muscles tight as he released the javelin skyward. The javelin arched in the sky and fell point first towards the ground, and fell some twenty paces beyond the fifty-pace marker. The crowd roared, and Gabir lifted his arms in triumph.

Osiris smiled and clapped his hands for his opponent. Osiris also took a run-up, but did not attempt the speed that Gabir ran at, as this imbalanced the throw. Osiris cleared his mind, *arch back, throw with your frame, not just your arm*, he recited in his mind, making the last two steps the speed of the leopard. Osiris now stripped to his short kilt and stretched, repeating the mantra in his mind. Running only five or six meters, he ran quickly only over the last two steps, his back arching and his arm stretching back, and then pulling forward the javelin from his whole torso, he released the javelin when his hand punched the sky.

Gabir watched in awe, even fear, as Osiris was an awesome athlete as many had told him. The javelin soared high into the air arched perfectly downwards and then speared the ground just beyond the hundred paces mark. It was a feat never achieved by a man before in competition; Gabir knew he could not win the event by a distance throw. He knew he needed to challenge Osiris to a death throw.

In the next round, both the man from Ta-Shemau and Gabir threw the javelin only sixty paces, and Osiris excelled again, throwing the javelin even further, perhaps even a hundred and twenty paces.

It was then that Gabir threw out his challenge of a death throw. "You throw well, my Pharaoh," said Gabir, "but the distance is of no consequence if you cannot hit a man."

"True, Gabir," said Osiris, knowing what would happen next.

"So I challenge you, my Pharaoh, to a death throw. We shall each stand at the others nearest throw, and the winner will be the man who survives," said Gabir.

Osiris now could see why he had thrown his second throw with less force: to make the target easier. His nearest throw was over a hundred paces, and therefore it would be difficult to be very accurate and kill Gabir. "I accept, Gabir, and you may choose either of my marks. I will stand at your nearest mark if you live. Remember, you can step aside with no disgrace, rather than die, if my javelin is accurate," said Osiris.

"My Lord, I will stand with my back to your throw; nobody can be accurate at that distance," said Gabir in disdain. He was confident that nobody—even Osiris—could hit a man at one hundred plus paces.

"As you choose," said Osiris.

Gabir strode to the furthest spear and counted the paces with his long stride. It was one hundred and twenty four paces, a throw from a god. He stood with his arms outstretched, confident that nobody could hit the same spot twice, and thought of the gold and jewels he would receive from Set when Osiris died. He heard the swish of the flight of the spear and then no more as the javelin speared his body pinning him to the ground. The crowd gasped in wonderment, and Thoth swore under his breath.

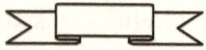

The next day, Osiris felt elated. At long last, he had been able to show the world his powers as a hunter and athlete. Today he was confident that none would prove better than him again. The loss of Bes was no longer heavy in his heart, and he already replaced him in his bed with Nefertiti, the maid provided by the household of Hakim. He stared at her naked body on the bed and marvelled at the arch of her back, the curve of her thigh, the whiteness of her skin, and the black lustre of her long hair. She was a marvellous woman and a good lover and good distraction for Osiris. Many thought Osiris was blessed to be married to Isis, and in many ways he was, as he loved her deeply and without reservation, but he could not love her sexually and could not make love to her, as he loved her like he always had, as his sister. Of course, he spread the myth he ploughed her daily, but the reality was she was a virgin. Osiris found his pleasure elsewhere, discretely, with girls and boys, as he liked them both.

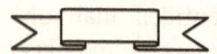

The first event was to be in the morning and would be a race around the city of Ta-Shemau. They would circle the city five times for a distance of about five miles. For Osiris, this was a long distance to maintain his usual speed, as he was muscular and more suitable for short and middle distance running, but Osiris did train occasionally over longer distances and had good stamina. He hoped he could keep pace with the two runners so he could use a sprint close to the finish line.

The Ta-Mehu and Ta-Shemau runners were both small, light men, built as runners, weighing less than girls. They had strong, skinny muscles on long legs with short-waisted bodies that took little effort to carry when running. Osiris probably weighed close to twice their weight and was built for strength and speed. He was not suited to a five-mile race, but still, he was Osiris and would run with his heart. They ran barefoot with just a short kilt for modesty on the streets of Ta-Shemau, and the sun was just rising in the cool of the morning. It would be fully set and hot by the time they were finished. The judge raised his flag, and when it fell, his two competitors immediately sprinted from the starting point.

Osiris cleared his mind and began to concentrate on his running action. Keep the back straight; let the legs do the work. Lift the knee shallowly and reach forward, keep the arms in time with the body, left leg and right arm together, right leg and left arm together, breathe shallowly, it is no effort, breathe slowly, fill the lungs. Osiris ran effortlessly, it seemed, behind the two smaller runners, their heads turning every quarter mile or so to see if he was still a few paces behind them. He always seemed to be effortlessly keeping up with their pace. The men ran within themselves for the first three circuits of the city, but in the fourth circuit, the man from Ta-Shemau, the better runner, began to lengthen his stride and draw away from the other runner.

Osiris saw the development and slowly increased his pace, overtaking the runner from Ta-Mehu, who lost confidence and begun to fall back. Soon, the race was between the two men, and as they approached the last lap, the smaller runner tried to increase the gap between them with a sprint, but Osiris lengthened his stride smoothly and kept pace. Osiris told himself: *Ignore the pain, it does not exist, lengthen the stride, concentrate, keep the arms in sync with the legs, don't over breathe, empty and fill the lungs, be ready for the sprint.* As they ran the last lap, they ran side by side, the crowd cheering until they reached the long climb up the hill to the palace of Set where the finish took place. When Osiris reached the hill, he changed his mantra: *Knees up, stride long, arms up, punch the air, keep the back upright, blow the air in and out of your body, burn the street with your speed, you are nearly there, run like the wind*! Osiris' sprint surprised the smaller man, and he struggled to keep pace with the larger, more powerful man, his legs and arms pumping and his body forcing forward like a leopard made for speed. The distance widened, and as they hit the flat area to the finish line, Osiris was already fifty meters in front and running away from the smaller man with every stride.

Truly remarkable, thought Thoth. *Osiris is surely a god*. Nobody can do everything perfectly, but Osiris seems to be perfect at everything.

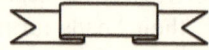

The next two events were to be held in the palace square and viewed by the court and public, who were able to crowd into the square. Osiris would wrestle two champion wrestlers, one each from Ta-Mehu and Ta-

Shemau, one after another, as the judges had drawn lots on the decision. Osiris suspected a conspiracy, but said nothing. The two men he would wrestle were famous throughout the known world. Shosheng was a man mountain and a giant of a man standing six foot two inches tall and weighing over three hundred pounds of solid muscle. He was undefeated in hundreds of contests until he fought Rameses, the man from Ta-Shemau, who defeated him with greater speed and agility in a match some two years ago.

Since then, Shosheng had regained some face in narrowly winning a return match and restoring some pride to Ta-Mehu, but his record of invincibility no longer existed. Rameses, like Shosheng, was tall a giant at six feet tall but weighed much less, perhaps two hundred and twenty pounds. Osiris was only about five feet eight inches tall and weighed one hundred and eighty pounds. Of the three men, Osiris looked the most symmetrical, with a classical V-shape body with eight ribbed abdomen muscles and symmetrical calf and bicep sizes, giving him a very balanced body shape. The other larger men looked bulky and cumbersome, but this was quickly dispelled in their warm up, when both men displayed lightening quick speed and agility. Rameses was the faster and lighter of the two and had many tricky turns and twists in his fighting style.

In wrestling, there was no punching or kicking the opponent, and no gouging or biting, and the match was to wrestle the opponent to the ground and pin his shoulders to the floor. Either opponent could retire by conceding the bout if the other man had him in a lock, from which he could not recover, but this rarely happened. The usual outcome was a throw, which left the opponent on the floor, having been picked up and thrown to the ground. Shosheng, with his superior size and strength, used the throw in most of his contests, as did most wrestlers. You needed three throws to win a contest.

Osiris would wrestle Rameses first. The giant Shosheng, regarded as the better fighter, would be used after Osiris had been tired by the first bout. Both men wrestled naked and were covered in oil, which made holds difficult to maintain. Whilst their genitals were exposed, it was illegal to grab the other man's genitals during the match. The speed of Rameses was legendary, and as the two men faced each other, Osiris was aware he was in for a mighty contest that day. Osiris spoke to himself: *Clear the mind, concentrate on getting a firm hold; twisting and turning, unbalance your opponent and then strike. Concentrate; make your body balanced like a rock of stone to lift and your arms strong. Lift your opponent like a feather with speed.*

They fought in a large square of sand, with the audience and judges surrounding the square. As the black flag dropped to start the contest, a deathly hush descended upon the audience. Rameses rushed across the ring in a lightning strike, which usually surprised his opponents. However, Osiris was ready, and using Rameses' momentum, he lifted him into the air, throwing him to the ground. In the second round, Rameses was more cautious, getting a firm grip on Osiris. They came together more slowly, but the outcome was the same: Osiris was impossible to move, and after a few tricks were tried and failed, Rameses tried a throw, and while unbalanced, Osiris picked him up and threw him to the ground. The third round was a similar affair, and the audience was a little disappointed because it was so one-sided. However, Osiris had been tired by the event and clearly was breathing more heavily.

Shosheng, the man from Osiris' own kingdom, entered the ring. "As is the ancient right of a wrestler, my Pharaoh, I offer you one bout to the death, no holds barred, no submission. The winner is the man who is alive at the end of the contest," said Shosheng.

This was a very unusual request, and was the second time Osiris would have to risk his life to compete. He was tired from the last contest and perhaps would not survive three bouts against the bigger man, Shosheng. "You ask for a fight to the death, Shosheng," said Osiris. "Why do you wish such a fate?"

"There is no risk; my Pharaoh will perish in the bout," said Shosheng confidently.

"No rules, any blow, any hold, to the death?" asked Osiris very quietly.

"No rules, any blow, any hold, to the death," confirmed Shosheng.

Osiris now knew that Set must be behind this and wanted him dead. The fowling and hunting incidents were not accidents, but somehow contrived by Set. "Very well, so be it," said Osiris, insulted that Shosheng had not called him "my pharaoh," as was required.

The two men faced each other, and Osiris could see that the sheer size of Shosheng was going to be difficult to lift and throw. The black flag fell, and Osiris leapt faster than a leopard across the ring and struck Shosheng with the side of his hand in the windpipe, and Shosheng fell to his knees choking. Osiris somersaulted over Shosheng, landing directly behind him. He grasped his head and turned it sharply, breaking the spinal cord and killing him instantly. Shosheng's body fell to the ground, dead. The crowd gasped in amazement, shocked at the speed of the outcome.

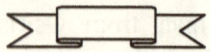

Thoth watched in horror. He had wrestled both Shosheng and Rameses, who had both dispatched him in seconds. He could not believe anybody could beat them both in a single day. Truly Osiris was a remarkable man, if not a god.

The weightlifting contest was anti-climactic for the crowd, as whilst the two giant men would contest against Osiris lifting rocks onto a stone plinth until they could lift no more; they expected Osiris to defeat anyone. He was obviously a god and had supernatural powers, so it was not a contest. So, even though Osiris was half the size of both men, when he convincingly beat them the crowd hardly cheered, hoping the underdogs from either kingdom would have beaten the god who competed with mortal man.

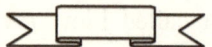

Set smiled at the reaction of the crowd and decided on how to dispatch Osiris the next day. He too was amazed by Osiris, but not completely surprised. As a boy, Set had never bettered Osiris at any sport, and he knew none who had. However, he knew Osiris was not a God and would bleed if cut, and would die if struck with a fatal blow. *Tomorrow*, he thought, *is your last day on earth, Osiris.*

Chapter Five

Unlike all of the other athletes, Osiris had been competing against the best athletes in each event for three days, and at a very high level, so as to avoid being killed each day. Most athletes would be stressed and tired from the excursions and dread the next day, but Osiris loved the competition and tension. He wondered what the next day would bring before the ceremony. He knew the Coffin of Destiny would be given to the man, who fit it completely, and not who won the most events—these were only events for the public consumption. What did surprise him was that the crowd was turning against him, because he kept winning against all odds. However, to lose was often to die, so he had to keep winning, regardless of the crowd's wishes. To be a dead hero was not in Osiris' plan.

The last day was to be the final three events of jumping, boxing, and fencing. Jumping was usually a ditch dug between two lines, and men would jump across; if they fell into the ditch, they were eliminated. Usually there were three or four ditches of different sizes. If there was a draw, they would dig a wider ditch until only one man cleared the ditch. The ditch usually was shallow and filled with sand to soften the fall. However, the event in Ta-Shemau was very different; each ditch was deep, and the walls sheer, so a man could not climb out without assistance. At the bottom were two fearsome lions that had not eaten for a number of days. Osiris' two competitors were tall and very thin; they had powerful legs for sprinting before they leapt over the ditch.

There were three ditches dug, the first was seven strides, the second, eight and a half strides, and the third, ten strides. Nobody ever had leapt the second ditch, and only the two men competing today ever had leapt the first ditch. To Osiris, it seemed the judges wanted something to happen at the event with the deep ditches and lions.

In the first round, much to the surprise of everyone, all three men cleared the ditch easily. The crowd was in a pensive mood, as all the men seemed in very good form and might clear the second ditch also without incident. The man from Ta-Mehu seemed untroubled by the second ditch, and he cleared it fairly easily by at least one pace. The second man also seemed confident in clearing the second ditch, and he ran confidently to the edge, but he seemed to trip, and then he tumbled headlong into the ditch. There was an agonizing cry from the man as the first lion bit clean through one of his arms, wrenching it from his body. The man miraculously stood, kicking the lion away, and ran away, blood pouring from the stump of his arm near his shoulder, but before he even could reach the edge of the ditch, the second lion's huge jaw snapped onto one of his legs, dragging him to the ground. The first lion discarded the arm and leapt on the grounded man, biting his other arm and tearing it from him. Now defenceless, the man screamed in terror as the lions tore him apart piece by piece. Osiris watched impassively, and when the man was dead and the crowd subdued, he leapt the second ditch by perhaps one and half paces, probably just not enough for the third ditch.

It was now Osiris' turn to go first, and he clearly saw that the plan in the event was for Osiris to fail on the third ditch and the remaining man to be the victor. Osiris cleared his mind and concentrated on a smooth run-up to the last five strides—to be all speed and power—until he felt the edge of the ditch, and then he sprung into the air and ran in mid-air, rotating his body forward. Osiris cleared the ditch easily, as if walking in mid-air, and landed a clear two paces on the other side.

The remaining athlete looked unamused at the jump and then prepared himself. He had practiced a few times on the ground, and mustering all his courage, he ran flat-out at the ditch. Because of the long run-up, Osiris could see that he slowed as he neared the edge and his momentum was downward, not upward, due to a lack of confidence. Even so, he nearly reached the other side, his outstretched arms clawing in the sky for the edge but missing agonizingly close in mid-air. There were two lions in this ditch that had not been fed for several days, and the athlete hardly hit the ground before the beasts began ripping him apart. The only consolation that could be said was that the death was quick and silent; he had hit his head on the ground and was probably unconscious as he was killed.

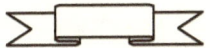

The next event was boxing, and as before with the wrestling, there were rules for the contest: No grappling or wrestling, no gouging with the fingers, but you could hit your opponent anywhere, including the genitals, as long as it was a punch. There were no rounds, and you beat your opponent until he no longer could stand or until he gave up and conceded the event. Both men were huge in size and had fearsome reputations, as boxing was often to the death, unlike wrestling, where submissions were common. This was to be the case with the two bouts that Osiris would box. He would fight Kemnebi from his own country Ta-Mehu first, and then Ponahasi from Ta-Shemau. Both men were huge, five foot ten or eleven inches tall, weighing perhaps eighteen or nineteen stones. As was customary, they had wrapped leather around the knuckles of their hands to protect them.

Osiris wore nothing on his hands, and as was the custom, both men would fight naked. Osiris had watched Kemnebi, whose name meant Black Panther, fight many times, and he was fast, ruthless, and very skilful. He would hit and keep moving, and he did not leave a vulnerable target like his throat open. Keeping his chin down, and his arms protecting his head, his body constantly was bobbing and weaving. Kemnebi saw the contest as a mismatch; as far as he knew, Osiris never had boxed.

Of course, Kemnebi was wrong. Osiris had been taught to box by an Ethiopian, which was where boxing originally had been invented, and he trained regularly. If anything, he preferred boxing to wrestling, but unlike most boxers, he hardened the sides of his hands for chops as well as punching with the closed fist. He did not use leather strips to bind his hands, as his hands were soaked every day in vinegar and a special mixture to harden them, and when touched, they were like a hard wood, not flesh.

Osiris cleared his mind. Concentrate, he told himself. Move, bob, and weave, and strike quickly. Hit each arm, one-two. Make each blow a hammer blow, tuck the chin in, guard the head, move out of reach, duck and weave, concentrate. The black flag fell, and Kemnebi, confident the fight would be short, rushed across the open space between them, determined to strike the first blow. There was no ring, just an open space, and no time limit. You fought until the other man was dead, and the two judges only ensured that you broke no rules.

The first blow from Kemnebi sailed harmlessly through the air as Osiris ducked and struck Kemnebi twice once on each arm and then danced away from him. Kemnebi advanced quickly, fighting with the left, and keeping his head protected with his right hand, but Osiris easily avoided him again, ducking low and striking his right arm with his left fist, hard. As Kemnebi punched with his right and guarded with his left, he hit his left arm with his right. The fight continued like this for an hour, Kemnebi pressing forward and trying to corner Osiris to strike a blow, and Osiris nimbly avoiding him and hitting his arms, unable to strike a telling blow to his head, which Kemnebi skilfully guarded with his arms held high in a classic defence. The crowd murmured their disappointment; expecting fireworks from the fight, they were getting a classic defensive fight. Both men avoiding being hit, save that Osiris landed blows on Kemnebi's arms at every encounter as he protected his head.

Kemnebi was patient; he was used to long fights, but had never gone this long before landing a blow. He also was confident that Osiris was too small to beat him, as all his blows had landed on his arms. Some had been aimed at his head, but Kemnebi concluded this was because of Osiris' reach—it was too short. After two hours, the crowd began to disperse, to go and have their lunch or go for a rest. Kemnebi now lumbered forward, hardly bothering to punch at Osiris anymore, hoping for an opening, and Osiris would dodge him and then strike each arm, punching hard each time. Kemnebi had been training to fight for hours all his life, and he had fought several matches that lasted two or three hours, but usually they exchanged blows and then danced away from each other, then attacked again. This fight was boring. No telling blows were landed, and Osiris only hit his arms, which now ached for rest.

Each blow from Osiris made Kemnebi wince, but he still held his guard high, protecting his head.

On the two and half hour mark, Osiris suddenly switched his tactics: He suddenly bent low and punched at Kemnebi's genitals, and as Kemnebi, surprised, lowered his right arm to strike Osiris hard, Osiris sprang to the right and chopped at his unprotected throat. At the beginning of this fight, Kemnebi easily would have avoided this blow by bringing his right arm back up and lowering his chin, but the constant assault of his arm had made the arm sore, and the muscles did not respond. The blow was not on the Adam's apple, and the windpipe was damaged, not crushed. It did not kill Kemnebi, but he was winded. Disoriented for the first time in a fight, his tired right failed, and his left arm came down exposing his face. Osiris spun in the air, his right hand striking a tremendous blow with the edge of his hand underneath the nose, breaking his upper teeth, his upper jaw, and caving in his face. It was a killer blow, and Kemnebi was dead before he hit the ground. The small crowd now sprang to life and cheered, some rushing back too late to see the action, and they began to chide the people who had stayed to explain what had happened.

Osiris was tired. Two and half hours of hitting a man's arms was tiring, as was concentrating on not being hit yourself, moving economically during the fight, so as to not tire, and remaining alert for that vital opening. Osiris could not fight Punahasi using the same tactics and then fence afterwards.

There was no rest between the bouts, and as Kemnebi was carried away, Punahasi, a barbarian, made ready to fight and the black flag fell to start the contest. This time, Osiris rushed Punahasi, raining blows on him, striking his genitals, and hitting his stomach and arms. Even his protected head was jolted.

Punahasi tried to strike back with a left hook, but the blow easily missed its target and the return blow broke Punahasi's nose and dazed him. His hands fell to his sides. Unprotected, Osiris punched Punahasi in the throat, crushing his windpipe and cutting of his air supply. Choking and dying on his feet, Punahasi flailed with his arms, and then Osiris rose into the air, swivelled, and struck him with the edge of his hand under the nose and caved in his face. He was dead before he hit the ground.

This time, the crowd saw the action and was pleased and applauded the brief contest. However, the admiration was muted; it seemed Osiris could not be defeated. He was a god, and men could not beat gods.

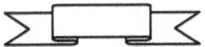

The fencing contest was a formality. Osiris, tired from his exertions for once, surprised everybody for demanding a fight to the death rather than using sticks. Of course, that was the contestants' plan all along, but it visibly shook both men.

Osiris, blade in one hand and fighting shield on his arm, dispatched both men in a few seconds in each contest. The fury of his attack was remarkable. He charged forward, and with one mighty stroke, he cut the man's lightweight shield in half together with his arm. The man, wounded and in shock, had no time to think, because the next blow cut off his head. It was clinical and effective, and it required immense strength and skill, both of which Osiris had in abundance.

Thoth watches the contests in silence his face resigned to the fact that nobody would kill Osiris in combat. No matter what the odds, the man was truly a god.

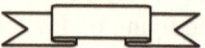

Osiris went back to his quarters in the palace and bathed with Nefertiti in a deep bath of warmed water, his muscles relaxing after the exertions of the day. Both naked, he mounted Nefertiti in the water, his manhood hungry to be satisfied, and he soon spread his seed in her willing crevice. Tired, he took her back to his bed and slept holding her soft flesh. The legend of Osiris grew. Every retelling was of how in ten competitions, against the best men at each event, Osiris had triumphed, a god against men.

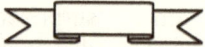

The feast and ceremony were going to be the crowning moment of the event. As Osiris had killed many of the contestants, or they were killed by animals, one person from each event could not be selected. Therefore, from those that survived, ten were taken, so the number was seventy-two men, all of varied sizes and from both Ta-Mehu and Ta-Shemau. The ceremony would be in front of an audience of the nobility from both countries, and many had travelled especially for this final day. The coffin was raised on a plinth, so it was high off the ground, and the dignitaries were seated in tiers around the coffin so that they could see the inside the bejewelled Coffin of Destiny, as it had been dubbed.

Set, with his long main of blond hair woven with jewels and ornate amulets, sat on his throne, his elder brother beside him. Taller than Osiris and paler, Set was an impressive figure, his powerful physique a testimony to the men's vigorous exercise regimes. However, Osiris shone, his light tan glinted, and his muscles were proportioned and pleasing to the eye. His strong face was friendly and open against the fierce stare of Set, who though handsome, looked reserved and unwelcoming in his stare. It was easy to see why Osiris was loved and Set feared, but who would you worship, one wondered? Osiris created envy, as every woman and some men adored him and sought him sexually. He seemed invincible in everything he did. He was creative, charming, and there was no flaw to identity except one: He was too good, too perfect, and therefore could not be a man, he must be a god. Therefore, he could be hated secretly for showing how weak and fickle mere mortals were, and he should be sent back to the skies.

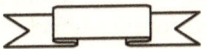

All seventy-two men lined up, and a priest and priestess conducted a ceremony with a manservant in attendance, as was normal. Each man was blessed and received a small piece of bread and a sip of wine held by the servant. This was to provide food for his journey in the Coffin of Destiny. If he fit the coffin, it would be closed and carried to the temple, and the man released, the coffin then becoming his for his journey into the afterlife when his time came. One by one, the men lay in the coffin. Some were too long, some too short, and others too fat or too thin; none fit the mould inside the coffin. When all seventy-one men had tried, Set turned to Osiris. "My brother Osiris, it's your turn to see if the Coffin of Destiny is to be yours," said Set.

Osiris did not reply, but nodded, his body alive and vibrant, his senses aware. He had seen the ceremony and could not fault any step, so he received the blessing, ate the small piece of bread from the loaf broken by the priestess, and drank from the same goblet as the seventy-one men. He then climbed slowly into the coffin and lay back, fitting into the mould in the bottom of the coffin exactly.

"The Pharaoh Osiris is the chosen one," proclaimed the priest, "and the Coffin of Destiny is his by right of combat, right of kingship, and right of celestial choice." The priest then sprinkled water on Osiris and Osiris tasted the water on his lips as Osiris watched from the bottom of the coffin. "The Pharaoh Osiris will be carried from this place to the Temple of Gleb, his father's, and declared a god to be worshipped in his lifetime. Then, when his journey to the afterlife arrives, know this, all men," the priest paused, "he who steals Osiris' coffin will be cursed forever. Only Osiris or the son of Isis may lie in the coffin, and any who defile the coffin will be cursed forever to be tormented by devils for eternity."

The words were spoken in a loud strong voice, and the hall hushed. Osiris felt somehow dreamy and slightly weak, and his body was heavy. His eyes began to grow weary. *Was the coffin responsible, or the priest's words*, thought Osiris, and before he could connect the thought, he passed into a coma. Thoth, the servant of the priests, had put an extremely strong poison in the water that that the priest sprinkled on Osiris which would kill most men instantly. Osiris' strong body, he knew, would try to fight the potion while he was in the coffin but it would be in vain. Osiris the god was now dead, but did not know. The coffin was closed, and six of the seventy-one men put poles in the coffin and raised it up from the plinth and commenced carrying it to the temple. The other men, each with a sword, formed an archway through which the coffin passed, the men exchanging places with those carrying the coffin so that every man carried the coffin and formed the archway of raised swords. The blades glinted in the flicker of torches and the oil lamps as the archway and the coffin made its way to the temple.

When the coffin was in the temple, it was placed on the ground, and the body of Osiris was lifted out of the coffin and placed in the ceremonial altar that was used for sacrifices to the gods. The priest anointed the body of Osiris, knowing he was dead, and then each of the seventy-one men hacked Osiris into seventy-two pieces. Thoth watched in horror over the part he had played in the plot to kill such a man. Blood and guts and intestines covered the altar, and they were gathered by the seventy-two men.

"Put the testicles of Osiris in the coffin with his ring and crown of pharaoh," said the priest, "and return them to Isis."

"Now, each of you go to your appointed place and scatter the remains of Osiris, the body never to be joined again," said the priest.

Thoth took the coffin, with the guards no longer in the ceremony, and covered it with a cloth to hide it from prying eyes. He was to take it by cart to a boat and set sail to Memphis, the capital of Ta-Mehu, on yet another suicide mission, this time on behalf of Set. He wondered again what would be his fate at the hand of Osiris' wife and sister Isis

Chapter Six

Bad news travelled quickly in Ta-Mehu, and within a half-day of the death of Osiris, a messenger arrived to inform the pharaoh's wife Isis that her husband was dead. His body was being sent by Set. Her brother with his envoy Thoth was at sea already, and Set was planning to march on Ta-Mehu within a couple of days. Even now, a fleet of boats were sailing to blockade the key ports, and Isis was to be detained pending Set's arrival.

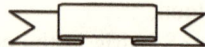

Isis was heartbroken. She loved her brother deeply, not as a husband, as neither had the stomach for the expected coupling of the pair, but as a, "beloved friend and brother." She had never loved Set and did not even like him, but as a brother she tolerated him. The news that he had killed Osiris stunned her, but did not surprise her, and she wondered how and who had given her such details of the event, which she assumed Set wished to keep secret until he controlled Ta-Mehu. The message asked her to await the arrival of the Coffin of Destiny and the envoy of Set before fleeing the country, but to make ready to leave with all haste. *Where to go was the issue*, thought Isis, as Set would now be the most powerful ruler in the region, and Isis would find sanctuary difficult to find.

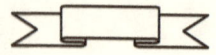

Thoth arrived to meet Isis with the Coffin of Destiny and the pieces of Osiris' body he could find. As haste was required, he left the body of men that were supposed to accompany him and told them to travel the next day. His total numbered only ten, including him, which was barely enough to carry the coffin from the boat to the palace where Isis met the party.

"Queen Isis, I bring the Coffin of Destiny and parts of the body of Osiris, your husband, hacked to death by seventy-one men on the orders of your brother, Pharaoh Set of Ta-Shemau. He travels now to your court to detain you from fleeing Ta-Mehu and will surely kill you, as it is rumoured you are with child," said Thoth.

"Who are you, envoy?" asked Isis, "and why should I believe anything you say to me?"

"I am Thoth your majesty," replied Thoth, "and if you clear the chamber, I will explain fully your dire position."

Isis hesitated. Maybe this was a gambit to kill her, but one look at the man, and she knew he could do that anyway if he was prepared to die, which clearly he was, bringing the body with such few men. "Very well, clear the chamber," said Isis, and she waved her beautiful hand and the court cleared.

"Let me explain what happened, Queen Isis, including my part in your husband's death," said Thoth. When he had finished, she was proud of Osiris, but saddened and hurt by Set's betrayal of Osiris and horrified the man before her actually had poisoned him.

"So why, Thoth, should I just not have you killed?" asked Isis.

"First, Queen Isis, let me say I betrayed the Eblan to Set because they thought by sending me as an envoy I would be killed. Secondly, I am betraying Pharaoh Set because he is a cruel and unjust ruler, and Osiris was the bravest and greatest man I have ever seen. I am ashamed of my part in his death, but if I had not been involved, another would have taken my place, and both myself and your husband would be dead," said Thoth.

"Perhaps," said Isis.

"Ammon, the chief advisor to Set approached me with a long-term plan that could see your future child, man, or woman, rule both Ta-Mehu and Ta-Shemau," said Thoth. "But first, you need to flee abroad to Palestine and hide among Pharaoh Set's enemies, until your son or daughter is fully grown," said Thoth.

"Thoth, there is one problem," said Isis, calculating that the truth was necessary.

"What is that, Queen Isis?" asked Thoth.

"I am not pregnant," said Isis.

Thoth swore under his breath. "Then, in all haste, you need to be, because without an heir you will lose all friends and be killed."

"How do you expect me to achieve that without arousing suspicion? Any man I lie with at some time will reveal the truth to progress his future."

"Perhaps you could create a story that you returned Osiris' body to being whole and he became the father?" suggested Thoth.

"That part is perhaps achievable with your help, but the pregnant part needs a man who will remain quite even under torture," said Isis.

"Only I can vouch for one man who is prepared to die rather than reveal the truth," said Thoth.

"And who is that?" asked Isis.

"Me, my Queen," said Thoth.

Isis was stunned. The man expected her to couple with him and then flee her country with the man's child in her belly, and make him the pharaoh of both countries? "Are you mad?" she asked.

"You know I am not," said Thoth. "It is now the only way."

Isis raced through the options in her mind. There were none. However, she had never been with a man, and now this large uncouth envoy was to deflower her in secret so that they could declare his seed was the son of Osiris and heir to a dynasty?

"When and where would you suggest, if I agree?" said Isis.

"On the floor, right here and now," said Thoth. "Most women I couple with are pregnant straight away, unless they take wild yum or pomegranate seed to stop the pregnancy."

"You expect me, a queen," said Isis, "to open her womb to you in her throne room, having met you only minutes before?"

"Yes, Queen Isis," said Thoth, "and then I expect you to sail to Palestine and hide until I bring the remainder of Osiris. You have minutes to decide all of our destinies."

Isis looked aghast at the man, and then, recognizing the truth of the situation, she got up from her throne and went behind the two thrones and lay on her back, not sure what actually was required for a man to mount her. Thoth took off his helmet and sword and loincloth, and now naked before her, she saw his erect manhood long and broad between his legs. He crouched between her legs, and licking his fingers on his lips, he first pushed them inside her, and she gasped as they penetrated her, and she felt an exquisite pain and a little uncomfortable. However, his experienced hand probed and pushed, and she felt herself open towards him, and as she did, he mounted her. She nearly cried out, but his hand smothered her cry. He thrust deep inside her with powerful strokes, and within less than a minute, she felt a strange sensation in her body, and as the exquisite pleasure captured her, she came for the first time in her life and Thoth planted his seed in her womb. Thoth withdrew himself from Isis.

"Keep your legs high in the air for a minute; let my seed reach your belly," said Thoth.

Iris remained on her back, doing what she had been told, her legs in the air, revealing her pubic hair and vagina and bottom, which no man other than her brothers and father had seen. She now knew why men and women wanted sex, and was resolved that when she had solved all these problems she would find a lover, even Thoth if he was still alive. A few minutes passed, and Thoth cut some cloth from a curtain.

"Bind your womb to keep in the seed, otherwise it will seep out and make your dress damp, and it may alert someone that something happened," said Thoth.

Isis stood up, and lifting her dress, Thoth brought the cloth between her legs and then around her waist to keep it in place. They both straightened up their clothes, and Isis looked at the man who would be the father of her child. "You returned his testicles," said Isis, thinking. "I will make a golden phallus and attach it to them when you return some of his body. We shall create a mummy for the afterlife and shall say he rose up and mounted me and so a child was born."

"Could work if I can find enough pieces of Osiris, especially his head," said Thoth.

"How will you find the pieces?" asked Isis.

"I asked Ammon to write instructions for those that could read, which were few. The others I gave the locations to, so I know every location," said Thoth.

"But how to get there in time," asked Isis, "before Set discovers your disobedience and has you killed, or worse, captures you?"

"Don't worry, I have already a plan in place," said Thoth. "I will see you in Palestine in one week. There is some advice Ammon has provided for you in Palestine," and Thoth passed a small scroll to Isis.

The ten men with Thoth had been charged to go to the ten locations in Ta-Mehu with body parts of Osiris and bury them, but Thoth had bribed them to leave the parts with Isis. Ammon was arranging a similar number of men to collect the parts from the ten locations of Ta-Shemau, and they would be ready tonight for Thoth to collect. Thoth bowed low to Queen Isis. "You are now my Queen and I will serve you all my life," said Thoth. "When your son is born, he will be the son of Osiris, and I will guard him with my life and heart."

He turned and left without another word, and waved the courtiers back into the throne room. Within thirty minutes of Thoth's departure, Isis had left the palace, and with the majority of Osiris' vast fortune already on the ship, she set sail for Palestine and an uncertain future.

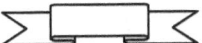

Ammon had been busy in Thoth's absence, gathering the parts of Osiris together to give back to Queen Isis. He was uncertain why he did this, considering the risk, but knew he had witnessed greatness, only to be defeated by treachery from a cruel and unjust pharaoh whom he loathed. One day Set would kill him and his wife, and he needed to know he had done something to redress the balance of power being returned to a just man and rightful heir.

When Thoth arrived late at night at the house of Ammon, the Pharaoh Set had not yet discovered his betrayal, as he still was busy preparing his army to occupy the larger kingdom of Ta-Mehu, which without a male heir to the throne, was his by birthright.

"Have you collected the parts of Osiris, my Lord?" asked Thoth.

"All of them," said Ammon, pointing to a simple wooden casket, "including the head."

"Good," said Thoth. "What news of Set? Does he know yet?"

"No," said Ammon. "When you are safely in your boat I will denounce you and reveal your betrayal."

"Good," said Thoth. "The Queen has made her plans and will declare she has been impregnated by the reincarnated Osiris, with a golden phallus being used to aid in the erection of his penis."

"Was she already pregnant, or is she to impregnate herself by another man?" asked Ammon.

"Did not ask," lied Thoth. "I did not think she would tell a servant."

"Understood," said Ammon, realizing that perhaps Thoth was not the easiest man to confide in for a queen as beautiful and pure as Isis.

"Well, I will be on my way," said Thoth.

"One more thing," said Ammon, "our mission shall remain a secret. Gather around you men you can trust and meet in secret. Never reveal my name, and keep the contacts in each country secret between just the two of us and one other. Here in the casket is gold and jewels, enough to live well on for many years. Be careful and invest it wisely, so you always have money to pursue our goals." Ammon paused and added in a almost whisper. "When the son of Osiris rules, remember me and my wife and my heirs, if I have any."

"You have my word," said Thoth, and the men parted friends and devotees of the son of Osiris for life.

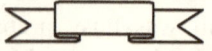

Isis sailed up the Nile into the Mediterranean Sea and then along the coast, reaching the port of Jaffa in Palestine. Isis did not wish to reveal her true identity, as she feared what might happen to her and her unborn child. She decided to follow the advice passed on in the scroll provided by Thoth from Ammon, the chief advisor to Set. He suggested Isis represent herself as a rich merchant's wife settling in Palestine in advance of her husband's arrival, and suggested she adopt the Jewish faith. Palestine was divided into walled cities that each ruled themselves, and there was no cohesive government or king of the land. Therefore, it was easy to move from city to city as a stranger, provided you had money and a convincing story.

Ammon had a contact in Jericho. Jericho was about eighty miles inland from Jaffa, about six miles north of the large salt lake called the Dead Sea that the Yardan (Jordan in Hebrew and Arabic) river ran into, and twenty miles east of Jerusalem. It was a large settlement of about twelve thousand people, so it would be easier to merge and not be too conspicuous with her large entourage. Jericho was a successful community because nearby it had a large spring of water called the Ein es-Sultan, which meant "the Sultan's Spring" in Arabic. It was the largest spring in the Lower Jordan Valley and was overflowing, providing a constant supply of fresh water. A large number of farmers planted groves of date palms around the spring, and the city often was called the "city of palm trees." Food was plentiful, and the people peaceful and friendly. A new ruler of the city, David, had pulled down all the housing and rebuilt the city within a wall on a grid pattern, and sewage was thrown outside the wall, keeping the city streets clean and disease-free. Ammon had come to learn about Jericho from a travelling merchant who had settled in Jericho because of its tranquillity. It was tolerant of foreigners, particularly if they converted to the Jewish faith, and it was far from the reach of Set.

The caravan of Isis was large, nearly two hundred people, and obviously difficult to hide. It carried merchandise that Ammon had been advised that the people of Jericho would barter for, items such as farm implements, ornaments, jewellery, cloth, carvings, oil lamps, spices, and perfumes. With the city being walled and the population having a form of government, it would make it easier to settle into the community, but with such a large entourage it would only be a matter of time before David, the ruler of Jericho, found out the true identity of Isis. The caravan stopped outside the walls of Jericho and made a camp of tents near the date palms at Ein es-Sultan. A messenger was sent to David with an invitation to visit the caravan.

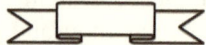

David, the ruler of Jericho, was a man in his early forties, and a devout Jew who believed in the strict following when possible of the laws of Abraham. However, he was tolerant of others and also wanted order and fairness. The city had a sort of town council, loosely elected by the people, of which David was the head. It was his decision some fifteen years ago when still a young man to rebuild the city wall and plan all the housing on a grid system, and to introduce the sewage being thrown outside the wall to keep the streets clean. He had heard of the large merchant caravan approaching Jericho from a local merchant the previous day, and was pleased it had camped outside the city and invited him to meet its leader. A man of average height, at five feet four, he was well built from many hours working as a bricklayer building the city. The city did not have an organized army or police force, but he had his work force who helped him build houses and acted like a police force, keeping the law under David's command. David took four of these men armed with swords with him and walked to the site of the caravan.

Isis had an open tent erected for the arrival of David, and had food and wine prepared for his arrival. She was dressed simply in a white dress with little jewellery, and a wig without a crown, and seated on the three-legged stool. David saw Isis and was stunned by her beauty, her white alabaster skin contrasting with the dark hair of her wig, and her slender figure untouched by age. He guessed she was no more than twenty and had never borne children.

"Welcome to Jericho, traveller," said David. "I am David, the city's leader, may I ask why such a large caravan travels to our city?"

"We come as merchants to trade and live in Jericho, with your permission, David," said Isis, "but please, sit and eat and drink," and she motioned with her hand and stools and a table was brought and filled with food and wine.

David sat with his men and ate some food and drank some wine whilst Isis watched the men. In the culture David had been brought up in, it was bad manners to discuss business whilst eating, and he and his men were hungry as they had not eaten their mid-day meal. Isis picked at her food and remained silent, waiting for David to finish his food. When David pushed his plate away from him, Isis asked, "Is there anything else we may serve you, David?"

"No thank you, my lady," said David.

"Then perhaps we can go to my tent and talk privately," said Isis. "Your men, I am sure, will be happy drinking more wine."

David looked at his contented men, continuing to eat and drink, and nodded at Asher, who always was happy, but alert, and it was understood that he would remain wary. When they were alone in the tent, Isis motioned David to sit, and she stood and spoke. "I am Isis, Queen of Ta-Mehu, the wife of Osiris, who was killed by his brother Set a few days ago, who now probably rules the whole of Ta-Mehu and Ta-Shemau, sometimes referred to as tWay."

"I have heard of these lands, and the great Osiris from merchants," said David. "Why do you come here?"

"To be safe from my brother Set, and hopefully to bear the son of my husband if the gods so will it," said Isis.

"Are you pregnant?" asked David.

"Of that I am not certain," said Isis.

"Very well, do you want to live within the city walls?" asked David.

"If you can provide houses for me and my caravan, we have gold and goods to barter," said Isis, "and we can live outside the wall until all is made ready. I also have a scroll from Ammon of Ta-Shemau, who knows of you," and she handed the scroll to David.

David read the scroll and said, "We can accommodate some of you very soon, as we have built new houses for future dwellers and we can build a larger house for you very quickly. But I think we shall promote the story that you are a rich merchant's wife, as Ammon suggests."

There was a commotion outside the tent, and then a servant came in the tent and whispered something in the ear of Isis. "We have a visitor," said Isis. "Let's go outside."

Thoth stood with two large wooden caskets and some smaller caskets.

"This is Thoth, one of our merchants," she said to David, and then to Thoth, "This is David, the leader of the city." Both men recognized their rivalry for Isis and hated each other on first sight.

Chapter Seven

Set marched with his full army from El-Kab in Ta-Shemau to Memphis in Ta-Mehu, taking several days, and entered the city without opposition or any greeting from the population. He knew by now that Isis had fled and Thoth had betrayed him and disappeared, perhaps with Isis, but he did not know to where. Ammon suggested either Palestine or Eblan, but could only guess. Even so, it would take several months to find them and mount a campaign to storm that city.

Set decided that first he needed to strengthen the joint army of the new country of tWay, as it was to now be called under his rule. His first act was to summon all of the generals of the former Ta-Mehu army to his court with their families. Set sat on the throne once occupied by Osiris with his wife Nephths beside him, both resplendent in silk robes and bejewelled over their whole clothing and hair. His face was passive as each of the generals from both countries were presented to him with their families. The last person presented was Nizam, the head of the army from Ta-Mehu, who was legendary for his loyalty and discipline. Nizam had three sons, all fully grown and married, with eight grandchildren. None of his sons had followed their father into the army, and all had very junior positions as scribes and merchants.

"Nizam, how long did you serve the Pharaoh Osiris?" asked Set, without any tone of threat in his voice.

"Nine years, my Pharaoh," said Nizam, standing straight, his body ready for death.

"Were you always loyal and truthful to Osiris?" asked Set.

"Always, my Pharaoh," said Nizam.

"Did you swear allegiance to him?" asked Set.

"Yes, my Pharaoh," said Nizam.

"What did you swear?" asked Set.

"I, Nizam, chief among generals of the Ta-Mehu Army, swear to the gods that I will put the pharaoh above all others and lay down my life and that of my family to preserve and keep him safe," said Nizam.

"And you believe what you swore?" asked Set.

"Yes, my Pharaoh," said Nizam.

"Then, Nizam, why was my army not here in Memphis to greet me, why were you not face down in the dirt to swear your allegiance to your new pharaoh?" asked Set, his face contorted in a wicked smile.

"I was away from Memphis with the army and did not know you were coming, my Pharaoh," said Nizam, knowing death was stalking him with every word.

"But did your spies not tell you I was coming to claim my birthright?" asked Set.

"Yes, my Pharaoh," said Nizam, "but not when."

"Um," said Set, seeing how Nizam was trying to wriggle, "is your loyalty the same to me as it was to Osiris?"

"Yes, my Pharaoh," said Nizam.

"Good," said Set. "Now, tell me who your favourite son is?"

Nizam was going to say all, but then realizing what that may mean, hesitated and decided to name his second son, who had no children.

"All my sons are special, but I favour Mdjai," said Nizam.

"Guard, take the general outside with Mdjai and his wife, and give the general a sword," said Set. "You are to kill your son and his wife and then yourself. If you do not obey, I will slaughter all of your family. Now go."

"Yes, my Pharaoh," said Nizam.

The court watched, fascinated, as Nizam went outside, his son and wife shivering with fear, he rock solid and fearless. When he was given the sword, he made his son and daughter-in-law kneel. Then, he cut off her head with one stroke of his blade, and then did the same with the head of his son. He turned and faced the place where he expected the pharaoh to be, saluted him with the sword, and sliced his own throat and fell to the ground dead.

General Jabir, a general who was second in command and renowned for his bravery, winced in horror at what had happened to Nizam and his family.

"General Jabir," said Set. "Of all the generals in both armies, who are the ten best generals?"

"There are some forty generals, but of these, only eighteen are active, the others are really retired, my Pharaoh. Generals do not retire, so we have nine active generals in both armies," said Jabir.

"Really?" asked Set.

"Yes, my Pharaoh," said Jabir, "and of the remaining number, I only know the generals of Ta-Mehu."

"But how do you rate the generals of Ta-Shemau?" asked Set.

"Very poorly," said Jabir. "If Nizam had been a hostile general, you would have been defeated. Taking your whole army across land without an adequate advance party and not using the Nile was a big mistake."

"Why?" asked Set.

"Because Nizam had the advantage of planning in advance and could have chosen ground on which you would have been at a disadvantage, and your army is already fewer than the Ta-Mehu army, and by land, the element of surprise is also lost," said Jabir.

"So we have twenty two generals who are retired, and now nine generals in my army who are useless?" asked Set.

"In my opinion, my pharaoh," said Jabir.

"Of the remaining nine, I have already killed one, and you are not going to select yourself as incompetent, so if you had to select any more for early retirement, who would they be?" asked Set.

Jabir did not hesitate. "Husani is vain and spends most of his time chasing after his soldiers' wives. Omari is proud and believes himself too important to tell junior officers how to proceed in battle, and Nkuku is fat and overweight and a bad example to his men, drinking and eating to excess."

"So I only have six generals left, Jabir. How many do I really need?" asked Set.

"No more than ten, my Pharaoh, for battle, and a senior general and his deputy," said Jabir.

"Good, take outside the three you have named and the Ta-Shemau generals and their families, men, women, and children, their servants, and any person loyal to them, and kill all of them," said Set, "including the entire family of Nizam. Let it be known henceforth, if I visit a city, if you and your family are not face down in the earth to welcome me with flower petals in the street and cheering crowds, I will kill every person in the city," said Set. "Select the remaining generals from the ranks of Ta-Shemau. By two days from now, I want a full report on the army and what needs to be done to make it the finest in the world. Now go and kill my enemies and use the selected generals to kill the generals and their families who mock me with their insolence."

Before protests could be heard, Set rose and left the chamber with Nephths.

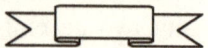

Set had been dramatic and cruel, but, Jabir reasoned, not without a rational approach to combining the armies. The retired generals had junior officers loyal to them in the ranks who could at a later stage be persuaded by Isis to rise up in a revolt of the army. Killing them was a necessity. The incompetent and other useless generals should have been killed or retired years ago. Killing them made every man think about his performance and behaviour in the army henceforth. Killing the generals' family, friends, and servants also was necessary, otherwise a vendetta against Set might arise at a future date from an aggrieved person related or linked to one of the dead generals.

In Jabir's view, the army of tWay was old-fashioned. They had no rapid advance troops, and their archers were static in battle and very vulnerable. Many of the soldiers were too old and not fit enough to fight and march more than one day, when often a battle might take several days to reach, and then the tWay Army would be too tired to fight. There was also no coordination between the navy and the army, and when it was more sensible to deploy by sea, the boats were insufficient and inadequate to take all the soldiers and supplies and equipment. Worse still, the machines of war were out of date. The soldiers used to weaken walls in a siege were very poor engineers and took too long to be effective. Jabir relished the thought of correcting all these issues in the army.

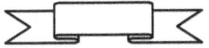

Isis was happy in Jericho; her house had been built rapidly and was surrounded by a small garden with houses for her servants and slaves surrounding the garden. Her house, though small for her, was twice the size of the largest house in the city, and the only one with a garden. Isis had set up both a pharmacy, a place of medicine, and a school to help the city, and soon she was famous for her generosity and her kindness. A little aloof from the community, they worshipped her from afar, and some even declared her a god under whispered breath, as this was blasphemy in the Jewish faith.

Thoth also prospered, travelling widely and trading goods and bartering, for which he had a natural talent. Reading whether a man was telling the truth or lying was something he had been able to judge all his life. To his skills, he only needed to add being able to value what was a good bargain. Of course, the ability to read and write and have a mathematical ability was extremely important, and Thoth astonished everybody by having all these requirements. He also quickly learned to speak in Hebrew.

The Jews had no written language, and the only written word was the tWay hieroglyphs, and this was very recent, so rarely could other men in other nations read or write. In counting, the tWay measured by portions a whole one, a half, a quarter, an eighth, a sixteenth, a thirty-second, and a sixty-fourth. Fractions greater than this were portioned again, starting with the smallest portion as the whole number. Thoth quickly mastered the system and could divide and count quickly and barter a good price because of his speed of thought. His talents went unnoticed by his only love,

Isis, who preferred the company of David, although she did not take him as a lover—of this he was certain.

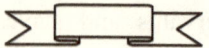

David was in love with Isis; it was plain to see whenever he was in her company. He watched her belly grow and envied Osiris each day for the miracle of his mummification and the golden phallus of his testicles. When Thoth returned bearing two large caskets, apparently the remains of Osiris, these were taken by the priests and embalmed and then they began the painful task of sewing the parts together to make Osiris whole again. Normally, for a pharaoh, the whole country would mourn, and embalming and mummification would take seventy days. As the courtiers had fled Ta-Mehu without mourning, Isis ordered that Osiris be made whole to mate with her in two days using a golden phallus and his testicles. The priests carried out the ceremony in her tent, and then over the next sixty-eight days, they completed the task. His body wrapped in linen, Osiris looked whole. His head and the golden phallus were left bare so that the followers of Isis could see the miracle of Osiris becoming whole again and believe in the legend of his miraculous mating with Isis.

Isis grew heavy, and David's heart cried out for her love, even if she carried another man's child. The year wore on, and they reached mid-December and nearly eight months into her pregnancy when shocking news came from the port of Jaffa by Thoth: Set had landed in Palestine and was marching towards Jericho. He would be there within one day.

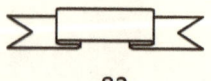

"Isis has to leave now!" demanded Thoth, "And she should flee to another city in disguise, her entourage going in another direction. Set will come and level this city and kill all in it," said Thoth.

"Jericho has withstood many armies and never been breached," said David. "Besides to get an army here will take days, not one day."

"Believe this now, the army of Set will be here tomorrow at first light and will level Jericho and kill everyone here," said Thoth. "Every man, woman, and child should leave now."

Isis considered carefully what both men had said. Thoth was brave beyond measure, she knew that, and he would not be so adamant about the danger unless he was certain. "Thoth, pack two mules with gold and jewels. I will take these with a small party," said Isis "Take the remainder of my wealth with the body of Osiris and the Coffin of Destiny with the main party. We will meet at a place we agree upon once we are on the road from Jericho. David, if you defeat Set, we shall return after the birth of the baby."

With that, Isis rose and began organizing her packing and selecting the small party that would accompany her. David watched as the party that had brightened his life and the woman who had made his soul soar fled Jericho, their caravan train swelling with perhaps over a thousand inhabitants joining the fleeing Isis. David began making the city ready; the people who remained were all prepared to fight. There were more men in the city than women because of Jericho's remote location, and they were able to muster six thousand men for the quickly-formed army, four thousand women, and some four hundred children who could use a sling. The remaining few hundred would stay in the walls of Jericho.

David had resolved that they would fight Set in one decisive battle on the plain just outside the city walls. He was confident that an army could not match his size in one day travelling by foot or mule. It took days to unload cargo and a couple of weeks to move that cargo eighty miles over the rough roads to Jericho. The population gathered stones for the slings, prepared arrows for the bows, sharpened swords and the tips of spears, and prepared the small shields of leather and wood. As a force, the population of Jericho had fought many times. Raiders often came to the city seeking wealth; so many men had been in battle several times, but always against another rabble, never the army of a pharaoh.

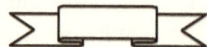

Isis watched as the main party turned north for the port of Haifa from whence they would find a new haven for her followers. Thoth would walk with them for part of the way before hiding the Coffin of Destiny and the body of Osiris and then join Isis outside Nazareth whilst she travelled to the small town of Bethlehem, which was about six miles south of Jerusalem. Isis felt exhausted walking and was very heavy with the child; it would not be long before it was born. She gazed upwards and saw that the sky was very clear and the stars shone brightly, but a single star she could not remember before shone to the south, leading them to Bethlehem.

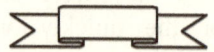

The army Set brought to Palestine was over one thousand men strong and was the core of the new army Jabir had built for the pharaoh. Jabir had been ruthless, and only young, fit, and brave men now existed in the army. New weapons of steel had been forged, shields of metal to protect against the arrows of archers, and the chariot and horse introduced. Some one hundred chariots with an archer and driver would be used in the invasion and conquest of Jericho. The remaining men consisted of eight hundred foot soldiers and one hundred archers on foot. Although the well-disciplined army had unloaded their weapons in less than half a day, Jabir realized that to rush to Jericho was folly; they could have a swift passage but must rest the night before the battle. Therefore, he force-marched the men for thirty-six hours, carrying the huge supply for the army of arrows, spears, swords, battering rams, towers, chariots, and horses to the outskirts of Jericho, and then they set up camp and rested.

The night of the fires from the camp of the Set army alarmed the men on sentry duty, and David was woken from his sleep. He decided he would scout the camp, and during the night visited the camp on the pretext of being an envoy from the city. Jabir and Set were seated together when they heard an envoy had arrived from the city under a flag of truce.

"Who are you?" asked Set.

"An envoy from the city, named David," replied David. "The city leaders want to know why you come here."

"We want Isis and her people. They have disobeyed their pharaoh and fled his lands with stolen gold and jewels," said Jabir.

"Isis and her people left two days ago at the news of your coming," said David truthfully.

"Then empty your city and let us search within the walls for Isis and her people," said Set.

"Your army is small against the city of Jericho," said David, "so your threat is empty."

"We will see you on the field of battle tomorrow, and will slaughter everyone who stands against Set, pharaoh of tWay," said Set, and he rose from his stool; the audience was over.

The next morning, the tWay army ate a hearty breakfast and prepared for battle. Jabir had been training with the army under the watchful eye of Set for months, and they were ready to unleash a new kind of warfare never seen in the world before.

David gathered his population. The men who were loosely organized in groups of about one hundred men, under the direction of one leader. However, these leaders were based on families and tribes, so some men had six hundred men and others thirty, so the command was very uneven. The population as a whole had never fought an organized army before. When they were threatened by other tribes, they simply picked up weapons and as a hoard charged they massacred them by weight of numbers. Today, David gave them some tactics: They would use slings first to kill as many soldiers as possible, and then arrows. Then they would charge and slaughter the tWay Army.

The city of Jericho was built on a mound, so the men and women of the city walked downwards and had the mound at their backs the valley in front of them. There was a slight rise to the left; it was on this rise that the tWay Army stood. David guessed that there were about one thousand men, so the Jericho army outnumbered them about eleven to one which would be sufficient to triumph even if they had superior tactics.

The children, women, and men all moved forward to within about one hundred paces of the tWay Army, which stood motionless, waiting on the small rise. They all loaded their slings, and as a multitude, they threw their stones. The tWay Army lifted their long shields above their heads, forming a canopy, and the stones bounced harmlessly off the shields. This was repeated several times until the Jericho stone supply was exhausted. The tWay Army remained motionless. The children, their part completed, retreated and started walking back to the city.

David raised his hand for the archers, and they loosed their arrows, but the effect was the same. Suddenly, before they could load another arrow, the front two rows of the army lowered their shields, and archers from the tWay Army loosed their arrows. Perhaps fifty or so people were killed or injured. This process of exchanging arrows was repeated several times by both armies. David could see that the tWay Army was not harmed, but hundreds lay dead or dying among the population from Jericho. He was preparing to change tactics, when suddenly from behind the tWay Army, at left, right, and centre, chariots and horses broke from their ranks and charged towards the Jericho army. The charioteers were firing arrows and repeatedly reloading as they raced towards the army, stopping short by about thirty yards and passing in front of the army.

The effect was stunning, and as the Jericho army watched, amazed, the archers from the main tWay Army began loosing off arrow after arrow in a frenzy of killing. The population, transfixed, was being slaughtered the dead falling on top of other men and women; more than a third of the population had fallen,

David guessed, that he was losing his numerical advantage. David decided to charge and raised his hand to charge. The Jericho Army, letting out an almighty roar, charged, and the chariots parted and raced left and right on the field of battle, all the time killing the Jericho people.

The crowd rushed forward, and the tWay changed shape, forming a V formation, with their tall shields held in front of them and their long spears poking out like a porcupine. The crowd surged forward, but were deflected onto the spears by the shields, which held firm. The army phalanx of tWay steel held firm, and the long spears kept stabbing and killing the oncoming crowd. The dead mounted, and to a barked order, the tWay Army stepped back two paces and then held firm again, killing more of the multitude. The process was repeated over and over again. As the battle raged, the inner core of the tWay Army would change places with the front row, stepping back so the front men only fought for a few furious minutes before being relieved to rest.

Archers in the centre also continued to rain arrows on the Jericho Army, and the chariots circled the Jericho Army, firing arrows into them. The children and several hundred men and women had run back to Jericho and now manned the walls, leaderless. David, always brave, had led the first charge and died like his many fellow Jericho population, speared by the steel phalanx of tWay. Set and Jabir watched the slaughter, impassively judging the tactics and measuring the effectiveness of the plan they had devised. Jabir had been surprised how astute this pharaoh was at warfare, and no longer underestimated his abilities at being a soldier and leader.

"How many do you think are still alive?" asked Set.

"Two or three thousand in the city, and perhaps two thousand on the field," said Jabir.

"Signal the advance party to charge," said Set. "Signal the main army to join the field of battle."

Jabir raised his arm upward and to his right and then left and then across his throat. The charge of the Jericho Army already had been halted, and the population now stood exhausted in the field. The tWay phalanx now threw their spears at the hoard, and men fell all around, confused. The tWay army lifted its shields and advanced, drawing its swords. The Jericho survivors turned and ran to the left and right, and then saw the frightening sight of a huge army, of perhaps twice the population of Jericho, which had joined the field of battle and swept down to cut off their retreat. It was a slaughter. The tWay main army was twenty thousand men strong and better armed and trained. They hacked the Jericho population to pieces within a few devastating minutes.

The crowd watching from the city walls watched in horror as the long towers and battering rams were now being brought to the field of battle, their army already slaughtered by the far superior army of tWay. It was hard to know what to do. Open the gates and plead for mercy? Fight? Run? Too late, as the battering ram was breaking down the gates of Jericho. The climbing towers were circling the city, and the soldiers were pouring over the walls. No mercy was shown; every man, woman, and child was put to the sword, except for about two hundred women selected for their beauty and youth.

The city was burned to the ground, and the clay brick walls shattered, levelling the city to the ground. The palm orchards were chopped down, and the roots pulled up and burned. The twenty thousand men worked remorselessly every day in their task of destruction. Every field was fouled, and the spring at Ein es-Sultan poisoned so that life could not be rebuilt at Jericho for a generation. Archaeologists five millenniums later would wonder what happened to Jericho, but every person in the whole region would know that to disobey Set was to be utterly destroyed. Nobody in any city would knowingly harbour Isis and her unborn child.

Chapter Eight

The small party skirted the much larger city of Jerusalem and headed towards the small town of Bethlehem, six miles to the south. The town was not much of a town, with a few scattered houses and farms and no real central point for meetings or worship. There was no accommodation available, and the only place of shelter was the caves used to keep animals in the winter months. Isis kept away from all the towns 'people and walked, one of her servants riding the mule. As she was clearly not pregnant or beautiful, she could not be mistaken for Isis.

Isis was sure that Set would vanquish David easily and would bring a mighty force to crush any resistance to his will. Although Isis despised Set for his cruelty and vanity, she never underestimated both his courage and skill as a soldier. Isis knew that Set was probably the greatest warrior in tWay, and but for Osiris, the greatest ever. No man ever had beaten Set in any combat sport, except Osiris, and even his tutors feared Set when they wrestled, boxed, or fenced, as he was both skilful and fearless, a deadly combination. David and his farmers, shepherds, and tradesmen would not be able to withstand Set; this she knew. However, she also knew Set would not stay in Palestine searching for Isis and her baby. He, of course, would destroy Jericho and kill everybody there; that was the obvious example to make to the people. Then, he would check major cities like Jerusalem on his return journey, plundering and capturing girls to become sex slaves for his army. If they could locate Isis they would, but as long as there was a strong message left behind that anybody standing with Isis would die, he would be satisfied. It certainly would mean that Isis must live in obscurity in a small town and become a poor housewife, not a regal queen if her baby was to stay alive.

After the birth of the child she planned to travel north to Nazareth, which was mainly Arabic-speaking, rather than Hebrew, and hide among the Arabs until the baby grew to a man. She and Thoth had agreed that he would wander for a few weeks travelling in different directions and burying false wooden caskets disguised as the Coffin of Destiny, whilst the real coffin had left after their departure with four trusted servants, headed directly to Nazareth.

The star she had seen in the sky seemed to stand directly over the cave in which she waited for the child to arrive, and the local shepherds came often to visit the cave to greet her and tend to their animals. They knew that the star was an omen of both significance and good for mankind, and they wanted to be part of the event, whatever happened.

On the day of the birth, Isis decided that before giving birth she must change her name and have all who addressed her called her that name. Her name in Arabic was Meri—Miriam in Hebrew—so she decided to adopt the name Meri, as she intended to live in an Arabic community. Thoth had agreed to be her husband, and they would meet before entering Nazareth, and he would change his name to Joseph to hide his identity. She had secretly agreed to marry him when he could prove his ancestry was of royal blood, albeit he was a bastard. Nevertheless, he was of noble stock and steadfast and true and Meri needed somebody who was prepared to live in obscurity whilst being a great leader and teacher for their child who was destined to be pharaoh.

The star had been identified as Sirius, and its helical rising, namely the day it becomes visible just before sunrise, usually was before the flooding of the Nile at the Summer Solstice. Now, Sirius was appearing in winter to herald the birth of her child, whom she was to call Horus if he was a boy. The night before, she dreamed an angel came to her and proclaimed her son would save the people of the earth from Set and would become a god. Meri told of the communication to her servants, but they thought her delirious and ignored her.

The birth was both quick and trouble free. Complications for a mother or child spelled death, even though Meri had a tWay physician in attendance to deliver the baby, a happy, healthy boy. He was the child of Meri and Joseph, for now, and was to be heralded the virgin birth of a god and called Horus in the future. The day was very cold, as it was the twenty-fifth of December, and the shepherds witnessed the birth as they tended their flock. As Meri was resting and feeding the baby, one of the shepherds asked Meri if three men might come and greet her, as they had travelled far and wanted to greet the baby.

The three men entered the cave and were all sun worshipers, dressed in golden robes and with wings across their shoulders sown in white silk to their robes.

"My lady we follow the star Sirus to fulfil a prophesy, that one day the son of a pharaoh will be born under the star of Sirus to lead mankind to the righteous path," said Baltasar. "I am Baltasar of Eblan, a priest of the sun god, and as an offering, I give you gold."

"My lady, I am the high priest of the sun god from Phoenicia, and bring you frankincense," said Faiq, and the priest bowed low and placed the gift close to the gold near the straw on which she lay.

"Thank you," said Meri, tired from the birth.

"My lady, I come from Mesopotamia. For four thousand years my people have waited for a prophesy to come true, the arrival of the saviour," said Ishtar. "I bring you myrrh."

Meri closed her eyes to sleep. The baby's birth had tired her, and the visit, though brief and pleasing, could not keep her awake, even with child suckling at her breast.

"One more thing, my lady," said Baltasar. "Set, the pharaoh of tWay has destroyed Jericho and declared any who harbour Queen Isis of Ta-Mehu will be destroyed. Herut, ruler of Jerusalem, is planning to send men to every town, city, village, and farm to kill all newborn babies, so my lady must with all haste leave this place."

Isis was shocked awake, and mustering all her strength, she rose up from her bed of straw and passed the baby to the maid. "Make ready for our journey," she said simply, and then staring at the three Deities of the sun god she said, "I must go whilst there is time. Thank you for the gifts; my son will treasure these in later life."

"What will you call the boy?" asked Baltazar.

"I will whisper it just for your ears," said Meri, "Abraham."

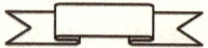

Herut was the leader of the city of Jerusalem, the largest and most powerful city in Palestine. He was an astute and cruel man of small stature, and he was portly from excessive eating and drinking. He had risen to power by cunning, carefully supporting each rising star around him. Through his spies, he heard of the invasion of Palestine by Set, and was made aware of both the advance party and main army that followed that could defeat all of the armies that Palestine could put in the field of battle. He sent spies to view the siege of Jericho and the battle that took place. As the location was close to Jerusalem, he heard the description of the battle and the burning of Jericho the next day, and he was resolved to make an ally of Set. Herut called his council together in the great hall used to govern the city. "The great Pharaoh Set has invaded Palestine and put to siege and destroyed Jericho, killing all of its inhabitants except girls for him to amuse his army officers," said Herut, smiling.

"I have heard this," said Hadar, an elder of many years and one-time rival of Herut.

"We need to seek an alliance with Set," said Herut, "and must give him gifts of gold, incense, cloth, and woman."

"We have little of gold and incense," said Hadar. "Cloth maybe, but no women of our own."

"Then we must give him some wives and daughters," said Herut. "Before he comes and takes all of them."

"Are you mad? We cannot give our own relations to be raped daily by tens of men as sex slaves," said Hadar.

"We must do more. I understand he seeks Isis, his sister, and her newborn baby," said Hadar, "so we must kill every newborn baby and mother in every city, town, village, farm, and dwelling in our region."

"My god, are you insane?" said Hadar. "Surely it would be better to die fighting Set, or flee the city and return when he has left Palestine."

"For a poor man, I would agree," said Herut, "but for a ruler, he would lose everything, so I suggest my plan."

"I cannot agree, and vote against this," said Hadar, outraged.

"I thought you might," said Herut, and nodded to the guards standing behind his council members. A soldier stepped forward and thrust his sword into Hadar's body, killing him. "Bring Hadar's family here," said Herut.

Hadar followed the Jewish faith, but was polygamous, with four wives and some sixteen children aged from twenty-five years to twelve. The family was hauled into the room, and Herut rose from his chair to go and inspect them like a cattle dealer. The eldest of his two wives were past their prime and no longer attractive, and with a wave of his hand, he dismissed them, and the guards ran them through with their swords. One of the sons, being brave, tried to stop one of the soldiers, and he was hacked to the ground, dead.

Hadar's other two wives were young and pretty, and Herut pulled up their dresses to look at their bodies and felt their breasts. He nodded, and they were shackled, and he did the same to all the wives of the men and daughters down to the age of about ten, and even some of the young boys. The remaining family members were hacked to death in front of their family.

Herut then looked at the cowed and shocked remaining women and boys, and found the prettiest daughter of Hadar who was about fourteen. "Adina is your name?" he asked.

The girl nodded in shock, and Herut took her to the table facing the other elders. "Bend over," he said, and the girl obeyed. Herut lifted up her dress over her head, revealing her bare bottom, which he slapped like you would a mare, and then pulled up his short toga and mounted her, sneering at his councillors. After a few short strokes, he gripped her, and his contorted face relaxed and he removed himself from the girl, who was crying quietly. He wiped himself on the frills of her dress and then slapped her bottom harder. "Go stand with your family; I will use you some more later. Now listen carefully, I will rape each of your wives and daughters in front of you and then cut off your testicles and put them in your mouths and send your women and young boys to be raped to death by the army of Set," said Herut, "or each of you leaders of the council can bring me fifty women or young boys that his army can rape in two hours from now. So, settle any grudges you like, kill who you want, but have those girls and boys here in two hours, or I cut off your balls."

The men were shocked at what they had seen, and none wanted that to happen to his family or himself. They walked away shaking from the council chamber.

"One more thing," said Herut. "Bring one extra girl. I think I will keep a small harem to remind me of this day." Herut then motioned to his head of the army. "Take your men and kill every baby under one year and their mothers, and pile them in carts we can take to Jericho." The soldier nodded and strode away to obey even though his own wife and son would now die.

The city of Jerusalem was a bloodbath within two hours, and wailing filled the city. The leaders were not at all happy but became immune to the wailing as they struggled to meet the deadline and killed friends, relatives, and colleagues quickly to achieve the orders of Herut. Within the two hours, over seven hundred women and young boys were in the square outside the council chambers, and Herut lost little time selecting the nine girls to be left behind for his return and leading this caravan of living and dead through the gates of Jerusalem.

Herut sent ahead an envoy to request an audience with Set, and he received a favourable reply, so they proceeded directly to Jericho. It was early morning when they arrived, and Herut could smell the rotting flesh of the dead and the smoke from the burned trees and buildings. The encampment of Set was large, and he took only a sample of his gifts to show Set the remainder being left outside the camps.

"I come to bear gifts, great Pharaoh of tWay, and to seek an alliance as your servant in Palestine," said Herut.

"What gifts do you bring?" asked Set, always greedy.

"Gold, incense, jewels, and cloth in abundance, some twenty cartloads," said Herut, pointing to some caskets being opened and bolts of cloth being displayed to show their quality.

Set nodded.

"Also, seven hundred girls and young boys as slaves for you and your men to plough and do with as you please," continued Herut.

Set smiled, and looking at the young girls, he was pleased. "Why the dead bodies?"

"All babies under one year old and their mothers have been killed in Jerusalem, and I will kill every one of them in the region. If your sister Isis is in my territory, she and her baby are dead," said Herut.

"What is your name?" asked Set.

"Herut, great Pharaoh," said Herut, whilst bowing low.

"And what do you want in return?" asked Set.

"That you leave my small city alone and march across other cities to plunder, and let me rule as your subject, for which I will pay tribute each year," said Herut.

"Very well, Herut, you are my subject," said Set. "Now, sit with me and my general, Jabir, and tell us where we can get more women to plough and gold and jewels," said Set.

The three men plotted the fate of cities and families across Palestine, which would become infamous for generations.

Meri and her baby, with her small entourage, walked to the edge of the Dead Sea and bought a boat to take them up the Jordan River until it branched eastwards. From there, they would walk to Nazareth and meet in a small oasis just outside the city. The small party walked slowly, as they had no pack mules and had to carry heavy caskets of gold and jewels and their belongings. Meri carried the baby Horus.

After several days late into the evening, they saw a fire glowing in the night, and it was the camp of her new husband Joseph. The Coffin of Destiny was already at the oasis, and Meri now relaxed a little for the first time since the birth of the child.

"What news do you have of Set and his army?" asked Meri.

"Last I heard, he was raping the pillaging cities and towns back to the port of Jaffa where his fleet is anchored," said Joseph, "but a new threat is Herut, who is killing all newborn babies and their mothers in all the areas surrounding Jericho."

"Who is this Herut?" asked Meri. "I heard the same story from priests who came to worship Horus, which is the reason why we fled so quickly."

"How did you escape past both Set and Herut?" asked Joseph.

"We went by boat up the Dead Sea and the Jordan River until it forked east. Sunk the boat in the river and walked without mules so nobody could betray our direction," said Meri.

"What about the person that sold you the boat?" asked Joseph.

"We had to kill him," said Meri, "but left gold in his pockets for his children."

Joseph could see Meri was sad that they had to kill to protect themselves. "Rest now, my wife, and let us prepare for tomorrow," said Joseph.

Isis then spoke to her entourage: "You must each choose an Arabic name, for tomorrow we are to be Arabs and will live simple lives until our pharaoh is fully grown. It is our duty and honour to serve him until our death. He will be known as Horus amongst us and Deyna Udeen, which means "brightness of the faith." Henceforth, we believe in whatever they believe in."

"I don't know," said Joseph, honestly. "I have been busy becoming a Jew, and we soon can learn to be Arab, but we need to have a sign so we can recognize each other without speaking."

Meri spoke with conviction, "The sign of the eye, which will be known as the Eye of Horus." Meri drew it in the sand.

"Why this sign?" asked Joseph.

"I don't know," said Meri, "but it seems right. Each person should have it tattooed on the palm of his left hand so we can look for this. We can say, 'Let me read your fortune, stranger, and they will offer their right hand, palm down. The Eye of Horus will become visible when the palm reader turns the palm upwards."

"And if the person does something else?" asked Joseph.

"Then something is wrong, and they should both part without any word of Horus and our mission," said Meri.

The next day, the party broke up into small family groups and entered the city separately. It would be over a year before Set would hear of Isis and the newly born Horus.

Book Two

Chapter Nine

David York was sitting at the desk in his study at his Mayfair London apartment, looking at a video of the infant of Mary and Joseph. He was a beautiful baby, and not yet one, he was crawling around on the floor, his parents laughing and smiling as they followed him on all fours. The Jesus bloodline was safe and happy at their secret location, and the first male first born in two thousand years was growing up in a safe and happy environment. David had found it difficult becoming the leader of the Sect, protecting the Jesus Blood Line and keeping the relics of Christianity and the Holy Grail.

The Templar's had been the forbearers to the Sect, which David headed, and their secrecy and discipline had been something both John McCallister his predecessor (and father) and he had sought to continue. After the death of his father by the Crusader, the Sect's own assassin, David had started to modernize the Sect and reinforce secrecy and discipline. He decided that rather than the single deadly assassin, a world organization needed regional operatives, and his Sect leaders would risk detection by meeting over the Internet on a regular basis to discuss strategy and plot the future.

He also had same problem with the Sect's objectives; what was its purpose? To protect the Jesus blood line, certainly – but for what? What was it they expected the infant to do? Preach and convert people to a new religion? There were enough religions and most of them reasonably sound in their teachings. Become a politician and change society? Perhaps, but many very good men had tried and failed, and many still were trying. Anyway, if you looked at society from an historical perspective, society has become kinder, more considerate, and more charitable over the centuries. We still have famine, war, poverty, murder, and atrocities, but gradually we deal with them in a better, more humane way. What would we expect a new Jesus to do? What would we expect him to achieve? What would a new Jesus expect the Sect to do? It had vast wealth and influence, but how to use it was the problem.

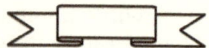

David's first action was to formerly appoint regional leaders and assign Sect societies to each of these regions. This would be the first time the whole of the Sect members would be known and documented. David believed that to achieve any goal, you needed facts, and he had none. Although the risk was high with computer records, a database of members was to be compiled.

The regions were important, and David divided the world into a number of geographical and important areas. The USA, Canada, and Mexico were the first region, and its headquarters would be the Sect Society in New York. The whole of the remainder of the Americas in South America would have its headquarters in Buenos Aires in Argentina. Europe would be divided geographically and politically. The European community and other Western countries with the Eastern European countries would form another region, with their headquarters in Zurich. Russia would be a region by itself because of its economic and political importance, with its headquarters in Moscow. The Turkish-speaking countries and the Middle East would form a region, and Istanbul would be the headquarters. Afghanistan, Pakistan, India, Nepal, and Bangladesh would be another region, with their headquarters in New Delhi. China would be a region by itself, with headquarters in Hong Kong. Australia, New Zealand, Papa New Guinea, and all the small islands in the area would be a region, with headquarters in Sydney. All the remaining Far Eastern countries would be in a region, with their headquarters in Tokyo. The whole of Africa would be one region, with the headquarters in Johannesburg.

This comprised ten regions, each that would have country leaders reporting into them. Each country leader would have city or regional leaders reporting to them. It was going to be a difficult job selecting the ten regional leaders, and among them a deputy to replace the leader, should the leader be killed or die in an accident. He also thought that the country leaders should all be reassessed, as he had no idea of their credentials or suitability for the post.

The demise of Paul Athers from the Newfoundland helicopter crash nearly a year ago obviously had been a defeat for the Cult. However, David surmised that with the resources the Catholic Church had at its disposal, the rogue element that controlled the Cult would recover and appoint another to lead their cause. He found it interesting that two organizations emanating from the Middle East had both had leaders based in London with MI6 connections, and thought it unlikely they would appoint another British citizen when their network was so vast. Other than the simple objective of killing the Jesus Blood Line and destroying all relics that supported the concept of more than one Jesus figure, David wondered what the Cult was used for; it seemed to be vast and powerful.

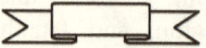

The Vatican is not a city, but the world's smallest state and the capital of Catholicism. It only consists of one hundred and six acres of ground located in Rome and is surrounded by high walls guarded by the Vatican Guard. The location is said to be the site where St. Peter was killed in AD 64 and was buried, and has been the residence of the popes of Rome ever since.

The Vatican is the only state that is ruled by a monarch with absolute power. Only five hundred people live in the Vatican, and the state has its own banks, post office, currency, judicial system, radio station, shops, and a daily newspaper. Unlike all other religious leaders, when the pope meets heads of state, he meets them on an equal footing as a head of state, not as a religious leader. As such, he is protected by diplomatic immunity from investigation unless very serious charges of genocide can be brought against him before the international tribunal.

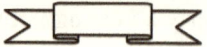

The pope sat in his private chambers in a simple white cassock and contemplated the report that Cardinal Castellano had provided on the Sect and its new leader, David York. As a member of the Pontifical Commission for the Vatican City state, those who draft the legislation for the pontiff and have executive powers, Cardinal Castellano was one of the pope's most trusted aides. Now in his late sixties, he was slow to move his heavy frame, but this belied a quick brain, greedy for position and power.

"So, he is a Catholic," said the pope.

"Yes, your Holiness," said Castellano, "but not practicing."

"Does he ever attend church?" asked the pope.

"Occasionally often at Christmas," said Castellano. "He likes the community of church, apparently."

"Don't we all?" asked the pope.

"Yes, I suppose we all love the church for that aspect, your Holiness," said Castellano.

"And this fellow," the pope looked briefly at his notes, "Giovanni Bellini, he is Italian or an American?"

"American, you're Holiness," and Cardinal Castellano moved uneasily in his chair, which the pope's quick eye spotted immediately.

"Of Italian descent, I presume?" asked the pope, probing. "Is he related to any one of note?"

"He is a distant cousin to my own family, your Holiness," said Cardinal Castellano squirming. *How did he suspect?*

"Really," said the pope. "What is his real name? Giovanni Bellini was the fifteenth century painter of the *Coronation of the Virgin*, altar piece in Pesaro."

"Antonio Castellano," said Cardinal Castellano, now aware he could not hide the relationship. "Pardon my deceit, your Holiness; he is the son of my brother. I thought to hide this so as not to spoil his chances of advancement, frightened of being accused of nepotism."

The pope already knew this and was pleased the cardinal at least had been truthful. He was pleased the young man would be loyal to the Catholic Church and had strong family ties at the highest level. The pope picked up a glass of water and drank it. "You may appoint the boy. If he fails, you will of course resign your office and retire," said the pope, very calmly.

"Yes, you're Holiness," said the cardinal.

"One more thing, Cardinal Castellano," said the pope. "The position the boy will hold will give him access to great wealth. I expect the Catholic Church to prosper as well as you and your nephew."

The pudgy hand of Cardinal Castellano gave an involuntary twitch, and the portly man squirmed in his chair very slightly. Obviously the pope was better informed than he thought. "Of course, your Holiness we will pay a twenty per cent levy on all our profits we make."

"That is most kind, your Eminence," said the pope. "Have you considered, however, that it is the church's money you use, and any losses are at the church's risk?" and the pope smiled and sipped his water again. The delicate, bony hand was pale in the brightness of the sun shining into the simple room of Pope John.

Castellano quivered. *He knows*, he thought. "What would you think was a fair portion?" he asked, his voice without confidence.

"The church has many projects, so all the funds we can get at this time are of great value to the poor," said the pope. "You should consider keeping only a small portion yourself, and rewarding the church for its generosity in giving you access to its resources which you put at risk with your ventures."

My god, he does know, thought Castellano, *perhaps everything*. "We have many hidden costs, Holy Father. The profit on some transactions is smaller than a person unfamiliar with the financial world would assume," he said, trying to probe and watching the kind, impassive, often smiling face.

"The church has many souls in its care, your Eminence, so don't worry, we can find one person to understand the intricacies of the prime mortgage rate," said the pope. "Particularly these schemes to bundle defaulted loans of middle-class Americans and sell

110

them to Europeans disguised as low-risk secured loans."

A bolt hit the heart of Cardinal Castellano, and he was about to answer, but the pope continued, "Tell me, your Eminence, from your front of the Savings Bank of America, do you still carry any of these loans?" The pope's voice did not change; it was always kind and never aggressive, but always probing.

"None, your Holiness, we sold them all to a German and French bank" said the cardinal, waiting for more revelations.

"Your bank still advertises, particularly in Arizona, that you can release money on your property, up to 120% of its value. Is that true?" asked the pope. "I am not a financial man, but that is a risk for the bank if they default, is it not?"

"Yes, you're Holiness, but we are selling those banks to a British bank," said Cardinal Castellano.

"Good. Remove yourself from this market. It may collapse, and you could be left with debt your family cannot repay," said the pope.

"Repay, Holy Father?" said the cardinal, startled.

"Of course, your Eminence. Should you lose the funds of the Fisherman, you and your family will only be too happy to repay any losses from your own resources." The pope sipped his last bit of water from the simple glass, easily purchased from any large supermarket in Rome.

"Of course, Holy Father," said the cardinal, now resigned to the fact he knew everything. "We shall count no losses of our transactions and provide a thirty per cent profit on all our dealings."

"That is most generous, Cardinal Castellano," said the pope, now going for the kill, "particularly when you have so many family enterprises. But as partners in the risk, perhaps fifty per cent would be more generous?"

"Your Holiness, fifty per cent of all profits would be a huge sum to repay," the cardinal was visibly distressed.

"We thank you for your generosity, your Eminence. I am sure you realize the unique position of trust you have as the Fisherman's banker, and will ensure we have the funds in our account by next Friday," said the pope finally.

"By next Friday would be impossible, your Holiness," said the cardinal, now close to collapse.

"With the capital returned, of course," said the pope. "You no longer need to risk this with our various sales of church assets."

It is over, thought Cardinal Castellano; *you cannot hide anything from the Fisherman.* "Please give us two weeks, and it will be done in full."

"Good, your Eminence, you may have these two weeks," said the pope, "and please remember, as your own capital is part of the church's profit, it expects your most generous original offer of twenty per cent to continue."

"Of course, you're Holiness," said the cardinal, the last dagger had been driven into his heart.

"Now, your boy, Giovanni Bellini, what does he make of this rumour of the Coffin of Destiny being real?" asked the pope.

"Just some resurrected cult hunting a mythical grail," said the cardinal.

"Really, your Eminence, you need to be more charitable; other religions can coexist with ours," said the pope. "Out of curiosity, send Bellini to see me. I want to question him about this mythical artefact. I understand he is here in Rome."

"Yes, Holy Father, in the Vatican," said Cardinal Castellano, no longer able to hide any secret.

"Good, send him to me," and the pope rose; the audience was over.

"He will be with you with all haste, Holy Father," and the fat cardinal knelt and kissed the pope's ring and watched as the tall slender figure, almost ghostlike from his pale complexion, turned his back on him to walk back to his desk.

As the cardinal left, the pope pondered how he would use the several billion of extra funds the church now would have available. It was perhaps as high as fifty billion with the thirty billion capital returned.

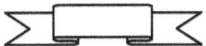

Giovanni Bellini looked exactly how you expected him to look. He was tall at six feet, three inches, broad shouldered and with a muscular build, which was highlighted by his tight fitting clothes. He always wore Italian-made silk suits, shirts and shoes cut and fashioned in the latest designs. He liked the designer Jane Barnes, an American from Maryland, because she obsessed over the detail; buttons, cuffs, pockets, collars, and even the thread used for sewing were all important to Jane. However, Gino, in spite of his wealth, would not pay designer prices, and bought from a small tailor in Rome who copied her designs exactly for Gino to wear. His shoes were less fashionable, and although expensive, were built more for combat rather than fashion, with steel heels and tips to hurt an opponent in a fight, rather than impress them with their design.

Gino did wear casual clothes if the occasion was appropriate, but usually wore a suit everywhere he went. He was now resplendent in a dark grey silk suit, a lighter grey silk shirt, and a multi-coloured black and grey silk tie. His golden sun tan and stylish short jet black hair was more suited to a man in his twenties, but Gino could carry it off because his aggressive and assured posture told you that he was perfect.

Gino contrasted greatly with his companion. He was small in stature at five foot six, and fat and overweight with a large paunch and chubby face and hands. His body was stuffed into an ill-fitting suit bought from a retail chain, probably at a discount to account for its lack of any redeemable feature. It had a bad cut, bad colour, bad cloth, and bad manufacture. Arnold Worth, "Arnie" to his friends, and "fat boy" to people who did not like him, had no attractive physical features, stuttered, and often smelled, as he sweated nervously in the presence of everybody, but he did have one talent: He was a financial genius. He could make billions appear and disappear in any set of books and deceive even the sharpest of financial auditors. Gino had found that theft by massive financial fraud was far more lucrative than any bank heist, particularly if you had the backing of the Vatican with its massive funds to manipulate.

Both men waited for Gino's uncle, Cardinal Castellano, and the outcome of his meeting with the Holy Father. One day, Gino hoped he could meet the pope so he could impress people with the meeting. A staunch Catholic, Gino questioned nothing in his absolute faith in the Catholic doctrine and his support of the clergy. Obviously it was very good for business as well. A Cult member since he was a teenager, he had benefitted from contacts in the Cult and his illegal dealings were protected by his contacts in politics, the police, and most importantly, the clergy. Now at thirty-three and the head of the Cult, he had a licence to print money for the Castellano family, of which his father had been the head and that he had inherited. Of course, Cardinal Castellano was an important member of the family, and often before he was head of the family, Gino would curry favour, but once his position as head of the family had been confirmed, he made it clear to his uncle that he, and not the cardinal, was the sole head of the family.

His father made sure he had the best education, and he had obtained a good degree from UCLA (University of California in Los Angeles) in Computer Science before obtaining a master's degree in accounting and management at Harvard University. His father had divorced his mother when he was three, so it was fairly easy to distance Gino from his father, and when his mother remarried, his name was changed to Bellini. It was simple to have the infant's birth re-registered with father being the stepfather, and his connection to the Castellano family expunged from the records. However, his father kept very close contact with Gino through the church, and his uncle, who was then a monsignor at their parish church, would take him regularly to meet him.

Anthony (Tony) Castellano was an old-fashioned gangster and he wanted his son not to follow the same path, but to be a more sophisticated and powerful criminal. The Cult provided this opportunity, and with help of his uncle, he became a member when he was barely sixteen. Fearless and resourceful, he was trained and used by the Cult to assassinate identified targets. Who would suspect a young, fresh-faced high school boy as a deadly assassin? Gino would never forget the lesson of, "Don't ever underestimate your opponent based on looks or background." His rise up the Cult mirrored the rise of his uncle, who always was positioned carefully to make Gino able to rise, Gino learning all the time.

Gino did have flaws, of course. He had a very bad temper and was very violent when he was young on a number of occasions, and those incidents had to be hushed up and their records lost.

Gino was very attractive and liked sex with both women and men, so he often was caught fucking somebody else's wife or husband, daughter or son, whom he should not, and was exposed. California, with its broader and more liberal approach to gay men was less of problem than when he moved to Boston to study at Harvard. As always, his indiscretions were covered up, and by the time he left Harvard, he had matured enough to be more careful and no longer be a liability with his behaviour.

One aspect was never a problem, and that was alcohol. He drank a little wine with his lunch and dinner, but never more than one large glass, preferring water. He rarely drank tea or coffee, and after discovering he loved keeping fit and training, he ate very sensibly, although he did have a weakness for his mother's pasta and his stepfather's desserts, both of which were delicious. However, he only visited their home briefly, and therefore that break in his disciplined life was never disastrous to his physique or training. He was a very loving son and truly loved his mother and both fathers and all his relations. However, he was also a cold-blooded killer, and was one of those rare individuals who could have normal emotions, but put in a compartment, those cold heartless non-emotions to kill and torture. He found this essential to be successful in the Cult and in business.

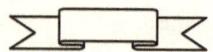

Cardinal Castellano arrived back from his audience with the pope, and when he entered the room, Gino rose from his chair, formally bowed to his uncle, and kissed the proffered ring. The less confident Arnie hid behind Gino until he was pushed forward to the cardinal. "This is Arnold Worth, your Eminence," said Gino, pushing the frightened man forward.

"Your Holiness," said Arnie, stuttering.

"Only the pope is called his Holiness, my son," said Cardinal Castellano "You may call me your Eminence or Cardinal Castellano."

"Sorry, your Eminence," Arnie stuttered quietly, and he saw Gino stare disappointedly at him and remembered he had already been told that several times before the meeting.

"Let us sit, we have much to discuss," said Cardinal Castellano. No longer under the gaze of the pope and unsure of himself, he now felt confident and assured. He explained exactly what had happened at the meeting with the pope, sparing no details. However, he did add five percent to the church's share, which he planned to pocket for himself.

"So the pope wants to see me," said Gino, very pleased with this aspect but not impressed with the outcome of the cardinal's other negotiations.

"Yes, with all haste," said the cardinal nervously, "but I suggest you stick to the quest for the Coffin of Destiny and leave the negotiations of the finances to me."

"Of course, your Eminence, I value your advice and will follow it carefully, " said Gino respectfully.

There was a knock at the cardinal's door, and a young priest entered with a small silver tray on which a small envelope lay. "A note for your Eminence from his Holiness," said the young priest.

The cardinal ushered the young priest forward and opened the envelope. It said simply:

"Please send Giovanni Bellini immediately."

It was not signed.

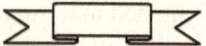

The pope, now dressed in his formal attire, would meet Bellini in a small reception room used to greet people in private but with formality. He had the advantage of course, of hearing the cardinal's briefing, as all the rooms in the Vatican were bugged and he could hear and see every conversation and meeting. There were no secrets from the pope in the Vatican. Whilst he was of course keen to resolve the business issues, he was also interested in the location of the Coffin of Destiny.

Chapter Ten

Giovanni Bellini waited outside the small reception room of the Papal palace that was used to meet dignitaries on a formal basis and felt a little nervous. Two Swiss Guards stood outside the door of the pope in their traditional Renaissance dress of red, orange, and yellow, armed with sword and the halberd, the four-sided pole, and Gino thought they looked very formal and he felt a little nervous. He had longed to meet the pontiff, but now that it was going to happen he wondered if such a meeting was going to be good for business. The huge percentage of the family's gains in the stock market and financial dealings had been halved, and effectively, their capital had to be repaid all in two weeks. All possible, of course, but nevertheless a hammer blow to both the Cult and the Castellano family plans. They did of course have the huge profits from the prime mortgage companies, but still, it was a blow.

The young priest appeared and summonsed Gino into the pope's room. Whilst small compared to the other rooms, the room was grand in the Vatican style, with high ceilings, and ornate walls festooned with paintings of the great masters of the art world. The pope was seated, dressed in his papal robes, and Gino crossed the room, knelt, and kissed the ring he proffered towards Gino. As he rose, the pope gestured towards a chair. "Please sit, Mr. Bellini," he said in a kind, quiet voice, "or may I call you Gino?"

"I would be honoured if you called me Gino, your Holiness," said Gino.

"Formality is such a trial, my son," said the pope, "but a necessity of the office. It is nice sometimes to drop the formality I find, but unfortunately, the office only allows certain boundaries." The pope left much unsaid. He did not need to explain that his Christian name could never be used again in public or private. The office demanded respect far above the feelings of the holder of the office.

Gino remained silent, and the pope, noting the pause, continued, "So, Gino, let me ask you. Did your uncle explain our acceptance of your offer of a share in your business and the return of the capital to the Vatican?"

"Some details were provided, your Holiness, but Cardinal Castellano did not provide all the details, as our time was brief," said Gino, fishing. "The major points seemed to be a gift of fifty per cent of the profits to date, the return of the capital, and twenty five per cent of future profits. I did not have time to ask what the Castellano family receives in return, your Holiness."

"Perceptive, Gino," said the pope. "But nothing."

"Nothing?" said Gino. "But your Holiness, why should we agree?"

"It is already agreed, Gino," said the pope, "but I have a small task, in return for which I will allow you to keep the capital to generate more funds for us both."

"What task, your Holiness?" asked Gino, seeing perhaps a way to rescue the situation.

"Bring me the Coffin of Destiny," said the pope simply.

"I know of the fabled Coffin of Destiny from 3,500 BC with the remains of Osiris, but believe this is a myth," said Gino.

"Gino, we don't have time for verbal fencing. We both know that the coffin is real and you paid one million dollars to locate its burial place in Palestine," said the pope. "Your men are digging for it now."

Nobody in his immediate circle knew this except Cardinal Castellano, so obviously he was the source to the pope. "Of course we search, your Holiness," said Gino smoothly, "but there is little hope of it being real."

"Pity, my son, as you have nothing else you can give me as a gift," said the pope dismissively, a hint of annoyance in his voice.

Gino saw he meant what he said. "If I bring you this gift you crave, your Holiness, what would you believe was fair in our dealings?"

The pope was now reawakened to hope and chose his words carefully. "We cannot demand the terms of your gift; the Castellano family must decide," said the pope quietly.

"I believe, your Holiness, that the percentages are over generous, and would hurt our ability to invest. I would suggest thirty per cent of our current dealings and ten per cent in future dealings, with the Castellano family keeping the capital to reinvest for a period of ten years and then returning it in full," said Gino, very carefully. The offer was very expensive, but generous to the church, and very affordable for the Castellano family.

"If you fail in finding and bringing the Coffin of Destiny to Rome, the church accepts your first very generous offer," said the pope.

"And if we bring the coffin to your Holiness?" asked Gino.

"The church was impressed by your skills in your financial dealings, and I am sure you would want to reward them in their faith in your abilities, so we would hope the fifty per cent gifts from your immediate dealings are still in your gift," said the pope, "and paid in two weeks."

"Of course, you're Holiness," said Gino. "That will be arranged immediately."

"The church will allow you to keep the capital for one year. If you fail in your mission, then you will return it with a twenty per cent profit plus a fifty per cent gift," the pope spoke very quietly.

Gino gasped, "And if we bring the coffin, your Holiness?"

"Then, my son, you will pay twenty per cent of the capital each year for each of the ten years it is in your keeping, and return it at the end of that period," said the pope.

"Thank you, your Holiness," said Gino.

"One more thing, Mr Worth, your financial advisor, ensure he is guarded at all times," said the pope. "It would be unfortunate if he fell into the wrong hands."

Gino understood. Arnie Worth was to be killed to ensure secrecy about the sale of the prime interest companies. The pope rose and the interview was at an end.

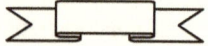

The first meeting of the provisional leaders was to take place, and they were going to use Skype as the medium. It was a risk, but David was determined to get started and then to improve security at every level.

The keeper of the scrolls for the Sect was William Osprey, a fifty-five year old banker and Swiss politician from Geneva. As one of the three wise men who attended the birth of the new Messiah, he would be one of the key men who certainly would keep his position and would shape the future of the Sect as David's deputy and heir should he die or be killed.

The European Sect leader was to be Aaron Wiseman. Now sixty-four, the Sect banker was a direct descendent of Francois Marriott (one of the founders of the Sect) and controlled one of the largest banks in Switzerland and companies all around the world. Another of the three wise men who attended Jesus' birth, his outwardly Jewish faith was also an attraction to David, as it hid often his involvement with the Sect.

Bill Travers, at forty-six, had been the final of the three wise men to attend the birth of the new messiah, and as chief of the Beothuck Indians, was not an obvious descendant of the Templars who came to America in 1314. The keeper of the Holy Grail, he would continue as the leader of North American region, from his new home of New York. On a daily basis, he also had the task of guarding the infant and Mary and Joseph, whilst the leader of the Sect travelled the world and developed the Sect's influence.

It was Bill Travers who had recommended Ignacio Rossi, having met him several times through mutual business and then through collaboration in the Americas. Like Bill, he was in his forties, but younger by three years at forty-three. He was of Italian origin, but his family had settled in Argentina nearly one hundred years earlier. Ignacio suited his name, which meant "fiery," and Rossi, the surname, was derived from the Italian *Russo* for a red-headed person. Ignacio was of medium build, and on the stocky side but not fat, standing five feet ten inches tall. He always wore smart casual clothes, rarely wearing a suit. His fiery temper often landed him in trouble, and the scars on his swarthy face told the story of his many fights. A successful businessman and generous philanthropist, he had been a Sect member from his teenager years and was highly effective. His outbursts hid a thoughtful and meticulous planner who had deep feelings for his fellow man.

The man who was the current head of Russia could not have been more different. Schooled under the Soviet regime as a child, he was evasive and mild in manner. Small in stature and modest in his dress, he spent very little on his casual wear and purchased his suits from a department store. He looked and acted like a minor official from a government department, which he once had been. Yuri Cheramisin, his family originally a member of the Mordivan people of Russia, was a self-made billionaire of the Russian elite. His fortune had come like many of his generation, from taking advantage of his knowledge of government and spotting a commercial opportunity. His had been in telecommunications before the liberalisation of the airwaves for cell phones was to be introduced. Quickly buying licences for very little and creating paper companies, he sold them on to other people or the public for a fortune, and then they had to do all the hard work of developing the network. In fact, Yuri never became involved operationally; he never had offices and only had very few staff. He was a facilitator who took a large margin up front in every deal and then moved on to the next deal.

Harika Kudret had the perfect name, as *kudret* meant power in Turkish and *harika* Lady. Harika could not be more suited; at sixty, she looked powerful stocky and strong squeezed into an elegant designer creation with her blonde-dyed hair tied back, her once beautiful face lined from the sun. She always spoke in a loud voice because she was hard of hearing but refused to use a hearing aid. She was one of the most successful women in the world, and appeared on several wealth lists as well as influential lists for her strong views on women's rights and education. A former prostitute, which she did not hide in her autobiography, she had made most of her money from banking and oil and several wise investments in technology.

Shreya Patel was very beautiful, and the youngest member at twenty-nine; she had classic features and a slim, curvy figure any man would lust for if he was heterosexual. The most devastating part of her appearance was her dazzling smile of perfect white teeth, which melted all hearts, male and female. Her wealth was inherited from her family's interest in steel, coal, and manufacturing. Shreya was very astute at business and continued to grow the family's wealth, following her inheritance upon the death of her parents when she was only nineteen. Her father, Vijay, and her mother were killed by an agent of the Cult, and ever since then, Shreya had been hunting and killing the Cult in India. Her beauty and charm belied her deep-seated hatred and ruthless streak, which made her the perfect head of the Sect in India.

Jin Tseng was very small, as so often the Chinese are, perhaps only four feet nine inches tall. She was very slim with a perfect figure maintained by vigorous daily exercise and a careful diet. She looked to be perhaps in her early thirties, and even younger from a distance, but she was in her late fifties. She was reserved and very polite, no matter what the circumstances. She was the daughter of a Chinese government official who was still alive and in the inner circle of the ruling body of the country and communist party. Jin (meaning gold or money) had become the capitalist in the family and closely followed her father's advice, as he always had inside information from his position and was close to all of the decision making in the country. Jin had been the leader of the Sect for over ten years in China, having joined right out of the university when she was only eighteen, still active nearly forty years earlier.

Liam Brown was a typical Australian character, just how you expected an Aussie to be: blond, bronzed, overweight with a beer belly, badly dressed in ill-fitting clothes, and a loud mouth and bad attitude. Liam had developed this persona carefully to hide a perceptive mind with an iron will to succeed in business and within the Sect. At only thirty-three, he was the second youngest regional Sect leader and one of the most outrageous and visible. All his money had come from pornographic web sites and financial scams that bordered close to being illegal.

Takuya Kato was tall for a Japanese man at six feet three inches, and had played basketball in the USA at UCLA, punching well above his weight, with his height still being short for the sport. Takuya was built very athletically and still exercised daily and played basketball with his grown-up children and grandchildren, even though he was now in his early sixties. A banker, he owned one of the largest and most influential banks having worked in banking all his life since he attended the university. He got control of the bank through artful and astute investments. His tactics and long-term, slow end-game plans were legendary. He only had been recently appointed to the Sect leadership in Japan, but had been a member for over forty years.

Laurette van Berkel was from a strong Afrikaans family who had been wealthy for nearly a hundred years. A very attractive woman with jet black hair and striking features with a dazzling smile, she had now started to gain weight in her late thirties and to lose that beauty the youth had in full bloom. She was the Sect leader for Africa, inheriting the position upon the death of her grandfather.

David York opened the meeting and introduced each of the regional leaders, giving a brief overview of each person. When he was finished, he introduced William Osprey, his appointed deputy, who would be the secretary for all meetings that David chaired. "Ladies and gentlemen, we have some important issues, the least of which is preparing the Sect for the present day and future. But before we start that planning, does anybody have any urgent business we need to attend to that may affect our primary goal of protecting the new Messiah or our relics?"

"The Cult have found something in Israel near Nazareth," said Harika Kudret, "My sources say it is something called the Coffin of Destiny."

"What the hell is that?" asked Liam Brown.

"If I may, honoured leader," said Aaron Wiseman.

"Go ahead, Aaron," said David York.

"The Coffin of Destiny dates back to 3,500 BC and is said to contain the body of Osiris, the husband of Isis, and the mother of Horus, the reputed ancestor to the Jesus blood line."

"I thought Set, Osiris, Horus, Isis, and all that gang of stories from tWayian mythology were just that, myths?" asked Liam Brown, intrigued.

"Ancient scrolls reveal these and several other myths to actually be real people with events exaggerated over time and made into myths. One day, I hope to publish some of these scrolls," said Aaron.

"For the moment, let us focus on the present danger," said David. "What do we need to do to obtain the coffin and destroy the Cult in your area, Harika?"

"The Cult is not like the Sect with a membership in the Middle East; there is no network to destroy," said Harika. "They rely on members from the Catholic Church, so unless you destroy every catholic, the Cult exists."

"But it has a head or at least an inner structure, otherwise Paul Athurs, my ex-colleague from MI6, could not have been its head," said David.

"It has a head, certainly, but when we cut off the head, it will be replaced," said Harika. "The problem is, David, we are talking about a religion that believes in its right to kill to protect itself. It believes that the Jesus blood line and the truth of the past are a threat, and seeks to merely protect itself from destruction."

"That is not dissimilar to our own role," said Sherya Patel.

"There is a big difference between protecting an infant from being killed, and speaking the truth about the past, and destroying relics and killing people," said Liam, "because the basis of your religion is built on a carefully constructed series of lies."

"I have always believed our way has been just," said Takuyo Kato, his voice serene and stern. "To my knowledge, we don't kill needlessly."

"Whatever we have done, or do, there needs to be a code which ensures our actions are just," said Sherya Patel.

"All killings and the use of force will be decided at this council," said David. "We can't have specific rules and codes, because our enemy, the Cult, has none."

"Darn right!" said Liam Brown.

"Very well, let's send a team to the middle east to investigate the Coffin of Destiny," said David. "They will be sanctioned to kill Cult members if necessary, but the objective is to obtain the coffin and destabilise the Cult, rather than eliminate the leader."

"We don't know who the leader is, do we?" asked Yuri Cheramisin quietly.

"No," said David, "but we will find out with all your help. Get our contacts to probe the Catholic Church."

"The Vatican is the key to unlock that mystery," said Yuri. "Is Aaron the Jew the right man to gain access to the Vatican?"

"We Jews have many friends, and the majority of the European Sect members are Catholics," said Aaron defensively. "But if you have an inside contact in the Vatican, we can use him."

"We have a cardinal from Russia appointed by Pope John himself," said Yuri. "Cardinal Bobrikov was a close friend of my family on my uncle's side, and a staunch family member. He is a devoted Catholic, but would be horrified by the existence of a Cult and the pope ordering killings."

"But would he help us?" asked David.

"That I don't know, but we could arrange to meet him in Rome and probe him to see if he is willing to help," said Yuri.

"Very well," said David. "Go with Aaron and find an excuse to introduce him. We need you not to be involved as the contact. Ensure all your meetings are outside the Vatican and you never telephone him or use a computer in the Vatican, as they will all be bugged."

"Where is the infant? When will we see him?" asked Laurette van Berkel.

"That we will keep secret until the infant is a man and ready to preach," said David, "but we will send some photographs each year over the Internet just for the regional leaders."

"Is that wise, David?" asked William Osprey. "Our security could be breached; a leader could be turned, and the infant could be traced and killed."

"We will be careful with the photographs," said David, "and we have to take some risks to communicate."

"I still think the risk is too high," said William Osprey, alarmed at David's reckless behaviour with the life of the Messiah.

"Who else thinks we should not circulate some photographs?" asked David.

"I don't need an image to believe," said Jin Tseng.

"Nor I," said Takuya Kato.

"Neither do I," said Ignacio Rossi.

"I would like to see the image," said Yuri Cheramisin, "but think the risk is too great."

The remainder were silent. "Does that mean the rest of you agree?" asked David.

"I say no to distributing photographs," said Bill O'Brien.

"I also say no," said Aaron, who felt guilty because he had seen the child.

"That seems a majority," said David. "What if we restricted it to one when he was a baby one year ago in front of a white background, and don't release anymore until he is grown up?"

"I would agree to that," said William Osprey.

"Any disagree?" asked David, and nobody answered. "Very well, I will arrange the photograph."

"Is there any other business?" asked William Osprey.

When there was no answer from the group, David closed the meeting, and the computer faces of his leaders disappeared from the computer.

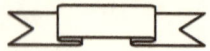

David looked at his two companions in his study, William Osprey and Bill O'Brien. "Do you think the traitor bought it?" asked David.

"Probably," said William.

"Any suspects from the meeting?" asked David.

"I am not good at espionage," said Bill, "so I have no clue, but time will tell."

"We will find them, but be careful, David, when you go to the Middle East," said William.

"I will be," said David. "I will take Veronica. She will scare the crap out of them," and they all laughed.

Just then, Veronica came in the room, unaware she was the butt of their joke, and David's face visibly lit up. The ex-ladies' man had become a one-woman man, sharing his flat and life with Veronica Goldsmith, the beautiful daughter of the billionaire Roland Goldsmith.

He had never searched for that special person most of us seek, that single person who makes your life worthwhile and whom you love unconditionally, but he had found her in Veronica. When she left the top of the toothpaste each morning, he did not swear and think *lazy bitch*, but put the top on and thought *how endearing*. When she left her clothes hanging on his trouser press he did not throw them on the floor in annoyance, but simply hung them up in her wardrobe. Every little thing he once found annoying in other women now became an endearing trait, treated with love.

Sex with Veronica always had been good, but now he felt far more relaxed about lovemaking, which no longer needed him to prove he was a sexual athlete. Now, the brush of his hand on her bare skin often was enough to let her know that he loved her and was there to hold her and keep her safe, in the arms of life's true love.

"Veronica, get packing, we are going to the Middle East. Tell the Nester family we need their help," said David.

"Another adventure, David?" smiled Veronica. "Does my dad know?"

"No, but he will," said David, and he laughed. "Thankfully, he won't approve," and they all laughed again, thinking of Rolly.

Chapter Eleven

Giovanni Bellini was dressed immaculately in a black silk suit, a white silk shirt with double cuffs, large gold cufflinks, and a blood-red tie with matching gold tiepin. His pocket handkerchief was a mixture of white and red silk to match the shirt and tie. Tight-fitting, it hugged his athletic frame and brought admiring glances from men and women alike in the outside bar of the Marriott Nazareth Hotel in Israel. He had decided to meet the man responsible for the excavation of the Coffin of Destiny for lunch at the hotel restaurant by the pool. Gino had never been a big drinker; he hated the feeling of losing control and rarely drank alcohol during the day except for a glass of wine with his lunch, so he chose a soft drink as he waited at the small table overlooking the pool for Abraham Levi. He watched impassively as girls in bikinis tanned in the warm sunshine beside the pool, their lithe bodies promising so much to the admiring men around the pool.

Abraham Levi had never met Gino Bellini, or for that matter heard of him; his contact had told him that an important Cardinal Castellano had asked him to check up on the excavation on behalf of a syndicate financing the operation. The syndicate was an obscure charitable trust chaired by Cardinal Castellano and had several New York luminaries on the board, but he had very few details about their objectives or work in the past. Strangely, there seemed no way to join, and communication with the site rarely received any useful information, simply a brief polite e-mail acknowledging receipt of any communication. Gino

Bellini also had very little on him on the Internet, with no background information other than his academic achievements and some business deals, for which he was a minor junior partner.

Gino rose from his table and put out his hand as Abraham approached, "Nice to meet you, Mr. Levi," said Gino. "Can I get you something to drink?"

"Yes, thank you, Mr. Bellini," said Abraham, feeling a very firm hand grip in Gino's handshake. "Perhaps a little wine and water."

"Perhaps you would like to select some food from the menu first," said Gino, "and then I can select the wine. Do you want still or sparkling water?"

"Either will be fine," said Abraham, "and I will eat meat, a steak I think, and some salad."

"I have not drunk Israeli wine, but understand Carmel Winery and Clos de Gut to be fine vineyards, according to the Wine Spectator," said Gino. "They recommend the Syrah/Shiraz, Carigon, or Petite Sirah; do you have a preference?"

"No, you choose please, I am not a great wine buff," said Abraham, impressed with Gino's knowledge.

Gino waved the waiter to the table. "Two fillets, both well done, with the chef's mixed salad, a large bottle of sparkling water, and a bottle of the Carmel, Kayomi Vineyard Shiraz, Upper Gailee 2005," said Gino. "Do you want anything else, Mr. Levi?"

"No, thank you," said Abraham, wondering how Bellini knew how he liked his steak.

"Perhaps you can give me a brief update, Mr. Levi, and then we can enjoy our lunch and enjoy the view of so many beautiful women," said Gino, nodding at the pool.

"Excavation goes well, and according to schedule, but we have not yet discovered the coffin, or any artefacts of any significance," said Abraham. "We will have completed the search in the area specified in two weeks' time."

"Is there any way of speeding up the process?" asked Gino.

"We could employ more diggers," said Abraham, "but it is very expensive, as they need to be trained archaeologists with some experience."

"Do it. We need to know if the site has the coffin, and if not, to search another site," said Gino. "Double the size of the area and let me know the extra funds you need."

There was a small group of young men dressed in colourful shirts and shorts approaching the bar, and Gino looked past Abraham and noticed the young men were a little drunk and becoming loud.

"Obviously not going to be as quite as I hoped by the pool," said Gino.

"Graduation celebrations, probably," said Abraham. "The universities have just been giving out their results; my daughter expects hers today."

"Well, I wish her well," said Gino, "but I understand she is a model student and will probably get a first-class honours degree, like her father, in archaeology."

"You are well informed," said Abraham. "She will be disappointed if she gets anything less than the top mark in her year, but I will be proud whatever she achieves. She is a fantastic daughter."

Gino looked across at the pool and saw a very beautiful woman with almost white blonde hair and a stunning figure take off her robe next to a much older man. The man was in stunning shape, his body rippling with lean, well-formed muscles. Both of them had light brown golden tans, probably from a spray-on tan rather than the sun. The group of men had seen the woman and were catcalling and whistling, but the couple ignored them. There were probably twelve in the group of men, and when they got no response, they decided to go to the couple. Gino could see one of the waiters try to stop them from going to the pool, but they pushed him to one side.

David York saw the group of men approaching the sun beds they were lying on and stood up. Veronica noted they had arrived and ignored them.

"Come on, love, take off your bikini top and let's see your tits!" shouted the ringleader, who was obviously an athlete of some sort, with large, well-developed muscles.

"Why don't you boys go back to the bar," said David, "and annoy somebody else before you get hurt?"

"Let's throw granddad in the pool," said the young man, and ten men lunged forward at David.

David struck the first man with a half-blow in the throat so as not to kill but wind him, and kicked his fellow student hard in the stomach; both men collapsed. The third and fourth man were chopped very hard under the nose and fell bleeding to the floor, but the remaining men rushed David, and he fell under the sheer weight of the remaining eight men to the ground.

Gino vaulted the rail surrounding the restaurant area, and with a few long strides, he reached the area on the opposite side of the pool where the men were pinning David to the ground. Grabbing the first man by the hair, he pulled him off, hitting him on the nose and smashing it into his face. He grasped a second man by the legs and picking him up as though he weighed nothing and swung him away from the fray and into the pool. Veronica had joined the fray and had pulled one man from David, and he pushed her to one side. Three of the men left David and turned to Gino. Gino kicked the first in the kneecap, smashing the bone, and he collapsed to the floor. As the second man threw an arm at him, he grabbed it by the wrist, swivelled, and snapped it behind the man, breaking the arm at the elbow. The third man ran at Gino in a rugby crouch, and Gino kicked him in the face, breaking his jaw with the kick. When Gino looked up, David York was on his feet again, and had dispatched the other three assailants, who all now were lying on the ground around the sun beds.

David had a swollen face, and his nose was bleeding, but otherwise he was unhurt. Veronica had her bikini top ripped off by one of the men, and it showed her magnificent breasts to the world. Gino looked around, and finding the culprit lying on the floor took the bikini top from his grasp and handed it to Veronica.

"Probably worth getting a beating to see you half-naked, madam," said Gino. "I am Giovanni Bellini." Picking up one of her hands, he kissed it formally.

David York came across to Gino. "Thank you for helping with the rowdy boys, perhaps I can buy you a drink or some lunch?"

"I am eating now," said Gino, "but I am alone in town and would enjoy getting to know a man who can dispatch so many men so quickly and attract such a beautiful woman. Why not have dinner together this evening, if you are not busy?"

"7 pm okay? I tend to eat early," said David, "and I insist I buy, for your bravery and help today. I am David York, and this is Veronica Goldsmith, my girlfriend."

"Any relation to Roland Goldsmith, the financier in London?" asked Gino.

"His daughter," said Veronica, "and thanks for helping and retrieving my bikini top."

"Well, delighted to meet you both," said Gino, "but I must return to my lunch guest. We will meet in the lobby at seven."

Gino returned to his table and David York watched him walk away. "We need to find out who that man is; he handles himself too well to be some businessman on a trip to Israel. Now, darling, do you want to continue sunbathing, or shall we go to the spa for a massage and face treatments?"

Veronica looked at his swollen face and laughed. "David, always the jokes, let's go to the spa," and she stepped over the man lying on the ground.

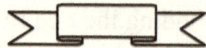

Veronica compared the two men as they met in the lobby of the hotel. David was older and a little shorter than Gino, but they both had very good builds, and like David, based on his exploits earlier, she knew Gino must train daily. Gino, being younger, dressed in very modern clothes cut very tightly to his athletic frame, and David more conservatively in clothes slightly looser. Gino was very handsome, but she would pick David every time; he exuded the sort of confidence only experience brings, and he now was being gracious as the host.

"Nazareth is not the culinary centre of the world, I am afraid," said David, "but they have a Sicilian restaurant that has good reviews, so if you like Italian, we can eat there."

"My name, Giovanni Bellini, is obviously of Italian descent, so naturally, I love Italian food," said Gino, looking forward to the evening.

"Good. I thought we could take the hotel limo, as I don't have a car," said David.

"Perfect," said Gino, "that way you can drink and be relaxed."

"Actually, I don't drink," said David, "never have, but being driven in a strange land is far more relaxing."

"I agree," said Gino, who also rarely rented a car, preferring taxis in foreign countries.

The Sicily Restaurant and Pizza was a takeout restaurant downstairs and a restaurant upstairs. The atmosphere was very plain, unsurprising and low key, but the food was reputed to be very good, and they served large portions with bread and salad.

The three of them looked out of place in their smart suits and ties, and Veronica in her silk yellow dress, but they were relaxed around the table and talked easily. David ordered a Barolo for Gino and Veronica, a powerful red wine from the Piedmont region of Northern Italy made from the Nebbiolo grape, whose flavours included chocolate, liquorice, figs, leather, and tar. It was considered by many people to be Italy's best wine. David had found some bottles of the Machesi di Barolo Barbera J 'Alba Paigal 2003, and had a case sent to the restaurant to serve his guests. The wine, with a caramel hint, was smooth and balanced with a red berry taste. In the glass it had the characteristic brick colour and hue around the rim typical of a Barolo.

David suggested that they order the pasta, which was highly recommended, as nobody wanted a starter. They all selected spaghetti with meatballs, which is really more American than Italian, as in Italy they do not serve the meatballs on top of the pasta. The sauce and meat balls were magnificent, and all three of them remarked on the quality and taste of the food.

"Tell me, David," asked Gino, "where did you find this wine? This restaurant has none on its wine list."

"It is from a wine merchant in Tel Aviv. I googled it when I found this restaurant," said David.

"For someone who does not drink, you have very good taste. Barolo is considered the king of Italian wines," said Gino.

"I am glad you like it. I took the liberty of sending half a case to your room just in case you liked the vintage, a 2003. I tried to get a 1988, but they did not have any in stock," said David.

"Pity," said Gino, "it is a fine vintage but I don't often drink Italian wines; I prefer the French Grand Crus, to be honest," said Gino.

"Which is your favourite?" asked David.

"That is really impossible to say. Laffite is gentle and light, while Latour is heavier and deeply satisfying. Margaux is marvellous also, but I prefer Mouton Rothchild if I had to select one, I suppose," said Gino.

"If you give me your address, I will ask my wine cellar to ship you a case with my compliments," said David. "I have maintained a small cellar in Bordeaux for many years."

"Really, why would you do that if you don't drink?" asked Gino.

"I invest in many things, wine is one of them, and I enjoy watching other people getting pleasure from a fine wine, so I took an interest in learning a few things about wine many years ago," said David.

"Fascinating," said Gino. "I must admit my own tastes are fine, but I rarely buy the Grand Crus except at Christmas and Easter. My family doesn't really appreciate fine wines, and I normally just buy good table d'hote wines."

"Nothing wrong with that," said David. "Can I pour you some more wine?" he said, noticing Gino's glass was nearly empty.

"No thank you, David," said Gino. "I never drink more than one glass of wine at lunch or dinner."

"Very wise," said David. "Overindulgence is extremely bad for one's behaviour, as we saw with those young thugs at lunchtime. By the way, where did you learn to fight like that?"

"Just a hobby at the university," said Gino, lying. "I was surprised any of it worked. I have only ever fought in the gym before."

"Really? You looked combat-hardened to me," said David.

"And you, David, must be a professional fighter?" asked Gino.

"Not really, I was in the army, and it was standard training for all troops," said David.

"Well, I hope I don't ever have to fight any of your soldiers," said Gino laughing.

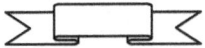

The evening continued, the two men talking about art, politics, wine, even clothes, but neither asked the other what he did or about his family. Veronica occasionally was included in the conversation for politeness, but otherwise it was mental fencing between two men who were unsure who the other really was and what were the other's capabilities.

David had researched Giovanni Bellini, but found little. He was rich, owned a smart New York apartment, drove a red Ferrari, and dabbled in the financial market. His academic records at UCLA and

Harvard were easy to find, but really, there was nothing more on the man.

The meeting had revealed a number of things which may become important thought David. In spite of Gino's obvious wealth he was careful with money, only buying table d' hote (as he referred to the wine) wine rather than fine wines for family. Secondly he was a snob about wine whilst not really understanding the basics, table d'hote usually refers to a fixed price for a standard meal and does not really refer to quality; a more correct term would be table wine. He was also hiding something regarding his past as you cannot become an accomplished street fighter unless you actually fight people in the street. All the practice in gyms and training count for nothing in a street fight, where there are no rules. Gino's knowledge of politics, finance and the arts were also impressive and he must therefore mix with the high fliers in society, David wondered why he had never heard of him when he knew most important people.

Gino had a similar experience trying to research David York; a special air service officer and philanthropist, he found very little about how he made his money or his personal life. There were a few clippings of him at society parties with beautiful women, including Veronica, but nothing that gave very much information about David that would reveal his true reasons for being in Israel.

When they parted at the end of the evening, neither man was any clearer about the other. However, David did note that Gino did not give him his New York address. This was of no consequence; he knew it already and would send the wine with a nice note the next day.

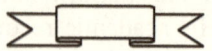

Benjamin Nester had been one of the world's greatest theologians most of his life, and worked from his beloved desk from his home in Jerusalem. He knew both Susan, his wife of thirty years, and his daughter Susan were Sect members, and he was not surprised when David York contacted him to help with the search for the Coffin of Destiny.

He was very sad when John McCallister, David's father, was killed, and he knew his daughter was distraught with the news, because she had been in love with him. She moved from England apparently because she wanted to get away from York University and the UK to America, and now lived in New York to forget about John and build a new life. He was surprised when she rang him up and asked him to meet David York in Nazareth about the Coffin of Destiny and the Horus fable. York had transferred fifty thousand dollars to his charitable trust, which funded his research, and there were no strings attached; the money was his whether he met him or not. He, of course, was delighted to agree to meet. A limo arrived on the day of the meeting and drove him to the small hotel on the outskirts of Nazareth where he was to meet David York.

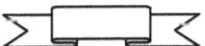

Small for a man at five foot seven inches, and wiry but fit for a man of sixty, he was dressed all in black. He had a *kippah*, the slightly rounded skull cap, wore his beard long, and had straggly, wispy white and black hair. He looked like what he was, a religious scholar.

"Mr. Nester," said David York when they met. "Thank you for meeting me on such short notice. Can I get you something to drink or eat?"

"No, thank you, Mr. York," said Benjamin. "It is kind of you to ask, but I have already eaten. I am happy for you to get to the point of the meeting."

"There is a team of people excavating in Nazareth for the Coffin of Destiny, which is rumoured to exist and contain the remains of Osiris, the father of Horus, who, it is rumoured, were real people, not myths."

"They both existed, certainly, about 3,500 BC," said Benjamin, "and probably the coffin exists. But not in Nazareth."

"Why do you say that?" asked David.

"My research would lead me to believe the resting place of the coffin has less to do with Osiris and more to do with Isis and Joseph, who returned to tWay now called Egypt with the coffin."

"Why?" asked David.

"I have read the heliographic scrolls of the period, and although Osiris and the coffin certainly went to Nazareth, the coffin was moved later by Isis to tWay," said Benjamin.

"Do you know where?" asked David.

"No, not really," said Benjamin, and his mind wandered a little as he remembered the scrolls he read, "I was not seeking the coffin, only interested in determining if Osiris and Horus were real or myths."

"Could you find the coffin in your research for me as a project? I will pay you two hundred thousand dollars for three months' work," said David.

"That is a lot of money perhaps for nothing," said Benjamin.

"How do you know I can find the coffin?"

"I don't, but if it can be found," said David, very assured, "you are the person who can find it."

"Three months is a very short period of time for such research," said Benjamin thoughtfully.

"Mr. Nester, we both know you will already have read more than any living person on the subject, so three months from yourself is worth ten years from somebody else," said David.

"Very well, I accept. My charity needs the funds, and I will enjoy the work," said Benjamin.

"The funds will be transferred today to your account," said David.

"Don't you want to wait until I start work?" asked Benjamin.

"Mr. Nester, we both know you started researching the location of the coffin as soon as your daughter Susan contacted you," said David.

"How perceptive of you" said Benjamin.

"Send me a weekly e-mail to keep me updated," said David, and he and passed Benjamin his details.

Benjamin rose; the meeting was ending and he wanted to rush to his research immediately. They hardly shook hands, and Benjamin left as quickly as his small frame could move. His curiosity, already high, was now raised even higher by David York's interest. The money was nice, but the reality was that he would have done the work for nothing.

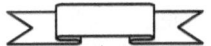

Giovanni Bellini had been monitoring the movements of David York and Veronica by bribing their driver, and he was intrigued by the meeting with Benjamin Nester. He resolved to have Benjamin investigated and watched until he discovered the reason for the connection. As to the current excavation, he had little hope, and they needed to look elsewhere, he believed. *But where?* He pondered this question and ordered all of his contacts in the Middle East to look for clues and report back in one week.

Chapter Twelve

There was a definite leak of information from the first regional meeting, but not from William Osprey and Bill O'Brien, because he knew Gino Bellini did not know who he was when they met in Nazareth. Only those two knew he would go himself, and that information was not passed to Gino, he knew. Of course he had not known he was part of the Cult at that time either, but since then, he had established he was part of the Cult through an informant. It would not then take much to link David York with the Sect, as they had an insider at the regional level within the Sect. However, David was confident he could lay a trap, both for the informant and Gino Bellini, but it would take time to set and spring the trap, so he must be patient.

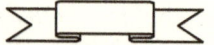

The rivalry between the two men also had increased before they left Israel. Whilst David was seeing Benjamin Nester, Gino Bellini called Veronica for coffee on the pretext that he was inviting both David and Veronica. Of course, Gino knew Veronica was alone. She politely refused, of course, but he did not give in and sent flowers to the room with a note:

> **"Very much admired you when we met.**
> **If you ever need a friend, please call me."**
> **Gino**

Veronica did not reply and gave David the note with the telephone number he had provided, which was a cell phone. When they returned to England, the flowers did not stop, but the notes were always the same:

"Thinking of you always.
Please call me."
Gino

At first, David was very annoyed, but then he got used to the flowers and notes and simply ignored them and treated them rather like a delivery from the florist.

Veronica was very flattered and enjoyed the fact for the first time, David had been made jealous, but the reality was that Gino Bellini had no chance for her affections. David York was the only man she actually loved with unconditional love and a passion that knew no limits. She was content just to be in the same room with him sitting, rather than to be at high society party, or film premier, or special event, which in her past she always attended. The only incomplete part of her life was that David had not proposed, because she desperately wanted to have his children and to marry him.

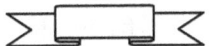

Gino Bellini had discovered that David York was the leader of the Sect through his informant in the Sect, who recently had turned to the Catholic Church and decided to help the Cult defeat the Sect. He had the information confirmed by his uncle, Cardinal Castellano, and was a little annoyed he had not been informed sooner by the Catholic Church's sources. Gino was not surprised, but had guessed from the information he received from the Israeli driver that

David must be a member of the Sect. He was shocked to find he was the leader. He expected a much older man than David, although when he received all of David's information, he realised that David, in his late forties, was nearly fifteen years his senior. Gino, at thirty-three, was at the prime of his life, and often thought older men slow in action. The David York he had seen was not like that.

He genuinely was attracted to Veronica, and would certainly date her if he was given the opportunity, but the flowers and notes received no response. He hoped they annoyed his rival, David. He did receive the case of wine at his home in Manhattan, and it was the very best wine money could buy and more. The Mouton Rothschild was from the year of his birth. David York sent a simple note:

"Thank you for your brave and timely help in Israel. As a token of my appreciation, I am sending you a case of your favourite wine from the year you were born, 1977. Hope you enjoy the wine."

Gino had not given him his address, nor had he provided any information about himself, so clearly David had him researched and had found this information. Of course, he would discover he was a member of the Cult, but not the leader, as people believed Cardinal Castellano was the head of the Cult, which Gino perpetuated.

The dig at the site in Nazareth proved to be a waste of time, and he needed a new site if he was going to satisfy the pope with the coffin. He did have numerous research teams pouring over scrolls for clues, but to date, there were no leads. However, the information he got from the bug placed in Benjamin Nester's small Jerusalem home was more promising.

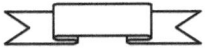

David smiled when he opened the small note sent to his London flat in Mayfair from Gino:

I have tasted the wine and it is wonderful. Thank you for the gift. Hope to see you soon in America.
Gino

David had thought hard what to send Gino, and then decided to send him a coded message with the Mouton Rothschild 1977. The wine, though very expensive, was from a poor year and considered a failure by most critics. David believed Gino would be impressed by the label and ignore the taste, unaware that it was a bad year. If he was correct, it was a flaw in his character he could use at a later date. He now had confirmed that flaw.

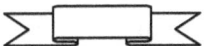

Benjamin Nester sat with his wife Susan on the roof of his home, sipping a cold glass of water, content and serene, overlooking his beloved city. His only worry was his daughter, but he had come to accept that he always would have a problem worrying over his adventurous daughter. His wife was his steadfast rock, and after his work, his only other passion. He loved her more every day they lived, and wanted nothing from life except her love in return.

The research, he was happy to say, was going well. It was clear to him that during the Third Crusade of 1187 – 1192, when Richard the Lionhearted recaptured the port city of Jaffa, several artefacts were found. Amongst those reported was a golden and bejewelled coffin, which the Templars were claimed to have taken as payment for supplies provided to the army. From there, the coffin was claimed to have been taken to France by the Templar fleet and never seen again until after the Templar fleet fled in 1314, which was before Louis IV of France destroyed the Templars. It was rumoured to be one of the artefacts taken by Francois du Marriott to Switzerland, and he is claimed to be the keeper of all the scrolls of the Templar secrets.

Through his daughter Susan, he knew William Osprey was a descendant of Francois du Marriott, a member of the Sect, and was the current keeper of the scrolls. He asked her if he could gain access to the scrolls for his research and was surprised when he was invited by William Osprey to Geneva.

He was sent a first class ticket and the details of a hotel that had been booked in his name, with a telephone number to call when he arrived.

"I am thinking of going to Geneva to complete some work I am doing to trace an artefact of ancient TWay," said Benjamin, broaching the subject for the first time.

"Really, when are you thinking of going?" asked Susan.

"Not sure, but as soon as possible," said Benjamin. "Do you want to come?"

"Not really, darling," said Susan. "You go and pore over your papers. I can go and visit Susan in New York whilst you are gone. She told me yesterday I should come, you as well of course, but I know you are busy so I said not now."

"Is there something wrong? Should we both go?" asked Benjamin.

"No, she is just missing us," said Susan. "You go to Geneva and I will go and visit Susan and have some girl time together."

"New York is very nice in summer," said Benjamin. "So you go and enjoy yourself and give Susan my love. When do you want to go?"

"As soon as possible; she sounded very needy," said Susan. "Let's find out what flights I can find on the Internet," and Susan got up and went to the study.

"Got a flight for tomorrow," said Susan, half an hour later. "So you can go to Geneva straight away."

William Osprey was a member of the Social Democratic Party, a centre-left party promoting social democracy. The party was the second largest in the country and formed part of a coalition government. Switzerland had been ruled by a multi-party government since 1959, with the four largest parties forming a coalition government using the *zauberformed*, or "magic formula," to decide who should occupy the seven cabinet seats. As leader of the Social Democratic Party, William had been in the cabinet since his mid-thirties. In Switzerland, there is no executive power rested in an individual like a president or prime minister; it is held by a committee. Since 1848 the Swiss cabinet known as the Federal Council has consisted of these seven members, and all decisions are reached by consensus. Quite often, William found himself at odds with his own party, as the Federal Council often made unpopular decisions against his party's policy. However, the Swiss constitution actually requires that the government take executive decisions collectively, and therefore all decisions must be defended by all cabinet members.

The seven ministries had not changed since 1848, and although attempts for reform had been made in the past, consensus had never been reached, so the system remained unchanged, providing each cabinet member with a huge workload. The seven ministries consisted of the defence ministry, economics ministry, transport ministry, environment communications and energy ministry, finance ministry, foreign affairs ministry, justice, police and interior ministry.

The Swiss presidency was rotated annually according to an unwritten agreement: Cabinet ministers take turns based on seniority. William already had one term as president, and would be entitled to another term next year, but was considering declining the invitation, as the role was largely ceremonial. Members of cabinet are elected by the house of parliament and serve for four years, and very rarely are removed from office. They are not allowed any other political office, so his role as party leader of the Social Democratic Party was completed by his deputy, and he had not completed this role for nearly twenty years. The balance of power was all important, and a law that banned more than one minister representing a Canton at one time was in place, but it was repealed in 1999. Today, the constitution merely stated that the, "geographical and linguistic regions must be appropriately represented." However, an unwritten rule still operated that Zurich, Bern, and Geneva should have a representative on the cabinet. Women were rare as cabinet ministers; only six ever have served and only two ever became President.

The magic formula for selecting cabinet ministers was brought into place when the Social Democrats joined the government with a 2:2:2:1 split, the three biggest parties having two seats and the fourth largest, one. Because of this, and coming from the Canton of Geneva, William Osprey would probably be a cabinet minister as long as he liked, and he was considered the elder statesman of the cabinet.

William had very little social life, as he always was busy, but was married to Christine, a staunch Catholic, and they had three children. They had two boys, Albert and Robert, and the girl Christine named after her mother. Their marriage had been dead for many years and was merely window dressing for the electorate and society. Neither he nor his wife had a mistress or lover, but he did occasionally use prostitutes for sex every now and then while abroad, but never in Switzerland.

Other than his work, his passion was the Sect, and his elevation to deputy of David York he took seriously and set aside time each day to attend to its affairs. When he was told about the need for access to the scrolls by Benjamin Nester, he was elated. He long had been an advocate of allowing the scrolls to be read by scholars and revealing whatever they held to the public. This had been vetoed by both John McCallister and David York without explanation. Nobody in the Sect could read the most ancient parchments, which dated back over six thousand years, and to have a scholar of Nester's reputation see the documents was a breakthrough. Of course, Nester would not read the real documents; they all had been converted some time ago into a digital format and were indexed electronically and online. Nester, in fact, did not need to come to Geneva, but before allowing unlimited access to the scrolls, William Osprey wanted to meet the famed scholar to judge his character.

They met at the hotel Nester was booked into near his home in Geneva, and although quite different in appearance and dress, immediately struck up a rapport over their interest in the search for truth about the development of religious thought and beliefs. Later,

William thought the rationale for their similar beliefs was the nature of their countries. Israel was made up of immigrants from different nationalities, and Switzerland had German, French, Italian, and Roman linguistic and cultural differences to accommodate.

William spent allot of time in Berne, the seat of the federal government, so following their meeting, Benjamin Nester was given a trusted Sect member to work with full time, William's trusted Geneva-based personal assistant, Suzette, and Benjamin started immediately. Benjamin was only allowed access from a controlled computer at William's Geneva office, and Suzette sat in the room at all times. Benjamin was in his element, immediately drinking in the information contained on the scrolls and scribbling notes in his notebook as he voraciously read scroll after scroll.

The collection was amazing and vast, the largest perhaps of pre-Christian scrolls in the world. Benjamin forgot about time, forgot about sleep, eating, anything, and just read and analysed the carefully indexed scrolls. Suzette had to remind him each day to go back to the hotel to sleep, otherwise he never would have moved from the office. After a time, Suzette made it a strict rule that he could not work longer than fifteen hours a day. She also made him stop for breakfast, lunch, and dinner every day after finding that he did not eat otherwise. They both got into a comfortable way of working, but rarely spoke, and he never discussed his work or his conclusions. After two weeks, he asked if he could speak with William or David York; he wanted to give them a short verbal report.

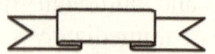

David York had tried to follow his progress by copying the notebook of Benjamin Nester, which he had to leave at the office each day after he had finished his research. However, it was useless, as he wrote in a mixture of several remote languages that none of the translation staff understood, so he was pleased when Nester decided he could make a report. David arranged for a video conference call, using the parliamentary secure link that William had in his Geneva office. He asked William, Bill O'Brien, and Aaron Wiseman to listen to the conversation, as he was certain that they were not the leak.

Benjamin sat in front of the computer he used and was able to see the four other men included in the conversation and greeted them. "Thank you for finding time to listen to my report, which will be in three parts," said Benjamin. "The first part is a summary of my findings. The second is reservations I have about the Sect, and some small favours I request for my further participation in your quest. The third part is the details of my recommendations. Any questions so far, gentlemen?"

"None," said David, intrigued by the second part.

"Go ahead, Benjamin."

"The scrolls I have read are truly amazing, and confirm the view I have held for several years that so-called myths about figures from ancient tWay and other civilisations like Mesopotamia are in fact accounts of real people that have been destroyed over time. I am pleased to report Geb and his wife and sister Nut, his sons and daughters Set, Osiris, Isis, and Nephths, and grandson Horus all existed. Further, there is strong evidence they are part of the Jesus blood line.

"Secondly, the Coffin of Destiny is real, and I am confident I know where it is buried. Thirdly, the few scrolls I have read reveal many other things that need careful translation and researching and cataloguing. A team of people are needed to transcribe, translate, and comment on such rare and important documents. Any questions?" asked Benjamin.

"None," said David. "Continue."

"I am, on a personal front, nearing my old age, so I would like my regular work funded without having to raise money all the time to fund my work, so my first request is that I and my small institute head the translation and interpretation project and funding for the next ten years is provided."

"Agreed," said David.

"My wife and daughter have been members of the Sect for some time, and carry out assignments on the Sect's behalf, which puts them and me at risk," said Benjamin. "I can't stop them from being members, but I would like them assigned to my project, removing them from risk for the next ten years."

"Agreed," said David.

"I would like five million dollars given to me so I can leave a legacy to my wife, daughter, and grandchildren, should anything happen to me."

"Agreed," said David again.

"Those are all of my requests. Please, draw up a binding agreement to sign to implement all these things, and bring my wife and daughter to Geneva to join me, as I feel lonely. When you have completed all my requests, I will outline my recommendations."

"Very well," said David. "Let's get the lawyers working on this and speak again in forty-eight hours, and well done, Benjamin!"

Chapter Thirteen

Giovanni Bellini had the location of where Benjamin Nester was, but he was unable to get access to the scrolls or any information on their contents. The parliamentary offices of William Osprey were comprehensively guarded, and all attempts to enter the building as workmen from the Telephone Company, etc., were rejected. Nobody had been able to find out the contents of the scrolls. He understood that Nester had found something and would reveal it in a couple of days, and he had to be patient until it was transferred to a wider audience to see if the secret could be stolen.

Gino now had a pretty good grasp of the Sect organisation, which was built in units of ten members with a leader; those ten leaders reported to a sector leader, who represented one hundred members. The centurion then reported into a country leader. Country leaders reported into the new ten regional leaders, who reported to David York. No records currently existed of the membership or even of the centurions. Only the country and regional leaders were known.

The Cult was far more difficult to penetrate because it used the Catholic Church and its hierarchy to organise and communicate, and it did not really have a strict organisational structure. Gino was its head, and his contact to the network was Cardinal Castellano, his mentor and uncle. The other cell leaders also used the clergy as a contact, like Gino, and on occasions the leader was their clergyman. There was no council or regional control or even country leaders, just cells within which they were organized by who ever happened to be the leader—a form of organised chaos.

Gino liked the structure; it had none, but worked effectively. In New York, Gino had over two hundred members in three families, each with a head, and Gino and the cardinal were the leader of the city. However, sometimes the lack of organization meant important information was not passed quickly enough to Gino (like the information on David York).

Gino saw the primary aim of the Cult as to protect the church, and therefore he decided on a two-pronged attack: getting the information on the coffin from Nester, or something valuable the Sect wanted so he could negotiate for the information. The thing they held most valuable was the Jesus Blood Line, so he would resurrect the search for the false Messiah. The failure of his predecessor to kill the parents Mary and Joseph and the infant in Newfoundland a year ago had been a blow to the Cult, and the worldwide search had ensued. However, the church tired of the quest, which showed no results, and when Gino was appointed, he cancelled the search and concentrated on establishing a levy to build funds for the Cult, in addition to developing more sophisticated, computer-based, surveillance detection methods. These aims achieved, he had made the Cult more sophisticated and deadly. Their activities were direct and brutal whenever the church required direct action.

A political leader had been tortured and assassinated and a rival terrorist group blamed. Women and men had been raped and tortured to get obedience to the Cult's cause. A number of clergy had disappeared, all assassinated by the Cult when they were too troublesome. However, there had been no major incident of note like the search for the new alleged Messiah, or a relic like the coffin, because Gino wanted a little time to reorganise and be ready.

Content that he was now prepared, he was happy to accept the pope's quest for the coffin, and relished the thought that his adversary was going to be David York. Of course, like David, he was a very fine athlete and trained every day at honing his skills. However, unlike Paul Athurs, he rarely was involved directly with any activity of the Cult. Gino worked in the background, organising and instructing; he rarely ever was the direct contact. The search for the Coffin of Destiny and the Jesus bloodline were different, as Gino's personal wealth was affected and he had this itch to get into Veronica's pants.

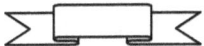

Gino was particular about his broads; he did not like hookers, instead preferring society women with class and style. He would woo and chase them and then emotionally ensnare them with his perceived attention and love, but once bedded, he would dump them dramatically. Because of his position, he could not do this in New York, and would carry on long-distance relationships with women all over the U.S. and a few women abroad. His main weapon was his charm and good looks, but his wealth and power were also good aphrodisiacs to most women. Of course, this had led to several problems with husbands, boyfriends, the family, and not least the women themselves, and most of these problems he had killed or quieted by bribery, threat, or torture.

His latest quest was the wife of a senator from California, an ex-beauty queen, and the daughter of a wealthy oil magnate. A real looker, she was very tall, nearly six feet, and at only twenty-three had the bloom of youth about her appearance. A keen basketball player at college, she still played as an amateur for a local team in California to keep fit and maintain her fantastic figure. The team, by chance, was to play a friendly match in New York for charity, and it would be mixed, men and women playing with all stars from the NBA among the players. Her husband was a man in his early forties, George Wiseman, a Jew of German descent who was considered very good-looking by women. His star was rising, and some thought him a possible Democratic presidential candidate.

His trophy wife, Patricia, came from a staunch Roman Catholic family, and the marriage to a Jew had been a shock, but George was charming and persuasive. The two families agreed the children would be brought up as Catholics, and the ceremony was in a Catholic Church. George did not convert, but would attend the Catholic Church as well as the synagogue. It was a smart political move, and George now attracted the Christian vote as well as having allies in the oil industry. However, there was one flaw: George was gay. He had been a closet homosexual since childhood, and his long-time lover was his personal assistant, who travelled everywhere with him.

Pat, as she liked to be called, was a strict Roman Catholic, and when she discovered the truth she was devastated, because she never intended to get divorced. Pat admired her parent's devotion to each other, and although they often fought, they always made up and stayed together. They worked at their marriage. Her father, Bill, was handsome and often was tempted, but remained faithful to his wife, Rosemary. Rosemary had been unfaithful once in their early marriage, but the couple resolved to stay together and Bill forgave her behaviour. The marriage and the family had been a success; all three of their children were married and successful in business. Pat was a fashion designer, and that was how she met Gino, at a fashion show for young designers. As Pat designed clothes for men, it was not unusual for her to have male friends, and she often had dinner or lunch with them, but it never led to any indiscretion on her part. Gino was perhaps the first man she felt an animal instinct to have sex with, and that troubled her somewhat. Pat always had elegantly refused advances and been able to retain most of her male friends, but she often thought being good-looking to be a curse as well as a blessing, what with men constantly trying to get into her knickers.

Pat played basketball as she conducted her life, strictly by the rules, but to the best of her ability. She practiced daily, had played most of her life and was an accomplished player. Being tall was an advantage, of course, but at nearly six feet, she was small even for a woman on any team. However, she played well against the all-star team of NBA retired players and women from show business and the arts. The game was played seriously, but the outcome was inevitable, and the all-star team won easily. Pat was towelling herself down when she spotted Gino in the crowd waving to her, and in spite of herself, she felt a surge of optimism and waved back uncharacteristically to Gino who smiled. She had agreed to have dinner later and was surprisingly looking forward to the event. However, she certainly was not going to give into her feelings and let him sleep with her; this she had determined.

Gino smiled as Pat returned the wave, and wondered how she would take the news breaking on television at this very moment, that her husband was gay and having an affair with his personal assistant. Of course, this would have stayed a secret, but for Gino. Discovering that George's PA could be gotten to, he arranged for the California Cult to turn the young man and persuade him to come out, denouncing George. This, of course, forced George to make a humiliating statement in advance of the declaration of his lover, to mitigate the damage.

Pat was walking up the player's tunnel when she saw Gino, and behind him lots of photographers. She put out her hand to shake it, but Gino turned to her and said, "Quick, come with me before you face the press."

A little shocked, they went back into the arena, and Gino took her up the stairs and into an entrance that led into one of the hospitality boxes, which now had emptied.

"What is it all about?" asked Pat, shocked at Gino's behaviour.

"Let me show you," said Gino and switched on one of the TV channels to the news.

There was George's face as the commentator was explaining George's statement declaring he was gay and having an affair with his personal assistant.

"Did you know?" Asked Gino.

"Yes, but we hoped to keep it from the press until we worked it out in our marriage," said Pat, in shock.

"George's statement says he is splitting from you so he can be openly gay," said Gino sympathetically.

"He can't!" said Pat, still in shock. "We married in church, it is for life!"

"Apparently not for George," said Gino, "I am so sorry, Pat," and he hugged her to his chest.

Of course, Pat was vulnerable, and Gino took advantage as he had planned. She lay naked on the bed of his Manhattan flat; her long, slender body was testimony to sensible eating and exercise. Gino always marvelled at the beauty of a woman's back, the curve of the hips, the roundness of the buttocks, and the shape of her thighs and calves. The sex had been frantic and explosive, and Gino had taken Pat in every position his extensive imagination had been able to muster, but she still craved more. Her husband liked fucking her in the ass, which Gino was not overly fond of, but obliged as part of the foreplay. Gino preferred the silken, smooth touch of a woman's vagina brushing his manhood as he strove to penetrate deep inside his conquest. That's how Gino saw any woman—a conquest—and Pat was no exception. He would, of course, exploit the situation to the fullest, and had a complete video: of Pat sucking his dick, her face contorted in ecstasy, her taking it bent over the table in his lounge, her dress hiked up over her luscious ass, her face screaming for more, and her legs spread wide on the couch, her vagina open and vulnerable as he probed her slowly with his large penis.

The photographs and video would be sent to her father today to persuade him to release his options on an oil site Gino wanted for a small exploration company in which he had shares. Gino would make a fortune when the company announced they had discovered large deposits at the site and they owned the rights to develop the field. Pat would not know about it, of course, and her father would not know Gino was involved, as his face was removed from the video. Careful editing would also make it difficult to identify the location, but of course, if Pat saw the recording, she would know instantly.

Bill and Rosemary O'Brien were devastated when they saw the news about their son-in-law, George Wiseman, on television, and were frantic to speak to Pat, but they could not contact her in New York. She was not at her hotel, and her cell phone was switched off. Bill received a call from his local priest, Father Murphy.

"Bill, sorry to trouble you, but somebody I know has some disturbing pictures of Pat having sex, which he threatens to expose to the media," said Father Murphy.

"What?" said Bill reeling already? "Are they real?"

"Yes," said Father Murphy. "I think you better come over; he is with me now."

"Okay," said Bill, and started looking for his handgun, just in case.

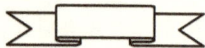

When Bill O'Brien arrived at the house of the local priest, he was surprised to see two large limos outside the building. He had brought his handgun, and was fully prepared to use it to protect his daughter. Father Murphy opened the door and let Bill in, but two large, bulky men grabbed Bill and searched him, removing the gun. Nothing was said, and Bill was ushered into the priest's sitting room.

Bill was shocked to see two high society lawyers whom he knew personally, Tony Montebello and Gerald Kauffman, sitting in the lounge. "What are you guys doing here?" Bill asked.

"Beats me," said Tony Montebello. "I got a call from Father Murphy."

"Me too," said Gerald Kauffman.

"You, Father, what is this about, and who are the heavies?" asked Bill.

"Patience, Bill," said Father Murphy, as a cell phone rang in one of the bodyguard's pockets.

"Yes," the large man replied and listened for a moment. "It's for you, Mr. O'Brien."

Bill picked up the cell phone and listened to the voice, which was distorted artificially. "Mr. O'Brien, let me give you a few facts: One, an assassin is outside your house, and at my order, he will break in, torture and rape your wife, and then kill her. When you finish this conversation and switch on the television, you will hear a horrific report about your business partner, Daniel Roberts, who has been brutally murdered by an intruder. Your son-in-law has been publically disgraced, and your daughter's reputation can be ruined by photographs I have obtained. Now, switch on the TV, watch the news, and ask Father Murphy for the envelope he has." The phone went dead.

"Can we switch on a news channel?" said Bill, in shock.

The TV was switched on and a news reporter was speaking: "Shocking news is coming from California. The billionaire oil man Daniel Roberts and his wife have been brutally murdered at their luxury home in the exclusive district of Beverly Hills…"

"Switch it off," said Bill, now anxious and in fear of what would come next. "Do you have an envelope for me, Father?"

The priest nodded and passed him the envelope, which lay sealed on the table. He scanned the first two photographs, which showed Pat having sex with some man, and felt sick. "Where is the bathroom?" he half-shouted, feeling vomit rise in his stomach.

Father Murphy pointed to a door just outside the room they were in, and Bill rushed inside, barely making the toilet before vomiting, retching loudly with the door still open. The photographs spilled from his grasp and scattered on the floor; when he looked up, he could see most of them. He wanted to scratch out his own eyes rather than see those images of his beautiful daughter being fucked by a man. However, it was too late, and they were etched in his brain forever. He gathered up the photographs and put them in the envelope. Bill washed his face and tried to compose himself. *They want something,* he concluded. *Think clearly, and make sure at some future date you can defeat whoever is doing this to your family.*

Bill now was calm, and the cell phone rang again. "Mr. O'Brien, you have seen what we can do," said the voice.

"What do you want?" asked Bill, steel now in his voice from his anger.

"First, let me tell you what will happen if you do as I ask," said the voice. "George Wiseman will be promoted as the first gay politician to run for the presidency. He will not win, but will become vice-president when Obama has completed his second term. Your daughter will stay married to him, and you will have grandchildren by genetically engineered insemination, which they will both promote, and stem cell research and receive many awards. Your wife will not be harmed. You will take over the holdings of Daniel Roberts and become an even richer man when they find a will leaving all his stock to you. As he had no family, it will not be contested." The voice then went silent.

"But what do you want?" asked Bill.

"We want the mineral rights to the land owned by your company in Malawi, and the mineral rights you have negotiated for Lake Malawi, and the mineral rights in Mozambique and Tanzania that border the lake."

"Why?" asked Bill. "No oil or anything has been found."

"There is a massive amount of oil under the lake, probably the largest single find this century. We want the rights transferred to the exploration company drilling for the oil," said the voice.

"Why?" asked Bill.

"Don't be stupid," said the voice. "We will buy up shares before the announcement of the find and make a lot of money."

"Why should I do anything you ask? Maybe you will kill my wife anyway and destroy my family," said Bill.

"Of course, we need someone to make the oil reserves more valuable, so your company will retain the rights to develop the oil reserves found. When the find is announced, you will simultaneously announce a joint venture with a company to build refineries in Malawi, Mozambique, and Zambia."

"That would cost billions, especially if we pumped the oil to the coast of Mozambique and built the refinery there for export abroad," said Bill.

"Among the documents you will be asked to sign is a loan document with an unknown financial company offering you ten billion dollars as a loan as part of the initial financing for the project. With that kind of initial backing, and your reputation, City Bank and Chase Manhattan already have agreed in principal to advance a further ten billion. The other five billion will be an advance payment from forward orders for fuel intended for American distribution companies. Letters of intent will be given to your once you agree."

"Twenty five billion dollars is certainly our internal estimate to develop the oil, should the find be as huge as you believe," said Bill, "but we would have no contingency if things go wrong."

"Agreed. Among the documents is a document selling twenty per cent of your company for two billion dollars, which is a fair price at its current valuation," said the voice.

"Sir, the alternative to not agreeing is disastrous for me and my family," said Bill, "and agreeing with you is attractive and even profitable. Why do I feel I am being somehow screwed?"

"Because you are, Mr. O'Brien, and you are a smart man," said the voice. "But if you don't do as I say, I would add you will be framed as the person who ordered the hit on Daniel Roberts, and even if you prove your innocence, you will lose your company and your life will be ruined."

"How will you prove I am the person who ordered the killing?" asked Bill.

"Tomorrow, the killer will be caught by the police," said the voice, "and he will confess he did the murder at your request, being promised a fee from your account after he had done the deed. If you don't do as we agree, that fee of one million dollars will be transferred from your company account to your personal account by your wife before she dies. He will also confess to killing your wife in revenge for not paying him."

"Why would he do that?" asked Bill. "He will be killed or at least be imprisoned."

"It does not matter what motivates people, Mr. O'Brien," said the voice, "only their actions, in this case. If you agree, he will still be found by the police from a tipoff, and will confess he broke in to rape and steal money from Daniel Roberts' house. His semen is already in the wife's body."

"Very well," said Bill. "I agree."

"Very wise. The two lawyers in the room will witness you signing, and both will appear in court if necessary to prove you were not coerced into signing. If you ever try to trace me or seek revenge in any way, we shall torture, rape, and kill you and your family, including your grandchildren. We will show you the footage before we torture and kill you," said the voice.

"I understand," said Bill.

"Well, congratulations Mr. O'Brien, you are now a richer man," and then the voice was no more.

He saw Father Murphy picking up bundles of documents, which he presumed were the documents he would have to sign, and he fully intended to read them, even if he had no choice but to sign the documents. At least he would know what those documents covered and the rules of business engagement, because he would continue to look for an opportunity to escape from this contract, even with the high risks to his family.

Chapter Fourteen

David York was waiting for Benjamin Nester to read the documents that had been sent to him. His wife and daughter already had been asked to go and join him, but for some reason his daughter did not want to leave New York. David decided to call her.

"Hi Susan, it is David York. How are you?" said David.

"Hi David, I am not sure how I am. I have a friend, Pat Wiseman, the wife of the senator from California who came out recently. She was very upset, of course, and called me, and I planned to stay and help her, but she called ten minutes ago and said everything is sorted and I should go to see my dad. I am not sure what is going on," said Susan.

"Okay. Come here to see your dad, and return if you are still needed," said David.

"What if my dad does not want me to leave?" said Susan. "He was adamant when we spoke; he needs me to help him."

"Leave that to me," said David. "I am going to America next week anyway, where is your friend, in New York?"

"No, she has gone back to her husband in Los Angeles," said Susan.

"Not a problem, I have some business in California anyway in the oil industry that I need to check out," said David. He never thought any more about it, but resolved to look up Pat Wiseman when he met his oil partner in California, Bill O'Brien.

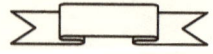

Benjamin Nester sat with his wife and daughter in the offices of William Osprey. Both David and William had travelled to Geneva, and Veronica had come as well when she learned that Susan Nester had flown from New York.

"So, Benjamin, are you satisfied with all your documents?" asked David.

"Yes. What is the status of the money transfer?" said Benjamin.

"Here is the bank transfer receipt to a Swiss bank account," said David. "It is deposited in your name. You need the account number and password I have provided to give the bank instructions. Your daughter and wife are here, what else do you want?"

"Nothing," said Benjamin.

"And the coffin?" Asked David.

"In one of three locations. In Egypt, Scotland, or New York," said Benjamin.

"I think for five million dollars and a multimillion dollar research contract, I need a little more," said David smiling.

"And you will have it, but I need Susan to help me translate many scrolls to give the possible location at each of these countries," said Benjamin.

"Why three locations?" asked David.

"Because the artefacts of the Templars were probably divided into three by the Templars," said Benjamin. "One location was to Newfoundland, one to Scotland, and one to Switzerland. The Scottish journey was completed by Guy de Buisson, who became Lord McCallister, your great ancestor, and took the Jesus bloodline. So he is the least likely to have taken the coffin. In Newfoundland you unearthed the Holy Grail, but did not discover the coffin, but perhaps the original knights who travelled to New York could have taken the coffin. Lastly, the most likely person was Francois du Marriott, the ancestor to William Osprey; he sent several documents back to Egypt to be hidden, and the coffin could have been among them. It will take about one week to know the location in each country, give or take a few days either way."

"Why so confident?" asked David.

"I think I could guess the locations from what I have read already, but let me check out the documents ancient and modern, so you are not sent on a wild goose chase, I think is the expression?" said Benjamin.

"Alright, I need to go to America anyway, so do New York first and you can let me know where to check out whilst I am there," said David.

"I think other people will be looking for the coffin," said Benjamin. "There was a dig in Nazareth, which was unsuccessful, which tried to recruit me to work on material in search of the new location."

"Really?" said David.

"Yes, so we need to hurry and be first and ensure our security is good on all those involved," said Benjamin.

"Don't worry about that. I am moving your call to the McCallister Castle in Scotland," said David.

"Is that not a Trust Castle these days?" asked William.

"Yes, it is, but the family still have accommodations in the castle and can use it when it closes in the off-peak tourist season for renovations," said David. "It will be easier to spot strangers there, and you will be right at the location my ancestors were in the fourteenth century."

That will be fine," said Benjamin. "I presume all the documents will be able to be accessed from computers there?" asked Benjamin

"Of course," said William. "David asked me a few days ago to make the arrangements."

"But I had not agreed then," said Benjamin.

"Lucky guess," said David, and they laughed.

The next day, the Nesters, William Osprey, and three aids flew to Scotland to begin the search for the Coffin of Destiny.

Giovanni Bellini had been meticulous in his preparation, as he always was when planning to entrap an unsuspecting victim is one of his complicated snares, and he awaited the outcome with relish.

He watched the lovely Pat with her born-again husband George Wiseman on television, being interviewed about their decision to have a child together and remain married. Gino always was amazed by how easy it was to manipulate the press and the media, and how gullible people really were.

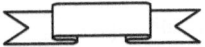

David York arrived in California and travelled to one of his favourite hotels, the Chateau Marmont. Tucked away in the lush enclave that hovers above the Sunset Strip, the Chateau Marmot was a famous destination for the rich and famous. The hotel had been a fixture in the Hollywood scene since the 1930s, when Harry Cohn, the original head of Columbia pictures, famously said, "If you must get in trouble, do it at the Chateau Marmont." The hotel was located in a garden oasis above the Sunset Strip, and was modelled after a castle in the French countryside, with a Gothic interior exuding bohemian flair. David always liked to stay in

173

one of the Spanish style-garden cottages located near the pool. The premier garden cottage had a separate living room and a kitchen, and David liked the arrangement, as he often had meetings at the hotel and sometimes needed privacy. At nearly six hundred dollars a night, the hotel was not cheap, but David did not begrudge the fee at the Marmont, as you always felt you were whisked back to the Hollywood of old and would meet Errol Flynn or Carol Lombard in the cocktail bar.

He decided to meet Susan's friend first, and invited Pat Wiseman and her husband to lunch before his afternoon meeting with Bill O'Brien. Although Pat had never met David York, she had heard about him from Susan and was intrigued and surprised when her husband George decided to join her on one of his rare visits home from Washington. The couple looked stunning together. George was dressed in a black pinstriped shirt, with a light pink double cuffed shirt with large gold cufflinks and a blood-red silk tie and gold tie pin. Pat had on a stunning red dress that clung to her stunning figure, and her hair was down, framing her features. When she smiled, every man's heart skipped a beat.

Pat saw David York seated at the bar, drinking what looked to be a cup of tea and smiled; she had been told he did not drink. He was dressed in a dark blue silk suit favoured by film stars and the more hip celebrities with a white silk shirt and a mottled tie of several shades of blue. Like George, he had double cuffs, but had gold and platinum cufflinks and a tiepin. His shoes were oxford full brogues in a light blue from Church, the English shoemaker.

When David saw them, he got up and confidently strode towards them, and Pat could see why Susan had the hots for him—he walked like a lion. Obviously lean and muscular under those clothes, he bounced forward, his face with a broad smile, and his hand outstretched in greeting. "Senator, Mrs. Wiseman, so glad you could come," said David. "David York, Susan's friend."

"Very pleased to meet you Mr. York, but please, call me George," said George.

"Pat." She shook his hand and felt power even though his grip was very light. "I am too young to be Mrs. Wiseman yet."

"Please, call me David. Let's go through and eat. I decided to eat in the restaurant rather than the pool, if that's okay," said David.

"That will be fine," said George.

"The food in the Marmont is usually good," said David, "but perhaps if you drink, I can recommend for a cocktail the fresh peach Bellini, a white peach puree, *mathilde peche*, and champagne," and he smiled at Pat.

"I will try one," said George. "What about you, honey?"

"Make that two," said Pat, thinking, *so he knows*.

David ordered the shrimp and avocado with garlic and lime to start and the seafood fry accoutrement, halibut, shrimps, and calamari, and the others asked to have the same.

"May I suggest the Marcassin Estate Chardonnay, if you would like white wine," said David.

"Obviously an expert, David, that is a very good wine. It is often compared to the Grand Cru White Burgundies," said George, who carefully read and followed wine reviews.

"I don't drink, but I do collect and sell wine for fun," said David. "The critics think that this Chardonnay avoids the common domestic pitfalls of excessive oak or insufficient acidity, which make it perfect for aging, so I bought some for my collection."

"What would you have recommended if we had selected meat?" asked George.

"I always try and select local wines, so I would have selected a California Cabernet Sauvignon from the Harlan Estate. The 1990 is very difficult to acquire, but I have some 1994, 1997, 2001, and 2002, all of which are world class vintages," said David.

"Where do you keep your wines, David, in the UK?" asked George, intrigued.

"No, I have rented wine cellars all over the world," said David, "often with the producers, and buy and sell annually. The Harlem Estate is a favourite of mine, and I have a cellar in Los Angeles for the West Coast of the USA."

"Fascinating," said George, "but what do you do for a living?"

"Investments and financing, really" said David. "I was lucky and made a little money, some of it in oil here, investing with some oil men."

"Really?" said Pat. "Daddy is in oil."

"Yes, I know, Pat. Bill O'Brien and his best friend Daniel Roberts have been my partners for many years," said David, smiling.

"My goodness, you are the secret partner they both talked about!" said Pat.

"Secret partner?" asked George.

"When Daddy and Daniel first started out, they needed money for their first deal. They got it from a secret partner. Daddy holds his shares on trust; he owns half the company," said Pat.

"Bill told me some time ago he had told you our little secret, I think on your eighteenth birthday?" said David.

"Yes," said Pat, now more confused. *He knew Daddy and about Gino?*

Just then, Bill O'Brien arrived, looking perplexed, and then walked across to their table.

"David," said Bill, "I did not know you knew my daughter and George," he said, shaking his hand and kissing his startled daughter.

"I don't, but I used her friendship with Susan Nester as an excuse to get us all to meet to discuss you being blackmailed by Gino Bellini and selling my shares to the Cult," said David smiling.

Bill O'Brien was visibly shocked. Just then, a large man dressed in an ill-fitting dark brown suit pulled a gun from under the table. However, before he could fire, a stiletto knife pierced his neck and he slumped to the table. A smaller thin man sat at the table opposite David, launched himself at David and by diving from his chair sideways he avoided him, but the table collapsed and his guests were scattered. David saw the young women who had thrown the stiletto pull another knife and throw it at another man, as he struck at the back of his assailant. The man easily avoided the clumsy blow of David and positioned himself between David and the woman before executing a death blow to David's throat as he was rising. David parried the blow and picking up a knife from the scattered cutlery from the table stabbed the man in the upper thigh. The man winced, but ignored the pain, parried a death blow by David with his left arm, whilst throwing a plate at David's head. David ducked below the plate, feigned a blow with his left, reversed and aimed with his right fist and as the man ducked brought his left knee into his face breaking his nose, as his right hand punctured both eyes with a two fingered punch into his exposed face blinding him. He then left handed a death blow to his

177

wind pipe and the man crumpled to the floor. The area around David was a complete wreck but the rest of the dining room was not affected. It had only lasted a few seconds, and some diners did not even notice. A young woman, not pretty, but attractive, walked calmly across to one of the bodies, pulled the knife from his neck, and wiped it on a napkin and then walked calmly to the second man and retrieved her second knife. David gestured to her an acknowledgment and Crusader turned and left the restaurant.

Pat looked in shock unable to move as Bill had thrown himself over his daughter to protect her. George was white with fear and still sitting in his chair

"Let's go to my cottage for a drink," said David smiling. "The assassin's are dead and you are all alive."

"How did you know about Gino Bellini?" asked Pat, as they sat in the small lounge of the cottage.

"It was complicated, and there was a chance remark Susan made that joined the dots together," said David. "Heard, of course, about Daniel in the news. Tried to contact Bill and then checked the company shares, and saw Daniel's shares had been passed to Bill. Then Bill sold twenty per cent of the shares to a trust company without my permission. That trust company has as a director, Cardinal Castellano, the uncle of Giovanni Bellini, the leader of an organisation called the Cult. Gino Bellini is a ladies' man who targets socialite women, and Bill has a daughter, whom else would he be prepared to protect? A little more digging, and I found him at the All-Star Game of basketball in New York. The fall from grace of George and sudden resurrection of George and Pat as a couple were all very strange and must be for a reason. Then it struck me that Gino must be blackmailing Bill, with pictures or something to do with an affair with Pat, or possibly George, but more likely Pat."

"Who is Gino Bellini, and what is the Cult?" asked Bill.

"Would you like a drink? It is a long story," said David, "I have some of the Harlan 1994 just for the occasion." David then spent the next hour explaining the Jesus Blood Line, relics, the Sect, Cult, and many other things as background to why there were involved.

"So really, this is all about luring you to the U.S. so that the assassin could kill you?" said Bill.

"Only in part," said David. "I am sure it was a coincidence that Pat was one of his sexual targets, and trapping and controlling a Senator is also pretty useful."

"So how the fuck do we get out of this man's grasp?" asked Bill. "Excuse my French, honey."

"That I don't know," said David, "but there is a way, I am sure. But before you agree to defeat Gino Bellini, you must know that it will be risky, and Gino Bellini will have to be killed to finish the matter."

"Good, kill the bastard" said Pat enraged that she had been used by Gino Bellini.

"First, we have to ruin his empire, discredit Cardinal Castellano, and destroy his network, which will not be easy," said David.

"Any tea total man who has a case of Harlan 1994 in case somebody wants red in his room can do anything," said George positively, and they all laughed.

David could understand now why Pat loved George; having met him, his sexuality was irrelevant. He was warm, very intelligent, amusing, and had inner warmth for other people. The guy actually cared about other people. You could see it in each little movement of his body language and gesture, towards Pat and Bill particularly. It was unconscious and not contrived, as there was no audience to perform to or plaudits to receive from the usual adoring crowd.

"Pat, you need to carry on seeing Gino and acting as you did before," said David.

"You mean sleep with him?" asked Pat, shocked.

"Yes," said David, "and behave as before; don't alarm him to your inner emotions."

"I was going to break it off," said Pat. "I confessed to George, and we agreed we should try harder, even if we have Brian, his personal assistant in our lives."

"Okay, that is natural, do that," said David, "but do it with breakup sex; he will expect that."

"Let me think about it," said Pat, "and discuss it with George."

"Okay," said David, "but let me know later when I call you. None of you can call me. Understood?" They all nodded.

"Bill, you hire this company," and David passed him a card. "Go to central Malawi and begin drilling for oil. Here is the card of the minister you need to contact to get the mineral rights transferred to that company. Put all the shares in your sole name."

"Why?" asked Bill.

"Don't ask now. Just do it," said David.

"George, I want you to lead a campaign from within the Energy and Natural Resources Committee, to stop drilling off shore in the USA completely and seek new sources elsewhere," said David.

"But I am not even a member," said George.

"I know, but you will be. The Democrats lost a senator recently, and the Chairperson of Energy, Maria Conwell, is canvassing for a replacement."

"I know, but lots of senators want that seat," said George.

"You have it. Call Maria. Here is her private cell phone number," and David passed the card across the desk.

"Okay. I have a plane to catch," said David. "My researchers tell me they have found something in New York."

"What did they find?" asked Bill.

"The Coffin of Destiny," said David.

Book Three

Chapter Fifteen

The people of Ta-Mehu did not accept the rule of Set, as the Ta-Shemau court used his rule to replace all the influential positions that controlled Ta-Mehu with people for Ta-Shemau. Even Jabir, the General who had reorganized his army, had been replaced by Set. Unrest also broke out in Ta-Shemau, and Set was forced to return to his homeland to impose his will on his people.

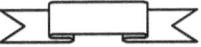

Meri and Joseph met in their small house in Nazareth. A year had passed, and they had settled easily into domestic life together. Joseph had become a carpenter and worked each day at the small shop fashioning furniture, and Meri looked after the infant Horus and managed the household. The followers of Horus met often and always used the greeting agreed upon, "Let me read your fortune," showing the right-hand palm with the Eye of Horus mark being shown. Reports reached Meri and Joseph from one of the Horus followers about the kingdom of Ta-Mehu being close to revolt, and Set having returned to Ta-Shemau to put down a revolt. Set decided they should travel to Ta-Mehu to assess the situation themselves, disguised as Jews. Meri would go to her close advisors in Ta-Mehu only if it was safe, and Joseph would send word to Ammon to get a report on Set.

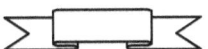

The journey from Nazareth to Memphis in Ta-Mehu was slow and long, as they rested often because of the infant. When they arrived in Memphis, they did not approach any of the influential people at court, and they stayed in the Jewish community like all the other traders from Palestine. Meri now was used to life as a loving mother and wife to Joseph and was very reluctant to return to being the queen of Ta-Mehu.

"Why can't we just be a simple carpenter and his wife in Nazareth and live a full life?" asked Meri, after they had rested for the first night in Memphis.

"Because you are a queen, my love," said Joseph, "and Horus should be the pharaoh of the whole of tWay."

"I would not risk Horus or ourselves if I did not know this was his destiny" said Meri. "I just hoped we had more time as a couple being unknown and happy."

Joseph reached across and hugged Meri, and holding her in his warm embrace said, "You are my one true love, Meri, never forget that. My life is only worth living because of you and little Horus. But he has a destiny we cannot deny him. We have had our rest; let's put Horus on the throne of Ta-Mehu."

"How are we going to do that?" asked Meri. "Set controls the army and the court."

"The court is weak, as it consists of Ta-Shemau members, so they are despised by the people," said Joseph. "The army is leaderless with Jabir gone and Set back in his capital El-Kab in Ta-Shemau. The generals do not hold sway over the officers, as they are all now from Ta-Shemau, and senior officers would revolt if they had a leader or figurehead. You, my love, as Isis, are that leader."

"How do you know that?" asked Meri.

"From Ammon," said Joseph. "His message arrived whilst you were sleeping."

"But Set would come immediately to kill us both," said Meri.

"No, not perhaps for a year," said Joseph. "His own army is in revolt about not being paid the plunder promised in the war in Palestine."

"So, why does not Set just give them what they want?" said Meri, puzzled.

"Because he already has," said Joseph smiling, "but they don't believe he has been fair, so fractions of the army keep revolting against generals, because they believe they have not received a fair share of the spoils."

"But that will die down quickly once Set chops off a few heads," said Meri.

"Usually, yes, but not this time," said Joseph. "There is unrest in the court, with officials believing they have not been rewarded for the conquest of Ta-Mehu or Palestine. These men continue to unsettle the army, and as Set has no plunder left to give, and is being stubborn, he makes the situation even worse by not explaining. We also have the help of Ammon, who secretly encourages and funds revolt against Set, to keep the court unstable."

"Why does he continue to do that?" asked Meri. "What would the advantage be to him?"

"Whilst the court is unstable, Set needs Ammon, and won't kill him," said Joseph.

"So what next?" asked Meri.

"Get your finest ready, and be prepared to be Queen very soon," said Joseph. "I am going to meet with the disenchanted high-ranking officers from the Ta-Mehu Army."

Joseph dressed as he did as a soldier when he was called Thoth and met as agreed in the army barracks close to the palace where Isis and Osiris had ruled.

There were six men. Hakim was perhaps forty-five and the most senior, and his son Heru was probably the most junior and barely twenty. Ikandar and Kushi, he had seen before, and were well respected senior officers, but the other two, Ptah and Sayyid, he did not know.

"So Thoth, or is it Joseph? We are here as requested," said Hakim. "What is it you want to speak to us about?"

"It is Joseph henceforth. I have a new life now serving Queen Isis and the Pharaoh Horus, her son," said Joseph boldly.

"So the rumour is true, she and the boy live?" asked Hakim.

"They live, and ask for your loyalty," said Joseph.

"They have our loyalty. When will they bring their army to retake Ta-Mehu from Set?" asked Hakim.

"You are their army, and we shall take Ta-Mehu this very night," said Joseph.

"Even if we revolt, take over the army, and kill the court in a coup, Set will march here and annihilate every man here," said Hakim.

"Set is weak now, and struggles to put down revolt in his own army. If we strike now, it will be a year before he could put an army in the field," said Joseph.

"But in one year, we would all die," said Ikandar. "Our army is weak and does not have horses and chariots like the army of Set."

"In one year we will have horses from Palestine and chariots to rival those of Set," said Joseph. "More importantly, the people love Isis, and Horus will be a symbol of unity so our army will fight with heart."

"Perhaps," said Hakim, "but why should we take the risk?"

"Because you are not satisfied with your lot," said Joseph. "All the generals are now from Ta-Shemau since Jabir retired and all the key posts at court are men from Ta-Shemau. Your families will lose all their wealth and you will only be servants, not rulers, whilst Set rules both Ta-Mehu and Ta-Shemau."

"This is all true," said Kushi, "but what are we promised if we take the risk?"

"Hakim, Ikandar, and Kushi will be generals," said Joseph. "The others I don't know, but will rise in rank. Your families will all be made rich by a grateful Isis."

"I am prepared to take the risk," said Sayyid. "You need not promise anything. Set is a tyrant and anything he gives can be soon lost when he loses his temper over some minor issue. We need a just and good pharaoh like Osiris, and Horus his son will be such a man." Sayyid opened his hand, and the Eye of Horus was shown. His fellow officer Ptah followed suit, as did Heru, the son of Hakim.

"That is three of you with me then," said Joseph.

"We are all with Joseph," said Hakim, "when could Isis be here with Horus? They need to be here if we are successful."

"They are here already," said Joseph.

"We need to kill the generals in the barracks first quietly, take the palace guard officers into our confidence, then kill the court imposed by Set," said Hakim.

"Let's go and kill the generals first," said Joseph, "then I will bring the queen and your pharaoh, when we take the court."

Hakim assembled fifty men and assigned ten men to each officer to lead. Each group would go and kill two generals in the barracks. Joseph and Hakim would go alone to kill General Mdjai, the most senior of the generals and commander of the army. The quarters in the barracks were modest but comfortable, and the generals were known to entertain the women of the court in their chambers, taking many of the wives of fellow officers and courtiers to their beds.

There were two guards outside the quarters of General Mdjai, and they straightened up and tried to look efficient on seeing Hakim approach. Both men were from Ta- Shemau, and therefore trusted by General Mdjai, and did not fear the officer from Ta-Mehu or his companion. When Hakim and Joseph reached the men, they looked as though they were inspecting them, but in a swift, silent movement drew daggers and slit their throats, covering their last sounds with a hand and holding their bodies so they gently went to the floor. They then went into the chamber quickly and saw Mdjai mounted on a young woman perhaps in her mid-twenties, ploughing her from the rear, her face contorted in ecstasy. Mdjai was a large man, but not overweight, with large powerful muscles, and he was ramming his large penis into the woman with gusto. In their passion, neither he nor the woman noticed the two men enter the chamber.

His sword drawn, Joseph chopped powerfully at Mdjai's head from behind, severing it almost completely, and his body collapsed on top of the woman, the blood pouring from his torso. Hakim pulled the body from the frightened woman.

"Get yourself away from here," said Hakim to the woman. "Go home now."

Joseph picked up the head of Mdjai and put it in a cloth lying on the bed. "Let's go," said Joseph. "Did you know the woman?"

"She is my wife," said Hakim.

Joseph said no more. When they reached the second corridor, they saw Ikandar and Heru carrying heads of generals under their arms.

"The others?" asked Joseph, and he saw Ptah and Sayyid appear carrying heads.

"Where is Kushi?" asked Joseph.

"He went to kill Malik, the deputy commander," said Heru.

"Let's go and see what has happened," said Joseph.

As they entered the corridor, there were about twenty armed men on guard outside the entrance. Dropping the head to the floor, Joseph drew his sword and shouted, "Attack!"

The surprised men turned and found over fifty men attacking them. Before they could strike back, they were cut and hacked to death.

Joseph entered the chambers and saw a naked man, his manhood still erect, whom he presumed was Malik, with Kushi; both men were armed, so he immediately presumed Kushi had betrayed them. "Kill them both!" shouted Joseph.

"Wait," said Kushi, "Malik wants to surrender and join us."

"Arrest them both," said Joseph, making a quick decision. "We will speak with them later."

"Get the heads, storm the palace," said Joseph. "I will bring Isis and Horus."

The taking of the palace was swift and bloody, the soldiers hacking to death every Ta-Shemau man, woman, and child. None survived except the regent and his family.

Huwayda cowered with his wife Nephthys and son Ramesses on the floor together, holding each other in the hope this would make them safer. The heads of their fellow countrymen and women were stacked on the floor, some of their headless bodies strewn on the floor of the throne room.

Joseph arrived with Isis dressed as the queen. She was with the infant Horus carried by one of her former maids who was now dressed as before for the royal household. The gathering soldiers bowed.

"Put the heads on spikes around the palace and arrange for the people to see Huwayda put to death," said Joseph.

"Mercy, great Queen," said Huwayda. "Spare our lives."

"That is not possible. You usurped our throne. The penalty is death," said Isis. "You will be stripped naked, flogged, tortured, and then killed in front of the whole population."

"Spare my wife and child," said Huwayda, now resolved he would die.

Isis wavered and then reluctantly said, "Your child will be cut in pieces in front of you, as will your wife, as I would have been. Your wife will be raped by men before your eyes, then flogged, tortured, and beheaded before you are desecrated in the same way."

"I beg you, great Queen, kill my child and wife quickly," said Huwayda.

Isis hesitated, looking at Horus. "I will give mercy to the child, but not you Huwayda, or Nephthys; you killed and raped my people and would have killed me and my child. Take these two to the dungeons and have the men rape the woman in front of her husband.

Kill the child quickly, but chop it up in front of the crowd for effect tomorrow." Isis waved her hand, and Huwayda, Nephthys, and Ramesses were dragged away.

Joseph turned to Hakim. "Where are Malik and Kushi?"

"In one of the dungeons," replied Hakim.

"Bring them both; the queen will decide their fate," said Joseph.

The faces of both men were bruised, and they looked a little dishevelled.

Joseph ignored their appearance. "Why shouldn't we kill you both?" he asked.

"Because I am loyal to Queen Isis," said Kushi, "and it was not wise to kill all the generals."

"Why?" asked Joseph.

"Because Malik served in Palestine and learned the art of chariots and horses," said Kushi. "He is dissatisfied with Set's rule and wants a new master."

"A man who can betray one master to save his own life can soon do that again," said Joseph.

"That is true," said Malik, "but Set is cruel for no reason and unjust; it is impossible to follow him with your heart."

"And you, Kushi, why disobey your order?" asked Joseph.

"Malik is related and often talked of living in Ta-Mehu before the invasion," said Kushi. "He will make a fine advisor to the army we need to build."

"Your betrayal was risky is spite of this," said Joseph, "and must be punished."

Hakim stepped forward and whispered in his ear, "We need to forgive him. If you must punish him, chop off a finger of his hand, but don't disgrace him."

Joseph nodded. "My Queen, this man disobeyed me and risked your life, but his deed was well thought out in our best interests. I say we punish him to remind him to follow orders, but also reward him by promoting him to general."

"Let it be done," said Isis.

Before Kushi could protest, Joseph and Hakim grabbed him and Joseph grasped his left hand. Prizing open the hand, he cut the smallest finger off. Kushi cried out in pain, but considering the alternatives, it was a small price to pay for keeping his brother alive and becoming a general.

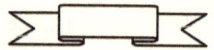

Set heard the news two days later in El-Kab and immediately ordered the army to be on alert. He wanted to invade, of course, but that was not possible, so he decided to torture and kill Malik's family, only to learn most had fled to Ta-Mehu. Set swore he would get revenge and retake Ta-Mehu and decided to imprison those family members who had not fled of the Malik family.

Chapter Sixteen

Joseph watched grimly with General Hakim as his troops fought a mock battle. It was being fought between General Ikandar, who was using Ta-Shemau tactics, and General Sayyid, who was using the standard tactics of the Ta-Mehu Army. It was safe to say that both lacked surprise, as they were predictable, but the Ta-Shemau tactics and weapons were superior. The larger shield gave a far better defence wall, and by pushing out spears or swords, it also was more effective than the shorter shield, which left the forward soldiers defenceless against the steel shields and points of the spear or sword. However, even with this disadvantage, it was possible to push down a line of soldiers as they came very close, perhaps less than a yard before being killed or wounded. A second line of soldiers or even a third was needed to support the front line, and the rotation the Ta-Shemau Army used kept the front line strong. The disadvantage was that the shields were heavy and they could not run far or fight long carrying the shields. The change, overall, left the front line vulnerable if you reach the front line at the point of changeover. Inside the wall of shields, the men were lightly armed with swords and spears, with only enough shields to create cover for arrows, so it was a softer centre. The tactic of raising their shields overhead to shield themselves from arrows also left the front line temporarily exposed.

The chariots and horses were also superior tactics, with the archers firing at the enemy on the move, to either side, and behind the enemy's main body of men. General Ikandar had to use chariots pulled by men, but it was plain to see this was very effective and would dishearten approaching soldiers as they advanced.

As a soldier and man, Joseph always had trained his body very hard each day, and he would run at least ten miles each day carrying two pails of water. Even as a carpenter in Nazareth, he would go outside the city gates each day and train his body. He practiced throwing a spear, knife, and using a bow and arrow. Of all the weapons, the bow was his weakness, and though competent, he was not a good archer. All of the other weapons he had mastered. Joseph also was a very good wrestler and boxer, and excellent in unarmed combat in a brawl or fighting in a battle. His strength, fitness, agility, and bravery were his strengths. His weakness, he knew, was that he was unable to change tactics and adapt quickly enough to the unexpected. He knew this was a weakness of most men, so he would need a surprise tactic to defeat Set and his generals in battle. The Ta-Mehu Army was weak in body and mind. They needed reorganising and strengthening to match the 20,000 men that Set would place in the field and rearm with shields, horses, chariots, and most importantly, re-training.

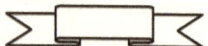

The generals sat with Joseph to discuss the tactics of Ikandar and Sayyid, and what to do to prepare for the inevitable attack by the Ta-Shemau Army.

"How many men do we have that we can deploy?" asked Joseph.

"Probably twelve thousand," said Hakim.

"Set has twenty thousand soldiers in his army, plus five hundred chariots with drivers and archers," said General Malik.

"How are they divided?" asked General Hakim.

"Two main armies, each of ten thousand, under a general," said General Malik.

"And within the two armies, how are they divided and managed?" asked Joseph.

"In hundreds," said General Malik.

"So, there are only two levels of command after the commanding general?" asked Joseph.

"Yes," said General Malik.

"You can only remember the names and history of fifty men," said Joseph. "We shall build our army on a platoon of fifty men, bottom up."

"We have six generals other than me," said Hakim. "Let us have four divisions each of five thousand soldiers, and one chariot division of one thousand men, each to be led by a general. I and the other general will dictate the battle plan, and he will serve as my deputy."

The generals nodded in agreement. "If we have twenty companies of two hundred and fifty soldiers, we shall have the next level of officers for promotion. Below this, we can have a platoon of fifty men led by a noble or even a soldier of merit," said Ikandar.

"That is a good plan," said Joseph. "It will create rivalry between the divisions within the army to be the best, and a structure for men to rise. But create deputies at every level, so if somebody falls in battle, there is a ready replacement to take over, and a hierarchy of at least five men below this deputy so there will always be a leader."

"That is one problem with the Set army," said Malik, "there are no replacements for the generals and middle officers in the two divisions."

"Good," said Joseph. "We will identify these and give the chariots these as their main targets to create confusion in their army."

"We need fitter, stronger men than Set has in the Ta-Shemau Army," said Joseph. "We need to create five separate barracks around the country and recruit and train the men."

"Easy to say, harder to do," said Ikandar. "When an army is idle, after they train for maybe four hours each day, they eat and get drunk and become fat."

"I will speak with Queen Isis about the payment of ten loaves of bread and two jugs of beer that the lower soldiers get now," said Joseph. "We need to reduce the beer the men drink and include vegetables and meat in the diet. We also need to provide them with work after training with some public projects so they are not idle."

"How about a tomb for the pharaoh, or a dam to hold water, or improving the water supply to the cities they are located near?" said Hakim.

"I will speak with the queen and report back on her decisions," said Joseph.

"Can I ask," asked Sayyid. "How is the Pharaoh Horus, the anointed one?"

"The pharaoh," said Joseph, "is well, and a lovely, bright little boy who will grow into a fine man and great ruler."

The generals nodded. Joseph had noticed they all had the Eye of Horus tattooed in the palm of their hands now, and the practice of getting the tattoo now was very much practiced by the population, if not the nobles.

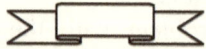

Queen Isis was playing with Horus the little boy, who was running around on the unsteady feet of a boy only eighteen months old. Isis loved watching him at play, particularly with other children. He seemed to have a built-in energy and spirit, but was always gentle and kind to others. He played with servant's children and even slaves' children, as well as nobles' children, but treated them all with the same respect. Of course, children at that age were unfettered by class divisions, so it was easy for the little Horus to not be affected by his position as the pharaoh of Ta-Mehu.

Joseph, her husband, saw the pair playing and smiled; Isis was a devoted mother and loving wife, as well as a great queen. He was blessed in his marriage.

"My Queen," said Joseph bowing, even though there were only servants in attendance.

"Husband," said Isis, smiling.

"The generals have advised me that we need to change the pay of the soldiers, increase their number, and find them work so as not to leave them idle after training each day," said Joseph, returning the smile.

"What work can soldiers do, husband?" asked Isis.

"They need hard, manual work, building perhaps a tomb, or a road, or irrigation, or perhaps a water viaduct for the cities," said Joseph.

"The afterlife soon arrives," said Isis thinking aloud. "How many projects do we need?"

"Five, my Queen," said Joseph, "one for each of your new divisions of five thousand men and one for the smaller chariot division one thousand men."

"Here in Memphis, we often suffer from the water supply, so pick two other cities with the same problem and build a viaduct system bringing water. Select a site and have a tomb designed for the Pharaoh Horus. I will be buried there when I travel to the afterlife with my husband. As for the smaller projects, why not build something in which the scribes can meet and teachers can sit with their pupils. One day, Horus can learn from within its walls," said Isis.

"Very wise, my Queen," said Joseph. "The people will love you for your generous thought of clean water and education in our capital," said Joseph, "but what about the payment of the troops?"

"Change the pay as you see fit, husband," said Isis. "As to the increase of soldiers, you have my blessing. But please arrange with our scribe to ensure we collect more taxes to pay the soldiers."

"It will be done as you command, my Queen," said Joseph, who bowed low to do her bidding.

The economy in Ta-Mehu only was just recovering from the reckless rule of Set and his courtiers. There was little grain in the storage granaries and little gold and jewels in the coffers. Joseph knew that the queen's advisors would not be pleased by the extra burden of more soldiers and more projects to drain their resources.

Joseph met with the queen's chief advisor, Quaashie, and his ever-present assistant Rashidi. Quaashie was of noble birth and tall and thin and walked and talked slowly and regally; he never forgot his place in society, or that of his master the Queen Regent Isis. Rashidi was small and fat and walked very, very fast, his plump legs pumping under his fat body. He only spoke when requested to by Quaashie, but then would speak quickly in a high-pitched voice. Most people said this was because Quaashie had his balls in his pocket and squeezed them when he talked to remind him who the boss was.

Joseph set out the plans for increasing the army, paying the soldiers more, and the new projects. The two men were silent.

"The great Queen Isis is generous," said Quaashie, "but I need to raise taxes to pay the soldiers and buy materials for the projects. Ta-Mehu is now poor from the brief rule of Set, as he plundered much from the merchants and nobles and took all the gold and jewels in the pharaoh's coffers."

"There is always a way, wise Quaashie," said Joseph. "I am sure you will find a way."

"Rashidi, what is our best course of action?" asked Quaashie.

"The nobles hate Set; their wives and daughters have been raped and violated, their sons killed. Ask each noble to supply a son for the army," said Rashidi.

"How will that help?" asked Quaashie. "We are short of wealth, not manpower."

"The middle rank of officers can share in the plunder," said Rashidi.

"We will not defeat Set and conquer Ta-Shemau easily," said Quaashie. "The nobles will see it as a ruse."

"Invade our weaker neighbours as practice for Set," said Rashidi. "Take the new weapons we need, take the gold and jewels to pay the nobles, and swell our own coffers again."

"We already have seven generals. We will have four divisions, with twenty companies in each for officers, and five times that for platoons. We are not sure of the structure for chariots," said Joseph.

"That is eighty high-ranking officers and four hundred low-ranking officers," said Rashidi. "If you divide the plunder in five lots, giving two-fifths to the pharaoh's coffers, one-fifth to the generals, one-fifth to the high-ranking officers, and one-fifth to the lowest officers, everybody will be happy."

"What about the lowest-ranked soldier?" asked Quaashie. "How is he paid?"

"Pay them from the lowest-ranked officers, asking them to pay half of their portion to the soldiers as they see fit," said Rashidi.

"It is a good plan, Quaashie," said Joseph, careful not to give the credit to Rashidi.

"My assistant and I will work on the details and will have scrolls prepared to issue declarations around the court by tomorrow," said Quaashie, instantly accepting the credit for the plan.

Rashidi held no bitterness towards Quaashie for taking the credit for all his plans and work. He was low born, a servant, not very good-looking, small in stature, fat, and even though he bathed often and applied scent to his body, he often smelled. Women avoided him, and men despised him for his quick brain, so he had few friends and lots of enemies because of his position as Quaashie's assistant. He adored women, and Quaashie provided a steady supply of nubile slaves for Rashidi to plunge his small prick into, which was as often as he could. He had no technique, guile, or intimate gestures for these women, just quick, furious sex from a frustrated giant of a man housed in a tiny body. Quaashie knew Rashidi's value and protected and helped him in exchange for his loyalty, and that meant receiving the praise and rewards for all his brilliant ideas.

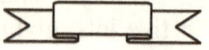

When the offer of soldiers' officer commissions were announced in exchange for plunder with the new taxes, there were few murmurs, as the nobles understood overall they would profit from the new army's triumphs in the field of battle. Most nobles had several sons from their wives, and lots of bastards from servants or slaves, so it was easy to find a suitable candidate for the army. The lower classes also responded well, as they saw a clear path to promotion and wealth by joining the army, and there were many more volunteers than there were vacancies in the army.

General Hakim sat with his fellow generals and Joseph, deciding whom to select from the hundreds of nobles applying for positions in the army.

"It is not easy, General Hakim," said General Ikandar. "We have already a core of people who can lead in the army, who should be promoted, but now must appoint some of these nobles, as well."

"It is simple," said Joseph. "Appoint one officer from the nobles, and then one from the army in every position. That way, nobody is offended, and we have ready-made replacements."

"But we have three or four times the number of applicants," said Ikandar.

"Then devise a way to eliminate those who are not suitable by a series of tests of running, wrestling, and mock fighting," said Joseph. "If we still have some left, then make them a deputy below the assistant."

"Sounds like a good plan," said General Hakim. "Let's get going with the tournament straight away."

The tournament asked all the men to run ten miles, and the last third would be cut from the officer cadre. They would then all fight an opponent. The losers would then fight each other, and that would continue until ten per cent were left, which would be cut from the cadre.

The same system would be used with the mock hand-to-hand fighting with wooden swords.

The tournament threw up anomalies, of course, as the luck of the draw meant you might meet all the best wrestlers, or swordsmen, but generally speaking, it was a fair method of selection. The army began to take shape. The soldiers were recruited at the various levels of officers, and the hierarchy to succeed them was selected. The training commenced, and the projects were started. After little more than six months, General Hakim informed Set that they were ready to invade one of their neighbours to plunder gold and jewels.

Chapter Seventeen

Joseph did not want to invade Palestine, where he had made many friends, so he looked to the Arab land of Libya, where they boasted a fierce army that included the Scythian women. The Maadi Libyan Atlanteans from the province of Madeira had been a declining empire since the loss of Atlantis, a large island in the Atlantic Ocean, which disappeared in 9570 BC. However, their culture and technology had been very influential in every land that they had conquered, and there had been periods when Ta-Mehu had been invaded and ruled by the Atlanteans. The Atlanteans were located in Libya at their city of Cyrene, and in this stronghold they ruled over the arid plains once fertile from the West Nile, which flowed into the Nile across Africa from Lake Tritonis. It was here that Joseph decided he would test his army. The much smaller army of Cyrene, believed to be around five thousand strong, would be a quarter of the size of the Ta-Mehu Army, but far more experienced and undefeated in living memory of any invasion. The invasion and battle plan would have to be flawless, and the battle plan creative, as they certainly would have weapons the Ta-Mehu army had never seen.

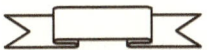

The army had trained well, and the five projects had been created in addition to barracks that had been built by the soldiers. The projects had all progressed but were far from finished. Joseph had changed the diet of the men, which had been a great success, by feeding the men directly three meals a day and then providing food daily for their families as their army pay. The traditional beer was changed to a watered-down wine, and vegetables were added to the loaves provided, as well as animals that they could rear and eat so they had meat. Joseph also provided a small plot of land for soldiers' families, so they could grow vegetables, and the following year they would receive some more animals to rear.

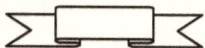

When Joseph met the generals to discuss his proposed adversary, Hakim was furious.

"You are mad! The Atlanteans of Libya are undefeated in centuries, probably never have been defeated," said Hakim. "Why not invade Palestine or attack Eblan?"

"If we defeat Palestine or Eblan, Set will expect that, as we always defeat them," said Joseph, "but the Atlanteans are undefeated, and we will shock the world."

"But what if they defeat us and invade Ta-Mehu?" said Ikandar.

"They have a smaller army," said Joseph. "If we are defeated, we will regroup and retreat back to Ta-Mehu, learn the lessons, and try again. The Atlanteans will not be able to fight a long campaign, as their soldiers are mainly farmers, and it will be the harvest in two months' time."

"So you mean we are going to attack now?" said the shocked Hakim.

"If we defeat the Atlanteans now, the tribute we receive will be larger," said Joseph. "We won't need to invade Palestine, Eblan, or Phoenicia to persuade them to provide our tax, because they will be willing to pay so as not to suffer the same fate. Also, Set will be shocked into delaying any invasion plans."

"But if our neighbours pay their tribute to Ta-Mehu instead of Ta-Shemau, Set will have nothing for his coffers," said Malik. "He will not be able to pay their promised remaining plunder from the Palestine campaign."

"Exactly," said Joseph.

"Ah, I see your plan now," said Hakim. "It is well thought through; I commend you."

"Let us attack Cyrene immediately. Make all haste, but prepare well. Ensure we are well stocked and armed, as they are formidable," said Joseph.

"It will take two weeks to prepare properly, and two weeks to arrive at Cyrene," said Hakim.

"Good," said Joseph. "In the next week we need a battle plan, and it should be well rehearsed."

"That is too short," said Hakim. "We need more time."

"We need to be more adaptable," said Joseph, "and one week is enough. Make all haste. I will go to the queen to get her blessing."

Hakim and the generals nodded; it was a good plan, and a whole week was enough, with one week to practice before departure. "If we sail from Rhakotis, we can sail along the coast to Cyrene and surprise them, which will give us an advantage," said Hakim.

"They will be ready for us," said Malik. "They have spies everywhere."

"Tell the men and sailors we are going to invade the Eblan. It is a similar journey, and the preparation would be the same," said Ikandar.

"Good plan," said Malik.

The generals all nodded and began making mental notes of what to do, thinking of a battle plan to beat the invincible Atlanteans.

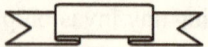

Isis was alone with her ladies in her chambers when Joseph arrived, and he bowed formally. "My Queen, the generals tell me they are ready for war and want to invade Libya and the Atlanteans at Cyrene."

"Tell them they are fools," said Isis, shocked. "They have never been defeated!"

"All the better to create a legacy of greatness for our son, the Pharaoh Horus," said Joseph.

Isis considered this for a moment, the shock subsiding. "Why Cyrene? There are easier Libya cities to take."

"If we take Cyrene, every city in the region will pay tribute without the need of a campaign. Set proved by defeating and destroying Jericho that tribute could be extorted from all the others with one example campaign. But it must be daring and unexpected, and Cyrene is such a war."

"Let me hear your plan," said Isis. "Ladies, leave us." After the ladies had left, she sat back on her bed and smiled. She had married a truly clever man in Joseph, who had proved to be a good lover and husband.

"Husband, your plan is risky and clever," said Isis, "and I am a little scared, particularly for Horus, but I agree."

"Good, my Queen," said Joseph. Then, unbuckling the belt that held his sword, he said, "Now, my wife, we have time before I make war to make love." Joseph was pulling off his short toga to reveal an erect manhood swelling before his wife.

Isis pulled off her long white shift dress and lay back on the bed, revealing her unshaven pubic hair, and opened her legs.

"Come husband, mount me," said Isis, "and sow seed for another child."

Joseph came on top of his wife, pushing himself inside her, feeling the warm grip of her soft inner lips around his manhood, and he sighed. Holding his wife, now inside her, her legs and arms wrapped around him, he thought, *what could be more complete*, and he ejaculated prematurely. His wife smiled; she had pleased him.

At the news that the army was going to war, Ta-Mehu sprung to life in preparation. Food for the journey and campaign was needed. Weapons were sharpened. Boats prepared. Men trained in the battle plan provided to the generals. Children wept, as their fathers were leaving, and women were ploughed as often as possible by their husbands.

The generals liked Joseph's battle plan. It had an unexpected twist, and to defeat the Atlanteans they needed a surprise as part of the battle plan, and none of the other generals' plans had any hint of surprise. They relied on a battle of attacking against a smaller army.

The four divisions would be led by Generals Ikandar, Kushi, Ptah, and Sayyid. Ikandar would be the most forward of the divisions and lead the initial charge. Heru would command the chariot division, which now had five hundred horses and chariots. This new division was the least trained and skilled, so it would play less of an offensive role than Joseph would have liked, but it still would be important. Hakim and Malik would command the battle from an advantage point.

The battle would be led by the pharaoh himself, little Horus, barely two, with his mother Isis, and the Coffin of Destiny would be paraded before the soldiers before the battle. They fought not just for conquest, but also for their Pharaoh Horus and the Coffin of Destiny, which held the fabled Osiris.

The fleet sailed on time and reached their destination some fifty kilometres from Cyrene so they could gain some advantage by choosing the ground.

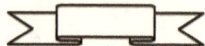

The elders at Cyrene met at the temple, where all decisions were made. The leader, Ahron, was old, now nearly eighty, and had guided the council for many years. Unlike other societies of the region, Cyrene was a democracy, and every person was free; there were no slaves. Each person cast a vote every two years for the council, throwing a pebble into a basket with the sign of each candidate pinned to the basket. The ten highest scores formed the council, which then selected a leader, and Ahron had been selected every time for the last thirty years.

The last vote had been only two months ago, and Ahron was considering retiring from leadership and not standing again as a council member. A woman, Bluma, had criticized his policies regarding the army and their foreign policy of no warfare and peaceful co-habitation in the continent. The woman was a member of the Scythian tribe, which was incorporated into the Cyrene population centuries before, and formed a division of the army used as an offensive thrust at the centre of the oncoming army to break their ranks.

Fierce and proud of their heritage, the tribe lived peacefully among the Atlanteans as equals, breeding as they did with the men of the population, but never marrying men. They married other women and lived as couples with their daughters. All male children used to be killed at birth, but were now given to the Atlanteans to be brought up. The Scythians did not farm or work like the Atlanteans, but followed their age-old customs of training for war: rigorous training every day and fierce mock fighting that often resulted in death or serious injury. Their number remained static, at about one thousand fighting women, as in spite of Atlantean's laws prohibiting the killing of infants who were deformed or sickly, the Scythians continued the practice. Only one thousand women were allowed to survive, and any child showing weakness during training was slaughtered.

Bluma was an exceptional leader of the Scythians, who were given one seat on the council by right by the Atlanteans. At five feet, ten inches, she was taller than most men. However, her shape was very much one of a woman, with large breasts and hips. Her rock-hard flat stomach and slender biceps gave her an athletic but definitely female physique. She was amazingly strong, but her greatest asset as a fighter was her mind.

Bluma had the one characteristic of all great hand-to-hand fighters: She instinctively spotted her opponent's weakness, and then exploited it in an instant. She was also very adaptable. If one tactic failed, she could quickly introduce another tactic. Very inventive, she often made up moves on the spur of the moment, without even thinking. Her weapon of choice was the sword, with a light, round shield used in the attack formation the Scythians employed, but she was equally gifted with the spear or bow. For many years, Bluma had been worried about tWay, with the rise of Set in Ta-Shemau, and was now concerned at the army being built by Ta-Mehu. It seemed inevitable that one of those nations would attack Cyrene, so she pleaded with the council to prepare, but her warning fell on deaf ears. The leader Ahron held sway at the council, and her motions always were defeated. Now, the worst news arrived from their spies in Rhakotis: The Ta-Mehu Army was marching to Eblan, it was rumoured, but could this be a ruse. She wondered whether they really were coming to Cyrene.

The Ta-Mehu Army landed on the coast as planned, and very organized, created a camp near the shore line to assemble. After two days of rest, the army, with the Coffin of Destiny paraded at the front of the army and a flag for each division flying its colours, had marched to the ground they had selected to fight the Atlanteans.

Cyrene was situated about six and a quarter miles from the port of Apollonian inland, in fertile land, and it was famous for its flocks of beasts raised for food of goats, cows, and sheep. Its crowning glory was horses, which were used both in farming to pull ploughs, and in war to pull chariots. Rich in metals, they used coins to pay for goods in gold or silver, rather than bartering labour or other goods. Joseph thought that they must choose high, rough ground with many rough rocks on which his troops must stand, otherwise the skilled chariots of the Atlanteans would have the upper hand countering their superior numbers.

The city, built around a river valley about eighteen hundred feet above sea level, was protected from the oppressive desert wind by the higher ground to the south. This is where Joseph would stand with his main army, deploying the first division led by Ikandar in front, and the three other divisions spread behind this division. The chariots would not be used until the second phase of the battle, and they risked everything by positioning them in the main division to the right. Only a few chariots and archers on foot were to the left, to make it look as though they had chariots on both sides.

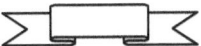

The news that the Ta-Mehu Army had arrived and taken the higher ground to the south did not concern Ahron, and he sat with his council to agree a defence of the city.

"Maybe we should barter a peace, rather than fight this day," said Bluma, aware they were on lower ground with fewer troops.

"Do the Scythian women fear the men of Ta-Mehu?" asked Atia, the General of the Army.

"We fear nothing, general, and will fight with all our might," said Bluma, "but we are outflanked and outnumbered. Better to fight another day."

"We Atlanteans have never been defeated in battle in thousands of years," said Atia scornfully. "We have defeated larger armies on better ground before, with better tactics and weapons. We will do so again, and will not barter peace."

"So we fight," said Bluma.

"We fight," said Atia and the council nodded. "We shall use the centre strike strategy, using our heavy beasts. They will not have seen this before, and it will break their centre. Then, our chariots will move left and right and surround them, and by attrition we will kill most of them, forcing them to retreat. We are stronger and more adaptable than them in the field, and will prevail."

"A full frontal attack through the centre is risky," said Bluma. "If we Scythian women are held, you will lose the day."

"Again, I hear Bluma, the woman who pled to prepare for war, question the plan that has served us well for thousands of years," said Atia.

"Thousands of years ago, your troops were battle-hardened veterans; today they are peaceful farmers," said Bluma. "In practice, you fight with wooden sticks, not swords like the Scythian women. If your plan fails, and the Scythian women do not destroy the line, your men will not stand and fight, and will flee the field, and the war will be lost and Cyrene will be taken."

"The plan will be used. It will work," said Atia, who was flustered, as he had no other plan.

Ahron looked at the council and nodded. "All in favour of General Atia's plan?" All of the council nodded except Bluma.

"I go to prepare the Scythian women for glory or death. I guarantee we will break the line," said Bluma. "Remember, your troops must rush into the gap we create, or the day is lost."

Atia ignored Bluma, smarting at her comments, and barked orders for the men to take the field of battle.

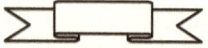

The worst time of the day to fight a battle was at midday, and Bluma saw the battle would commence at this time. The army of Ta-Mehu did not look twenty thousand strong, she thought maybe fifteen thousand, and there were very few chariots left and right. The centre was forward of the left and right divisions, which she thought was a mistake.

The battle plan would be simple: The heavy beasts would smash through the centre of the first central

214

division, and the Scythian women would charge through, cutting the centre to pieces. As the gap was widened, the main army would pour through and reach the higher ground behind the division to the left and right. The chariots would attack left and right, keeping the enemy occupied until they had the higher ground, and then they would kill the bulk of the army until it retreated.

As they prepared for battle, a small number of men were seen carrying a box of some sort to the front of the army, and a small boy and woman went to the front of the army with a soldier. The cloth covering the box was removed, and it glinted in the sunlight as it was golden and bejewelled. The small boy was held high above the man's head, and the army shouted as one: "For Horus, the only true pharaoh!" and then the field was silent. The golden box, or perhaps coffin, was covered again, and the boy and the woman melted into the front ranks of the army and disappeared from view.

So, the battle now will commence, thought Bluma.

Chapter Eighteen

The Cyrene Army took to the field of battle dressed in shiny breastplates, which Joseph knew were light armour designed to protect their men. Their shields were not as large as those of the Ta-Mehu Army, perhaps two-thirds the size, exposing the legs of the soldiers. They wore light armour on the lower legs to compensate for this. He had heard a sword blow would not break a man's leg easily, and the armour was very effective. The Cyrene Army took the field as he had read in chronicled accounts of their exploits, with their inferior numbers facing the centre of the opposing army. As predicted, the centre of the Cyrene Army parted, and five large elephants ridden by two soldiers burst forward, followed by the Scythian women, who were perhaps one thousand strong.

Joseph knew that woman against man; these women would win every time in hand-to-hand fighting. As the elephants thundered forward, he saw Hakim wave his red flag, and archers from the centre and either side fired arrows at the oncoming elephants and running women soldiers. The arrows bounced off the elephants' armour, but some stuck in their sides, enraging the elephants to rush even faster at the force in front of them. At one hundred yards, the bowmen released more arrows, this time lit and a stretch of ground eighty yards from the front row of the Ta-Mehu Army was lit with arid smoke. The elephants were splattered with oil which came alight, making them uncontrollable. The thick smoke made it impossible for Cyrene's General Atia to see what was happening, and he hesitated not sending his main body forward. When the uncontrolled elephants reached the front of the Ta-Mehu Army, the front rank parted and let the beasts through. When they reached the other side of the army, a deep ditch had been dug with spikes, and the blinded elephants fell into the ditch to be speared by waiting soldiers.

The on-rushing Scythian women flew into the centre of the gap in the front ranks of the army, to be faced with a wall of steel shields with very long thirteen foot spears pointing at them. The army closed around them, having an inward-facing square as well as an outward-facing square.

Bluma realized too late that they had followed into a trap they could not escape from; their superior hand-to-hand fighting skills were no match for the men thirteen feet away spearing her helpless brave warriors. They fought as they should, by rushing the ranks, trying to break through, and keeping the centre busy. *If Atia advances quickly*, she thought, *the front line is thin and we can still win the day when the chariots attack.* She fought as never before, hacking at the spears forcing her dwindling force forward.

Atia, unable to see properly, still ordered the chariots to attack, and they flew into battle, unable to see the ground. As they reached the rocky ground, the chariots, unable to see the rocks, unseated their drivers, sending them crashing to the ground. Atia, unaware of the disaster, signalled the army to advance slowly.

When Hakim saw this, he sent his three unused divisions, and they rounded the first front division and would meet the oncoming army on the plain flatland just in front of the tiring first division. The arrows were now raining left and right from the Ta-Mehu

Army; therefore, Atia positioned his left and right flank defence evenly.

As they reached the phalanx of the Ta-Mehu Army, the left flank was attacked by the fifth division of chariots, and it broke under the pressure. The front rank met the thirteen-foot spears, and although better equipped, they were fighting standing in burning oil. The soldiers broke ranks, not noticing the left and right divisions had outflanked them, and they cut them down as they tried to flee the field. It was slaughter, not a contest. They had been out-planned and out-fought at every stage of the battle. The city was at the mercy of the Ta-Mehu Army.

The Atlanteans still alive stopped fighting and put their arms on the floor, throwing their arms. At a signal from Hakim, the Ta-Mehu let them surrender, and perhaps half of the army surrendered.

The women of Scythian had lost nearly eighty per cent of their number, killed or wounded, when Hakim signalled to the division surrounding them to stop the slaughter. Bluma, her wife Kadia at her side, was covered in blood from the wounds and blood of people she had killed, and the remaining few women were surrounded by a steel shields and the long spears. The shields parted, and Joseph, dressed as an imperial general, and Isis, carrying the Pharaoh Horus, appeared before the women.

In a clear voice, Joseph spoke, "Women of Scythian. The Cyrene Army has been defeated and surrendered. You have fought bravely. Now is time for you to stop fighting."

Bluma spoke in the Ta-Mehu language in a clear voice: "We women of Scythian fight to protect our children and our city. We would rather die than see Ta-Mehu rape our women and kill our children."

Isis spoke for the first time, her voice clear. "I am Isis, Queen of Ta-Mehu. I come to the field of battle to salute you Scythian women. Your city and women are safe from harm. Leave the field of battle and pay tribute to my son Pharaoh Horus of Ta-Mehu, and we shall not harm your city or your people."

"I can only speak for the women of the Scythian tribe, not the council of Cyrene, but we accept your terms," said Bluma. "We have no gold or goods to offer as tribute, but offer myself and one hundred of my warrior women in your service for five years as tribute."

"Ten years would be acceptable to the queen," said Joseph, before Isis could speak.

"Who are you, Lord?" asked Bluma.

"I am the man who read your tactics in your chronicles and will treat you with honour and dignity if you serve my queen well. They call me Joseph, and I am Queen Isis' husband."

"The gold box or coffin we saw at the beginning of the battle; what was it?" asked Bluma.

"The Coffin of Destiny," said Joseph. "If brought before an army of Ta-Mehu by the Pharaoh Horus, the army is invincible."

"Why the boy, Pharaoh?" asked Bluma.

"Because the boy is blessed by the gods," said Joseph, "and only he can use the power of the Coffin of Destiny, which contains the divine Osiris.

"Then, Queen Isis," said Bluma. "We are yours for ten years or until we die in your service." The women laid down their weapons and walked from the field back to the city of Cyrene.

The army of Ta-Mehu stayed out of the city of Cyrene and sent a messenger to meet with the leader of the city and its council.

Ahron came with his council and defeated General Atia and Bluma was amongst its number. Joseph greeted them with dignity and respect, and when they were all seated inside the tent for the meeting, he commenced his opening statement: "Gentlemen, and noble Lady Bluma, you were defeated in battle and your city lies before us, to rape your women, kill or enslave your men as we please, and plunder your city," said Joseph, "or, you can form an alliance with Ta-Mehu. If you do, we will protect your way of life and set up trade between our two great nations, to our mutual benefit. Of course, you will need to pay a tribute each year to our Pharaoh Horus, and we will require a suitable tribute today."

"Thank you great Lord," said Ahron. "I am old, and my life is over, but we have many young men you still hold captive. What will happen to them?"

"If we are comrades in an alliance, your men are free to go. If you do not form an alliance, then they will be killed," said Joseph, "but we keep our word to the Scythian women that their children and homes will not be harmed. Everybody else will be tortured and killed, and their homes made rubble."

"It is not really a choice then," said General Atia. "We have to agree to an alliance."

"In an alliance, you will need not just to supply Scythian women to advise us on warfare, but to show us how you make your viaducts and remove waste from your city, and other marvels we have heard of," said Joseph.

"How do you know of these things?" asked Ahron.

"From scrolls describing Atlantis when I served the Eblan king," said Joseph.

"Is that how you defeated our tactics in the battle?" asked General Atia.

"Partly," said Joseph, "but your general also delayed his advance at the vulnerable stage of our plan, as we suspected. If that had not happened, we don't know what the outcome would have been."

Atia was silent, so Ahron spoke, "We cannot refight the battle with words. What is the tribute we Atlanteans need to pay?"

"One half of all your gold, silver, and jewels you have in the city and one quarter of your harvest," said Joseph.

"That means our granary stores will have no reserves," said Atia.

"We are not here to debate and bargain," said Joseph. "It is fair, and you still have gold, silver, and jewels to barter with your neighbours for reserves of grain."

Ahron was silent, and then spoke: "What else do you want?"

"I will lead a delegation of officers and scribes to the city. You will show me your marvels, and we shall require you to give us craftsmen, who can create these wonders in Ta-Mehu," said Joseph.

"Anything else?" asked Ahron.

"The men would rape women to death, so I will station them away from the city and give them duties to perform," said Joseph, "but our officers will need to be satisfied before we return to our barracks, so if you can supply maybe one hundred prostitutes that the officers will plough during our visit to the city," said Joseph.

"We have no prostitutes in the city," said Ahron, "only wives and daughters."

"Then we have a problem we must resolve," said Joseph. "Let me speak to the officers."

Joseph met with Hakim and the generals after Ahron had returned with the council to gather the tribute.

"Sorry, my Lord, but conquest has certain rituals for officers and men, and if there is no rape and pillage, we need paying," said Hakim.

"I agree, but if we take any more, we will kill the goose that lays the golden egg," said Joseph. "Let us keep an open mind at least until we have seen the city and assessed how their miracles can help us make Ta-Mehu a richer and greater nation."

"When he said officers," asked Ptah, "did he mean generals?"

"I am afraid he did, General Ptah," said Joseph.

"I don't have a problem with the request," said Ikandar. "I don't fight men to rape their wives and daughters. I don't think that's the way of the Pharaoh Horus. I don't want a woman unless she is willing. So, all I would ask is if officers have a desire, are there any willing maidens?"

"Very considerate I will relay your request," said Joseph, "but let us first have our visit to the city. I will take half the generals. General Hakim, you will stay here with the other half. Keep the men on alert and watch the captives carefully until we return. I will take half the scribes."

"Why don't you take all the scribes?" asked Hakim.

"If we are killed or don't return, you will slaughter the captives, storm the city, and kill all but the Scythian women and artisans who can help build Ta-Mehu, and you may need them to write down everything you find," said Joseph carefully.

"Very considerate and well thought out as always," said Hakim. "It shall be done as ordered."

Joseph toured the city and was amazed that every house had a place to defecate and urinate, and this was washed away by water down clay pipes outside the city several miles to a central collection point. The resulting waste then was mixed with rotten vegetation to create manure used in farming. Water was fed to the city viaducts, which he had seen before, but these created individual wells at each house so that water was available all the time at each dwelling. The streets were clean, and refuse was collected daily in carts and taken outside the city and made into manure or burnt. The metal or wood was sorted and made use of in some way.

Different tradesmen made goods and sold them for gold or silver coins to merchants, who displayed them in stalls called a market. These merchants were paid with these metal discs, or coins as the Atlanteans called them, so it was easy to calculate any transaction.

Much of what Joseph saw just simply was superior to what was done in Ta-Mehu, but some things were revolutionary, such as a tomb planned to be built for the population called a pyramid. Each was taken a careful note of by the scribes and an artisan who could come to Ta-Mehu to show the artisans of Ta-Mehu how to build these wonders.

At the end of two days, the tribute had been paid and the artisans assigned, and the scribes had recorded all the details sufficient enough to leave Cyrene. "Our work is complete Ahron, and I am satisfied in all respects except for the one in which we asked you to consider use of your women for a night of lust for our officers," said Joseph. "Did you have any volunteers?"

Ahron was silent and then spoke, "My Lord, you know I cannot ask a man to give up his wife or daughter. I would rather die than live with that on my conscience. So, if it will please you, you may kill me."

"Old man, your death will not appease my generals," said Joseph. "Surely you have some women they can plough this night before we return?"

"And you, great Lord, what girl do you want?" asked Ahron.

"None," said Joseph. "I am content with my wife; I need no other."

"By drawing lots, we have twenty women your officers can use, but they must not be harmed or abused," said Ahron. "They are all young and pretty, but infertile, so their husbands have abandoned them, as is our custom."

"I assure you, the women will be treated well, but with only twenty, they will be ploughed many times," said Joseph, "that is unavoidable."

"I understand," said Ahron, sadly looking away as he thought of his granddaughter in the party. "You have my trust and goodwill for the way you have behaved in your conquest. Don't lose that trust for one night of lust."

"I cannot guarantee, Ahron, how men behave. I can only tell you I will tell my generals to keep order and to return the women with respect and thanks," said Joseph. "The majority will obey, but there is always one or two who will not, and they will be punished, but that will not repair the hurt to the girl or her family."

"You are a wise man, my Lord," said Ahron. "Demonstrate your justice to my people, and you will retain my trust."

"I will always treat you and your people fairly, and keep my word, but my loyalty is to my Queen Isis and her son, our Pharaoh Horus. If there is ever a conflict of interest, I will always side with my queen and the interests of Ta-Mehu, even if they are wrong. Remember that fact, Ahron," said Joseph.

"I will remember," said Ahron, and the men parted, still friends and trusting each other's word.

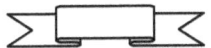

The night of debauchery passed without incident following a stern warning from Joseph to all officers, including the generals. In the morning, the women gathered as a group and Ahron came to collect the women with Bluma. The Scythian women had supplied five of the women, who wanted children and wished to mate with a man; they did not care if five or ten men ploughed their furrow, as long as they were not harmed.

Ahron counted his women and all seemed in order, but one of Bluma's women was missing. "One of the Scythian women is missing, great Lord. Can she be fetched from whoever keeps her from her duties in Cyrene?" said Bluma.

"General Hakim, who was this woman given to?" asked Joseph.

"General Ptah, my Lord," said Hakim, looking for the general, whom he could not see.

"Send someone to the general and get the girl now," said Joseph, a little annoyed, but he decided not to make an issue over a small delay in returning the woman by the general.

Hakim sent his son Heru to General Ptah, and he returned after a few minutes with General Ptah looking the worse for wear, with cuts and bruises to his face.

"Where is the Scythian girl, General Ptah?" asked Joseph.

"She is gone, my Lord," said General Ptah. "She left last night following a fight we had. She did not like being mounted doggy style." He smiled, as did the other generals.

"Arrest General Ptah," said Joseph. "Mount a search through the camp and outlying area for the girl. Can I ask you, Ahron, to return with Bluma and search the city, and bring her here if you find her?"

"My Lord, I protest! I am a general!" said Ptah.

"General Ptah, if any harm has come to the girl, I will have your penis cut off first, and then your head," said Joseph. "If you defy me, you defy your Pharaoh Horus."

Ptah went ashen, and the generals were grim-faced.

Chapter Nineteen

The Scythian woman was found bound to a tree, her throat cut and her body full of bruises and cuts. Bluma carried the girl back in her arms, her eyes wet with tears. She shed them at the death of Kadia, her wife and lover. As was the custom, one of the pair every two years would mate with a man until she was pregnant. They would continue this until the couple had given birth to two girls. The family then complete, they would stop the ritual. If a child died, such as the child of Kadia who had in an accident in training, and the mother was still able to bear children, she would mate again. Kadia volunteered to be one of the women used by the soldiers for sex. The interbreeding of the smaller population of the Atlanteans did not always produce strong women, so the Scythian women would seek out men visiting Cypress to mate with whenever possible. Bluma had no fears for Kadia when she told her of her wish for another child and thought it a good idea, mating with a foreign soldier. Now grief-stricken, the love of her life had been killed by the Ta-Mehu General Ptah.

Joseph watched in horror as the body of Kadia was placed at his feet as he sat with Queen Isis and the generals.

"My Lord, I demand justice," said Bluma. "My wife Kadia has been tortured and killed by General Ptah.

"Lady Bluma, we sympathize with your loss, but demand is not a word used to the queen of Ta-Mehu," said Joseph. "You are forgiven because you talk in haste and anger. However, before the queen decides the fate of General Ptah, let him speak. Well, General Ptah?"

"The girl was uncontrollable," said General Ptah. "She fought me when I tried to plough her, and would not allow me to enter her in the ass."

"So how did she come to get tied to a tree?" asked Joseph.

"I called my men at arms and we held her down," said General Ptah, "but she continued to struggle and fight, so I cut her. It had no effect, it just enraged her, and she broke free and killed one of the soldiers. The woman was immensely strong, my Lord, one man could not hold her down, so we bound her and took her to a tree. She had killed a soldier; the punishment under army law is death. So after we had all ploughed her, one of the men killed her, as is our custom."

"Who are these men, General Ptah?" asked Joseph.

"My personal guards, my Lord," said General Ptah.

"Bring them here now," said Joseph.

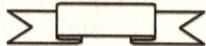

The five burly soldiers were brought and questioned by Joseph, and the events were very similar to those described by General Ptah, except that Ptah had been beaten up by Kadia and humiliated, it seemed. The girl had killed a soldier in self-defence, as General Ptah had said, and the penalty was death, which any officer could enforce. Ptah could not be put to death for killing the girl.

"General Ptah, you have disobeyed my order, and for that you will be punished," said Joseph, but he could not think of a suitable punishment.

"Lord, may I speak?" asked Bluma.

"Speak, Lady Bluma, but speak softly in the presence of our queen," said Joseph.

"These six men held down my wife and tortured her, cutting her body; she fought in self-defence. I ask not that you punish them, but that I fight all six of the men in mortal combat," said Bluma.

"My Lord," said General Ptah, "none of us is equal to this woman in hand-to-hand combat. It would be suicide."

"I will fight all six at once," said Bluma.

"No warrior can beat six prepared men in mortal combat, my lady," said Joseph.

"I accept the challenge," said Ptah.

"Lady Bluma, the men will be punished, but they cannot be killed; do not sacrifice yourself for this challenge," said Queen Isis.

"Queen Isis, I am also the leader of my people, and our law demands justice by combat. I would rather die than live in defiance of our laws," said Bluma.

"I grant your wish, Lady Bluma," said Queen Isis. "Go and prepare yourself; you shall meet at sunset."

Joseph saw the men smile; they were used to hand-to-hand fighting in battle. Often, there would be one exceptional warrior, and they were taught to surround him and attack simultaneously. An exceptional warrior could perhaps fight three people, but not six. Regardless of skill or agility, you could not parry and dodge six simultaneous blows. Bluma surely would die. As the challenge had been made by Bluma, she could choose the weapons, and she selected the sword and shield.

At midday in the clear ground in front of the royal tent, the combatants faced each other. Bluma was dressed in the light armour for battle, with a breast and back plate, moulded plates to her legs and arms, and she wore a light helmet. She had the small light shield the Scythian women preferred in battle. The six men all had the larger, heavier shields used to defeat the Cyrene Army. General Ptah was not a great hand-to-hand fighter, but he did train every day and was competent and a very good tactician. *He will have drilled the other five men how to defeat this lone woman*, thought Joseph.

"There are no rules in mortal combat other than these," said Joseph. "You cannot leave the field of battle unless quarter is given by your opponent; you can only fight with the weapons in your hands now; any weapon picked up by somebody from the crowd is not allowed; and nobody from the crowd can interfere with the combat. The combatants fight to the death."

General Ptah could choose his ground, and the six men stood in a V-shape with their backs to the sun, the sun shining directly into Bluma's eyes. When the red flag fell, the contest would begin. The six men inched forward as the flag fell, seeking to corner Bluma within the circle of soldiers who watched the contest. Bluma ran full tilt at the six men, and they grounded their shields and stuck out their swords as they had practiced in battle. Bluma jumped high in the air, and with her left arm, slammed it in the gap between two of the men and vaulted over the men. Bluma swivelled before the startled men could move the heavy shields and cut left and right killing two men, then retreated as the other four men turned.

"Keep a gap between the shields!" shouted Ptah, thinking quickly. "Drop the shield if she tries to vault you!" But as he was speaking, Bluma had somersaulted behind a man who instinctively grounded his shield. Turning rapidly, she cut off his head with a single stroke.

Bluma retreated in the open ground, and the men chased after her, her three fallen soldiers being dragged from the field of combat, their weapons lying on the ground. The three men now adopted a new formation: two were facing Bluma, and one was facing the other way just in case she vaulted them again. Bluma circled the battle area, quickly taking up position at speed, and the men ponderously followed her, carrying the heavier shields. General Ptah, older and less fit than the other two men, struggled to keep up, and there was sometimes a gap between him and his other two soldiers.

The use of the swords stuck out from the shields in a wall of hundreds of men was effective because the oncoming troops were pushed onto the swords. In hand-to-hand battle, the shields were very heavy and difficult to move, and men tired. Bluma saw that Ptah was very tired now, and she exploited the gap between the two men. She ran forward and then jumped at Ptah's shield, feet first, his shield collapsing on top of Ptah, exposing the man with his back to Bluma, who she cut with a blow to the back of his head, killing him. Ptah struggled to his feet, now frightened. The two men were standing back to back, now looking to defend not attack.

Bluma discarded her smaller shield and picked up one of the larger shields and charged the two static men, crashing into them and sending them to the ground. The soldier sprang up, sword in hand, and Bluma attacked him. The soldier parried her sword blow, but missed the dagger in her left hand as she spun and stabbed him in the throat. Ptah rose, dizzy, picking up his sword, too weak to use the heavy shield.

"General Ptah, you seem to have lost your army," taunted Bluma.

"I am going to cut off your head you bitch!" said Ptah, charging.

Bluma easily parried the blow and cut Ptah on his back; it was a shallow blow, and blood poured from the wound. The contest now became a ritual, Ptah lunging at Bluma, and her cutting him until he was covered in cuts and would die from loss of blood.

"How does it feel, General Ptah," asked Bluma, "to know a woman has defeated you and humiliated you in front of your whole army?"

"May you rot in hell, you bitch!" cried Ptah weakly, and made a final attempt at attack.

This time, Bluma knocked the sword from his grasp, and as the shocked Ptah looked up, she cut off his head.

Bluma although tired, had not been injured by any of the soldiers; her only cuts and bruises were from the battle a few days earlier. Joseph watched fascinated, but did not see how he could adapt anything Bluma had done for the army. Few individuals could fight like Bluma.

Queen Isis rose from her chair, and taking a necklace of gold with a medallion, she walked to the armed Bluma in the field. Joseph was quickly at her side, sword drawn.

"Lady Bluma, you were magnificent," said Queen Isis. "As a token of my esteem, I award you the medallion of Horus," and she placed the necklace around her neck. "I release you from your ten years' servitude; you and your people are free."

"My Lady does me great honour, and I thank you," said Bluma. "What say you, great Lord?"

"My queen's words are law," said Joseph, "but I offer you service as one of my generals in the Ta-Mehu Army with your women, for which you will be paid. You need to fight, and we will have many battles."

"We are a strange people," said Bluma. "We have customs of our own that we must keep, one of which is we don't marry men, but women."

"Lesbians and homosexuals are common in Ta-Mehu," said Joseph. "Most people are bisexual if they are soldiers, so it won't be a problem."

"And you, great Lord? What are you?" asked Bluma.

"I am heterosexual. I have never wanted another man, but there is nothing wrong if it pleases other men," said Joseph.

"And other women, do you take them to your bed?" asked Bluma.

"Not anymore," said Joseph. "I am married and need only my queen."

Isis smiled and squeezed his hand.

"Great Queen, it is our custom to request permission from the wife of the man we mate with," said Bluma. "I therefore ask your permission when we return to your land to mate with your husband, the Lord Joseph, so I can replace my fallen wife's child."

Isis was shocked. Men, even husbands, had sex with whoever they wanted; fidelity was not common in marriage amongst the nobles. She did not mind if Joseph took other women occasionally. "My husband is my Lord when I am in his bed," said Queen Isis. "He may choose who he ploughs for recreation. So you and he have my permission for him to mount you once."

"Our tradition is to be served for a week, great Queen, to ensure the child is sown," said Bluma.

"So be it, then," said Queen Isis. "My husband can decide."

"Lord Joseph," said Bluma, "before you say no, this will bind my people to you and your queen and young pharaoh, so grant my wish."

"If it is my queen's will," said Joseph, and turned to his wife, who nodded. "So be it." *This is going to be trouble*, he thought.

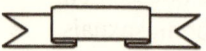

Joseph sent envoys to all major Palestine cities, the Eblan, and the Phoenicians, each accompanied by a Scythian soldier and an Atlantean diplomat. The message was clear and simple: Pay tribute to Queen Isis and her infant, Pharaoh Horus, or Ta-Mehu will invade and destroy your city. The tribute was one-tenth of their silver, gold, and jewels, as calculated by the Atlanteans, and one-tenth of the harvest each year. The land of Ta-Mehu and Cyrene also offered to trade with each city, and opened an account by which they could exchange goods or labour. News of the defeat of the Atlanteans by Ta-Mehu had travelled swiftly, and people were scared of the story of the invincible army led by the Coffin of Destiny and an infant god called Horus. It was rumoured that soldiers with the Eye of Horus tattooed on their hands fought like ten men. Even the fabled Scythian woman had been humbled. The rumour became true when the envoys told of the annihilation of the Cyrene Army and Scythian women in the battle. The feared Scythian women joining the Ta-Mehu Army made then even more formidable.

Joseph insisted all envoys, whether Atlanteans, Scythian women, or Ta-Mehu, had the Eye of Horus on the palm of their right hand. He was surprised that Bluma had her whole tribe adopt this symbol at her promotion to general and the freeing of her people. The Atlanteans were different, and within their population, Horus was the cult of the few. So, it was from these willing people that Joseph selected envoys to accompany the Ta-Mehu main envoy. The cult of Horus grew very quickly after the victory, and in Ta-Mehu it was rare to find somebody without the Eye of Horus tattooed in the palm of his right hand. Joseph heard from Ammon in Ta-Shemau that there was an underground cult of Horus, and Set put to death any who had the Eye of Horus in the palm of their hand, so a few had the tattoo instead on their inside thigh. It was less easy to see, but more embarrassing to reveal.

Joseph recognized that having every follower with the Eye of Horus generally was a plus, but it also meant they easily could be identified, and he ordered groups of people he trusted as spies and infiltrators not to have the Eye of Horus tattooed on their bodies. Many refused, and had it tattooed above their genitals, over which they grew pubic hair. Those secret Horus followers became known as the Society of Horus, and began to develop rituals and sign language so they could identify and communicate with each other.

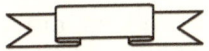

Many cities' sought to test the value and strength of the legend of the Scythian women, often by mortal combat against their best warrior. In every case, the women triumphed, killing their opponent easily. Their speed, agility, and power were a marvel to all who witnessed the contest. Joseph knew this would be the outcome, but how could he use these skills to his advantage? *Perhaps I could have elite bodyguards to protect the queen and the Pharaoh Horus*, he thought, *or as a strike force in battles to fight through and kill a commander or break a line, as the Atlanteans used the Scythian women, and include them in the Society of*

Horus as undercover agents for assassination. He would talk to Bluma after they had mated and had a child. The problem was that he suspected it would be a boy. All his life, he had produced boys and had bastard sons whenever he had sex with women regularly.

Isis was an exception; she would have no further children, as she took a potion using pomegranate seeds to prevent pregnancy from developing. Both he and Isis had agreed there would only be one heir to the throne to avoid the rivalry that blighted the rule of Osiris and Set. They also agreed that Horus should marry outside the current blood line and father an heir who was healthy and strong by finding a bride from another land. Joseph was constantly assessing who would be a good candidate to produce the perfect future wife for Horus.

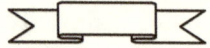

Set was furious; he had sent envoys to the cities of Palestine, Eblan, and the Phoenicians, but they all had returned empty-handed. In two cases, their heads had been returned as a mark of disrespect. Everybody talked of the fabled Coffin of Destiny he had created and the body of Osiris having special powers. The soldiers of Ta-Mehu were supposed to be invincible, having the Pharaoh Horus as their mascot and the Eye of Horus as a mark on each of their hands. Set could not believe how people quickly forgot that it was he was who had the coffin made; it was not a divine object. However, everybody remembered how Osiris fought, easily defeating everybody and the legend grew, and soon the coffin had been made by the gods, and any soldier who marched behind it could not be beaten.

Set also found some of his people changing alliance to Horus, believing him divine and risking death by having the Eye of Horus tattooed on their body. He decided he needed to end this farce and raise an army to defeat Ta-Mehu in battle and crush the myth. He knew he needed a huge army, the biggest ever in the world, and decided he would hire mercenaries and enlarge his own army. Set would put fifty thousand Te-Shemau soldiers in the field and hire eighteen thousand mercenaries that would make his force three times the size of the Ta-Mehu Army, and he would make them well armed and trained. His General Jabir had retired, but still advised on training and appointments, and they would recruit a new young group of generals bold enough to fight the Ta-Mehu Army. He planned to invade Ta-Mehu with this mighty force within two years. Set would send spies to study the Ta-Mehu tactics and training and would devise a battle plan to surprise the fabled Ta-Mehu Army.

Chapter Twenty

Joseph and Isis sat on the balcony of their chambers in the palace, with Horus playing at their feet, looking out onto the city of Memphis, as the sun was setting in the sky and the light just fading. It had been over a month since they had returned from Cyrene and they had returned very naturally to family life in the evenings in their chambers, even if their responsibilities during the day made that part of their lives quite different. However, Joseph found no difficulties in accepting and respecting Isis as his queen and working as her servant during the day. With Isis, certainly every evening and when in private, they spoke as equals. Their child was loved by them both, and although Joseph was regarded as a stepfather, he had no problem in this regard, and even if this had been true, he still would have loved Horus.

Joseph reached across the couch they were lying on together and pulled Isis towards him and wrapped his strong arm around her shoulder and held her soft flesh close to him. He loved this time of day after they had eaten together, just sitting together and watching little Horus play, he being a husband, father, and lover, she a wife, mother, and temptress. They often made love on the couch, Horus playing on the floor, and Isis always made Joseph feel complete with her wonderful, slim, shapely legs wrapped around him, her tight pouch a perfect fit for his manhood. Isis was the perfect lover, always ready for sex, soft and silky, wet inside, warm and soft outside, but not flabby as some women became as they got older. Isis exercised each day, even copying some of the Scythian women's exercises to keep trim and fit and ate sparingly each day. Both she and Joseph drank very little wine and no beer. They drank mainly water from a spring in the garden. Vegetables and fruit also came from their own gardens and meat from their own farm along the banks of the Nile.

Every servant that touched any aspect of the life of Isis or Horus, no matter how minor, was checked carefully by Joseph, and spies were allocated to watch them constantly. The Society of Horus, although embryonic, was very useful in this respect, and it was a regular occurrence to catch a spy from Ta-Shemau trying to infiltrate or become friendly with farmers, labours, servants, cooks, gardeners, soldiers, or anyone connected to the royal family. Joseph had each of them carefully interrogated, all contacts dismissed from service, guilty or innocent, and unfortunately for them, tortured and killed. Nothing was allowed to come close to harm the royal family, which included Joseph. Security at the palace was changed, as Scythian women as well as elite solders guarded the royal family. Scythian women were ever-present in the chambers at discrete positions even as the couple mated, but at a distance they could not hear their whispered words. Royal guards guarded every entrance and the palace and Joseph constantly changed routines and guard rotas so they could not be memorized and used by any enemy. All food and drink was tasted by servants before being eaten by the royal family, and the royal gardens and well were tested every day for contamination.

Even with these precautions, Joseph would buy produce from the markets and other farms, and cook three different meals and then select which meal the family ate. The tasters were constantly changed and had to eat all food one hour before the family ate so as to test that the food was not poisoned. It was a cumbersome and difficult process to undergo daily with all the precautions, but they thwarted many attempts on the royal family's lives from Set's assassins.

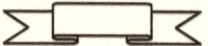

Bluma had become invaluable to the royal household, and often would stand and watch Joseph and Isis making love in the chambers hidden from view. Bluma recognized Joseph really loved Isis, and she really loved him, and their love for Horus was also evident in everything they did. The Spartan lifestyle of the Scythian woman did have love, but home life was more about monitoring the progress of their children on strict training routines. There were no cuddles, kisses, and hugs, which Horus got in abundance from Isis, Joseph, and even the servants.

Everybody loved Horus; of course, even Bluma, but she never showed her feelings ever in public. She was ashamed that she cried in public when her wife was killed by the coward General Ptah. When she watched Joseph and Isis in private, she understood why people married now, as Joseph and Isis were completely different as husband and wife than as queen and lord of the realm. She marvelled at how they changed roles so easily. Isis was very lucky. Though Joseph was a strict man and ruthless as her servant when she was queen, he was gentle and kind as a husband and father. He would play with the boy Horus, all the time teaching him how to play a game, or do an exercise, always with love and affection.

It was clear Joseph loved Isis. Joseph always was always attentive to his wife in their private chambers, and sex came naturally to both of them. He never seemed to demand sex, but regularly mounted Isis as part of the way they cemented their love physically. He was a good lover, being well endowed, his manhood was long and thick, so Isis always was satisfied, and cried out in ecstasy on nearly every occasion. Unlike many men, he often performed oral sex on his wife, and she lay on the couch, her legs apart, enjoying the experience. Being from an all-female couple Bluma found oral sex was often the highlight of the sexual experience, as ebony, wood, or even ivory phallic toys were not the same as the feel of a man. Still when she considered everything in balance, she preferred being a lesbian to being a wife to a husband. It was demanding being a wife, and she was not prepared to give anyone that kind of commitment or attention. Still, she thought it would be interesting having Joseph plough her for a week. She was going to ask the queen if it could be next week.

The integration of the Scythian women had been easier than General Hakim had envisaged, and General Bluma was a joy to work with, always disciplined, and any order was carried out instantly. She had other duties guarding the royal family from time to time, and spent time with her daughter's training officer occasionally, but other than that, she worked on her duties for the army. Her women were completely obedient; there was never any disobedience or argument, and every one of them was excellent at whatever role they were assigned.

Hakim was pleased that General Bluma had killed the stupid and arrogant General Ptah, as he was the weak link in his chain of command. Malik was resourceful, and clearly had the best command brain of all the generals; only Joseph had better battle plans.

Ikandar, Sayyid, and Kushi were solid commanders in the battlefield; they did not panic, and they carried out commands. His son Heru was the bravest of all these commanders, and although competent, was over confident sometimes and need careful handling. General Bluma would command the strike force division of the Scythian women, so Hakim had a vacancy for a general for one of his divisions. He needed to think about whom to select, as a weak commander could result in a lost battle and death to most of the army.

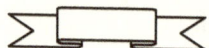

Joseph also was thinking about the replacement general when General Bluma asked for an audience with Queen Isis and Lord Joseph. Joseph was a bit surprised, because she had been on duty the previous night.

"General Bluma," said Joseph. "You wanted to see the queen and me in our chambers?"

"Yes, Lord," said Bluma. "You may recall, you promised to mate with me for one week, so I could conceive a child."

"Yes, I remember," said Joseph.

"It is now time," said Bluma. "I would like to mate together tonight."

"Oh," said Joseph, "why now?"

"We feel the right time instinctively," said Bluma.

"My Queen," said Joseph, "do I still have your permission?"

"You do, my husband," said Isis, "but where will you actually mate?"

"I don't know. Bluma, where do you suggest?" asked Joseph.

"I had not thought of that," said Bluma, "but if the queen does not object, why not in these chambers?"

"What? In front of me and the child?" said Isis.

"The boy is too young to understand," said Bluma, "and I watch you mate when I am here on duty."

"Really?" said Isis. "Don't you turn away embarrassed?"

"No," said Bluma, "it is normal, like defecating or urinating, so I am not embarrassed to plough Joseph in front of his wife and the child."

"You may not be embarrassed, but I may be," said Isis. "I don't know how I am going to react."

"Joseph is not my lover, my Queen, he is yours," said Bluma. "He does this as a duty to bind us together and to provide sperm for a new child in my belly. People, particularly nobles, often couple openly at parties in the palace."

"It is true," said Isis, "but your husband coupling with another in your own bedchamber may be different. I won't know until it happens."

"Let us do it now and get it out of the way," said Bluma, "not have the thoughts festering before the event."

"Very well," said Isis, "I will sit where we normally do on the balcony. You both can be on the bed together."

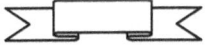

It was not unusual for nobles to take servants or slaves to their wife's bedchambers and have sex with both women at the same time. Even male servants were taken to the bedchamber to service the wife and husband, so it was not an unusual event. With intermarriage in the family allowed, sex was very open in Ta-Mehu and not considered a taboo subject. The concept of fidelity and abstinence were uncommon among the nobles and merchants, but couples did differ widely in how they treated wives and husbands with regards to performing sex with other people in front of each other. Osiris, her first husband, had never had sex with her, nor had she seen him having sex with a woman, or a man. She understood that he liked both men and women.

Bluma took off her uniform and weapons and stood naked near the bed. She was a magnificent specimen, perhaps taller than Joseph, but slimmer and with defined muscles that clearly showed her strength. She was nevertheless a woman, and her blond pubic hair in a perfect triangle could be clearly seen. Joseph, broader and darker-skinned, had also stripped; all his muscles were bigger and more powerful. Ignoring Isis watching them, he gently guided her to the bed. Isis could feel his touch, not just see it as he gently opened up Bluma with his fingers stroking inside her, his mouth gently sucking her breasts in turn. Joseph mounted Bluma, her legs spread wide, her vagina open and inviting, and he thrust his manhood inside; her cry was that of contentment. He rode as he did Isis and all women, very hard, gripping her bottom, forcing his finger in her rear, and thrusting deeper and deeper inside her. He held his rhythm, until clinging to her frame, he ejaculated inside her, and Bluma cried out in ecstasy.

Isis listened quietly as they mated for the first time, and seeing Horus was happily asleep, looked to her husband, who now held Bluma in his arms on the bed.

Isis rose, and her husband motioned her to come to the bed, and she crossed the room and removed her simple sheath dress and lay on the opposite side of Bluma beside Joseph.

Joseph smiled, and releasing Bluma, he kissed his wife. Opening her legs with his hands, he gestured to Bluma to join him in pleasing Isis. Bluma came between Isis' legs, and opening the lips of her vagina, gently licked her inner core as Joseph gently kissed her nipples. It was a strange feeling Isis felt, having two people pleasuring her at the same time, particularly as one of them was a woman, something she had never experienced before. Bluma was an experienced lover, and stroked and probed with her fingers, as well as skilfully used her tongue to tease her vagina into an orgasm.

As she was nearing a climax, Joseph moved Bluma away and mounted her, and with hard, swift strokes, his manhood brought her quickly to a climax, her arms and legs pulling Joseph inside her. As she opened her eyes, her husband still inside her, she saw his hand now probed inside Bluma, and feeling an affinity towards her, she reached out and they clasped hands lovingly. Joseph moved Bluma's head between Isis' legs, and mounted her from behind, and as he rammed himself into Bluma, he could see Isis' lovely face contorted in ecstasy as he brought both Bluma and himself to a climax. The night was long, and the three of them slept little as Joseph mounted both of them often in every position.

Joseph noted that Bluma often pleasured Isis, but Isis never gave Bluma oral sex, even though she often gave Joseph oral sex, and they both licked and sucked Joseph's manhood at the same time. Eventually, as the night was becoming daybreak, all three of them fell asleep.

Joseph awoke to his penis being sucked by Bluma, and as his eyes opened, she climbed on top of him and pushed his penis inside her. When he spent his seed inside her, she moved to his side and held him. Joseph wrapped one arm around each woman and held them to his body.

"What do you think of the officers?" asked Joseph of Bluma.

"Many are really nobles pretending to be officers," said Bluma, "but the core is good and applies themselves correctly."

"Are there any that stand out suitable to be considered as a general?" asked Joseph.

"Maybe two: Semerkhet and Menes," said Bluma. "Both men are good soldiers and well thought of by the men. But of course, I don't' know how good they would be commanding a division with twenty officers below them."

"What about the officers nominated as substitutes in the event of death in battle of one of the generals?" asked Joseph.

"All useless," said Bluma. "They have been picked politically, not on merit as a soldier."

Isis was still asleep or pretended to be. "Thank you, Bluma. Well, I need to bathe before my duties for the day, but first, let me do my duty to you again," said Joseph, and he turned Bluma on her front so he could mount her from the rear. Unlike most of last night, Joseph was quick and efficient, spilling his seed in her after a few strokes and withdrawing swiftly.

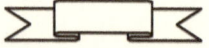

He learned that the two officers, Semerkhet and Menes, were very much rivals, not nobles, but soldiers who had attained the level of company commanders by bravery, hard work, and exceptional leadership qualities. Both men had much to commend them, but were very different from each other. Semerkhet was a large man, nearly six feet and built like an ox, and was very broad shouldered, with large muscles. He spoke very quietly, was slow to lose his temper, and he considered things slowly but usually was right. Menes was small in stature and wiry. Immensely brave, he would fight any man and would triumph often with speed and guile. He was quick-witted and loud, brilliant sometimes, but occasionally completely wrong. He once had picked a fight with his rival Semerkhet, and that had been a mistake, and all his guile and speed could not prevent a sound beating.

"Hakim, have you considered the general's vacancy?" asked Joseph.

"Yes, for some time," said Hakim. "There are several worthy nobles who all command respect and would make excellent generals."

"Hakim, we both know if we lose against Set in a battle because we select a noble for a general who is not good enough, we will regret it the hard way, by having our balls cut off and stuffed in our mouths," said Joseph graphically. "So who can actually do the job?"

"Either Semerkhet and Menes, both are very good," said Hakim. "Menes is bright; Semerkhet is steadier."

"Who would you select in a last-ditch battle with your balls on the line?" asked Joseph.

"Semerkhet," said Hakim.

"Very well," said Joseph. "We shall appoint Semerkhet. Bring him here so we can talk together."

Having been wrestling, Semerkhet was naked when he arrived to see the general, his toga over his shoulder.

"Forgive my appearance, Lord Joseph, General Hakim, I was training the men," said Semerkhet.

"Put your toga on man," said General Hakim, "and don't come into the tent like that again."

"Yes, my General," said Semerkhet.

"We have a vacancy for general. Who do you consider equal to the task?" asked Hakim.

"Other than myself, only Menes," said Semerkhet, not humiliated.

"Why not some of your noble officers?" asked Joseph.

"Merely window dressing," said Semerkhet. "They shit themselves in battle and rely on their platoon commander to carry them through. We need clear, decisive action at the divisional level."

"You have been recommended to me by General Hakim," said Joseph. "Who would you appoint as your deputy?"

"Nobody, unless it is a proper position with pay and status," said Semerkhet.

"What pay and status is required?" asked Joseph.

"The deputy divisional general should have three-quarters of the pay of a general," said Semerkhet. "If the general falls in battle, he will lead, but should be selected to compliment the general."

"Who would you choose as your deputy?" asked Joseph.

"Mendes, without question," said Semerkhet.

"Why Mendes?" asked Joseph.

"Quicker in thought than me and can be brilliantly right," said Semerkhet, "but also wrong, he will be proud to show me alternatives to consider during the battle."

"Good," said Joseph. "General Hakim, replace all the useless nobles; we don't need their wealth anymore. Appoint Semerkhet and Mendes, and find deputies for every general, commander, and platoon leader based on merit."

"Yes, Lord Joseph," said General Hakim, smiling. He would enjoy booting some of those nobles out of his army.

Joseph made his way to the palace, and wondered if he would enjoy both his wife and his general again another night.

Chapter Twenty-One

Nearly two happy years had passed since the battle at Cyrene, and Joseph and Isis were still blissfully happy, their harmony untouched by the birth just over a year ago of Nabiti, the golden lady. Nabiti, her blond locks from her mother, and her golden skin from her father Joseph, had come from the week of coupling with Bluma after nine months. A healthy and stunningly pretty child, the girl had been a joy to all the Scythian women's children. The child was being brought up within the palace playing with the Pharaoh Horus, and officially was adopted by Isis and Joseph. Isis adored the little girl she always had wanted, and played with her all the time, lavishing love and affection on her. Bluma now spent every evening she was in Memphis at the palace, a second wife of sorts to Joseph, sleeping with Isis and Joseph quite naturally. They ate together, made love, and played with the children.

Horus, now approaching four, was becoming competitive, and Bluma trained him in the arts of combat she would only reveal to Scythian women, and the little boy was adept at every skill even at the tender age of four. Horus, large for his age, his physique a miniature of Osiris many said, was slimmer than Joseph, but muscular, a real future Adonis. Horus played often with the baby, liking the fact she was a girl, and often sitting with his mother Isis entertaining the toddler with handmade toys in her cot or crawling on the floor beside her to encourage her to walk. He very quickly grew attached to Bluma as a second mother, and watched, fascinated now in their private chamber, as Joseph ploughed both his mother Isis and his second wife Bluma.

Of course, having more than one wife was not uncommon in Ta-Mehu, and many men had more than one wife. Even some noble women had more than one husband, but that was more unusual. There were no laws regarding marriage or divorce in Ta-Mehu, only custom. The first wife was the head of the household domestically, and any other wives must obey her. All children she produced were to inherit the wealth of the family. Any children of other wives must make their own way in the world, although they often were given land, or gold to make the journey easier.

Bluma never had intended to become a wife of Joseph; the plan was to spend a week coupling, and then return to her lonely existence in the Scythian Army. Her daughter Zahra was already sixteen and a soldier, and like Bluma, she was a remarkable woman soldier, athlete, and leader. Isis persuaded Bluma to sometimes bring Zahra to the palace, but Zahra found it awkward in the presence of the queen and Joseph, and preferred the company of her friends in the army barracks. At seventeen, she would become of coupling age and become pregnant by a man following the Scythian tradition. Bluma continued to fiercely defend all traditions regarding the Scythian women, but outlawed punishments any more for taking a man as their partner. The choice was now the woman's, but few took this course, preferring to marry women and live as they always had, as soldier women.

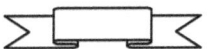

The army had developed into a formidable force since the battle of Cyrene. The cadre of officers had changed, so the company and troop levels were efficient and effective officers dedicated to their profession. The nobles largely had left, except those who clearly had the aptitude to be soldiers.

Training was harder; they had to be able to run twenty miles carrying two heavy shields, a spear, and their sword, and fight a mock battle on arrival. The fighting skills of the Scythian women could not all be employed by the men, but some fighting skills were added to training, as were a greater number of battle plans to be drilled.

More archers on foot were added, as were chariots and horses to the army. The heavy shields only were used in training now, and were replaced with the lighter steel shields and all the soldiers were armoured with the light steel breast and back plates with arm and leg coverings. Elephants were introduced also, as heavy cavalry, but they had only twenty, and like the Cyrene Army, they would be unpredictable in battle. The use of fire, digging ditches, and spiking the ground all were practiced endlessly, and became second nature to the army.

Semerkhet was a popular replacement for General Ptah and got on well with his fellow generals as did Deputy Menes. The other five generals soon had able deputies, and soon the generals and their deputies became a pair, going everywhere together.

The projects kept the men busy and fit, and with the help of the Atlanteans, viaducts were built into three of the major cities, providing water for the population. A tomb in the shape of a pyramid was built at Sakkara to the wonder of the world, and another was planned at Abydos. The learning temple in Memphis was contracted and become operational, with the scribes providing scrolls in a library for others to read; this became popular. Schools of learning grew around the temple, and a loose collection of scholars formed an alliance of learning, teaching different subjects and exchanging students. Atlanteans' culture and technology was one of the subjects most sought after, and their influence developed the culture and tolerance within Ta-Mehu.

Joseph met with Quaashie and Rashidi to discuss the queen's coffers and he met two very happy men revelling in the glory of their wisdom.

"So Quaashie, how do the queen's coffers grow?" asked Joseph.

"Well, my Lord Joseph," said Quaashie, "tribute arrives from all over the region as the battle of Cyrene grows in magnitude, and the power of the Coffin of Destiny and the Pharaoh Horus grows daily."

"And you, Rashidi, what do you have to add?" asked Joseph.

Rashidi looked to Quaashie before replying, and Quaashie nodded approval. "Our grain stores are full, and we build more grain stores for our own harvest. Water is stored in wells for a drought, the cities are becoming cleaner with this new sanitation being introduced, and our buildings are more organized and planned within our expanding cities. We have made much progress," said Rashidi.

"What else do we need to do to improve our economy and the lives of our people?" asked Joseph.

"For now, we have enough change," said Quaashie. "Some families marry more. More men are taking second wives to follow the Lord Joseph. The knowledge of the Atlanteans is much to absorb, and our greater power and army brings us wealth to distribute."

"Rashidi, what do you think?" asked Joseph.

"I agree with my master Quaashie: We have enough progress for now. Expansion would be a mistake and destroy all we have built to date. Expanding too fast will dilute all our wealth, and our focus will be lost," said Rashidi.

"What if Ta-Shemau invades our lands and we defeat them in battle?" asked Joseph.

"Defeat them and send them packing," said Quaashie, "but if we occupy, we will overreach ourselves like Set did and soon lose the colony again and have a weaker homeland, one beset with troubles."

Joseph looked at Rashidi for his contribution and he looked again to Quaashie, who nodded. "Our society needs a generation to develop these new ideas and have them firm in our culture, and then we can spread them abroad," said Rashidi. "If we occupy defeated territory, we will not have enough leaders to rule and develop those territories to our culture."

"Very interesting, gentlemen," said Joseph. "I will ponder on your thoughts and discuss them with the queen."

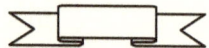

Joseph was sure the army being built by Set would invade Ta-Mehu in the near future. From his sources, he heard the army was to be thirty thousand men strong, a larger force than the Ta-Mehu Army, but he was unconcerned about being out numbered. The weapons and tactics, he understood from his spies, were to remain the same: the heavy metal shields and the shorter spears and swords. Joseph decided to discuss Set with Isis and Bluma.

"Set will invade Ta-Mehu soon, my love," he said, touching the shoulder of Isis as he watched the two children playing on the floor with Bluma.

"I know," said Isis, "and our idyllic world will be disrupted."

"If we lose the battle, Set will try to kill you and Horus," said Joseph.

"Of course," said Isis, "but we shall win."

"If we win, will you leave Memphis for El-Kab to rule there?" asked Joseph.

"No, our rule is still very young here, and we have much to do in Ta-Mehu. We need to remain here and develop our country," said Isis. "Leave Ta- Shemau to Set or whoever to rule for now; it will be Horus who will unite our country when he is a man."

"Are you sure?" asked Joseph.

"I am sure, husband," said Isis, "but what of you, Bluma, would you rule Ta-Shemau if we defeat Set?"

"No. Rather they pay tribute like the other nations. Like you, I worry over expansion," said Bluma.

"And Set, would you let him live?" asked Joseph.

"Yes. He will provide the strong rule to raise and pay the tribute," said Isis.

"Let's hope we win then," said Joseph, "because we don't seem to have another plan," and they all laughed.

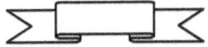

Set carefully spread the rumour that the army was thirty thousand strong, a huge number, when in fact it was nearer to forty-five thousand. It was difficult to keep it from Ammon because of the cost, so he bluffed about the figures when Ammon came to see him.

"You say the general has disobeyed me, Ammon?" said Set.

"Yes, Lord, they lie. The army cost is for about forty thousand men, and beasts must be over ten thousand," said Ammon. "The rumour is it is for an invasion of Ta-Mehu."

"They are wrong, Ammon," said Set. "Leave this with me and send any rumour monger to me to be put to death."

Of course, Ammon would send none, and was confused about Set and his intentions. Then, an envoy from Eblan arrived to announce that ten thousand warrior mercenaries had arrived at the port of Amarna and would be ready in two days to set sail again to invade Ta-Mehu. Set gathered his generals. Like the Ta-Mehu army, the army of Ta-Shemau was divided into five divisions: four of foot soldiers and one of chariots. The four divisions now had ten thousand soldiers in each, and there were five thousand horses and chariots. When they took to the field they would outnumber the Ta-Mehu Army two to one. To make the Ta-Mehu position more difficult, he would strike at the rear of the Ta-Mehu Army with his Eblan Army. All his generals concluded that the simultaneous strike would be impossible for the much smaller army to resist.

"Generals, we march on Ta-Mehu with all haste," said Set, "our battle plan is drawn, and our men ready for battle."

The generals nodded in agreement; it was a good plan, and over two years of planning, they had remodelled a much larger army.

"My Pharaoh, we outmatch them, but they have the divine one, Horus, and march behind the Coffin of Destiny," said General Nakhte, the commander of the army.

"These are myths created by the Ta-Mehu," said Set. "We made the coffin for Osiris to lure him to his death; it is not magical."

"It is well known, the story of Osiris, my Pharaoh; however, the men believe when he was hacked to death and reassembled in the coffin it got magical powers," said General Nakhte.

"Make an example of all men who tell that story," said Set, "and torture and kill them."

"My Pharaoh we would have to kill all the men," said General Nakhte. "The only way we can dispel the myth is to strike quickly in the battle and decisively, then the men will gain heart and fight like lions."

"Does not my plan please you, General Nakhte?" asked Set, furious.

"My Pharaoh, it is too cautious. Even with the better ground, we wait for the foe to attack; this will weaken the men's resolve in my view," said General Nakhte, as always, brave and unafraid to die for telling the truth.

"General Ponahasi, how say you?" asked Set of the barbarian. The general was feared for his bravery and ferocious tactics.

"My Pharaoh, I will follow any command to the death," said General Ponahasi, "but I agree with General Nakhte: Our first move must be offensive to raise the spirits of the men."

"General Nuri, what say you?" asked the pharaoh. Nuri was regarded as the master of tactics, small and slender for a soldier, but his brain was quick and decisive and he was brave to a fault.

"I disagree. Use the better ground, fight an attrition battle, and take no chances; the pharaoh's plan is a good one," said Nuri.

"And Bakari, your view?" asked Set of the oldest general, who at nearly fifty was a veteran of many campaigns.

"The men need to see the foe defeated quickly, or will lose heart. Battle plans and tactics are important, but will and determination will win the day, regardless of numbers," said Bakari. "Punishment, threats of death, even the demise of his family will not stop a soldier running from the field. I say attack simultaneously on the plain in front of Memphis; don't use the ground advantage and hope the Ta-Mehu Army attack us."

"Ahmose and Eso who do you agree with Nakhte or Nuri?" asked Set, cleverly now giving Nuri the plan he had devised now that there was doubt from his generals.

"General Nakhte," said Ahmose. "My men fear the Scythian women, the Coffin of Destiny, and the divine Horus; they need to charge, not stand and defend."

"General Nuri," said Eso, "the pharaoh's plan is sound; there is no need to change the plan."

"So we have a dilemma," said Set, "but I agree with General Nakhte, we outmatch the foe, so perhaps I am over cautious. We shall follow his plan and attack the army from the rear with the Eblan Army, and ourselves from the front and sides, and encircle them on the plains of Memphis."

"My Pharaoh, what are our plans for retreat if our plan fails?" asked General Nuri.

The other generals nodded grimly. They knew their fate if they failed, but there was no need to tell them, that was no encouragement to the generals, thought Nakhte, but he was pleased that they would attack and not wait for the oncoming Ta-Mehu Army. One aspect he was unhappy about as he commanded the field was that he would have no contact with the Eblan Army. Their involvement in the battle was uncertain in his mind, and the pharaoh only spoke to their leader, Ashai.

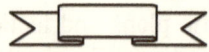

Ashai had a name from the Ta-Shemau people, as his mother was from this land and his father an Eblan, so he had reason to side with Set against the Ta-Mehu Army. He was an inflexible and arrogant general who would not ever admit he was wrong, even to a superior. He believed with their numbers and outflanking the smaller army of Ta-Mehu, they should attack, not defend, even going onto the plain in front of Memphis and risking defeat. His argument was that the Ta-Mehu Army would be surprised by the plan and even with their Coffin of Destiny and divine Horus, would lose heart when their twenty thousand men faced fifty thousand soldiers surrounding them on an open plain.

When Ashai received his battle plan, he smiled; Pharaoh Set had changed his mind. They would make history on the plains of Memphis, and Ashai would become a legend for all time. His men, being the nearest to the city of Memphis, would reach there first at the end of the battle, and he planned to rape and plunder as much as they could from the rich city. He hoped Isis and Bluma, the wives of Joseph, were still alive, as he wanted to plough them both in front of Joseph before he chopped them to pieces before his eyes.

Chapter Twenty-Two

When news came that the Ta-Shemau Army had arrived and were positioned on the hill facing the city, Joseph was not surprised or alarmed. The count of the army exceeded the estimates he had of thirty thousand and was close to forty-five thousand. The news that the Eblan Army was behind them with a force of ten thousand soldiers was a surprise and required a revised plan, which he quickly prepared. It was a daring and extravagant plan. Preparation of the plain in front of the city walls had been made over the last two years, and nearly all the mock battles were based on the Ta-Shemau Army taking the better position on the hill opposite the plain. The army generals gathered in a conference led by Hakim.

"We face two forces that are twice our size and surround us," said Joseph. "We shall deploy the division of Semerkhet to face the Eblan Army, and deploy the heavy beasts and Scythian women against them in the hope they defeat them quickly. Half the foot archers and half the chariots will be used in this battle. The remaining three divisions will face forward, left, and right in a square, as we will be surrounded. The front-facing rank will be Ikandar. Malik, you relinquish your rank as deputy commander and take the right flank, were I expect the main thrust. Sayyid, you will take the left flank; if what I say is correct, give the order of one in five of your platoons to deploy to the right. Kushi, you will replace Malik as deputy to the field general, who will be myself. General Hakim, you will act as an advisor to your son Heru. Heru, you will deploy three-quarters of your remaining chariots and all your archers on the right of the field. They will not be used until I give the order. I will take the field from the centre of the army and have posted lookouts on the city walls to signal the enemy's movements. All of you will follow my commands to the letter. Understood?"

The generals nodded grimly. They were grossly over matched and it should be a formality if Set used the correct tactics.

"Bluma, I want you to command your troops and break the Eblan Army so our troops can pour through and defeat them quickly and return to the field to help against the Ta-Shemau Army," said Joseph. "I want two suicide groups of warriors to risk all to attack the position of General Nakhte and Set and try and kill them, twenty in each group, supported by chariots and archers. They will circle the field of battle and attack at the peak of the battle."

"I will choose the best women," said Bluma.

"Hear me well, Bluma," said Joseph. "This is a direct order: Your daughter Zahra is assigned to guard our Queen Isis and Horus, who will take the field with the army. The Coffin of Destiny and our royal family are her priority. Tell her to come to me for special instructions."

"I understand," said Bluma, relieved.

The Ta-Mehu Army took to the field and arranged itself very carefully in the centre, too far away from archers close to the city walls or from the Ta-Shemau position. The armies of the Eblan and Ta-Shemau would need to come to the plain and attack, as Joseph was relying on the arrogance of Nakhte and Ponahasi, two generals he knew of as offensive in strategy. He considered Set and their tactician Nuri conservative, and would hold position and wait on the better ground. If he was wrong, then they had lost already. The next gamble was the thrust; it was a feint to the front and right, which would leave the Ta-Mehu Army facing the Ta-Shemau Army. Then, they would surge on the left, which would be the right-hand side of the Ta-Mehu Army. He needed his best general, Hakim, in command of the archers to execute the volleys at the exact moment of the surge and the chariots to attack exactly, otherwise he was lost.

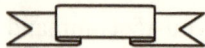

The Ta-Mehu position looked strange to Nakhte, and he murmured under his breath. He could see the Coffin of Destiny and the infant boy Horus paraded in front of all the troops, and there were gasps from his own troops at the sight. He was going to triumph today, he thought, they are surrounded and out matched, and they had a spy in their camp. He saw the movement of the men to the right and knew this was where they expected the attack. He knew of the ditches in the ground and the boards marking positions over which you could pass. His troops were prepared, and they would not use the attack chariots until the Eblan Army had defeated the rear of the army. Even if they were not successful, they would occupy one quarter of the Ta-Mehu force. Of course, he knew of the elephants, and the Eblan was prepared, they would open their ranks as the Ta-Mehu Army did and let them through. *What a waste of time.* They would then kill the women as the Ta-Mehu Army had with long spears. *Pity though*, he mused, *ploughing those women after they were defeated, would have been fun.*

General Nakhte raised his arm, and the messengers flagged the advance. There was no signal to retreat, and every man knew retreat was death. He watched as his men moved forward, the main column to his right, which the Ta-Mehu expected; they would change just before the charge.

Joseph saw the oncoming columns and nodded to Zahra; her sword already drawn, she cut off the head of Kushi with a war cry. A women warrior beside Malik, supposedly to guard him, stabbed him in the throat, killing him. Joseph threw up his right hand, and a blue and yellow flag was waved. The gates of the city opened and the elephants came charging towards the rear of the Eblan Army. Archers appeared at the wall ramparts, and under the order of Hakim, began raining arrows on the troops at the rear of the Eblan. The troops, as Joseph had guessed, knowing archers were positioned left and right to fire on them, positioned themselves out of range and too near the city walls. As the arrows fell and the soldiers realised they were vulnerable at the rear, the soldiers with the shields and long spears at the front tried to retreat to the rear, confusing the army. The elephants then hit the troops, trampling them underfoot. They stabbed the beasts with spears, and the beasts went wild, trampling them everywhere, and the soldiers, in their panic, collided into each other, knocking each other down. The Scythian women arrived at the unguarded, confused rear and began the slaughter with two swords, one in each hand, and no shields. The soldiers at the front with the big shields and long spears were now in the middle, trapped by their own men. The division led by Semerkhet walked to the enemy in a line of steel and began killing the defenceless men with the long spears. It was a massacre.

From his right, an arrow flew and killed an officer in front of Nakhte, and he turned to signal a change to the attack, only to receive an arrow in the throat and more raining on his body. He died realizing both assassination teams had been sent to kill him, as his

263

troops already had captured the group they thought had been sent to kill him.

Menes had been sent to the right, and took command of Malik's division, and he ordered half the division left to bolster the side to be attacked by the Ta-Shemau Army. The slaughter of the Eblan Army was nearly complete, and Semerkhet was breaking away with half his troops to back up a charge to be led by General Hakim to the rear of the Ta-Shemau main army. It was a move Menes had suggested in secret to Hakim and Joseph, when he secretly was told of their plan to kill the traitors Malik and Kushi when the battle started. Hakim was a wonderful brave soldier, a man you would follow, and Joseph knew he needed such a man to win the day.

Set watched the battle from a vantage point, and was a little disturbed to see the attack of the Eblan Army vanquished by a far inferior force. The main attack was on the right, and aware of the ditches, they carried planks of wood to cross the ditches, all the size of ten feet in length to cover the eight-foot ditches. The men seemed startled, and he saw them falling into the ditches, pushed by their comrades. *What was the problem*, he wondered.

Joseph saw the soldiers falling into the ditches because they were fifteen feet wide and twenty feet deep, dug secretly by the Semerkhet division. Their planks reached the other side because they had built columns in the middle in certain positions that could use ten foot planks. Both Malik and Kushi thought all the ditches were the same width. At the bottom of each ditch were oil and spikes, so the men falling first were killed by the spikes and soaked in oil. At Joseph's signal, they now fired lit arrows into the ditch, and the men falling on their dead comrades were being burned alive. The column now turned and pushed to go back, shouting for the men of the right column to retreat and they pushed against each other in confusion.

The men under Hakim now attacked, cutting through the centre of the Ta-Shemau column in a V-shaped formation with long spears and the lighter shields; they were fresh. Whilst carrying the heavier shields and shorter spears, the Ta-Shemau Army was tired and disheartened. Ta-Mehu men shouted for Horus and the Coffin of Destiny, and the Ta-Shemau men tried to flee, being killed easily as they dropped their shields, exhausted by the rush of the long attack from the high position on the hill they originally had occupied. The right of the Ta-Mehu column now advanced, and crossing the ditch with longer planks, and using the correct crossing points, they reformed and advanced as the right flank of Ta-Shemau Army fled. Heru, under his father's orders was now harrying the rear of the Ta-Shemau, so the soldiers were being killed from three sides. The weaker front and left attacks were now advanced upon by the Ta-Mehu Army, and the soldiers, seeing the slaughter of the main army to their right, dropped their weapons and fled the field of battle.

Set had seen enough, and defeated, fled the field, furious he had not stuck to his original plan. He had been outsmarted by a bloody woman, Isis, and her bastard husband, Joseph, *a dammed Eblan himself.*

The battle had been a disaster for both the Eblan and the Ta-Shemau armies. Of the ten thousand Eblan who had taken the field, only three thousand survived, all of whom were sold into slavery, except Ashai, who was captured alive to face Queen Isis. The Ta-Shemau

Army fared even worse: Some fifteen thousand men were killed in the battle, and over twenty thousand were captured, as they feared death by Set for retreating. All the generals were taken.

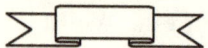

The Ta-Shemau generals were stripped of their weapons and armour and whipped naked, tied to a tree, and then in chains brought to the palace to see Queen Isis and Lord Joseph. When they arrived at the great hall, the Coffin of Destiny was on a plinth, and Queen Isis sat on the throne of the queen, her small son Horus on the throne of the pharaoh. Lord Joseph stood beside them.

The Ta-Shemau Generals Ahmose, Bakari, Eso, Ponahasi, and Nuri were bleeding from their whipping, and humiliated, they stood sullenly before their conquerors.

"Generals of the Ta-Shemau Army, you come to invade Ta-Mehu with ten thousand Eblan and forty-five thousand Ta-Shemau soldiers. Eighteen thousand men lie on the battlefield, and some twenty-three thousand are captured, destined for slavery. Your pharaoh has fled the field and your other soldiers run to hide," said Joseph. "Now we have to decide what to do with you."

"Lord Joseph, we are soldiers and expect to be killed," said General Ponahasi, "so make it quick, and with the dignity you would expect at your end."

"You are a brave man, Ponahasi," said Joseph, "we all knew that, but foolhardy and headstrong. Before I kill you, tell me how you knew Malik and Kushi would betray Ta-Mehu."

"We had some of Malik's family who did not leave El-Kab in time, and Kushi was his brother, so neither really needed much persuading," said Nuri.

266

"Who are you?" asked Joseph.

"General Nuri," replied Nuri.

"Nuri, you have a reputation for battle tactics; what went wrong?" asked Joseph.

"I recommended we stay on the hill and let you come to us. In that way we would choose the ground and have the better position, which would have meant our poorer tactics would have prevailed based on numbers," said Nuri. "We relied too much on the information Malik fed us, much of which was wrong, and obviously you gave him that information to feed us with false tactics, incorrect sizes of ditches, and positioning of troops."

"Of course, General Nuri," said Joseph.

"Now we all know the truth, do as Ponahasi asks: Kill us quickly, with dignity," said Nuri.

"I am not going to kill you, Nuri, but you will remember the day you lost in battle to the Ta-Mehu Army, who is invincible. Take these generals outside, whip them again, and throw salt in their wounds to close them. Then, chop off their sword hands and bind them so they don't bleed to death. Then take them and send them with an envoy to the Pharaoh Set with a list of our demands," said Joseph, pointing to all of the generals except Nuri. "Take General Nuri to the dungeons; we have a special way for him to meet his end."

The next day, Nuri, bathed and dressed in a linen toga, stood before Joseph.

"Let me introduce you to two special women," said Joseph, and he waved a hand. Two very beautiful women under twenty came in the room. "This is Ebe and Femi," said Joseph, "they were the lovers of Malik and Kushi and were ploughed and abused by the two men daily. We know all about the plot, because these women belong to the Society of Horus. Show him," said Joseph.

The two ladies pulled up their shifts and showed their naked bodies below the waist. Their pubic hair had been shaven, and there was the Eye of Horus tattooed there.

"Normally, pubic hair would cover this sign, and lovers and husbands would never know they are ploughing a spy," said Joseph, "and when a man has spent his seed in women, he is weak and talks too much, with wine or beer to help him to be indiscreet."

"Why do you tell me this?" asked Nuri.

"We need people who have nowhere else to go to work for the Society of the Eye of Horus, people who can set a trap, read a plot, be resourceful, and I think you are such a man," said Joseph.

"What would I get in return for my allegiance and work, other than my life?" asked Nuri.

"Well lots of willing girls to plough, some gold, and a life away from battles, planning, and conniving the downfalls of kings and pharaohs," said Joseph, smiling. "Of course, nobody will know you exist, and you will not receive any honours or attend royal functions, and you cannot have a prominent place in the court."

"Why choose me?" asked Nuri. "You seem very adept at sleight of hand and plotting against your enemies."

"In this life, we have only so many things we can do in a day, and the more people you have helping you, the better," said Joseph.

"Horus and his legacy will live for centuries, and hopefully his children will rule a united country in peace and bounty for centuries. Somebody in his formative years needs to guide him to that destiny, and that task has fallen to me. When people only think of Horus as a myth and the dynasty of pharaohs has disappeared like the Atlanteans' demise, and the followers melt into another culture, as they now do with ours, I want the secret society of the Eye of Horus to keep the symbols of Horus and Osiris safe, and the truth of Isis, Horus, and Osiris alive in the hearts of men."

"What about the Lord Joseph?" said Nuri? "You are an exceptional tactician and general, and a great and wise leader, what about your legacy?" asked Nuri.

"I have no legacy. It will confuse the true messages of Horus if we start giving credit for the victories to many people," said Joseph. "The Society of the Eye of Horus must concentrate at each event to mould the story positively to Horus, Isis, or Osiris; all around them must be incidental."

"But what does Horus stand for? What is the message?" asked Nuri.

"All that is good in man: fairness, kindness to each other, bravery, sacrifice for others, and abstinence. All the things we men find hard to follow in life," said Joseph. "But I cannot say what Horus will say when he speaks as a man; that must develop naturally."

"What if Horus is not such a man as you believe he will become?" said Nuri.

"Then there will be no legacy. No Society of the Eye of Horus, no myths to preserve, no symbol of hope for all men and all women to follow," said Joseph. "You cannot make a person good, or manufacture a myth; they must come from within a person. Horus is a very special boy and will be a very special man."

"Let me be honest, my Lord Joseph. I need convincing to believe such a man can exist," said Nuri.

"Come," Joseph said to Nuri, and he led Nuri to the garden were the children were playing with Isis and

Bluma. They had invited other children to the garden as they did occasionally, and the children varied in age from about twelve to crawling infants like Horus' sister Nabiti.

"Let us sit here and watch the children for a moment," said Joseph.

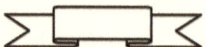

Bluma was teaching the boys to throw a discus, an object used in sports competitions and in training to strengthen the arms. Horus was four and large for his age, and perhaps could be taken for a boy of six, but the boys of twelve were twice his size and weight and therefore naturally stronger. The Atlanteans had brought the discus as a present to the court, and Bluma showed the children how to throw the wooden discus, standing still with just her arm, and each of the children tried to varying degrees of success. The largest boy threw the discus nearly halfway the length of the garden, and was applauded with his effort, his chest swelling with pride. Horus was the last to throw, and he held the discus easily in his right hand. Unlike the other boys, who simply threw with their arm, Horus spun his whole body in a circle, his arm releasing the disc when his rotation was complete. The disc flew over the wall of the garden. The other boys gasped in admiration, but Horus did nothing to celebrate; instead, he went to fetch the disc he had thrown over the wall.

Coming back to the boys, he touched the larger boy on the shoulder and gestured for him to throw the disc again. When he began with his stance to throw the disc with his arm, Horus stopped him and demonstrated how to swivel his body with the disc to get more speed and a better fulcrum to throw the disc. The boy struggled to get the rhythm, and several times failed, but Horus persevered, and eventually the Boy threw the disc nearly the length of the garden. Horus applauded and patted the boy on the back and the boy was pleased and laughed with Horus. After that, the boy followed Horus everywhere, copying how he completed every game. He and the other children were never as good as Horus, but they were always better than they were when they tried their own way.

"When your way is difficult, and one man shows you an even more difficult path to follow using a better way, most men will try and succeed to different degrees," said Joseph. "Maybe no man will ever attain the special position of Horus or Osiris in life in following Horus, but they will achieve more following his way."

Nuri was changed that day; the goodness in Horus was easy to see. Nobody needed to explain his natural goodness or compassion for others; his actions did that in abundance. Even at four, Horus was by far a better athlete than children some three times his age and twice his size. Everything was based on technique and quick thinking and creatively inventing ways to approach a problem to succeed, and Nuri could see this with Horus. That in itself was impressive. However, the most impressive aspect of Horus was his willingness to share his invention to make his fellow children better. If Horus became half the man he was as a child, he would be very special.

"I will follow Horus, Lord Joseph. You have my allegiance and I will melt into your court as a shadow and guide for the Society of the Eye of Horus," said Nuri.

"The Coffin of Destiny and Osiris are no longer needed as the child Horus grows and can speak well already," said Joseph, "but as precious symbols, take them and guard them well for a time we may need them again at court. The Gift of Osiris is in death he will live forever through Horus and his coffin."

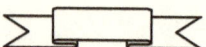

The envoy Akil to the court of Pharaoh Set of Ta-Shemau came with the generals who had been captured in chains. "Great Pharaoh, I bring you back your generals defeated in battle by the invincible army of Queen Isis and the divine Pharaoh Horus," said Akil.

"I see you have brought some back, but where is Nuri?" asked Set.

"Nuri would not bend to the will of the Pharaoh Horus and Queen Isis, and is no more, and I bring you his ashes," said Akil, gesturing to an urn of ashes that was placed on the floor at Set's feet.

"I am sure you come with more than words of dead and defeated generals," said Set.

"Queen Isis and the Pharaoh Horus are displeased that you have twice invaded Ta-Mehu, which is rightly their land. Much cost and hardship have been endured by this action," said Akil. "In compensation for this, you will pay the Ta-Mehu people one-tenth of your harvest in tribute. Further, you will take back your soldiers and generals and promise not to kill them and treat them well. Third, you will pay over half your entire wealth of gold and jewels, which the Ashai leader was promised and not paid. Bring him forth," said Akil, and motioned for Ashai to be pushed forward. "Lastly, you will honour Horus and not pursue or kill his followers and the wearers of the Eye of Horus will not be punished."

"And if I do not accept?" asked Set.

"Then the Ta-Mehu Army will advance," said Akil. "You have no army, and your people will rise up and destroy their pharaoh rather than be put to the sword of an invincible army."

"Very well, I agree," said Set, and he rose and left the details to Ammon to complete.

Ashai was taken by the envoy with the defeated generals to every nearby land, and tribute increased, with the Eblan having to pay the most for their invasion. No level was requested that could not be met, which meant the people of the lands saw this as a reasonable tax by a superior nation. The Eblan Army was sold carefully as slaves to each nation, and they spread the story of the battle and Horus to many lands.

The generals and soldiers were returned to Ta-Shemau and they were discharged from the army and became civilians. Set kept his word and did not kill them, and they merged with society, spreading the word of Horus and becoming part of the Eye of Horus followers. Set was furious, and vowed he would rebuild the army and in time invade Ta-Mehu again and crush the infant Horus.

Book Four

Chapter Twenty-Three

David York loved New York; it was his favourite city after his home in London. It was difficult to compare cities, David found, because they were a composite of so many things: the architecture, layout, infrastructure, culture, people, customs, language, weather, history, and atmosphere, all intertwined and hidden within the perception a traveller found as his experience. One traveller's view differed very much from another's because of each one's background and preconditioning. One would marvel at the simplicity of a village of straw huts in Africa, another marvel at Rome, and another at Sydney. Taste is all about preconditioning, perception, and what you get to know about a city. David loved big cities; you could be famous but melt into the background of the city very easily. Anonymity was relatively easy, just dress differently and don't be ostentatious. York was neither famous nor well known, but people instantly recognised that he was important and rich and deferred to him, particularly in New York. Americans love a truly English accent, clear and precise with good diction, but not the contrived accent often mimicked as upper class by some people from the upper classes of the UK. Unlike the perception some people have of America, it has history, art, and culture to rival those of any European city. You merely have to look for it and accept that like their wines it is younger, fresher than the older European vintage, but definitely not inferior.

Their hotels were a good example. David always stayed at the Algonquin in the heart of New York, located at West 44th Street. The Algonquin had been an iconic centre for the literarily elite since it opened its doors in 1902. The Round Table, which a group of twenty-something's formed in 1919, founded the *New Yorker* and influenced writers like F. Scott Fitzgerald and Ernest Hemingway. Long disbanded, David still liked dining in the Round Table after a drink in the Blue Bar. David, of course, ordered a pot of tea Rooibos (red bush in Afrikaans), which was a very good anti-toxin tea that he often drank. To his surprise, Pat was on the same plane to New York, and she decided to stay at the Algonquin. He wondered how well planned the trip was, but thought that he soon would find out, as she had invited herself to have dinner with him.

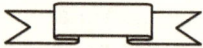

Pat came into the room, and heads turned, as she was a stunning woman.

"What can I get you to drink?" asked David.

"Not a Bellini," said Pat, laughing at her own joke.

"Have you spoken to Gino yet?" asked David.

"Yes," said Pat, "I am meeting him here tomorrow."

"Ok," said David, "that is good, but don't mention me. He will know soon enough that I am in New York."

"Don't worry; I will stick to the planned breakup. But I don't know about the breakup sex yet."

"I will leave that to you, Pat," said David. "My girlfriend is coming tomorrow, so once you have finished with Gino, all three of us can meet up."

"Veronica Goldsmith is a very beautiful woman. I read all about her and her father Oliver, a real high roller worldwide," said Pat.

"Yes, they are both remarkable people," said David noncommittally.

"The article called you a reclusive playboy billionaire," said Pat teasingly, "who dates younger women. Says you may marry Veronica, as she has lasted the longest ever."

"Who knows what may happen in the future?" said David. "What about you and George and the boyfriend?"

"I am reconciled to it," said Pat. "I just need to find somebody discrete whom I can have a long-term affair with. George and I don't plan to have sex again."

"Why?" asked David. "Don't you want children?"

"Yes," said Pat. "We will have some by artificial insemination; it is more certain than sex."

"I understand," said David.

"I don't think you do," said Pat. "Why do you think I am here?"

"To meet Gino?" said David, lying. He knew why she was there.

"I know you don't believe that," said Pat. "I am here to be with you, no strings attached. I am asking if you are interested in occasional sex."

"Why me?" asked David.

"You know why," said Pat. "You are a bastard who can be fucking me and talking sweetly to your girlfriend. You are like Gino Bellini, but more polite."

"Don't you think I should have a say in this?" asked David.

"Not really," said Pat. "If you want me to fuck Gino, you are going to have to fuck me first. Sorry to be so blunt."

"Okay," said David, "but let us eat first. I really like dining in the Round Table."

"Okay," said Pat. "Eat first, fuck later."

They ordered the colonial shrimp cocktail, followed by the citrus salmon fillet, with grilled yellow vine-ripe tomatoes, Portobello mushrooms, and cilantro corn salad.

"Can you recommend something they make locally, a sparkling wine perhaps?" said Pat.

"The Pleasant Valley Wine Company under their Great Western label produces an extra-dry sparkling wine. They call it champagne, but of course the French say that can only be produced in France," said David.

"Why is that?" asked Pat.

"Because firstly, champagne is the region the wine comes from in France, and secondly, the method of manufacture is *methode champenoise,* created more naturally, whereas sparkling wines use a sealed tank method that keeps the wine under pressure all the time, that is why the bubbles don't last as long," said David.

"Really," said Pat. "Is the wine any good in the U.S.?"

"It won a prize in 1867 for U.S. champagne in Paris, and they say the soil is similar to the French region, so it is fairly good," said David.

"Okay, let me try a bottle," said Pat.

David drank sparkling water while Pat drank the full bottle of the sparkling wine David recommended, and then Pat said she wanted desert in the room. David signed the bill and went to his room.

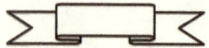

Sex with Pat was fast and furious; she seemed determined to have as many rides on David as she could before Veronica arrived. He wondered what she was like with Gino. He thought the swearing and wanting sex with David were all part of the shock of recent events, a way of coping with the heartbreak of

George being homosexual and Gino merely using her to blackmail her father. It must be a huge shock for someone as pretty and successful at Pat to discover men were deceitful and could just use her body for sex without any feelings. He looked at the naked Pat, asleep, lost in her dream world, and hoped she was happy in that place. He touched her thigh in affection and rose, as he needed to exercise before the day started.

He had joined the New York Sports Club Gym, as it had fifty-five gyms in the borough, all of which he could use, but he generally used the 62nd and Broadway gym, reasonably close to the hotel. David had a planned routine of exercises to hone his body into the shape that kept his body hard, flexible, and strong. The six-pack that men strived for was only achieved with a diet as difficult to maintain as the exercise regime. David did both by carefully keeping track of his daily diet allowance and food categories to eat and the rotation of exercises to perform daily in a small notebook.

He maintained flexibility by various inner core exercises using a gym ball and standard mat exercises like full sit-ups, wide-arm push-ups, planks, and dips on the nearest bench. Pull-ups, both close-arm and wide-arm, must be repeated each day. He always warmed up with stretching exercises, gently warming up the body, and a short run of one to three kilometres at high speed. He liked to run under three minutes and thirty seconds a kilometre, even if he was running on pavements to the gym. David rarely used machines to exercise, using free weights for his weight training, but some machines he found did work, like the rowing machine, static bike in a spinning class, and cable exercises. All his other exercises with weight training used free weights. Free weights not only forced the muscles to exhaust by increasing the weight, but the inner core gained balance because you needed to keep the weight steady and firm, which is what the machines did for you when you used them.

As David had trained all his life and maintained a balanced and healthy diet, he often looked amused at the men past forty, fat and overweight, with their personal trainers trying to convert eighteen stone of blubber into twelve stone of lean, hard muscle in twelve weeks before they went on holiday. You could certainly lose a lot of weight in twelve weeks, but to attain the perfect physique takes a lifestyle change that you must want to maintain. There was no magic bullet or recipe for the diet; the old adage you are what you eat was true. The most important factor was how much you ate. The size and the weight of the food determined how big you were going to be. How someone could believe that they merely had to stop eating junk food and eat vegetables and fish and would suddenly be slim was beyond him. You needed to reduce your portions to the size you wanted to be. Of course, eating the right foods also was required for a healthy body, and to reduce fat percentage and exercise to tone and change the body shape, but the key was the control over the amount of food you ate. If, like David, you travelled a lot and ate in many restaurants, you could follow simple rules: always select steamed vegetables, fish, or chicken, and eat only half of what was put on his plate. Always leave some food on the plate was his mantra. He took no artificial stimulants, but he did take a pre-gym shake and an after-gym shake to replace vitamins he would lose in his rigorous routine.

David always trained for a minimum of two hours, and tried to catch a class of self-defence, boxing, Thai boxing, or game of squash each day for thirty to forty minutes to break the monotony. He had played squash as a child and practiced, often alone, honing his skill as opponents of his standard were hard to find. Unlike many of the people at gym, he tended to keep to himself whilst he exercised, not seeking to talk to men or women. However, if he wanted to play squash, he needed an opponent unless he was going to train alone, so he often rang the manager at the gym to arrange a match with the best player. He had done that before he set out from California, and today after a rigorous training session, he would play some young player.

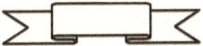

He was playing at court one, and as he looked through the glass wall, he saw Gino Bellini warming up the ball. He watched for a minute, noticing the stance of the player wrist action and how he struck the ball. Gino was a power player, hitting the ball tremendously hard and low just over the tin. His shots, close to the wall and deep to the back wall, made them difficult to return. David could see he was a very good player and figured he must play often.

David took his Wilson racquet from his squash bag and tapped on the glass wall, and Gino turned and faked a smile as he saw David. Gino opened the door and put out his hand. "I wondered if it would be the same David York I know," said Gino.

David shook the firm hard grip. "Surprised to see you, Gino, did not realise you played squash."

"From when I was a little kid," said Gino. "I used to play competitively for a while, but I only play for fun these days. And you?"

"Never above club level, but also have played since school because it is an excellent aerobic exercise and breaks up the run so it is good for the physique."

"What are you doing in New York?" asked Gino.

"A little bit of business and some pleasure, going to take in some shows with Veronica," said David.

"Well, we must meet up and have dinner if you have time," said Gino. "This is my hometown, the Big Apple."

"I have your card," said David. "I will give you a call. Let's play."

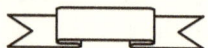

After warming up, they spun the racquet for service, and Gino won and served. As David suspected, it was a power serve and the speed would deceive most players. David let the ball go past him, and turning, boasted the ball off the side wall into the corner directly in front of him and furthest from Gino. Gino already had moved to the T at the centre of the court, and although the ball was weighted perfectly, he smashed the ball and hit it very hard close to the wall to the rear of the court. David had moved to the T and now retreated back, boasting it again, and Gino made the same return. The cat and mouse play was repeated until Gino made an extravagant killer stroke into the opposite corner at the front of the court, which David failed to reach in time. The first match was close, but Gino won it fifteen to thirteen.

They broke for the ninety seconds between games and drank some water together outside the court, both of them having brought bottles of water to the gym.

"You are a good player," said Gino.

"But obviously not good enough," smiled David.

"The game has a long way to go. Best of five we play here, or first to three games," said Gino.

"That's fine, I like American rules, scoring on every rally rather than only winning points when you serve in the British game," said David.

"Why don't we spice up the game a little? Loser pays for that dinner we are going to have," said Gino.

"Are you a New York Knicks fan?" asked David.

"Of course," said Gino.

"Last game of the season is against Toronto, and you will have tickets?" asked David.

"Of course, front row, the best," said Gino.

"Ok, let's make it dinner after the last game of the season. Loser pays, but the winner gets your tickets. I presume you have two," said David.

"Of course two, always take a girl," said Gino. "Generally by watching the game it makes it easy to get them into bed."

"Don't count your chickens before they hatch," said David, and went onto the court.

Like all power players, Gino liked that satisfying sound you got when you hit the ball very hard; he was used to long rallies as the ball bounced higher and his opponent could return the ball. David had played Gino so he could win narrowly, also playing a power game, but dropping the ball about one foot from the back wall so it bounced back, making Gino return it before it hit the floor again.

David now changed his game. His high lobbed serves Gino had to volley, which like most power players, he smashed, and David then lobbed again into the far corner, but now with no bounce, right in the corner. Gino, being a superb player, would get some, but the return was weak, and David killed the ball over and over again. He frustrated Gino, constantly changing his game, from a touch game, to power, back to touch, and back to power and back again, even within rallies unbalancing Gino and making him lose

285

confidence. David easily beat him fifteen to ten, fifteen to six, and fifteen to thirteen in the next three games. Gino's confidence dwindled as David kept him under pressure and won the match three games to one.

David smiled at the end of the game. "Well played, Gino, I really enjoyed the game," and David held out his hand.

"I will send the tickets around to your hotel," said Gino.

"Thanks," said David, noticing that Gino already knew he was at the Algonquin, so he also would know Pat was there. "I am in Room 312; shall we say 22h00 at the Del Posto on 85 Tenth Avenue? Do you need directions?" he smiled inwardly, as he knew this was Gino's favourite restaurant.

Gino winced but said nothing, ashamed he had lost. He shook hands reluctantly, and lost in thought, forgot to ask David at which hotel he was staying.

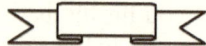

David ran back to the hotel, and when he got to his room, Pat had left, so he called her room to let her know Gino knew she was already in New York, but she already had left the hotel. He suspected Gino already had called her. *Now*, he thought, *will it play out as I suspect, with all the fallibilities of women's and men's egos unchecked?*

David looked forward to seeing Veronica again. He did not really want to fuck Pat, but it was necessary to infuriate Gino, and he hoped Veronica would understand if she ever discovered it had happened. He was firmly of the opinion that openness in a relationship, sharing the negative feelings we all have about our partners, was a big mistake. Telling your partner she left the top of the toothpaste was annoying and a mistake; just accept it put the top on yourself and move on. Nobody likes being told to pick up your clothes, dress differently, or that he or she is fat. If you don't want to be with that person because they have some annoying habits, make your excuses and leave the relationship and move on, don't try and make them perfect; they never will be.

Sometimes, in a long relationship, one of the partners strays and has a fling. The worst thing that can happen is a big analysis of the relationship with a marriage counsellor. What the injured partner needs to do is pay more attention to their partner, try and concentrate on the positives if you want to save the relationship. The other partner either will stop the extra relationship, or return in spirit to his old love, or will leave them. In either case, you get a positive result amicably. Being told in a meeting with a stranger that you are crap at sex, or fat, or fart in bed, etc., does not do your esteem any good when you get left anyway by your partner and need to find a new partner.

David heard the key card open the door, and instantly alert, he positioned himself near his handgun. Veronica opened the door with a porter pushing in her luggage on a trolley.

David smiled. "Hi, honey, hope you enjoyed your visit to see your dad? How is he?" Veronica had left David, as arranged, to briefly fly to meet her father in Boston where he was negotiating a deal for a hedge fund.

"He is well and sends his regards," said Veronica with a dazzling smile.

"Don't lie, Veronica," said David. "Your father hates me."

"We can always pretend," said Veronica. "What's on the agenda?"

"A meeting with Susan and Benjamin Nester for lunch," said David, "and then front row seats to see the Knicks and dinner at Del Posto with Gino Bellini."

"Really, how did you get the tickets? They are gold dust," said Veronica. "It is the last game of the season against Toronto."

"Beat your young friend at squash", said David.

"Does he know Jahangir Khan has coached you?" asked Veronica.

"Of course not! Nobody knows that. How do you know?" asked David, shocked.

"Daddy had it in his file on you. Jahangir is one of his clients," said Veronica.

"Keep that to yourself," said David. "That is my secret weapon, lessons from the worlds best-ever player, undefeated for five and half years in five hundred and fifty-five consecutive games."

"I will keep your secret," said Veronica. "I presume you set him up?"

"Of course," said David. "Let him know I would be here by taking no precautions; he is watching me and reacted the way I wanted."

"I presume you fucked the woman, Pat, to annoy him as well?" said Veronica.

David was silent.

"I knew you would; of course, it does not matter," said Veronica. "Just don't fuck her again or start an affair with her. Using her as a pawn is one thing, having a proper affair is another."

"What are you going to wear?" asked David, trying to change the subject.

"A black cocktail dress. It is simple and good to look at on TV. Gino will be infuriated he can't get in my knickers," said Veronica, "and you are fucking Pat."

"Sounds good," said David. "Take off your clothes before you unpack. I have a deposit to deliver," and Veronica saw his manhood was rising to attention. *Lucky me*, she thought, *makeup sex*.

Chapter Twenty-Four

David York was not a great basketball fan, but Veronica really enjoyed the game. She shouted and applauded all the way through. There is no other game where the spectators can get so close and see their heroes in the flesh, and in this sport, there is a lot of flesh because of the athletes' size. Earl Barron and Danilo Galinari were seven feet and six feet ten inches tall, weighing in 250 pounds and 225 pounds, respectively, dwarfing the dominating Chris Dalian at a mere six feet tall and 190 pounds. Men were big in this game and swift, moving the ball quickly, with sweat pouring from their bodies and dripping to the floor. David always thought Veronica liked the muscles and sweat more than the game. David admired the athletes and endeavour, but never really the game, which for him was not as compelling as rugby and soccer, which they played in the United States but were not national sports like the NBA, American football, ice hockey and basketball. David looked now, as Veronica was on her feet shouting at Earl Barron, the forward centre, but it was to no avail, and the Knicks lost to Toronto one hundred thirteen to one hundred thirty-one.

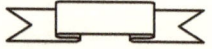

David had the hired hotel limo take them to Del Posto on 85, Tenth Avenue, and he wondered what the evening would bring, as he knew Gino would have met Pat by now. The Del Posto had been built to have an airy feel, but retained an Italian flavour by using towering columns and tall curtained windows in a darkly glowing room created by the dark wood and golden decor. Space had been provided, and many critics thought the restaurant lost the intimacy of the Italian bistro but David instantly liked the atmosphere. The tinkling piano music in the background he found pleasing, not disturbing, and the space between tables logical. Gino was seated with Pat, and his face was not happy and relaxed. Pat looked stunning as always and was drinking red wine.

"Hi Gino," said David, "I am sorry, but your team lost one hundred thirteen to one hundred thirty-one."

"I know, I watched the game," said Gino.

"Yes, he was a real grouch," said Pat. "He does not like losing and is having a bad day," and she laughed.

"Well, let's eat," said Veronica. "I am starving. Thanks for the tickets, by the way, but don't play David at games; he never loses."

The owner, Mario Batali, was of the Bastianich family fine dining empire, and seeing Gino, came across to greet him.

"Mr. Bellini, how nice to see you," said Mario. "How did your squash game go? I saw you going to play at the gym."

"He got his ass kicked," said Pat, "by a much older but superior man."

"Oh sorry to hear that," said Mario, "and pity about the Knicks, did you watch the game?"

"Yes," said Gino, annoyed with Pat. "There is always next year."

David sensed the tension between Pat and Gino and wondered what had happened when they met. "If you don't mind, Gino," said David, "let me choose the wine. Do you like champagne, Pat?"

"Of course," said Pat.

"Well, let's celebrate the end of the season for the Knicks and this meeting at this wonderful restaurant. Two ice-cold bottles of the Bollinger Vielles Vignes

Francaises 1992, I think to start, and some sparkling water." David knew Gino hated spending money, and the extravagant purchase of wine at two thousand U.S. dollars a bottle would annoy him, as he was paying. "What are we all eating?" he asked. "I hear the seafood is very good."

"Let's start with some caviar, Beluga, don't you think?" said Veronica. "We must with the champagne."

"I love caviar," said Pat, "let's have lots."

"For the main course, I would suggest their spaghetti Vignola," said David, "with the Romano Dal Forno 1993; they have a magnum."

"That sounds wonderful," said Veronica. David smiled. Gino would not get out of paying over ten thousand dollars for the meal, as the Romano Dal Forno was six thousand U.S. dollars.

David, Veronica, and Pat were happy and animated during the meal and chatted gaily, but Gino seethed at the extravagance at his expense. Gino always chose modest meals and wines, never drinking very much. Now he felt compelled to get some value from his own expense, and overindulged in the wine, drinking far too much.

David, not drinking, ate very little caviar and only half the plate of spaghetti, which was as good as the review he had read. "My compliments to the chef," said David to the waiter, as he cleared the table. "Is it still Mark?"

"Yes sir, Mark Ladner," said the waiter.

"Tell him David York says well done, an excellent meal," said David.

A few minutes later, Mark Ladner came rushing to the table dressed as the chef. "Mr. York, how nice to see you!" said Mark, and the men shook hands warmly.

"Another triumph, Mark. How many more menus will you create?" said David.

"Who knows, but with customers like you, Mr. York, we shall always be inspired," said Mark. "Do you know this man is a superb chef and came to our kitchens a few years ago at Lupa to learn about our Roman trattoria fare?"

Gino was astonished. How the fuck does this guy know the chef and food better than me? He poured himself some more wine.

"Maybe when I have more time, I could spend a little time here. The trans-generationalism of *cucina classica* flavours are delicious," said David.

"Maybe I should tag along and learn, too," said Gino.

"Alas, Mr. Bellini, I extend a courtesy to Mr. York as a fellow professional who owns restaurants, vineyards, and wine cellars all around the world," said Mark. "Mr. York is a trained chef, having trained in France, Italy, and Spain. We don't allow amateurs in our kitchens, most sorry," and the chef turned and walked back to the kitchen.

David enjoyed the expression on Gino's face when he received the bill a little later, and he had to admit to himself he was going a little over the top goading Gino. He was surprised, however that Gino had drunk so much; that was not characteristic of his behaviour, but never having been beaten at anything and then losing sometimes unhinges people. David had been humbled many times by the best at everything he tried; Jahangir Khan could probably beat him blindfolded at squash, Mark was a far better chef, Tiger Woods a better golfer, and the list was endless, but you could learn from the best in the humbleness of defeat. Defeat for David was an inspiration to strive harder and improve at each thing he did, but people like Gino found little positive in the experience.

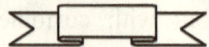

Veronica was a little drunk, he saw, but he had begun to realise she was probably the closest person in his life now, and he felt a pang of jealousy every time she even looked at another man. The great lothario was being tamed, like all men, by a woman.

"Honey, do me a favour, will you?" asked Veronica in one of those enticing voices.

"What is that?" asked David, always wary.

"Go and sing me a song," said Veronica.

Pat looked shocked. "Does he sing as well?" she asked surprised.

"Of course, and plays the piano beautifully," said Veronica.

"Well, it is late, we don't want to spoil the evening," said David.

"Go for it," said Gino, thinking, if he fucks up, he will look foolish.

"Okay, let me ask the pianist if he will let me sing and play one song," said David, "but you must come to the front so I can sing to you, Veronica. You will distract the audience," and he laughed.

David rarely was nervous when asked to sing. He always cleared his mind of the audience and sang to one person. He thought carefully about what he really wanted to say to Veronica to show her how he felt, as finding the words in daily life was difficult.

"Hi," said David to the pianist, "Do you mind if I sing a song to my girlfriend?"

"Well, I don't know," said the pianist, who then hesitated when he saw the stunning Veronica. "Okay, just one. What are your names?"

"David and Veronica," said David.

"Just going to take a short break, folks," said the pianist. "All in the interest of love, while David sings a song to Veronica."

"Thanks," David said to the pianist, and then had a little practice, which instantly told everybody that this guy could play. "We all want to tell someone special in our lives how we feel, but life tells us to be careful, and sometimes the love of our life never hears the words in our heart. For all you lovers out there, this is what we would like to say, in the words of Kenny Loggin," said David to the audience.

David sang in a light, low, tenor voice, phrasing the words carefully and looking directly at Veronica; his playing of the piano was perfect and his voice enchanting. The people in the restaurant stopped eating and listened as the feeling in his voice touched them and men squeezed the hands of their companions to tell them that the words of the song were how they felt.

**"Are those your eyes, is that your smile ,
I've been lookin' at you forever,
But I never saw you before,
Are these your hands holdin' mine ,
Now I wonder how I could have been so blind ,
For the first time I am looking in your eyes,
For the first time I'm seein' who you are ,
I can't believe how much I see ,
When you're lookin' back at me ,
Now I understand why love is...
Love is... for the first time.**

As he finished the last phrase, **"Now I understand why love is... love is... for the first time,"** he meant it, and it was obvious.

Both Pat and Veronica had tears in their eyes, and the audience a lump in their throat. They rose as one and applauded.

As Pat sat down, her heart also changed; she knew she was behaving badly out of hate and revulsion for George and herself, and Gino was not worth those emotions. She would end the affair in a dignified way; there would be no sex or tantrums, and she would divorce George in a year or so when the media had lost interest and find someone else she could really love, just as she saw true love in the eyes of David and Veronica.

Gino now was completely infuriated; his only consolation was that he would be able to take his frustration out on Pat with rough sex. First, he must have that fucking annoying man David York killed.

They all parted smiles and kisses. David and Veronica got in the hotel limo. Pat went across and asked them to wait a few minutes. Pat was now sober, and Gino a little bit tipsy and he really should not drive. "What I have to say is quite hard, Gino. You won't like it," said Pat. "I am ending our affair. It was entirely my fault, and you were trying just to be there for me. I thank you for that, but I want true love, not just platonic sex, and I need to look for that elsewhere," said Pat, and before Gino could reply, she got up and left the car.

Gino speed dialled the number. "It is me," he said. "Go and kill that fucking man," and he ended the conversation. It was foolish sending a message on his own cell phone in a public place, all of which could be traced, but he was so mad that he was not thinking. The killer, an Italian hit man, noted the order and set off to the hotel.

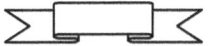

The limo had taken them just out of view of the restaurant and slowed for traffic lights when David leaned forward to the driver. "Just pull over here please, we want to walk for a little and will make our own way back," said David. "Please excuse us, Pat; we will see you in the morning."

David and Veronica exited the limo and walked hand in hand along the road. Pat thought, *how romantic*.

The limo returned to the hotel, and when the concierge saw the driver parking the car and Pat returning, he assumed they all had returned and called the number he had been given.

The man nodded and said, "Thanks," when he got the news. He packed his firearms in a small case and set off to the hotel. He wanted to finish the job as soon as possible. When he got to the hotel, he used the staff entrance. He made his way up the emergency stairs exits, which had no video cameras, covering his face when he reached the hallway. He made his way to the room David and Veronica occupied. He opened the door with a hotel pass card for the electronic lock and quietly entered the room, letting his eyes become familiar with the darkness. As he ventured further forward, he felt a sharp sensation in his spine, one of excruciating pain, and he tried to call out, but his voice was silent. He died falling forward into a laundry trolley. The maid who had struck him from behind bundled him fully into the trolley and then covered him with dirty linen. She then calmly pushed the trolley to the staff elevator and took the trolley down to the laundry room in the hotel, and parked the trolley with the others ready for the morning washing of bed linen.

Crusader then left the hotel, as David York had ordered.

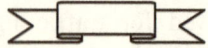

David and Veronica picked up the rented car that was parked as instructed and then drove out of New York, headed for Boston. His and Veronica's clothes and personal items would be picked up at a later date. He suspected they would try to kill him once they knew he was in Boston, and therefore believing the hotel bugged, he spread a lot of false information through acting out scenes with Veronica. He supposed that Gino had bugged his room and the limo they drove around New York in from the hotel. There would be no easy way to trace the Nesters, who already were in Boston, or himself, as they were all booked under false names and had forged documentation.

Gino seethed and drank some more wine, his normal iron will disoriented. When he woke up in the morning, he had passed out on the couch. He had been sitting alone and had drunk two more bottles of wine. His head ached and he felt dizzy; it was his first hangover since he was a teenager and discovered he could not drink. He felt sick and ran to the bathroom and threw up. He felt a little better and searched for some aspirin for his headache. He found the unrecorded cell phone he would use for contacts and phoned the paid assassin. "Is he dead?" he asked simply.

"Sure," came back the reply, and then the phone went dead.

Gino felt a little peeved at the discourtesy, but heartened by the news, he went to his bedroom to lie down again as he felt dizzy. He would not be breaking his one glass rule again for quite some time.

Crusader put the phone back in her pocket and smiled, she was good at accents, and the deep-sounding voice was fine for a few words, but she found it difficult to maintain the depth in a conversation. The body would be discovered later today, but Gino would be sick for a few days, she thought. It had been easy to get a job at Del Posto, and knowing Gino always ate the spaghetti and meatballs, to put something in the rich sauce before it was served to him by the waiter. He accelerated the effect by uncharacteristically drinking, and the food poisoning he was suffering he thought was a hangover. Either way, Gino was going to be one sick puppy for a couple of days, enough for David and Veronica to meet the Nestors and get out of the country.

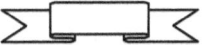

Susan and Benjamin Nester were seated across from David and Veronica in one of the premier suites named after important historic Boston figures. The Omni Parker Hotel was on 60 School Street in Boston and had been built in the nineteenth century. The bronze sculpted doors at the entrance beckoned the traveller into America's oldest continuously-operating hotel, which opened in 1855. The hotel, now with modern amenities, was decorated tastefully. The blends of reds and gold fabric and light wooden furniture and the high carved ceilings in the lobby with chandeliers gave you the feeling of Victorian luxury. Situated on the Freedom Trail, David could have guessed Benjamin would have chosen this as the hotel to have their meeting.

"So, what have you found Benjamin?" asked David, excited at the prospect of finding the Coffin of Destiny.

"We all know three men, Charles de Chevalier, Guy du Busson, and Francois Marriott escaped the slaughter of the Templars by Louis IV in 1314. Charles de Chevalier, we know, buried the Holy Grail in Newfoundland, which you found that with your father and Bill Travers, who was a direct descendent of de Chevalier. What is not often known is de Chevalier had a fellow officer, an English serf named Thomas Lesley. When the burial place was complete, he took his Indian bride Soft Blanket, renamed Rachael, and some others to Quebec (with de Chevalier), and they waited, hoping settlers would arrive. That did not happen until 1497, when John Cabot rediscovered Newfoundland. Those Crusaders did not bury all the artefacts they had with them. In documentation written by the Templars, they had many relics, amongst which was a golden coffin. This golden coffin had within it a mummified body, but the Templars did not know the origin of the coffin, or the body. That is lost in the ancient scriptures they did not understand. As the coffin was valuable, they painted it with pitch tar, sealing the coffin, and always carried it around in a nondescript wooden crate. Thomas Lesley was the custodian of the coffin, and his son of the same name, when he became the leader of a cell of the Sect, decided to leave Quebec and venture into America. As the box was conspicuous in their small community, they thought Lesley should take it with him, and maybe, as it was valuable, it could be used to barter a loan, using it as collateral in a more civilized community. So, Thomas Lesley takes the Coffin of

Destiny to America, and we think to Boston," said Benjamin.

"But where are they then, these Sect members?" asked David. "Why have they never made contact?"

"That we don't really know," said Benjamin, "but we know the original signs were overlapped triangles, in the form of a pentangle for men, and the women wore a cross and the greeted each other as Templars and Crusader."

"That's not going to help," said David. "We no longer use all the old traditions."

"But you still use some," said Benjamin, "like using an assassin called Crusader who is a lesbian or homosexual in each cell."

"True," said David, "but they no longer need to be of any sexual persuasion anymore."

"Really?" said Benjamin. "I did not know that."

"Dad thinks if we look in Boston for societies that meet, maybe we will find the Sect," said Susan. "He thought they would recruit from people interested in history or religion."

"Possible," said David. "How do we start looking?"

"By going to meetings," said Benjamin, and he handed a list to them.

"Lots of meetings," said David, looking at the piece of paper.

"So, we need to start straight away," said Benjamin, "each of us going to as many as possible, starting this afternoon."

David looked down the list, and his eye catching a group called the Historical Crusades of Christianity, he decided he would go to that event.

Chapter Twenty-Five

David went with Veronica and purchased pentangles and crosses for them from a local jeweller, favouring a lapel pin for the men and a small broach for the women. They were very small and discrete and made in gold, and the jeweller told him they were moderately popular, but he could not remember the last person he sold one too. David noted he wore a small pentangle in his jacket lapel.

Veronica was not going to a lunchtime meeting, but as she made her way back to the Omni Parker Hotel with David, she changed her mind and decided to go to David's meeting for lunch in one of the meeting rooms. When David and Veronica arrived at the designated room, they saw Benjamin and Susan waiting for them.

"We have nothing better to do so we might as well join you," said Benjamin.

"And is lunch included with the talk?" said Susan smiling.

"I think so and you better both wear your sign," said David, and gave them the small gold pentangle and brooch he had bought.

He saw the jeweller arrive with a woman and two young men, and saw they all wore the small pieces of jewellery. The couple who were at the reception desk also wore the same small pieces of jewellery.

There were perhaps forty tables, each of which seated eight people, which meant three hundred and twenty people potentially could be seated, and the place was about three-quarters full when they entered the room. That meant that there were about two hundred and forty people. David noted that nearly all of them wore the jewellery. The format was very simple, and there was a small, four-page photocopied agenda and information on the talk that was to be given. The society chairperson was Rachael Lesley-Worthing, and she gave out some information about the society for guests and then a few administrative highlights about the report that members could download from their website. The guest speaker then gave a very boring lecture on the impact of crusaders on Christian and Muslims in today's society, and then lunch was served.

The meal was pre-set and included a seafood chowder or seafood salad. David and Veronica both selected the salad. This was followed by sole or steak, vegetables, and potatoes being placed on the table. David and Veronica went with the sole and only ate a few vegetables. A set wine was served, but they preferred the bottled water on the table. David noted that Benjamin and Susan ate the exact opposite way, and both drank one glass of red wine. Both ate the Parker House Rolls, which were famous, but David and Veronica only ate a very small corner of a roll, just to taste the bread, which included sugar in its recipe but was delicious. For dessert was the famous Boston cream pie with chocolate icing, but David and Veronica again only ate a small corner of the dessert.

"Oh, you folks must eat all of our wonderful dessert," said Rachael Lesley-Worthing, noticing how sparingly they had eaten the famous pie.

"David York, from England," said David, and he stood up smiling and held out his hand. "Sorry to offend you, but trying to not put on the pounds."

"Well, you can see I didn't try," said Rachael gesturing to her ample hips and laughing.

"What would you say if I greeted you, Crusader?" said David, as he shook her hand and whispered the last word.

"Templar," she whispered back, looking shocked. Then, recovering in a louder voice, she said, "Why don't you visitors to Boston come to a real family home for dinner?"

"We would love to," said David.

"Say tonight at 7 p.m. sharp? It is in the old part of Boston. Here is my card, it has my address," said Rachel and then she moved on. He saw that she moved confidently, greeting regulars and stopping to speak longer to guests.

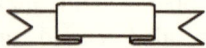

David tried to persuade the other three to stay at the hotel, but they were having none of it, and they travelled to the suburb to find a superbly restored house with a large extension added.

They were greeted at the door by the jeweller they had met with a warm handshake, "Welcome, Crusader," he said.

"Templar," replied David.

"I am John Lesley," said the jeweller. "My sister is Rachael; she and a few of the Sect are in the lounge."

Rachael greeted them warmly, and they sat facing perhaps ten people.

"So let me explain briefly who I am, and why we are here," said David. "Let me begin in 1314 and with the Templars." It took over an hour to describe the journey to the meeting in Boston, and the three separate Templars making separate lives in Scotland, Quebec, and Switzerland. He explained the Jesus Blood Line, Holy Grail, Templar gold and secret scrolls, finishing with the recent events and the search for the Coffin of Destiny.

"Wow, that is some odyssey," said John Lesley. "Makes our story quite ordinary, really. Our ancestor, we understand, brought the artefacts of the Templars here to Boston in the early-sixteenth century. We settled in Boston and became part of the community. We carried on some traditions of the Templars, wearing the cross if a woman and the pentangle if a man. Even the greeting you used, but gradually over time the reason for our existence disappeared. Our late father began researching our past in the 1940s and started the society as a focal point for the group, and we bought a jeweller's shop that would produce the pentangle and crucifixes the way we decided they should be worn. We did try to trace other groups, but did not try very hard in Quebec, I must admit, believing the Templars would have moved on like our family. We know from papers our father had that the coffin contains a mummified body, but we have never seen any scrolls, only the ones written by the Templars themselves."

"Where is the coffin?" asked David.

"In an obvious place," said John Lesley, smiling. "Guess where?"

"King's Chapel, probably in a family mausoleum," said David.

"Bingo," said John.

"Has the coffin ever been opened?" asked Benjamin.

"Never, it was placed there after the building of the stone church designed by Peter Harrison in 1754," said John. "He also designed and built the Lesley Mausoleum we still use this day."

"So you are not Catholics, then?" asked David.

"No, we are all members of the Unitarian Universalist Association. The Sect members were loyalists to the monarchy and became puritans, as were the majority of the people at the time," said John.

"That will make the search for you by the Cult more difficult, but once they link the Lesley name, they will find you quickly as we did," said David.

"Our intention has always been to be found someday," said John. "We wanted our congregation of Sect members to join with the other original Sect members. Our society's wearing of the pentangle and crosses, and always having a Lesley as the chairperson were supposed to be a sign, eventually to be found by a fellow Sect member. Now that has happened, these signs can be removed," said John Lesley.

"Changing the name of the society, not wearing insignia, and having a different name as the chairperson won't stop the Cult from coming to get the coffin and any other artefacts," said David. "We need to move everything to a safer location."

"What will be safer, though?" asked John.

"That I need to give some thought," said David, "but make your changes without delay, and I will have Bill Travers, the country Sect leader for America, contact you."

"Can we see the coffin in the crypt?" asked Benjamin.

"No, it is built into the wall so it is not visible," said John.

"Is there any security at the King's Chapel?" asked Susan.

"No, not really. It is a tourist venue, so there are always people there during viewing hours, but not at night," said John reflectively.

"Let's have somebody watching the place twenty-four seven, discretely, with my cell phone number, so they can alert me if somebody starts trying to enter the crypt," said David.

"We can arrange that tomorrow," said John Lesley.

"Do you have a Crusader member in your Sect?" asked David.

"No," said John, "the Sect abandoned the use of force several generations ago. We don't have anybody with those skills in our community."

"Okay," said David. "Let me arrange somebody to guard the crypt. Excuse me," and David left the room and went outside and called Crusader.

"Are you close?" asked David.

"Watching you from the street," Crusader replied.

"Go to the Lesley crypt at King's Chapel. Do you have the details?" asked David.

"Yes," said Crusader. "Picked that up from your conversation with John Lesley, already got the location and found the location of the crypt using Google."

"Good," said David. "Only kill if necessary, but don't lose the coffin."

"The old Sect members, do they live?" Crusader asked.

"They live," said David, "for now, we need to find out more about this group before deciding their fate."

The van down the street marked as a TV repair company moved from the curb. "I am on my way and will contact you for instructions if there is any approach to the crypt." Then the line went dead.

"Okay, somebody will be watching the crypt within the hour," said David, "so there is no need to assign somebody from your Sect. It has been a long day. Let's end the meeting now and meet again tomorrow at the hotel."

The group shook hands with David and his party, and David searched their faces but saw nothing suspicious. He decided to go back to the hotel. Crusader would monitor the members of the historical society now known as sect members and their homes, which now had listening devices already in place.

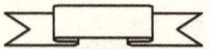

Gino Bellini was sick for two days and cared little of David York or the Coffin of Destiny. When he recovered after the second day, his energy returned, his mind forgot his defeat, and he returned to being positive again. He was furious that David and Veronica had disappeared without a trace and that Benjamin and Susan Nester could not be found. The body of their assassin was found at the Omni Parker Hotel and the incident was covered up by the police, as the man was a secret agent for the U.S. Government and thought killed by another spy.

Gino also had a message to contact his uncle, Cardinal Castellano, regarding developments with their oil project. "Your Eminence?" said Gino.

"Gino, we have a problem," said the cardinal, "the Senate is putting a ban on offshore drilling again. So our field cannot be brought in, or sold."

"Shit!" said Gino. "We need that field to be active to sell it."

"Can our senator contact anyone or do anything?" asked Gino.

"George is on the committee, but he said he can't sway the general consensus for now," said the cardinal. "He called me just now to tell me. In a few weeks or a few months, he will try to get it lifted."

"Fucking try! We need to fucking sell our interests now!" shouted Gino.

"My son, losing your temper will achieve nothing," said the cardinal, "but tell me, what is Bill O'Brien doing in Malawi? I heard he had new oil rights and was drilling inland."

"I don't know," said Gino. "I will find out."

"Won't the ban on offshore oil drilling make our field in Lake Malawi more valuable?" asked the cardinal.

"Yes, but we need the money from the sale of our offshore interests to fund the Malawi investment," said Gino.

"Can't we use the money from the Vatican?" asked the cardinal.

"Perhaps, but we need to be careful," said Gino, "Let me talk to George first."

"Don't forget, we borrowed the money for the Malawi oil fields and the offshore fields, and that money falls due shortly," said the cardinal.

"I know," said Gino. "Let me deal with it now." Gino seethed at his extravagant plan, which was unravelling because of one Senate committee temporary ruling. He decided to find out what Bill was up to in Malawi, and he sent one of his men to investigate.

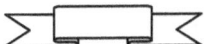

Bill O'Brien was on site at the drilling rig when his foreman came running excitedly to Bill, his face elated with a broad grin.

"Boss, boss!" said Joe. "We have struck oil again!"

"What?" said Bill. "I don't believe it!" and he rushed from the cabin to see the gusher spilling oil from the strike. Not able to contain himself, he threw his hat in the air, and all the men followed his lead, including the Malawians.

Of course, you could not keep a find like this a secret, and before he had returned to the Capital Lilongwe to seek the permits for exporting the oil, Reuters was broadcasting the find on the newswire. The claims of the largest strike in the world sent the price of the shares in the company Bill held for David York through the roof and sparked a plunge in the shares in offshore and deep-water drilling companies. Maria Conwell, Chairperson to the Committee of Energy and Natural Resources, announced a review of all offshore contracts to drill oil off the coast of the United States, with the report not being due for eighteen months. She announced that the U.S. had negotiated an option to buy the oil discovered in Malawi to make up for the shortfall of supply in the U.S., with the company Bill O'Brien owned receiving funds to develop the oil business in Malawi to include refining, distribution, a pipeline to the coast, and a transportation network in Africa.

The Malawi Government was to suspend licences on oil exploration of the Lake of Malawi, in line with the offshore drilling review of deep-water drilling, due to the concerns regarding the effects on the environment. The disastrous events of the BP oil leak from offshore drilling in 2010, which lasted months, were cited again and again. The future looked bleak for anybody owning shares in companies with deep-water drilling.

Angelo, the executive sent by Gino, stood out in Lilongwe like a sore thumb in his shinny Italian suit and thick New York accent. Bill O'Brien ensured that he was made aware of the huge find and all the information necessary of ownership of the company being in Bill's sole name.

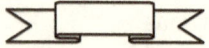

Gino was under pressure; he had borrowed money from the Italian Mafia and the Chinese, and used all the money from the family resources in his speculation of the oil fields. His shares were now worthless. His only hope was to apply pressure to Bill O'Brien using the photographs of Pat and himself to reveal her affair, which would ruin the image of the reconciled marriage.

He was rehearsing his telephone call to Bill when a newsflash caught his attention on CNN news. A news conference was being held by George and Pat. He watched, fascinated, as Pat spoke. "My husband and I have decided to part, having considered our mutual behaviour following the revelations of my husband's homosexuality," said Pat. "My husband has been nothing but loyal and honest in his behaviour to me, but I had to confess to him that my behaviour was far from exemplary, and I had carried on a torrid and degrading affair with a prominent businessman who disgracefully took advantage of my weakness in a time of stress to take photographs and a video of me in compromising positions in the act of intercourse. It is therefore with regret that my husband and I have decided to divorce and rebuild our lives in public service separately. I have nothing but admiration for the honesty and integrity my husband has portrayed throughout the ordeal of announcing his homosexuality and supporting me even in my betrayal of our relationship with another man. He will always have my love and support in all his endeavours." Then Pat, wiping tears from her eyes, walked magnificently from the podium with George holding her hand.

When Gino called Bill O'Brien, the conversation was distantly frosty. "Hi Bill, it is Gino," said Gino.

"What do you want?" asked Bill in a distinctly irritated voice.

"Want to buy some shares in your new company," said Gino.

"Gino, go fuck yourself, threaten away. I have the photographs with the FBI and CIA and half of the government; touch me or my family and they will hunt you the rest of your life," said Bill, and he put the phone down.

Chapter Twenty-Six

Cardinal Castellano had been at the heart of a paedophile ring since his days as a lowly priest, using the power given to him as part of the criminal activities of the Castellano family. His elevation to cardinal and leader of the Cult meant he had even more power to suppress allegations of abuse against him or his ring of clergy paedophiles. Accusations did not make a case, and people would disappear before a hearing, and the accusations would be unsubstantiated. The new pope, to his credit, was against this practice, and was ruthlessly crushing the practice by dismissing clergy and paying off the victims to minimise the bad press to the Catholic Church.

From the parish of which Cardinal Castellano was a bishop, Saint Patrick's Catholic Cathedral in New York, the Archdiocese of New York and the pope had received a complaint from the archbishop. The complaint was from twin brothers from a well-respected family, who were now both lawyers in a prominent law firm in New York. Both men were married in the Catholic Church and had young children, not yet at school age, less than three years old. The men were married to good Catholic girls, both of whom were from very well-connected Catholic families, and the complaint, which was well documented, had supporting testimonies from over twenty young men of a similar age also providing affidavits, of the cardinal's sexual abuse of the men as young children. The complaint had not been made public, and the archbishop had been approached to do two things for the accusers: First, the church was to hear the accusations against the cardinal, and if found guilty, to strip him of his office, pension, and priesthood, excommunicating him from the church for abuse of his power. Second, the church was to pay compensation to all the abused men except the twins, who wanted no money from the church, only justice. The compensation they sought for each man was two hundred thousand U.S. Dollars as a one-off payment. Some of the men did not want the money for themselves, and nominated charities who would receive the money.

Both men were concerned for their safety, having heard of what happened to other men who complained. They therefore only supplied fifty per cent of the details of the men's identities. It was made clear that if any "accident" happened to a single man, the remaining men would take their case to the press. Documents and audiotapes recording the men's fears for their safety would be sent to the press. A court case immediately would be pursued by all the families jointly, and as they numbered over thirty families, they could not all be killed or silenced by the Cult. More importantly, those names of families were extremely rich and large contributors and fundraisers for the Catholic Church. They threatened not only to stop their contributions, but to campaign against the church to persuade others until the abuse charges were resolved.

In honesty, the pope thought the men seeking justice were mild in their requirements, based on the evidence they had on the cardinal. Taped conversations, videotapes of abuse, affidavits, and bank accounts proving he paid for paedophilic information and sold paedophilic information. The cardinal had overwhelming evidence against him, and the pope had very little time within which to act, just forty-eight

314

hours. The pope decided to grab the bull by the horns and ask the cardinal about the allegations.

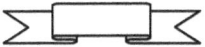

The pope sent for the cardinal. Cardinal Castellano came quickly and was out of breath when he was summoned. He knelt and kissed the pope's ring.

"Your Holiness, you wanted to speak to me?" the cardinal asked.

"Yes, you're Eminence," said the pope. "First, what is the news on the Coffin of Destiny?"

The cardinal looked uncomfortable. "No news, your Holiness, the people who we are tracking have disappeared."

"Really?" said the pope. "How careless of your nephew. Now I hear he has invested badly in deep-water drilling and lost all your investments, including money borrowed from the Italian Mafia and Chinese Triads?"

"I think that is an exaggeration, your Holiness," said the cardinal. "It is just a temporary setback."

"Well, as a precaution, ask him to return our funds plus our interest in one week, or Hell will seem like a holiday venue," said the pope.

"Yes, your Holiness, I shall pass on the message," said the cardinal.

"The last point is more serious. Let me show you a video," and the pope pressed a remote control button and a film of the cardinal abusing a young body appeared on the screen.

"Your Holiness, this is a fake tape concocted by actors!" said the cardinal, blustering.

"Maybe," said the pope, and handed a thick file, neatly indexed by each known family and unknown accuser, each with a sworn affidavit.

"This is just a way of extorting money out of the church, your Holiness!" said Cardinal Castellano, visibly wilting before the pope's eyes.

"Many of the accusers don't want any money, merely justice," said the pope.

"A ruse to make a claim at a later date," said the cardinal.

"That we can establish at a later date. In the meantime, you are discharged as a cardinal and demoted to a priest. Second, you may not leave the Vatican until your trial is complete. Third, all your worldly wealth in confiscated until the outcome of the trial is known," said the pope.

"Your Holiness, that is harsh! I am innocent until proven guilty," said the cardinal.

"In the Vatican, the rule of law in New York and Rome is of no consequence, and the pope can override ecclesial law and common law for the good of the church which I do now," said the pope.

"Please, your Holiness, give me a chance to defend myself before taking these measures, I beg you," and the cardinal crawled on all fours to the pope, a pitiful sight.

"Your Eminence has pleaded mercy, and it is granted," said the pope. "You have one week to prepare your defence, which will be heard within the Vatican by your peers and me. If you try to contact, coerce, harm, or threaten one accuser, I will excommunicate you without a trial. You can tell your nephew not to interfere on pain of excommunication and ruin," said the pope. "Now you may go."

The cardinal crawled away like a crab, deflated, and unsure of what to do next except call Gino.

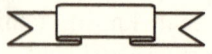

Gino was in his apartment contemplating what move to make against Bill O'Brien when he got a call from the Italian Mafia. The Genovese crime family was the most influential since Paul Gotti had been sent to prison. Believed to be the most powerful and wealthy in America, they were led by an acting boss who seemed to change frequently, to confuse outsiders, but Gino knew him as Patrick Gianvie.

"Hey, Gino how is it going?" said Patrick.

"Very well, Godfather," said Gino, surprised he had been called by the head of the Genovese family.

"Not what I hear on the street, Gino," said Patrick. "The family want their money back, plus interest. You have one week." Then the phone went dead.

Gino was considering the devastating effect of repaying the loan when he was called by an unknown Chinese man who he said represented the United Bamboo members of the Chinese Triads. This group was the largest in New York, with over ten thousand members, and was by far the most feared.

"Mr. Bellini," said the man, "I represent the United Bamboo. Their leader does not like the news we hear, and wants our investment back."

"Sorry, I don't know who you are and what you are talking about," bluffed Gino

"No matter, you have one week. Pay in full with our agreed fee, and you will have our gratitude," said the voice. "Don't, and you will be killed." The man rang off.

The call from his uncle, Cardinal Castellano, demanding the Catholic Church's money back and telling of the indictment was equally challenging. Bad news seemed to be coming from every quarter, and there seemed no place to retreat, so he decided to attack. He had nothing to lose.

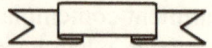

Pat Wiseman felt relieved at long last following her frank confession on television. Gino Bellini could no longer hurt Pat or George. His days were numbered by all accounts of her father, as he had sunk his money into offshore and deep-sea drilling, both of which were now banned. Far from hounding her father out of business, he was going to watch Gino fry whilst he exploited the biggest land-based oil field find in decades. Not only did he own the oil field, he had a U.S. senate grant to exploit the discovery as a form of aid to Malawi. *My father has outsmarted everybody big time,* she thought. As she walked to her car in the shopping mall car parking lot, she felt a hard jab in her back.

"Keep calm, Mrs. Wiseman, and you will not be hurt," said the man. "Call out, and you will be killed where you stand. Now, get into your car slowly." Pat saw another man with a gun get into the passenger seat beside her, dressed smartly in a suit.

"Drive out of the lot slowly and don't look alarmed. No one will hurt you if you cooperate," said the man sitting beside her, and he put his hand inside his open jacket to hide it from view. "I will tell you where to go outside the lot."

Gino Bellini was elated when he received the news from his two henchmen that Pat had been abducted without incident and she was at a safe house in Boston. "Call Bill O'Brien and tell him the fee," said Gino.

A few moments later, one of his henchmen called Bill on his private cell phone.

"Is that Bill O'Brien?" said the henchman.

"Yes. Who is this, and how do you have this number?" Bill asked.

"Shut up and listen," said the man.

"Daddy, it is me, Pat. These two men have abducted me at gunpoint; unless you sell your shares to Gino, they will kill me," said Pat. Then the phone was taken from her hand

Bill, shocked, called Gino Bellini. He was not very tactful. "Bellini, if you harm one hair on my girl's head, I swear I will personally cut off your balls and shove them in your mouth."

"Good day to you as well, Bill," said Gino, amused.

"I can't sell you the shares of Lighthouse Oil. I never owned them, merely held them on trust for a Jersey-based investment house. They have sold them already for forty billion U.S. cash," said Bill, "so release Pat now!"

"Have they paid the money yet?" asked Gino.

"No," said Bill, "I hold the shares in escrow in my name until the money clears. I can't assign the shares, as a precondition of the owners, and the bank holds the share certificates, so unless you have more than forty billion in cash, you can't get them, even if you kill Pat," said Bill.

"What about my offshore shares and shares in the company drilling in Lake Malawi and all the companies surrounding the lake," said Gino?

"Worth billions if we could get drilling permission, but we can't," said Bill. "Worth nothing in today's climate."

"I have forty billion in cash. I can match the offer of the other company," said Gino, thinking he may as well risk everything and bet all of the wealth of the Catholic Church.

"Won't work. They already have the first offer at forty billion. They can only sell to you if you top that offer," said Bill, "that's the law."

"Okay, all my oil assets, the forty billion in cash, and the Bellini property portfolio, worth an estimated two billion dollars," said Gino.

"Will need a formal offer in writing signed by you in the presence of Judge Carter, with all the transfer documents, completed and signed affidavits from Cardinal Castellano and all fellow directors that they agree unanimously with your decision. Additionally, I will need copies of filed company minutes stating those facts with copies of receipts of the registrar's office receiving those documents. The cash will have to be transferred non-refundable, so that when we sign, the money is passed to us, and only if we don't sign is the money returned to you. Pat will have to be returned unharmed for me to sign, and she will have to be returned now. So the deal cannot be said to be coerced, she will need to sign as one of the directors, which she actually is, so it is not fake," said Bill, very calmly.

"Okay, I will have the documents and money to you within two hours with Pat. If we can get the right connections, we can file before the close of business today," said Gino.

"Only filing properly listed shares will be transferred to you, Gino, so I suggest you stop fucking talking and start organising," said Bill. "I will wait in my office with the share certificate ready to sign."

Pat arrived two and half hours later with documents, which appeared superficially okay to Bill, but he passed them to a room of lawyers who scanned and read the documents several times while the broker's bank account was checked for funds and the registrar checked for the correct filing. Bill and Pat then signed the share certificates, gave the two thugs the signed copies, and called the broker to advise the exchange. The company had been sold for forty six billion, forty billion in cash, two billion in property, and four billion in shares of various companies. The shares were valued at face value, even though the quoted price for all companies was less than 200 million dollars.

When they had conducted everything, they left the office relieved. On his way home, as arranged, Bill called David York.

"You are forty-two billion dollars richer," said Bill.

"Good. Is it done?" asked David.

"Yes, all complete," said Bill.

"Are you sure no missing document or minute?" asked David.

"No, none, no hole for him to crawl in," said Bill.

"Okay, did you release your press release yet?" asked David.

The following release was sent to the press:

Lighthouse Oil has been purchased by Gino Bellini's Golden Lake Oil Company, chaired by his Eminence Cardinal Castellano, for forty billion in cash, two billion in property, and four billion in a package of shares, including all the offshore and deep-water drilling company shares owned by Golden Lake Oil.

Bill O'Brien said the deal meant he still had faith in the long-term future of the deep-water drilling technology, which would overcome the fiasco of the BP spill by the higher standards of quality assurance of an American company. His faith, he said, is deep-seated, and he and his partners were prepared to put up substantial guarantees in cash to commence re-drilling.

His group of companies is to be renamed Clean Oil Incorporated.

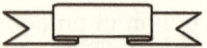

As the statement was released, George Wiseman asked for an emergency meeting of the Energy and Natural Resources Committee.

"What is this meeting all about George?" asked Maria Conwell.

"Let me show you a CD sent to me anonymously in the mail this afternoon," said George. He pushed the CD into a recorder and the small subcommittee saw a naked Cardinal Castellano abusing a young boy. "Can I ask you, gentlemen, do we want to be seen supporting a company with a paedophile as its chairman, and its chief officer as Gino Bellini, secretly his nephew, I am told, which is deceitful to the market and suspicious?" said George.

"But the fact of the matter is, we need oil," said Maria.

"I cannot propose the logical suggestion to restart drilling offshore again and encourage Malawi to drill in Lake Malawi, because my ex-wife's father is the joint owner of that company, so you must excuse me for the debate on the alternatives," said George, and he left the room.

"He is right, you know. No American company screwed up, and the company offers billions of dollars up front in guarantees," said the senator from Texas.

"Very well, let's cancel the grant to Lighthouse because of inappropriate management running the company. Give the tapes to the police, and have a warrant issued for Cardinal Castellano. Raise the non-disclosure of Gino Bellini as the nephew of Castellano and refer this to the stock exchange as a breach of disclosure. Bar him as a director, pending investigation. Offer the grant to Bill O'Brien's renamed group of companies of Clean Oil Incorporated, provided he puts up ten billion dollars, and sign the Malawi development deal on the basis of an environment friendly approach. In the short term, offer oil re-drilling offshore to all companies who put up a bond of ten billion dollars" said Maria.

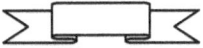

The next morning, when the announcement was made by the Energy and Resources Committee, all oil shares were suspended until mid-day. When they opened, Lighthouse Oil was wiped out, the shares plummeting to a few cents a share. The shares in Clean Oil Incorporated soared to over five hundred billion before dipping to a more realistic three hundred billion. As this was owned three ways, thirty per cent by small market shareholders, thirty per cent by Bill O'Brien, and forty per cent by David York's investment arm, David had made himself one of the richest men in the world with the twenty two billion he kept of the forty-six billion he had received.

Financially, the Castellano family was wiped out, and worse than that, they owed the Catholic Church, the Italian Mafia, and the Chinese Triads.

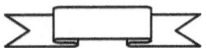

Gino still had the Cult under his control and had been tracking David York and found him in Boston. After very careful research, they found the path to the John Lesley organisation and the hurried removal of insignia. The attempt to remove the records of the

Lesley crypt led them to the conclusion that the Coffin of Destiny was in the crypt.

With all the problems he had with the Catholic Church, the Coffin of Destiny could maybe delay the inevitable and control two of the direct threats to his life. He called the pope directly.

A young priest answered the cell phone. "His Holiness' private cell phone, who is speaking please?" said the young priest.

"Gino Bellini," said Gino.

The pope nodded when the priest said his name. "Gino," said the pope.

"Your Holiness, I want forty-eight hours' grace. Call off the Catholic Church and the Italian Mafia, and if you have any influence the Chinese Triads..." said Gino.

"Why would I do that, Gino? Have you not wasted all our money on worthless investments, being led by the nose like a fool, because of your own greed?" said the pope. "Worse still, your uncle has disgraced the church and must be punished."

"Because I have found the Coffin of Destiny," said Gino.

The phone went silent. "Gino, if you play games with me, it won't be the Italians or Chinese gangsters who I will give you to, but your own Cult followers, and you know what that means," said the pope.

"Your Holiness, I have found the coffin, and will bring it to the archbishop in New York. From there, do with it what you will," said Gino. "From there, I want safe passage out of the country, and an assignment abroad until I can figure out how to recover the money we lost."

"Gino, only you lost money," said the pope.

"My uncle lost the money, your Holiness," said Gino.

"Gino, we both know that is a lie, but if you bring the Coffin of Destiny to New York, we will promote that lie, but you must crawl away and hide for a few years," said the pope.

"What about the Italians and Chinese, your Holiness?" asked Gino.

"They will not trouble you until after you recover the Coffin of Destiny," said the pope.

"And after?" asked Gino.

"If it is real, we will blame Cardinal Castellano and give him to the gangsters," said the pope. "You will be allowed to run away and hide."

"Thank you, your Holiness," said Gino.

"One thing, Gino, don't underestimate David York and the Sect. He is very clever at setting a trap," said the pope.

"I understand, your Holiness, but this time, no more being subtle. We will go in numbers and break doors and heads, and take what we want," said Gino.

"Good luck, Gino," said the pope, and he ended the call.

Chapter Twenty-Seven

David York sat with Veronica in their room at the Omni Parker Hotel in Boston. Crusader had been briefed regarding the Coffin of Destiny and the measures that they had discussed had been implemented. Gino Bellini was in a corner and would come out fighting, that David knew, and he would deploy every bit of muscle available to him to seize the prize and win the day. However, he would only be able to use the Castellano family's resources, which Gino estimated were only thirty to forty men. David very carefully had trapped Gino, using his own greed, into returning the shares in the valuable oil fields and paying a huge amount of money for a worthless piece of land in the middle of Malawi. There was no huge find in that part of Malawi. There were some small pockets of oil his exploratory company had found, but the bulk of the oil was under the lake. The exploration company merely tapped into a small oil find and created the mirage of a massive find to convince the impetuous Gino to return what was rightfully Bill and David's.

The acquisition of the offshore oil company property and Catholic money was a huge bonus. David had no intention of keeping either. He gave the twenty billion needed as a guarantee for the oil drilling offshore and in Lake Malawi, but asked for it to be invested and for any profits to develop the environment in both areas. The twenty billion effectively became a fund to help all environmental projects. The property portfolio was donated to a housing charity in the U.S. to help the homeless, and the remaining twenty billion was divided amongst a long list of charities worldwide. David wanted to make it clear what the Sect had done with the money, so he made the transactions visible enough for the Catholic sources, identifying the funds so they would know their destination. David thought, ironically, *perhaps this was how it should have been used in the first place.*

The huge success of the Lake Malawi find and the acquisition of the offshore oil field made David very rich, but he always was, and his trust fund bulged with investments in every sector of the economy worldwide. He wondered what would happen to it all when he was gone. David's ambition to become indecently wealthy had been achieved long ago, and money had not been an issue even decades earlier. His entire father's wealth was given to charitable causes, universities, and the Sect and David did not inherit any wealth. David had no dependents, nobody who relied upon him, and he had never been engaged, married, or lived with a woman until Veronica.

He found women distracting, annoying to his equilibrium, his carefully planned days ruined, his strict routines disturbed. Women shook him out of perfect habits and forced him to be spontaneous. He should have hated it. Veronica would come and kiss him when he was writing, immersed in some complex issue, breaking his concentration, ruining the flow. He would be showering and she would join him as he rushed to get ready for his next appointment, delaying him, distracting him with her beauty. She had annoying habits, like leaving the top off the toothpaste, putting her clothes on his trouser press—particularly that fluffy dressing gown that left bits of fluff all over his black Armani dinner suit. However, David somehow loved all of it, the annoying habits that became endearing, and when she was not around, he missed her, particularly her smell and touch.

It was reassuring to reach out in bed and find there was always someone there. David was never very tactical, and lying together in each other's arms happened rarely. His sexual exploits often belied a lack of feeling and emotion he felt inside, and his sexual adventures were a form of physical exercise with a woman. With Veronica, it was becoming different. He actually did lie holding her, their naked bodies entwined. Their touch was one of love towards each other. David had slept with countless women and had sex with many more, and he wondered, *did they all feel like this to some man? Did they all have the same desire to be loved unconditionally?* Because that is what it is, the other person becomes blind, deaf and dumb. They don't see imperfections, don't hear any negatives, and never tell you what is wrong with you. Of course, he knew love changed over the years, but this was the first flicker of the candle in the gentle breeze of new emotions.

Veronica—perhaps wisely— never put any pressure on him about their relationship, but now he thought they should perhaps do something that tied them together.

"Do you ever think about the future?" David asked, probing.

"Sometimes," she said smiling, "but not often. We always seem to be on some wild adventure."

"What do you think?" he asked, really interested.

"Oh, I guess what all girls think about, getting married, having children, growing old, and seeing your grandchildren," she said, a little distant.

"Do you want those things with me?" asked David.

"Of course, but you don't want those things, do you?" she asked, surprised. "You have always been a fuck them and leave them kind of guy with women."

"Probably," said David, "but I am getting older, and I think I want children."

"My god, that would be something: David York and kids, pushing his pram on the way to the church, or the shopping mall," said Veronica laughing. "Who are you planning to breed with, have you decided?"

"I thought I might marry you," said David.

She now was suddenly silent; it was no longer a joke. "Really?" she said quietly. "When?"

"We could get engaged when we return to London," said David, "and then perhaps plan a wedding six months later I know you would want lots of guests to come."

"There are lots of things in the past you may not like, you know, I fucked around a lot before you," she said, hoping it would not matter, but desperate to make sure it would happen.

"Well, we will have to do a list, but mine will be longer," said David laughing, "I know all about you. Every person is researched before I bed them."

"I suppose we both know we had a lot of sex before with other people," said Veronica, "but if we get married, I want the full commitment thing. You won't be able to fuck people to gain an advantage in business or for the Sect."

"Is that what you are prepared to do as well?" asked David. "I am a lot older than you; there will be lots of younger men to love you."

"David, you are the one," said Veronica. "I have not looked at another man since we first met."

"I don't have a ring, but think I should do this properly," and he got down on his knee. Holding her hand, he looked into her eyes, smiling. "Veronica Goldsmith, will you marry me?" asked David, smiling.

"David York," she said, smiling back and pausing for a tantalizing second to saver the moment. "I will. But you know you will have to ask Rolly, and my mother will need to get out of rehab to come to the wedding."

"How is your mother doing?" asked David.

"She is cured, we hope. She has not had a drug for six months. She sounds completely different, talks completely differently, even actually seems to like my dad again. Do you know he has gone on a diet and started to go to gym?"

"Really?" said David. "I can't picture Rolly in normal gym clothes. Somehow my mental picture is with a red-striped shirt and braces on a running machine," and they both laughed.

"He has lost three stone already. He won't be Rolly Goldsmith anymore soon," said Veronica, "My God; my whole family is becoming respectable."

"Do you prefer respectable?" asked David

"No, not really," said Veronica. "It was good to have other experiences, but I really want children, and to bring them up in a balanced environment. One problem though, is you and my mother. My dad knows you were fucking her. You will need to clear that little mess up with him when you ask for my hand in marriage."

"Do you mind about your mother?" asked David.

"Not really, I already knew before I had even met you," said Veronica. "In fact, you have fucked half the girls that I will probably invite to the wedding," and she laughed.

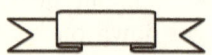

Roland Goldsmith was stunned to silence when David York called him. York was a presentable man, of course, tall, good-looking, athletically built a perfect specimen. Rich, perhaps richer than himself, after the oil riches he had acquired. A model in society with his charitable causes, with an impeccable army record, and he knew a period as a spy in MI6, perhaps destined for a knighthood this year by all accounts.

There was an age gap. He would be forty next year, and Veronica was only twenty-one later this year, half his age. A brilliant girl intellectually, she was any man's equal in intelligence, and well-read; she could discuss literature and poetry in great depth and with passion. Her taste in music was also extensive, and she enjoyed classical music and the opera, which Rolly had no time for, preferring jazz and rhythm blues. She also had a great grasp of business, and when he discussed any financial issues, she was extremely perceptive and intuitively knew the correct decision to take. However, David York was the leader of the Sect, of which he was an integral part, and one of the most dangerous men in the world. Did he really want his daughter to marry him? Then there was the personal issue of him fucking his wife Vivian, Veronica's mother. Recently, they had reconciled, and Rolly had been trying to become more attractive to his beautiful wife by dieting and exercising. However, it was hard to change a life time of physical lethargy into a finely-tuned body like David York's when your muscles had no muscle memory of exercise. Still, he was trying and feeling better for the effort. Vivian was also becoming normal now, she did not drink, and even took some interest in him, and they were rebuilding a relationship that they only had briefly when they first met.

He, of course, gave his permission gracefully to David York, and his wife called York to give him her best wishes and blessing. There really is never any other course of action to take. He knew women were attracted to men like York, and if he wanted any of them, they would marry him, so he could not stop his daughter and no threat would deter her. Therefore, he decided to grin and bear it and try to make the best of events.

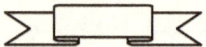

The pope was amused at how David York had donated the church's money to the charitable causes, and gave the property of the Castellano family to the homeless. He was aware the Sect leader was a man of principal and always followed his own strict code of conduct. He regretted that his elected Cult leader had so many frailties and wallowed in greed and avarice. The church was wrong to so quickly pass the responsibility of such an important mission to such a young man, and his mentor, Cardinal Castellano, was perhaps also another huge mistake. He was determined that the mistake would not be repeated. The celibacy laws that were introduced partly to protect the church from priests' children inheriting the church's wealth and then not becoming priests, causing the church to lose the wealth, would need reconsidering. In the meantime, the endemic paedophile element within the upper echelons of the Church needed to be stamped out. The pope felt he must protect the church, and if necessary use the Cult to kill priests if they have the potential for major embarrassment and for large claims against the Church.

However, first he must prevent an artefact from being revealed to the world. He no longer had confidence that Gino Bellini could outwit David York, who clearly had played him very easily at every juncture. His choice was a man of similar age to York, nearly forty, Raymond Mason. Mason was an assassin for MI6 and he had spent a period seconded to the CIA for two years and was based in New York. Tall and muscular, he was very capable of killing a man with his bare hands; he was a seventh dan karate champion and a crack shot, having represented Great Britain at the Olympic Games in the pistol shooting.

Highly decorated and admired, he was on the fast track one day to lead MI6 when his operative days were over. He had been a candidate to take over from Paul Athurs after David York had killed him using an explosive device, but the influence of Castellano had swung it towards Gino Bellini. Now, with Bellini unpredictable and perhaps mentally flawed, throwing Ray Mason into the mix would ensure that David York was killed and the Sect stopped for some time. Preventing the Coffin of Destiny from reaching the public's attention would protect the myth that Jesus was the only genuine messiah, and that these stories about Set, Osiris, Horus, Joseph, and Isis were all myths and fairy tales. The Catholic Church spent time and money posting a counterargument every time new research revealed some new fact about the Jesus blood line. However, confidence in the Catholic Church's teaching was dwindling, and even church goers were non-believers in much of the Catholic doctrine. The pope was confident that Mason would kill York and his girlfriend Veronica, and much of the Sect in Boston, as they would be busy watching Gino Bellini.

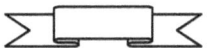

Raymond Mason had prepared all his life for the calling from the Catholic Church to be its protector. Unmarried, he was celibate and had been for over sixteen years. He found any human contact contaminated his mind, and at the age of twenty, he stopped all human sexual activity. As well as being a martial arts expert, he studied yoga and meditation extensively to train his mind in abstinence, and he no longer had sexual desires.

He knew David York by reputation and had seen him fight in the gym once, during a training class, and knew him as a formidable opponent. York did have weakness: He was not spontaneous. He was a planner, and having identified Gino Bellini as the opponent would bait him, entrap him, and kill him. York did not know about Mason, who would at the key moment surprise York and kill him.

He would then destroy the Coffin of Destiny, melting the gold into gold bars, re-cutting the gems, burning the mummified body of Osiris, and destroying any scrolls. His allegiance to the church was absolute, and an order given by the pope was a message from god's representative on earth. He would take with him his best men, who were all of a similar mind. They numbered about twenty, and if hidden correctly, would be formidable.

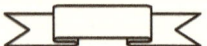

Gino Bellini gathered all his soldiers. There were nearly fifty people.

"We have been watching the crypt the last two days," said Gino. "There is a young woman watching the site who is probably an assassin from the Sect. There are also four or five more visible members from the Boston Sect, all heavily armed. We think at most they could master twenty to thirty people, so we will outmuscle them and will have superior firepower."

"Where is the coffin we need to get?" asked one of his captains.

"Built into the wall of the crypt, we imagine, so we need to kill the guards, break into the crypt, break the walls, find the coffin, and transport it to New York," said Gino.

"That will all take time," said the captain.

"Yes, which is why we need to have superior firepower," said Gino.

"We need to have a fallback team held in reserve, which tracks our progress, of maybe ten guys who can come in to the fire fight at any time, maybe deployed by helicopter?" said the captain thoughtfully. "We keep the bird out of sight until we are out on the road."

"Okay, agreed," said Gino. "Now, let us rehearse how we shall attack this crypt."

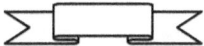

The Sect had deployed their most able people to guard the crypt and had a small team of people, numbering fifteen, who could be called up in addition to the five people guarding the crypt all the time. They were well-armed and would be effective, as they were members of the police force or ex-army or navy servicemen. David had included one woman to watch the position from afar, and instructed the four men not to interact with her. She was a backup to provide them with a warning signal if an attack was to commence. David also had seconded ten people from the New York Sect members to prepare an ambush on the road, should the Cult manage to steal the coffin and take it by road to New York.

The Lesley family was heavily involved in the planning, and David expressed his doubts about their capabilities to the New York team so that they would be ready to retrieve the situation.

Much to David's surprise, Benjamin and Susan Nester stayed to help in the defence of the coffin, and he appreciated their dedication. Whilst he recognised that Susan was quite handy with a gun and knife, Benjamin, to put it mildly, was useless and more useful alive. He assigned Benjamin to the team on the roadside and Susan to the key lookout role on the night he thought they would come. Veronica had been sent to New York with a special assignment, as had Crusader. David would lead the assault team himself.

Chapter Twenty-Eight

John Lesley was on guard outside the Lesley crypt, guarding the coffin, and the night was cold in late April, so he shrugged into the warmth of the thick collar and pushed his hands deep in his pockets. John could see the other three men shivering in the cool of the evening, not used to sentry duty. David had told them to be alert, but it was already four hours into their shift and was midnight, and John was already sleepy and hoped the shift was soon be over. Susan Nester would call if any bad guys arrived, anyway.

He looked across and noticed that Police Sergeant Towers had moved behind one of the other gravestones away from the three of them, which seemed odd, so he instinctively crouched lower to the ground for some reason. A thud hit the headstone behind John and he saw the two other men fall blood pouring from their bodies from multiple wounds and he rolled behind the headstone, as though he had been hit, and he remained still. He speed-dialled David York using his cell phone with the right hand, and then switched it off completely. He could see several men, perhaps twenty in all with weapons emerge from the night, and Police Sergeant Towers and Susan Nestor greeted them and entered the crypt. Heavy crowbars were taken inside the crypt, and some loud banging was heard, and then the sounds stopped.

"Bring up the scanner," he heard someone say. After a little while, during which he imagined they had scanned something, he heard, "Okay, it is clean, take it away."

337

Then he heard a truck arriving, with lots of banging, and then the truck drove away again. Then there was complete silence for a number of minutes. When he looked up, the two dead men lay in the cemetery where they had fallen. The other people had all disappeared. He went inside the crypt and saw that the wall had been broken into and the coffin was gone. For nearly seven hundred years, the Lesley family had guarded the Coffin of Destiny, and he had lost it under his watch. He then heard trucks arrive and looked up to see David York.

"What has happened?" asked David.

"We had no warning. Susan and Sergeant Towers were working for the Cult, so we got no early warning," said John.

"What was the vehicle?" asked David.

"A black van with some sign on it for flowers," said John Lesley.

"Okay," said David and he speed-dialled the team placed on the highway. "The package is on the way to you; stop it. It is in a black van with an advert for flowers."

The team leader nodded and deployed his men waiting by the roadside. It was 20 minutes before the van arrived, and his orders were to stop the van, so he nodded to his squad. They fired a small charge from a rocket launcher, which destroyed the front of the van and caused it to crash into the embankment at the side of the road.

About six men firing automatics came from the rear of the truck, and two from the front, but the carefully-positioned men mowed them down and they fell, bleeding to death. They approached the van, slowly advancing, and opened the back door, but no coffin was in the van. A helicopter flew overhead, and as they looked up, a bomb was detonated that was in the van, sending the eight men close to the van into the air, their bodies shredded, and killing everybody within thirty yards away with shrapnel.

Gino Bellini had detonated the bomb from the helicopter and could not believe how easy it had been, and how easily David York had been outsmarted. Of course, Susan Nester and Sergeant Towers were a great help as insiders. Susan had contacted them, as had Towers, disgruntled with the changes to the Sect, and offered to help them get the Coffin of Destiny.

He only wished he had had the help earlier and he would not have been in such a mess. However, Susan Nester was not aware of any plans until she arrived in Boston, and the financial setup was never even discussed with her. The Sect had killed Professor John McCallister, and she just never forgave them for killing its leader and her lover. Sergeant Towers was turned by Susan very easily with sex, kind words, and a few false facts. He would be killed and dumped at the end of the journey. Susan, with her knowledge, would be invaluable in interpreting any documents they found. Her father, Benjamin Nestor, did not know anything about Susan's plans apparently, and his daughter's departure would be a big surprise. The scanner to ensure there was no bomb in the coffin was Susan's idea, and he thanked her for that, but there was nothing seen in the coffin except the shape of a mummified body and some vague impression of scrolls. Still, he was wary of David York, and expected him to have provided for a response once the coffin was taken, hence the switch to the helicopter and the bomb being placed in the van for any roadside response team to be blown up. Gino smiled; he had outwitted David York in the final game.

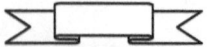

The coffin was to be taken to the archbishop's residence beside St. Patrick's Cathedral, which was located on the east side of Fifth Avenue between 50th and 51st Streets in Midtown Manhattan, facing the Rockefeller Centre. They had to land at the MetLife Building at 200 Park Avenue. The MetLife Building had a helipad, as it was used to use to ferry messengers to the John F. Kennedy Airport in the 1960s, but a traffic accident in 1977 stopped the service, so the helipad was not used. Gino arranged to use the helipad to land and then transport the coffin by road to its final destination. As the helicopter landed, Gino looked around, anxiously waiting for men from the Sect to spring out to attack them, but none appeared. The coffin was unloaded onto a trolley and moved to the service lift and taken to the waiting television repair van. The drive to the rectory was uneventful, but Gino was anxious all the way, waiting for the pre-emptive strike by the Sect. He was to hand over the coffin at the rectory and his job was complete. Raymond Mason and some men were to take over the keeping of the coffin. He suspected that Mason was his replacement as Cult leader.

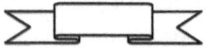

They took the coffin into a de-robing room were the clergy could prepare for services in the Cathedral, and the coffin was left on the trolley they took from the MetLife Building. Raymond Mason, whom he knew by sight, was not there, nor was the archbishop, but

340

Cardinal Robinson was, representing the pope, and there was some man from the crew Mason had handpicked.

"Where is Mason?" asked Gino.

"He was at the crypt in Boston, watching you," said the cardinal, "so I guess he is still there."

"I see," said Gino, smiling. "So I guess he will be a long time coming. Okay, you have your coffin," said Gino. "I have completed my mission. Where is his Holiness sending me?"

"That I don't know. I was told to give you this envelope," said the cardinal.

Gino opened the envelope, and inside was a passport in the name of Anthony Vinzetti, an Italian, with an airplane ticket to Sicily. There were credit cards, traveller's cheques, a hotel voucher, and some typed instructions about the man's background and his new role a holiday tour guide. Gino shrugged. The role would be fine for a year or so until he figured another way to redeem himself.

He shook hands with the cardinal and went to a small bathroom and changed from his combat clothes into his travelling clothes, an off-the-rack pair of slacks from Sears and casual crew neck sweater and a black leather jacket. None of these were to his taste, but he could no longer dress in designer clothes, and these were the clothes a tour guide could afford. He picked up the small case he had prepared for his journey and walked out into the cold night air. He felt suddenly elated and recharged as he walked towards the cathedral, where he would give thanks before taking the tube.

A young girl smiled at him as they passed each other, and he thought, smiling back, *I will still get lots of pussy.* His thought was frozen in his brain as he felt the stab in his spine and his body fell to the ground.

The syringe Crusader had stabbed into Gino was lethal and incapacitated and killed the victim slowly, and Crusader looked into the frightened eyes of Gino, whose body was going through spasms as the poison killed him slowly.

"You will die slowly, Mr. Bellini. The poison is killing each organ, and you will lose control in a few seconds and defecate and urinate uncontrollably," said Crusader quietly. "You will die in the gutter and be buried in an unknown grave with no absolution from a priest, and go to Hell, if there is one. In death, you will remember you are a loser." Crusader smiled as Gino's body contorted and the pungent smell of defecation and urine came from his body. She removed the lethal syringe from his body and walked across the road.

Gino tried to call out, but he could not control his vocal chords. He had shit himself and pissed his pants and felt uncomfortable and ashamed. A frightening pain reached his body and he wiggled uncontrollably on the ground.

Gino saw a couple walking with a dog were approaching him, and the dog ran towards him. Lifting its leg, it pissed on him. The couple shouted for the dog to go away and looked at him in disgust.

Crusader watched, unmoved. Any autopsy not completed within four hours would conclude a heart attack unless they found the telltale pin prick. However, Crusader guessed that nobody would care what happened to a tour guide.

Raymond Mason arrived, angry at missing the helicopter escape route, and had been driven to New York. His men reported that the whole of Gino's crew were dead, except the men that left in the helicopter.

Still, it was a successful mission, although Gino was not to be killed by him or Susan Nestor; the bum was to be sent into exile. As he drove, he noticed the man lying in the street being taken into an ambulance and thought nothing of the event. Yet another drunk who collapsed on the pavement.

The coffin was still in its wooden casing, untouched, as he had ordered until he arrived.

"Has it been scanned for bombs?" asked Mason.

"Several times," said Susan.

"Alright, let's get it open and check inside," said Mason.

Two men broke open the box, removing the lid and sides so the coffin was revealed. Covered in black pitch, the coffin looked unimpressive.

"Open the lid," said Mason.

The men delicately started scraping the tar away and prying open the lid.

Susan Nestor became agitated. "We should do this more carefully; we may damage the coffin," she pleaded.

"Shut the fuck up!" said Mason. "Open the fucking coffin!"

The men pried the lid open with crowbars, and the lid opened.

"What's inside?" asked Mason.

The men handed down large, rolled-up pieces of modern architectural drawings of buildings. The mummy appeared to be a plastic skeleton of a body wrapped in normal bandages.

"What a fuck up!" said Mason. "Did we let that prick Bellini go already?" he asked, and his phone rang.

"Hi, Raymond, long time since we have spoken," said David York. "No need to worry about Bellini, he is dead, and so are you."

David pressed the remote, and a massive explosion from below the coffin killed everybody in the room. The collapsible trolley David had placed at the helicopter pad was too convenient for the henchmen of Bellini to resist, and they of course checked the false coffin, but not the trolley they had chosen. Really, there was no other location they could land without permission close by, so it was the only location available. A helicopter really was the only choice Gino had other than road, so both options were going to be covered by David. However, his bet was on the final destination as well, and both had been correct.

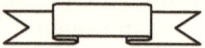

David York had watched the Crusader killing machine in action from a distance, and always was surprised at how easily you can kill, provided you planned correctly. It was over an hour before Raymond Mason arrived at the rectory, and he listened carefully from the car he occupied.

Susan was no surprise; he had long had suspicions about her, and careful surveillance proved to confirm his doubts. To get an early heads up on the plan to remove the coffin was very useful. Of course, the real coffin was removed by Crusader within hours of discovering its true location. It was safely deposited in the Museum of Egyptian Antiquities in Cairo, Egypt, and would be announced to the world once the events of today had played out.

Veronica and Crusader had planted most of the bugging devices as tourists, and in the event the trolley was not taken, they had planted a smaller bomb in the rectory just in case. It would be destroyed with the blast of the larger bomb already. The car was owned by a resident on the street who parked it overnight each day. It was easy to get a key and use it as a listening post. David now walked to the nearest subway station 47th – 50th Street at Rockefeller Centre, and caught the tube to the Algonquin Hotel. David entered by the service entrance, and although they would see him on video footage in the hallway entering the room, he would say he went for a walk.

David was surprised to see Veronica and Roland Goldsmith and her mother Vivian waiting for him in the lounge. It was nearly three in the morning. David instinctively threw himself to his left side, and drawing a handgun he had in his right pocket, he rolled and aimed at the door he had entered and fired. A shot had been discharged as he was throwing himself forward; it had hit his upper thigh, but he ignored the injury. His instinctive shot had killed the assassin by the door, and a man hiding behind the couch had stood up to receive a bullet fired by David in the middle of his forehead. The bathroom door began to open as David began firing, coming forward and picking up the weapon of the man by the couch, he smoothly adopted the kneeling position, adjusting his position several times to fire at all angles into the bathroom. He then, within the space of a couple of seconds, kicked open the door to see one wounded man adjusting his position to fire a sub-machine gun, and he shot him in the head. The other man was clearly dead, having been hit directly in the middle of his face. David then immediately somersaulted back into the lounge, and in one bound cleared the couch and crashed through the bedroom door, but his keen eyes saw no more men. He kicked open each cupboard, checked that the bed had no space underneath, and then calmly walked back into the lounge.

He reached into his belt and opened the pouch on his cell phone and called a number. "Clean-up operation, four dead, probably Cult members, Algonquin Room 406, moving to Room 309."

"Sorry about that Rolly, Vivian," said David, holding out his hand. "Not a nice way to be greeted when meeting your new son-in-law to be."

Roland Goldsmith had sat transfixed on the couch whilst Veronica had dragged her mother to safety on the other side of the couch. It had all happened in seconds, and four men lay dead, bleeding all over the floor. Rolly had never seen a dead man before and felt physically sick, but with two corpses in the bathroom, there was nowhere to go and puke privately. He held back the bile and fear he felt. He had seen York before in action, beating up his bodyguards, but never with a gun killing someone. He knew he wished never to see it again. He killed clinically with almost unbelievable speed and accuracy, with an innate sense of where everybody in the room was going to be.

David looked around the room satisfied. He spent time when booking into a room, setting it up in case of an ambush, and always rearranged the furniture to position the assassin to be facing him over an armchair or couch entering the door. He found out which way the door opened, and knew which way to throw himself, which way to fire his first shot, second shot, and secondary shots, in case they had backup. He rehearsed his moves in his mind in every location at all times; it was second nature. "Are you okay darling? They did not hurt you?" David went across to hold Veronica and kissed her forehead.

"No," said Veronica. "They came about 1 a.m. We were still talking having decided to wait for you. A little bit scary, but I knew somehow you would handle them. But how did you know where they all were in the room? It was uncanny how you fired exactly where they were."

"Rolly's eyes looked in fear as I entered the room towards the door. The rest is where I would have positioned myself if I had set up the assassination," said David. "Look, let's go straight to the room."

"Come on Rolly, Vivian," said David, and when he got in the elevator, he pressed the third floor.

They got out, and David took them to the employee staircase to floor two. They just followed, perplexed. David led them to Room 206 and let them in. It was not a suite, but a room with two double beds for a family. It was not the type of room he would normally book, and he had nothing of his in the room. "Stay here," said David. "Let me just check the other room."

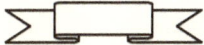

Crusader waited patiently in the dark in Room 309, and the two assassins entered from the window using the hoist, which lowered the window cleaner to each window. They were silent, removing a pane of glass rather than breaking the window. The two men dressed in black were professional and silent. Crusader, using a wind pipe, fired a small dart in the neck of the first man, who stumbled, and as the second man reached out to help him, she fired the second dart, hitting the second man close to his ear in the face.

The first man was dead, and the second now incapacitated. She commenced tying the stricken man to a chair quietly in the dark. Then she carefully took the first man and put him back in the window hoist, which they would use to remove all the bodies. The eyes of the stricken man glinted with fear in the dark as she sent an sms to David York. He had climbed onto the ledge outside the room and now entered the room from the hole in the window. The short term poison was fading from the assassin's body, and he had a tingling feeling in his arms and legs, which were now tied.

David switched on the television quite high, and then he took a small washcloth from the bathroom and rolled it into a ball and stuffed into the man's mouth.

"What is going to happen to you will not be pleasant, and in any case, you will die anyway," said David. "It just depends on how much pain you would like before you die. Tell me what I want, and it will be quick and painless."

He nodded to Crusader, and she held the man's hand in hers and with a pair of pliers, she ripped off a nail. The man's scream was caught in the washcloth in his mouth. "Would you like to tell Mr. York what you know?" asked Crusader.

The man looked wildly at her and York, unsure of what to do. Crusader ripped another nail from his finger. "Would you like to tell Mr. York what you know?" asked Crusader calmly.

The man was now in real pain and disoriented, and hesitated again. Crusader ripped another nail from his finger. "Would you like to tell Mr. York what you know?" asked Crusader.

This time, the man was given a few extra seconds, and he nodded.

"Okay, what are all the Cult members you know, names and addresses?" said David. "Before you answer, know this: We will track each one and kill them and torture them. Any false names, and we shall cut off each one of your balls and make you eat them. Understand?"

The man nodded. He knew perhaps ten contact names and addresses; the rest were vague. Crusader set up a laptop and began tracing each person. It took about two hours, and the assassins from all over the world brought in to kill everybody in the Cult were dispatched to each address. David attached wires to the man, and a lie detector, but looking at the man's face, he knew he was broken and telling the truth. When he was finished, and David satisfied, Crusader gave him a lethal injection into his neck.

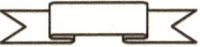

The bodies of the six men would become part of the New York foundations of one of the new buildings, and the rooms would be restored to their pristine glory without the hotel ever being aware of what happened. A few complaints were received about Room 406 from nearby occupants, and David York apologised for the television being too loud.

Exhausted, he joined Veronica for early-morning breakfast with his in-laws to be.

"Well, I suppose we better set a date," said David.

"When would you suggest?" asked Rolly.

"I suggest we announce the engagement and have an engagement party on Saturday, June 5, that way people going to the World Cup in South Africa won't be affected," said David.

"Where shall we have it?" asked Veronica.

"Why not the Grosvenor? I more or less used to live there," said David.

"Could we get the Park Room and the Library perhaps, and it would be like a homely feel as they both are like stately home rooms?" asked Veronica.

"Not a problem," said David, and he picked up his cell phone and phoned a number.

"Hi, David York. Can I book the Park Room and the Library for the 5th of June for an engagement party, and perhaps another room to dance in?" he listened for a moment. "Okay, thanks." Turning to Veronica, he said "fixed."

"Let's get married on the 25th of September at Westminster Cathedral at midday, have the reception at the Savoy, and holiday where?" said David.

"South Africa," said Veronica. "Cape Town, Johannesburg, and Durban, let's see some of the country."

"Okay, done, let me book now." David called his various contacts and was busy for about thirty minutes. "Okay, all fixed, they are all emailing the details. We can look for a house in the UK when we get back home, somewhere in Mayfair, and choose a designer to refurbish it."

"If we are done, I think I would like to go and rest for an hour. We are booked to fly out later today," said David.

Rolly stood up. "We have had our differences, but I want you to know I admire you as a man, and wish you all the best in your marriage to my daughter," he said, and David could tell it was from the heart. Vivian just kissed him, and Veronica and David returned to their suite at 406, which had been restored remarkably in record time.

David stripped and had a quick shower, and Veronica joined him. Exhausted, they just soaped each other and then dried each other; they were spent of energy.

They put the "Do Not Disturb" sign on the door, set the alarm system that the team had installed, and lay together on the bed, drained. David held Veronica close, and as her soft flesh melted into his, he wondered what it was going to be like married to Veronica. Would he be the same man?

Veronica saw his eyes closing and closed her eyes, wondering what adventure would be next, and what it would be like married to a man like David York. They fell asleep together wrapped in their love, the words of the song he sang at Del Posto, "For the First Time," ringing in Veronica's ears.

The news about the Coffin of Destiny's return to Egypt was sensational news, particularly as it was said to contain the mummified remains of the fabled Osiris.

Benjamin Nestor was in shock with his wife Susan for several days following the death of their daughter, and found it hard to understand how she could deceive her own parents. He, of course forgave her in his heart, but her mother Susan seemed full of hate for her own daughter now, which Benjamin believed was a mechanism his wife was using to cope with the loss.

The head of ancient history in Egypt gathered a worldwide team of scientists together, and it would take several months before they could provide forensic evidence on the dates on the coffin, the body of Osiris, and the scrolls in the coffin would be translated.

Benjamin, after a few weeks, travelled to Egypt and became part of the team and soon lost himself in his work.

A preliminary report was prepared by the group of scientists after three months, and David York and Veronica travelled to Egypt to hear the results.

The professor of ancient Egyptian history, Professor Abduh from Cairo University, chaired the meeting. "Ladies and gentlemen, let me open this press conference with some sensational news. The contents of the Coffin of Destiny contained a body that is confirmed to be of a male who is at least five thousand five hundred years old. The scrolls in the coffin vary in date, but some are from this date also. What we can say in outline is that the body is of Osiris, and it would appear Isis, Set, Horus, and Joseph were all real people, according to the scrolls. Horus is a Messiah figure, and in later scrolls would appear to be an ancestor of Jesus," said Professor Abduh. The room hushed and was stunned.

"We need much more time to read translate and verify all the information in the scrolls, but it would appear that we have the body of an Egyptian God believed to be a myth, now proving to actually be a man who existed. We will need to rewrite our history and revise everything we have written in the period 3,500 BC and beyond. It would also appear that the all-seeing eye often depicted in the Middle Ages as the all-seeing eye of God is in fact that of Horus, whose life and works appear to be those of a messiah, a Son of God," said Professor Abduh.

"Are you saying," asked a reporter, "that Horus is a Jesus figure from five and a half thousand years ago?"

"Put simply, yes," said Professor Abduh.

The room went silent, and David York spoke. "Professor, many people have promoted this concept in the past, and the Catholic Church has simply said that all the information is fake and the relics not real. Why should we now believe this Coffin of Destiny and the body of Osiris and these scrolls are real?"

"Because you cannot fake carbon dating," said the professor, "and the scrolls are verified as genuine, as is the mummified body and the gold coffin. The facts can't be disputed: Horus is not a myth, he was the Messiah before Jesus, and in a few months, we will have the full account of his life."

"Where is the Coffin of Destiny and mummified body?" asked a Catholic priest in the audience.

"Right here," said Professor Abduh. "We will end our presentation now, and in a few months produce a comprehensive report of all our findings." The professor nodded, and the curtain behind the scientist was dropped and two boxes moved forward.

He then removed a cloth from the first box, and a closed coffin of gold and jewels appeared. The audience gasped. It was amazing. The jewels were very large, the size of two fists in some cases, and the patterns were intricate and pleasing to the eye. Immediately, reporters were snapping photographs and film crews were scanning the surface of the coffin to record its beauty.

"Ladies and gentlemen, this is the fabled Coffin of Destiny, which is the greatest find ever found, except for one other," and the professor walked across to a coffin-like box that was upturned and pulled the cloth from the box. "I give you Osiris, pharaoh of Te-Mehu, and five thousand five hundred years old!" said the professor.

The audience gasped. The mummy was in a glass case, and the face bandages had been removed, and you could see the man's face. Whilst slightly discoloured with age, it appeared handsome, not the usual leathery look of a mummy shrunken into the bones of the skull.

The body also looked intact, and was very well shaped, but was covered in what appeared to blackened bandages, except for a golden penis, which stood erect from the mummy's crotch.

Osiris was a truly well-preserved mummy, and had far exceeded anybody's expectations. The audience now was lost in admiration at the find, their heads spinning with the questions to ask. The scientists already had left the stage, and the two artefacts were being covered again. The presentation was at an end.

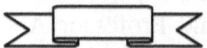

David York and Veronica were truly amazed to see their find was real, and wondered how his next adventure to find the Eye of Horus would take shape.